The Winds of Change

Merlin in Moab, Book Four

CARYL SAY

Cover Design and Author Photo by Ginger Aaron.

Front Cover Image: Dark Angel, Arches National Park (source US Gov.)

Front Cover Image: Fiery Furnace, Arches National Park (source Caryl E. Say)

Interior Layout by StandOut Books

Contact the author via email at carylsay.author@gmail.com or on her website, carylsay.com.

Printed in the United States of America

ISBN (paperback): 978-1-7348537-3-5

ISBN (ebook): 978-1-7348537-4-2

Caryl Say's MERLIN IN MOAB series

ACKNOWLEDGMENTS

As always, there are many people who I would like to thank for their support:

Lisa Albert and Karen Feary for taking the time to read through the manuscript (several times!), make corrections, and provide constructive criticism. Publishing this book would not have been possible without their help.

Brad Weis at Moab Internet for ongoing website maintenance and Ginger Aaron for cover design.

The Grand County, Utah, Sheriff's Department for assistance with law enforcement procedural information.

Alan Hay in Aberdeenshire, Scotland, for checking my use of the Scots language, and the rest of my Clan Hay extended family in America and Scotland, for their support of my literary efforts.

And, of course, thanks so much to everyone for buying my books! I'm so glad that you enjoy my stories.

Lastly, thanks once again to my sister and traveling companion, Peggy Di Mauro, for another wonderful trip, this time to Scotland (including the Shetland Islands and the Orkney Islands) and England in August, 2022.

AUTHOR'S NOTE

In writing the Merlin in Moab series, I have created a new approach to a legend that has persisted for many centuries.

I have always loved the legend(s) of Merlin and King Arthur, but there are aspects and much debated details of those legends that always bothered me, so I changed them.

My characters are real to me. I dream about them. I know exactly what they look like, sound like, and act like. And sometimes they do and say things I don't expect, or agree with. But this has been one of the most amazing experiences I've had as a writer.

I tried making an outline before I wrote the first book, and I never finished it. I just started writing and the characters took over.

In response to questions and comments I've received about the sometimes convoluted relationships between the characters, I have created a comprehensive and descriptive List of Characters that should provide some clarification.

In addition, I have created a Glossary of Terms and Phrases to help you navigate through the various snippets of Irish Gaelic, Scottish Gaelic, Welsh, Scots, and archaic English words you will find in this novel.

I've placed both the List of Characters and the Glossary of Terms and Phrases at the end, rather than at the beginning of the book, for a very good reason: *they contain numerous spoilers!* But please feel free to refer to them at any time.

Occasionally, you may find a few errors in my books, but it can't be helped; sometimes we just miss things. As a friend of mine once told me, "You can only sweep a dirt floor so many times. You'll always find more dirt." So any errors are mine alone.

I hope you enjoy reading this book as much as I enjoyed writing it!

PROLOGUE
Arthur

I have existed for centuries in the Other World as a disembodied spirit, protected by the Elven Fae. I have no real sense of the passage of time. It seems like only recently that I warned Merlin of an ancient adversary plotting to thwart his mission to return me to the human realm. In reality, it was many years ago.

That adversary is still striving to prevent my return, according to the Elves, and I must be protected at all costs.

One would think I was important.

In truth, Merlin is the one the world needs, and the one who will ultimately save it.

But apparently, my return is inevitable. I will be back in the human realm once again, corporeal. I anticipate with great pleasure my first breath of air through new lungs, my first sight of the earth through new eyes.

The man who has always loved me as a father loves a son, will be my father in truth.

I will be the son of a god and a part-Elven woman, not entirely human. I will have two brothers and a sister to spoil me, and many of my knights of old to protect and serve me. I will grow fast and tall and, hopefully, be worthy of my new family.

I wonder if anyone suspects that Merlin never threw my sword, Excalibur, into the lake at Avalon upon my death. That he has had it in his possession all along.

I look forward to holding it again.

I look forward to living again.

And I look forward to finally having magic of my own, through my father, Myrddin Emrys, the god of magic and healing—also known as the mighty sorcerer, Merlin Ambrosius.

1

CHAPTER 1
Moab, Wednesday, January 30, 2019

"Merlin, he's coming…" Emily panted and groaned, experiencing wave after wave of pain as our baby came into the world in the traditional way.

I'd offered to make her labor pain-free but she'd refused—she wanted to experience Arthur's birth to the fullest, pain and all.

As I held her hand and brushed her sweat-soaked hair back from her face, I knew she wouldn't appreciate the fact that I had ignored her request and eased the process considerably. My sometimes erratic knowledge of the future had forewarned me that the birth would be a difficult one, and I could not allow her to risk either her life or the baby's. Nor was there any point for her to endure needless suffering.

The long night gradually succumbed to the light of day as our child finally made his appearance at seven twenty-five, and I beheld the face I'd been waiting so long to see.

Exhausted yet triumphant, Emily sat up and reached for Arthur. Rae helped her open the front of her gown so that she could hold the baby against her bare skin, even before he was cleaned. I clamped and cut the umbilical cord and soon after that, Em delivered the placenta with a small gush of blood. I checked it to make sure no part of it had been left behind in the uterus.

When Em could bear to part with Arthur for a few moments, Lumina and Rae dried him and wrapped him in a soft blue receiving blanket.

"Oh, well done, Em," Sarah murmured as she replaced the water-proof pad and soiled bedding with clean sheets.

I stood close as Lainie gently sponged Em's body with warm water, dried her, and helped her into a fresh gown. I grinned when I noticed the word "magical" printed on the fabric, surrounded by magic wands and shooting stars.

Settled once again, Em glanced up at me with elation. I smiled as I lovingly caressed her face and simultaneously sent Light into her body to heal her of the rigors of childbirth.

Em reached again for the baby, and when Lumina handed Arthur to her, she guided him tenderly to her breast. He was ready to nurse and latched onto her turgid nipple, suckling enthusiastically.

She sighed contentedly, glowing with love. With one hand still touching her face and the other cupping Arthur's downy cheek, I called upon the Light of the gods, which surrounded the three of us in a bright golden glow.

* * *

Later, as I held my newborn son in my arms, I could scarcely contain the overwhelming joy I felt that Arthur was here at last. As I gazed raptly at his perfect features, his eyes slowly opened, and rather than the typical unfocused look of a human newborn, he looked up at me with the awareness of an older child.

"Ah, there you are, my lord. How does it feel to be back in the land of the living?" I whispered, hoping I wouldn't disturb my sleeping wife.

Arthur smiled and waved his tiny arms excitedly. I laughed quietly and lightly kissed his forehead. Lumina had done much the same thing at two weeks old when the knights had visited her.

"Do you remember, Arthur, in your previous life, before you were aware of your true parentage, that you wished I was your father? I always did love you like a son, all those centuries ago in Camelot. And now, my lord, you *are* my son."

I was talking to myself. Arthur had fallen asleep. I rocked him gently, singing ancient cradle songs under my breath in several different languages.

* * *

Emily quietly watched her legendary husband rock their child, his long black hair falling forward over his shoulders in a silken mass, and the Light of the gods shining golden white around him. As she listened to him sing to Arthur, her heart swelled with love and pride. This was the first time she had ever heard Merlin sing. He had the voice of an angel, which was appropriate, since that was precisely what he was. He generally insisted he was a god, but it was just semantics, really. She still called him "god man," and "wingman" when she was being flippant, but ever since he had finally told her the truth, that he was actually one of the original sons of God, and she had seen his angel wings, she had been awestruck.

Emily had treasured her entire pregnancy, but the moments when Merlin had spread his large elegant hand on her belly and the child within her had seemed to communicate with his father, had been particularly poignant. The delivery, while long and arduous, had not been as painful has she had feared. She suspected Merlin had helped with that, which was contrary to her request, but she decided it was a good thing he had intervened after all.

Originally, her husband and her mother were to have been her only attendants, but her daughter Lumina, Derek's wife, Sarah, and Morry's wife, Lainie, had begged to be part of the whole experience. Emily decided she would enjoy having everyone around to help her bring Arthur into the world, and graciously welcomed them all.

She was the mother of the future King of Albion—Arthur Pendragon Ambrosius. Em shook her head. Unbelievable.

Merlin stopped singing and was watching her. "You're awake." His pleasant baritone seemed to reverberate in her mind, calm yet exuding an undeniable power.

She smiled and beckoned to him to hand her the baby, who took that moment to awaken and cry out hungrily.

Merlin carefully handed Arthur to her. She settled him at her breast and he immediately began to suck. Emily gave a satisfied sigh and met her husband's intense green gaze. Without warning, his aura flared so brightly she had to shade her eyes to see him.

"Could you please tone your Light down some, god man?"

"Oh, sorry, Em." He modified his brightness. "Is that better?"

"Much, thank you."

Emily smiled. Ever since Merlin had fully transitioned, he'd had to monitor and make adjustments to the brilliant god Light that naturally shone through him.

* * *

I couldn't take my eyes off of our son. I hadn't realized the extent of my longing for another child, particularly this child. I had missed Arthur terribly since his death at the Battle of Camlann in the fifth century, and although the pain had gradually subsided, it was comparable to a losing a limb—the ache from that missing appendage never wholly disappeared.

Over the centuries, my raison d'être had been the search for a way to bring Arthur back from Avalon—that special corner of the Other World to which his body and soul had been taken upon his death. Though I knew his soul resided there, it had never occurred to me to try and contact him.

Then, in early 2013, I was awakened from my self-imposed slumber through time by a voice that urged me to renew my commitment to bring Arthur back by finding a new portal to Avalon. The original portal on Glastonbury Tor had disappeared long ago.

After an unexpected meeting with Arthur in the Other World that summer, and for many years afterwards, I had searched for the new portal here in the glorious red rock country around Moab, Utah, in a cave or a cavern, or under an arch. But the endeavor proved fruitless.

In June of 2018, when I returned from my unplanned trip to the past—during which my brother Beli and I had mended our long-broken relationship—it became clear to me that the portal was not a place at all, it was a person. It turned out my wife was the portal through which Arthur would arrive in the current century, his soul residing in the body of my newborn son.

* * *

I looked closely at Arthur's tiny face, somehow expecting him to look like he did in the past and in the vision I'd seen at his conception. Now, his features were similar to mine; his face narrow and his slanted eyes a startling green. However, his hair was the familiar sandy blond I remembered. Most newborn babies' hair and eye color changed as they grew older. I knew that Arthur's would not.

My phone, which I'd muted hours ago when Em's labor started, vibrated urgently. I smiled and accepted the call.

"Hello, Gwen. Yes, Arthur has arrived. Would you like to see him?"

"Are you kidding? Of course, I want to see him!" Her excitement was palpable, even over the phone.

"Shall I take a photo and send it to you?"

"Yes, please!"

I touched the camera icon on my phone, took a picture of Arthur, and texted it to her.

"He doesn't look like he used to." She sounded strangely disappointed. "He looks like you, except his hair is light."

"Which is understandable, Gwen, since I'm his father this time, not Uther Pendragon. However, his soul is the same. Lancelot is large and blond, rather than slender and dark-haired as he was in the past, and yet you recognized him, didn't you? Come over and see Arthur; you'll know him. And he will remember you, Gwen. Even this young, he'll remember."

She and I spoke quietly for a few more minutes, and then ended our call.

"Gwen is coming over soon, I take it?"

I grinned at Emily. "She'll be here shortly, along with the knights. I'll make sure they don't stay long. After all, you and Arthur need your rest."

She gave me an eloquent look. "They've all been waiting impatiently for this moment to arrive, so I doubt we'll be able to hustle them out of here so peremptorily. Besides, Arthur will let us know when he's tired."

We both looked at our son, who seemed to be waiting for his old friends, and his former wife, to arrive.

A few minutes later, I sensed the Hummer pull up at the curb and heard my daughter's voice in my mind.

Dad, they're here.

Invite them in, Lumina.

Emily handed Arthur to me and I stood waiting for his subjects to enter the room.

Gwen walked in first, followed respectfully by Sir Lancelot, Sir Gawain, Sir Percival, and Sir Leon. All five bowed at my feet in a show of respect to both their god and their king. I couldn't help but remember when these knights had last kneeled to Arthur centuries ago, their red and gold cloaks with the Pendragon emblem draping their powerful frames, while Queen Guinevere observed their deference with approval.

Returning my thoughts to the present, I accepted the fealty they offered, and indicated by a quick telepathic message that they should stand. I held Arthur so that he could see the faces of his loyal subjects and he waved his tiny arms enthusiastically, particularly when he noticed Gwen hovering to the side with her hands over her mouth and tears in her eyes. She approached me humbly and searched my face for permission to hold my son, who would one day be her husband again.

I smiled and held Arthur out to her and she gingerly took him from me.

"Oh, you sweet thing," she murmured. As he lay cradled in her arms, she crooned to him in a voice thick with emotion. He smiled his newborn, toothless smile and reached for her curly hair, which was nearly as long as it had been in Camelot. Gwen laughed, delighted that he seemed to recognize her.

"Naturally he does, Gwen," I murmured. "And he never stopped loving you."

She looked into my eyes briefly, knowing better than to linger, then gazed at Arthur once more.

Emily and I exchanged a look, and beckoned to the knights to come forward.

INTERLUDE
Arthur

I had been in a warm, wet environment, held securely and safely inside my mother, her heartbeat a constant source of comfort.

And then I was forced out of my haven, propelled through a narrow, tight channel and out into a world of sensation.

Bright lights and strange noises dazzled me. I was cold then I was warm then I was hungry.

What had happened? Where was I?

I heard a voice I recognized. Although I did not understand the words, I knew who it was. I opened my eyes and beheld a dazzling light surrounding the one who had always been the center of my world.

Merlin. The name emerged and settled in the forefront of my mind. I smiled happily and moved my arms, pleased to be held by my father.

I must have slept, only to awaken when a sharp pain in my body made me cry out.

I was held in my mother's arms and offered a firm round object that fit perfectly between my questing lips. I automatically began to suck and a sweet warm liquid flowed into my mouth. As I drank, the gnawing pain gradually disappeared and I was satisfied.

I slept again and awakened to hear another familiar voice. Female, but not my mother's voice. The sound of it brought back memories of a life before this one and I perked up, somehow understanding that the person whose voice I recognized would be here soon, along with others, the faces of whom were familiar and dear to me.

Then they were surrounding me with greetings of love and respect. And the woman I had traveled an unimaginable distance to see again took me into her arms and sang to me. I laughed and grabbed at the soft curls tickling my face. Guinevere. Oh, Gwen, my love, I'm back.

CHAPTER 2
Moab, Wednesday, January 30, 2019, Noon

Derek Colburn closed his front door and jogged across the street as the Jeep Patriot pulled up behind a long line of cars. He waited on the sidewalk as his son got out of the car.

"Jeez, what is this, Grand Central Station?" Morry groused as he joined his father.

"Yeah, well, it's a big day for this family," Derek said, noticing that Merlin's house seemed to pulse with energy. He glanced at the younger man quizzically. "Ya seem on edge—what's goin' on?"

"I don't know. I've been feeling out of sorts lately."

Derek was anxious to go in and see the new baby—*Arthur was finally here*, he thought excitedly—but he was concerned by his son's attitude. He and Morry had not spent much quality time together recently, since they were both married, but even so, he had no trouble sensing Morry's dissatisfaction.

Derek tentatively reached out with his mind and encountered a solid wall of resistance. Morry was effectively blocking him telepathically, which concerned him greatly. He put his hand on Morry's shoulder in what he hoped was a sympathetic gesture.

"Ya can tell me anythin'."

Morry looked briefly into his father's eyes. "I know. We'll talk later, okay? We need to get in there and greet the new arrival."

* * *

I sensed the tension emanating from my grandson as he and Derek approached the house and knew the cause of it, but I was too caught up in the pleasure of holding my newborn son to focus on any kind of negativity. However, in the back of my mind, I was aware of everything that happened in my house—every action, every thought, every word.

* * *

Gwen and the knights were hanging out in the kitchen, where the women were setting out a buffet lunch, and all of them looked up and smiled as Morry and Derek walked into the living room.

"Hey, have you guys eaten?" Lumina asked.

"I'd be glad to fix you two some sandwiches if you're hungry," Rae added, as the men's wives greeted them with hugs and kisses.

"I want to see the baby, but after that, yeah, I could eat, thanks," Derek said as he gave Sarah another quick peck on the cheek and headed towards the master bedroom.

"Roast beef and Swiss cheese on sourdough, if ya have it, with mayo, mustard, lettuce and tomato," he tossed back over his shoulder.

"You got it. It'll be here waiting for you." Rae received a 'thumbs up' as Derek disappeared down the hallway. "And you, Morry?"

"I'm not very hungry, Rae."

"Okay, honey. Let me know if you change your mind." The older woman turned away to get Derek's lunch ready.

Lainie watched her husband with concern. He hadn't even thanked Rae for her generous offer, which wasn't like him. She steered him back into the living room and sat him down on the couch. "What's going on?"

"What do you mean?" he asked, evasively.

She pursed her lips. "You're upset about something. Talk to me."

Looking into her lovely, violet eyes, he admitted what was bothering him. "I want *us* to have a baby."

She blinked and looked down. "I know you do, Morry."

He was tired of her evasion, so he cupped her face in his hands and made her look directly at him. "Don't you?" He was tall, but so was she, so even sitting down their gaze was almost on the same level.

She paused for a moment too long. "Uh, sure, I guess...some day." She cut her eyes away from him.

He gritted his teeth. "You're going to have to decide what you want, because I definitely want a family, and I won't wait forever for you to make up your mind." He dropped his hands abruptly.

"I'm going to see Arthur," he said flatly, then got up and stomped towards the bedrooms. He didn't look back.

Lainie watched him go and knew she was going to have to do some soul-searching. She was afraid of taking that next step, of getting pregnant, and she didn't understand her reluctance. She loved Morry and knew the two of them were meant to be together. He was an excellent lover—she'd never had such electrifying sex in her life—so that wasn't the problem. Hell, they'd had children together before, in other lifetimes that they both remembered. So what was it? She—

"Lainie, what's the matter?"

She turned around to face Sarah. "Oh, nothing. Morry and I had a slight difference of opinion," she said airily.

"I can tell something's wrong, honey. You have tears in your eyes." Sarah's sympathetic observation was too much for her and Lainie started to cry in earnest.

Lumina and Rae paused in their culinary pursuits to turn and look at her with alarm and Gwen and the knights stared at Lainie, concerned.

"Is everything okay?" Lumina started to put down the knife she was using to spread mayo on the bread, but Sarah shook her head to indicate she would handle the situation.

She grabbed a couple of jackets off their hooks next to the back door and hustled Lainie outside, over to the stone bench under the leafless mulberry tree in the corner of the yard. They both hurried to don their outerwear as a cold breeze hit them and they shivered involuntarily. Despite the fact that they both wore jeans and sweaters, neither woman had considered they would be sitting outside. Once they were properly clad and had pulled their hoods up to cover their ears, Sarah pointed to the bench and said, "Sit."

Lainie obeyed meekly and Sarah squeezed in next to her, hugging her close.

"Tell me what's bothering you."

"I...I can't."

"Okay. We could just sit here together for a few minutes and revel in the solitude."

Lainie wiped her eyes. "Yes, we could. Thanks." She closed her eyes.

They were quiet, listening to the distant sounds of traffic from downtown Moab, and the occasional clatter of dishes and laughter from inside the house.

After a few minutes, Sarah said, "We women have to help each other out, give each other emotional support when we need it, wouldn't you say?"

Lainie nodded and acknowledged to herself that she'd be able to cope with her issues with a little assistance from her sister-in-law. After all, she was a strong woman, a witch, and a shapeshifter. She could do this.

"Why don't I come over for coffee tomorrow morning and we can talk, say seven forty-five?"

Lainie smiled. "I'd love that."

Sarah shivered. "Great. Let's go back in before we freeze to death."

CHAPTER 3
Moab, Wednesday, January 30, 2019, Night

Merlin held Arthur in his arms while Emily got ready for bed. She lingered in the shower, knowing that her husband cherished every moment he spent with his newborn son. She stretched luxuriously, glad that the long painful labor was over. But she quickly reminded herself that it could have been worse. She hadn't realized how agonizing birthing a child would be. Lumina had teleported directly out of her womb, so she'd never endured that level of pain before.

Which raised the question, why hadn't Arthur done the same? Em pondered that thought for a few minutes, until she came to the conclusion that it must have been because Lumina was a goddess and Arthur was only a demigod.

Only a demigod! About six years ago, before she met Merlin, she had read about magic, demigods, gods, and angels at Derek's insistence, since that normally wasn't her thing. Now, they were a part of her daily existence.

Em grinned as she finished rinsing and turned off the faucets. She squeezed the excess water out of her long, thick mane of golden-brown hair, and stepped out of the shower onto the plush mat. Grabbing a towel off the rack, she started drying herself, careful not to brush the terrycloth against her sensitive nipples.

Unbidden, a memory popped into her head. Five years ago, shortly after Lumina was born, her daughter had experienced a growth spurt that caused her to go from newborn to three-year-old practically overnight, so she hadn't wanted to nurse any longer. Em's breasts had been engorged with milk and she'd had to ask Merlin to magically relieve the pressure, easing her discomfort. The sudden loss of her infant had caused her a great deal of distress, both mentally and physically.

She fervently hoped that Arthur's inevitable accelerated growth would hold off at least until he was a toddler, but she had no control over how or when it would occur.

She made an effort to shake off the sense of melancholy she felt. This was her destiny, and Arthur's. She couldn't change it, so she was determined to relish every last second of his childhood. After all, the plan was for Arthur to grow to manhood in the next five years, because the world needed him desperately. It would be inexcusably selfish of her to want to keep him a child with the world on the verge of destroying itself. But…

Her emotions surged and tears threatened to fall. Emily struggled to contain them. She didn't want Merlin to feel badly that he had put her in this position, so she took a breath and let it out slowly, focusing within until she calmed down.

* * *

I had put my son down tenderly in his cradle as soon as he'd fallen asleep, and was sitting in the big rocking chair reflecting on the reality of my transition, when I felt Em's emotions threaten to overwhelm her.

I waited, smiling fondly as she dammed her emotional flood by distracting herself with thoughts of making love to me. Desire surged through my body as it responded to her mental images.

"Ready for bed?" Em inquired with a gleam in her eye as she stepped into the bedroom. She looked like a Valkyrie standing there, magnificently naked, her lush curves inviting me to touch her.

I couldn't look away from her. I hadn't showered or brushed my teeth yet, but as much as I valued the ritual of getting ready for bed in the traditional way, the occasion called for magic. Instantly, I took care of my ablutions, dispensed with my clothing, and stood facing her, as naked and ready as she was.

"Absolutely, but are you sure you're up to it?"

Em walked over to the cradle, lightly stroked her hand over our child's downy hair, and turned to me confidently. "Yes, I'm sure. You already healed me, Arthur is sleeping soundly, and I want you inside me, husband."

She came to me and pressed her warm body sensuously against mine. Without delay, I guided us to the bed, whereupon we collapsed in a writhing jumble of entwined limbs, touching and kissing until the urge to join our bodies overrode everything else. As I slid inside her, Em wrapped her legs around me, increasing the angle of penetration, pulling me in deeper. I couldn't move for a moment as our bodies and souls became one. Then nature prevailed. I had no choice but to move, thrusting into her moist heat repeatedly, until we both achieved that ultimate pinnacle of sensation, coasting gradually down the other side with heartfelt sighs of completion.

Even after my wife had fallen asleep with her head on my shoulder I continued to hold her, kissing her hair and running my hand down her back to her sweet round bottom. She was my darling and I loved her beyond reason.

Eventually, though, I became restless lying in bed. I was constantly aware of my unique connection to the universe—it was the source of my endless energy and the reason I no longer required sleep. I eased out from under the covers and stood next to the cradle gazing down at my son. My vision blurred and our newborn baby disappeared. When my sight cleared, a tall, regal man with green eyes stood at my side while we worked to bring the world back from the brink of disaster.

CHAPTER 4
Moab, Thursday, January 31, 2019, Morning

"Honey, what's going on, is Arthur okay?" Em's concerned voice broke through my trance.

I had been standing there for hours. Golden rays of early morning sunlight peeked through the drapes and Arthur was awake and fussing.

"Merlin?"

I turned to face her with a smile. "Sorry, I was caught up in a vision of the future." I picked up my son and cuddled him as my wife quickly donned her robe, then handed him to her when it became apparent that Arthur was hungry, something I was not equipped to handle.

"I think our boy needs a dry diaper first." She quickly changed him and put a clean onesie on him. "Okay, sweetheart, time for breakfast," she murmured, sitting down in the large rocking chair next to our bed. She opened her robe and bared a breast, settling our son at her nipple.

We made eye contact and grinned at each other.

* * *

"That was the most amazing thing I've ever seen." Lainie took a sip of coffee and glanced over at the stunning woman sitting across the kitchen table from her.

"It was beautiful, wasn't it?" Sarah smiled dreamily as she recalled the moment when they put the baby in Emily's arms and she held him to her breast for the first time.

"I don't know about beautiful." Lainie looked doubtful. "It was smelly, messy, and noisy and must have hurt like crazy. But it was... miraculous."

Sarah frowned, and then her face cleared as she realized Lainie was referring to the delivery itself. "Oh, yeah. That was pretty gross, but you're right, it was a miracle." She remembered how Em had described her first birthing experience. "Are you aware that Emily didn't actually deliver Lumina? The baby teleported out of her womb, so she didn't have to go through any of that."

"Why didn't Arthur teleport?"

Sarah shrugged. "Maybe he couldn't. In reality, I think Em wanted to experience the entire process, start to finish, conception to birth. So that's what happened."

"Do you think Merlin orchestrated the whole thing?" Lainie asked as she got up and walked over to the coffeemaker on the counter, intent on making a fresh pot.

"He might have." Sarah looked thoughtful. "How would we know?"

"I guess we wouldn't, and it's none of our business anyway."

Sarah looked sheepish. "You're right, it isn't."

They both paused, unsure whether they should pursue that sensitive topic.

Lainie elected to finish what she'd started with the coffee. "Would you like another cup?" she asked as she filled the reservoir with water.

Sarah checked her watch and shook her head regretfully. "I have to get going. Since Emily's home with the baby and Rae and Lumina are taking turns helping her, it's going to be up to me to run the shop for a few days. What are your plans for today?"

"I have a dentist appointment early this afternoon in Price, so I took the day off. With a total of four hours of driving, plus a couple of hours for the appointment, there was no point in trying to go to work today. And I figured I'd go to Wal-Mart while I was there." She turned to the other woman and debated whether she should blurt out the truth. She thought better of it.

"Thanks for coming over, Sarah. Since I married Morry, and you and he are close, it worked out nicely that you and I became friends."

Sarah got up and put her arms around Lainie. "It did, and I'm glad. It's fantastic that he found someone who makes him happy." She pulled away and grabbed her purse, pausing as she remembered the real reason they had decided to get together this morning.

"Oh, shoot, I'm so sorry. We never talked about what's going on between you and Morry."

"Don't worry, I think I've decided what I need to do." Lainie forced herself to sound confident and plastered a sincere smile on her face.

"Wonderful," Sarah said, relieved. "I felt so sorry for you yesterday. By the way, where is my stepson this morning?"

"He said he had to be at work earlier than usual to write a high priority article, so he left shortly before you got here. I think he was anxious to get away from me."

17

"I doubt that, although he did seem distant and not his usual self yesterday. Anyway, I have to run. We'll talk later, okay?" Sarah waved as she hurried out the back door, closing it behind her firmly as a gust of icy wind twined around her ankles and up under her coat. She was wearing a green cable-knit sweater, brown wool pants, and fleece-lined boots with heavy socks, but she was still cold. She checked the time again and winced.

Sarah shivered as she walked briskly up Aspen Street to the intersection with Doc Allen Drive. She paused for a brief moment to admire the wall of red rock that rose like a sentinel behind the housing tract, and checked both directions for traffic. She waited impatiently while a single vehicle drove slowly by, then jogged across the street, cutting across the swath of winter-brown grass that was her lawn. She walked up the slight slope of concrete driveway to her car, settled herself in the driver's seat and started it, turning up the heat with anticipation.

As she backed out and drove towards the downtown area, she thought how pleased she was that Morry and Lainie had been able to find a house within a couple of blocks of both hers and Derek's, and Merlin and Emily's, homes.

* * *

After Sarah left, Lainie finished setting up her coffeemaker and pushed the button. As she leaned against the counter, waiting for the process to finish, she thought about the major topics the two of them had never gotten around to discussing: their own plans, dreams, and fears regarding motherhood.

She wished they had, because she knew Sarah was pregnant. Lainie didn't know how she knew, but she did. Perhaps her heightened sense of smell, courtesy of her shapeshifter magic, enabled her to perceive what Sarah herself wasn't aware of yet.

It was ironic, really. She and Morry had gotten married in a rush the previous August because they thought she was pregnant. The pregnancy test she'd used had shown a false positive.

Lainie didn't regret marrying Morry since she loved him dearly. But she wasn't sure how she felt about not being pregnant—now and then she felt sad, but mostly she felt relief. Despite the fact that she was going to be thirty-seven years old in May, she wasn't ready to be a mom. Maybe it was Merlin's doing, or even…God's. A quiver snaked down her spine as she remembered that God was her husband's great-grandfather—literally.

After Morry's declaration yesterday, however, Lainie knew she was going to have to take that step to motherhood soon, whether she was ready or not, if she wanted to keep her husband. She doubted he'd really leave her, but she didn't want to push her luck.

She decided to suggest they have a date tomorrow night.

She shook herself free of all those perplexing thoughts, poured herself a fresh cup of coffee, and carried it into the bathroom. Time to get her day started.

* * *

Sarah unlocked the front door of The Moab Herbalist and recited the words—infused with her magic—that released Merlin's protection spell on the building. As she stepped into the room, she flicked her hand and the overhead lights came on. She grinned smugly.

She had just divested herself of her heavy coat, warm hat and gloves, opened the blinds and turned on the computer when the phone rang. "Good morning, The Moab Herbalist."

"Sarah, it's Em. I wanted to tell you I hired Chris Colburn." She chuckled. "It's kind of ironic, since it used to be her shop. Anyway, she's not starting until tomorrow, so I hope you'll be okay alone until then."

"Oh, I'm sure I will," Sarah said confidently. "I can always use magic when the customers aren't looking."

"Fine, but be careful, don't let anyone see you."

"Don't worry. And I'll make up a list of things Chris can start on when she gets here tomorrow morning."

"Great. I appreciate you taking care of the shop until things get settled here. I'm hoping to bring Arthur with me at some point, but I won't be ready to do that for a while yet. Oh, and if you do get swamped, give Merlin or Lumina a call and one of them will pop in and help you. Thanks, Sarah."

"You're welcome...'Stepmom,'" she said glibly.

"Gah, don't *you* start with that!" Em exclaimed, referring to the teasing she and Derek had done with each other for years after they had found out Merlin was Derek's father, making Em his stepmother.

They laughed, then said their goodbyes.

Sarah sighed. Of all the people in Moab to choose from, Em had hired Chris. It wasn't as if Sarah actively disliked her, but she still couldn't quite let go of her jealousy. She knew it was ridiculous to feel that way, for several reasons. One, Derek and Chris had been divorced long before she came on the scene. Two, she and Derek had been married since August of 2017. And three, Chris and Seth had been living together for the last six months, so she clearly wasn't interested in Derek anymore as anything but a friend.

Sarah brightened. Working with Chris rather than some stranger meant that she wouldn't have to hide her magic. *Okay*, she thought, *it will work out after all.*

CHAPTER 5
Moab, Friday, February 1, 2019, Early Morning

The headlights of the oncoming cars pierced the darkness and then disappeared one after the other as the vehicles rushed past, heading north to the intersection with I-70. The line of cars had become a never-ending blur.

Fatigue caused Cathy Grant's eyelids to droop and her concentration to waver. A loud piercing honk startled her to full alertness and she jerked the steering wheel to the right, narrowly missing the oncoming eighteen-wheeler. Heart pounding frantically in her chest, she braked quickly, swerving onto the shoulder of the road. The guy behind her leaned on the horn in irritation as he passed her.

Shaking, she closed her eyes and gulped air into her lungs. She could have been killed in a head-on collision! She groaned and leaned back in her seat. She was so damn tired. What had possessed her to drive from Denver, Colorado to Moab, Utah in the middle of the night in this weather? She could have waited at least until the sun was shining. Admittedly, the roads were clear and dry at the moment, but it was overcast and cold and felt like it could snow.

In her heart, she knew why she'd done it. She hadn't heard from her sister in months and she was worried sick about her. They'd had no more than sporadic contact for nearly a year after Chris's return to Moab, due partly to Cathy's participation in an experimental drug program.

Cathy had been optimistic that it would take care of her chronic health issues and the drug had worked—she was no longer housebound with limited mobility. But she had severely underestimated the effect this drive would have on her stamina.

She flipped on the dome light so she could see what she was doing and shuffled through her CDs. She fed her favorite old Air Supply CD into the player and cracked the window open for some fresh, cold air.

She still had thirty miles to go before she arrived in Moab and she was determined to get there in one piece.

She poured herself a cup of coffee out of the thermos sitting on the seat next to her and pondered Chris's latest text, which aroused her curiosity yet again about the guy in her sister's life.

The way Chris described him he was the perfect man. He was good-looking, tall, an accomplished lover, and had a killer Scottish accent. And he had long, sexy legs he showed off when he wore his kilt. All of that sounded great.

But she also said he was a fairy.

Cathy snorted derisively. Sure, uh huh. A six-foot-three fairy with long black hair and huge white wings.

Chris's "perfect" boyfriend must have gotten her hooked on some serious hallucinogens.

This was the real reason she was risking her life, driving recklessly through the dark hours all the way to Moab when she should be in bed sleeping.

Cathy took the last swallow of now-tepid coffee and shook off the rationalizations for her behavior. She screwed the cap back on the thermos and adjusted her posture, ready to continue her journey.

She switched off the light and patted the dashboard of her old Toyota. "Good girl," she murmured. At least her car was running smoothly.

As she drove back onto the highway, her favorite song, "Making Love Out of Nothing At All," came on and she cranked up the volume and started singing. So what if her taste in music was hopelessly outdated?

Thirty minutes later, as she slowed entering the north end of town, she noticed a Maverick station on her right and decided to stop. The car was low on fuel and she badly needed a restroom. She pulled up to the gas pump and shut the car off. As she opened the door and stepped out, the cold jolted her and she reached back inside for her coat. After quickly tugging it on, she stretched with a groan and a sigh. She got the gas pumping before going into the convenience store, finding it difficult to put one foot in front of the other since she was stiff from sitting so long.

A few minutes later, Cathy headed back to her car with a bottle of apple juice in hand. She paused to inhale the invigorating air and took a sip of her drink. The clouds had lifted, the sun was coming up, and she gazed appreciatively at the cliffs on each side of the valley. The red rock shone like a new penny in the early morning light and she recalled why she had always loved this area: it had an otherworldly quality that spoke to her soul.

She topped off the tank and hung up the nozzle. After replacing the gas cap, she slid into the driver's seat and fastened her seat belt. She felt revived as she headed into downtown Moab and grinned when she saw that many of the shops she remembered from the past were still there.

Like the one she was passing on the right-hand side of Main Street —The Moab Herbalist. It had been her sister's business years ago, in the building she'd inherited from their paternal grandfather, until Chris had sold them both to some English guy. Or was he Welsh? What was his name again? Merle or Mitchell, something like that. She couldn't remember. In any case, the business appeared to be flourishing; the exterior of the building had been repainted and the sign redone.

She glanced at her watch. It was still early, and she didn't know if Chris had found another job yet, so she might still be in bed. She undoubtedly wouldn't appreciate her dropping in unannounced, but Cathy hoped that by surprising the two of them, she might catch Chris's boyfriend at a disadvantage. Like, with his wings on display. Right.

* * *

"Chris, how is yer—" Seth paused midsentence and glanced towards the door.

"How is my what, honey?"

"I was going tae ask how yer sister is faring, but we'll soon be able tae ask her, as she's walking up the sidewalk the noo."

"What? Are you joking? I—" Chris jumped nervously as there was a loud knock on the front door, and she looked over at her lover, hoping he had disguised himself. She was relieved to see he'd created an effective glamour to hide his wings and pointed ears, but he'd forgotten one thing.

"Uh, are you going to do something about your eyes?"

"Weel, shite," he muttered, and his yellowish reptilian eyes became light green with round pupils.

"That works. You look very handsome, almost human." She smiled and pulled his head down for a quick kiss.

Seth looked disgruntled. "Ye needna insult me, lass." He glanced towards the door as a second knock sounded.

"Coming," Chris raised her voice and gave Seth a worried look. "What she's doing here?"

He shrugged. "Let's find oot."

Chris changed her expression to look welcoming, then disengaged the deadbolt and opened the door, allowing a gust of cold air to enter. "Cathy, hi, what a surprise! Come on in. It's so good to see you, you're looking fabulous!" As she gave her sister a hug, Chris knew she was babbling. She'd never expected Cathy to drive all the way to Moab without informing her that she was coming, showing up at such an early hour, no less.

* * *

As Cathy gazed over her twin sister's shoulder at the tall man with long wavy, black hair, his gaze seemed to mesmerize her and she had difficulty answering.

"Oh, uh, I'm feeling better so I thought I'd, ah, drop by. I mean, it's been a long time since I've seen you, so…" Cathy was overpowered by Seth's blatantly sexual presence. He didn't appear to have wings or pointed ears, but he was every bit as attractive as Chris had claimed. Particularly since his chest was bare and his black jeans rode low on his hips. And she hadn't had sex in years.

Chris noticed her sister's reaction to Seth's innate sexuality and it irritated her. "Sooo, you decided in the middle of the night to drive for five-plus hours after you've scarcely recuperated from a long debilitating illness, because you missed me."

"Well…yes." Cathy looked at the floor and shifted uneasily as she lied to her sister.

"Will ye excuse us a moment?" Seth asked politely and pulled Chris across the room, conjuring a soundproof bubble around the two of them.

"She wanted tae catch me without ma glamour, lass, which leads me tae believe ye told her the truth aboot me." He raised his eyebrows and waited.

Chris flushed in embarrassment. "I figured she'd never see you, and wouldn't believe me anyway."

Cathy finally raised her eyes when the two continued to stand there, evidently talking, but in complete silence. She looked back and forth between them, wondering why she couldn't hear them. She was getting hot standing in their warm apartment with her coat on and debated taking it off.

Seth pondered the situation solemnly for a moment with his head tilted at a distinctly inhuman angle until he heard a familiar voice echo in his mind.

Cathy's here for a reason. Go ahead and show her what you actually look like.

Are ye sure?

Yes.

Ye ken best, Da. He dropped his glamour. Who was he to argue with the god of magic and healing?

Cathy gasped out loud at the shock of seeing Seth's suddenly altered appearance. The man—er, fairy—before her now sported graceful white wings attached to his back, pointed ears, and the yellow-green eyes of an unusual reptile.

"Seth, what the hell are you doing?" Chris demanded.

"Obeying ma father's instructions. She apparently needs tae ken the truth."

Chris took a measured breath and blew it out in exasperation. "I'm sorry I told her without your permission."

He gave her a wry look. "'Tis alright, Chris, if Da is fine with it, I am as weel." He glanced at Cathy, who was staring blatantly at his eyes and ears in wonderment, and dropped the magical barrier so they could all communicate again.

"This is amazing," Cathy exclaimed. "You look exactly the way she described you. I thought you were both on drugs."

Seth chuckled. "Nay, lass. We dinna take drugs." He stuck out his hand. "Seth MacAdam. Nice tae meet ye."

She clasped his slender hand firmly. "Cathy Grant. It's nice to meet you, too. It's a little overwhelming to meet a real fairy, especially when I was expecting it to be a hoax." She glanced between Chris and Seth apologetically.

"No' a hoax, I assure ye. And my race prefers the term Fae. I'm from the land of Faery, wi' an 'e,' or ye could call it the Fae realm, but I've lived in the human realm, in Scotland, for many years."

"Ah, okay." She was surprised at his eagerness to reveal his personal information after his initial reluctance to do so.

The conversation halted abruptly and an awkward silence ensued.

Finally, Chris made eye contact with Seth and asked him a question subvocally, using a technique he had taught her several years ago since she couldn't communicate telepathically. He nodded.

"You can stay in our extra bedroom, Sis. When do you have to go back to Denver?"

Cathy looked guiltily at her sister. "Ah, I don't. The truth is, I brought some stuff with me, and the rest is in storage. I was considering moving back to Moab, and I was hoping...."

"What, that you could move in with us? Nooo, huh uh, sorry, absolutely not!"

"Aw, Chris, please, just until I find my own place?" Cathy hated to be reduced to pleading, but she was so exhausted and light-headed all of a sudden she was ready to collapse.

"'Tis alright lass, ye can stay," Seth said softly, aware the woman was on the verge of fainting. He glanced eloquently at his lover, who glared back at him and then sighed dramatically.

"Okay, Sis. Where are your keys? I'll go get your stuff out of the car."

"Thanks. They're in the outside pocket of my purse," Cathy said weakly. She took Seth's arm gratefully as he steered her down the hall and through the door of a sparsely furnished bedroom, which was apparently used for storage, given the neatly stacked boxes in one corner. She shrugged off her coat and he guided her to the bed to sit down. As Seth kneeled on the floor in front of her to remove her shoes, his wings rustled in front of her face and she could barely restrain herself from touching them.

Before he stood up, he took her small hands between his two large ones, looked deeply into her eyes and said a few words in a language she didn't recognize.

Instantly, Cathy relaxed and fell into a dreamless sleep. Seth gently eased her down onto the mattress and put a pillow under her head. He pulled a warm blanket over her, got to his feet, and then stood looking down at her, noting the differences between the two sisters. They weren't identical twins, but each woman was attractive in her own way. They both had blond hair but Cathy's was a shade darker than Chris's. Cathy's nose was slightly larger and straighter, and her lips were thinner. Seth smiled. The two couldn't be more dissimilar in personality, but he sensed they loved one another, despite Chris's negative reaction to her sister's unanticipated visit.

He finally left the room. Cathy would be unconscious and healing for several hours and there was no point in standing there watching her sleep.

As he was closing the bedroom door, Chris dragged the last of Cathy's belongings into the apartment and dumped them unceremoniously in the center of the living room.

Seth crossed the room to join her and put a hand up as he sensed Chris's irritation. "Afore ye get cross wi' me, ye need tae ken that Cathy's had a reoccurrence of her ailment, caused by the long drive she made tae make sure ye were alright."

Chris looked properly chastened. "I wasn't very welcoming was I?"

"I ken ye aren't pleased tae share our home with anyone else—even yer own sister—but she may have tae bide a wee in order tae recuperate. I've used a healing spell on her, but it could take some time tae work correctly. And I should do a few follow-up treatments for a day or two."

"Oh, Seth, I love my sister, but she's always been so needy and it gets on my nerves." She stared at him miserably.

He didn't reply, but took her into his arms and kissed her, his dark, wavy hair falling around them like a black satin curtain.

Chris caressed his handsome face and reluctantly pulled away. "I wish we could go back to bed and make love, but I have to go to work. I'm going to be late as it is, which isn't a good thing on my first day. And I'll be working with Sarah, who, as you know, is not my biggest fan."

"I ken that, but she's family, sae she'll understand," he said as Chris ran into their bedroom, hurriedly donned her work clothes, and made a mad dash for the bathroom.

When she emerged, makeup applied, Seth held her coat while she slipped it on. "Ye never had yer breakfast, lass. Here." He conjured a sweet roll in a white bakery bag and coffee in a to-go cup.

Chris quickly slung her purse over her shoulder, then took his offering and stretched up to kiss his cheek. "Thanks, Seth, I'll see you later."

* * *

Sarah looked up as the bell over the door tinkled and Chris slunk guiltily in the front door.

"You're late, Chris," she said, annoyed that the woman couldn't even make the effort to be punctual her first day.

"I'm so sorry. My sister showed up unexpectedly this morning and ended up collapsing. She'd driven all night from Denver, which was dreadfully hard on her since she's had a chronic illness for years." She was using her sister's condition to justify her tardiness, but it was the truth, damn it.

"Huh, I didn't know you even had a sister. Why hasn't Derek ever mentioned her?" Sarah let go of her self-righteous attitude in light of Chris's extenuating circumstances.

"I guess he never thought about it," Chris said, hanging her coat up on the rack in the corner. "Oh, and Seth surprised me by relaxing his glamour and showing her what he really looks like."

"*What?*"

"According to Seth, Merlin communicated with him telepathically and told him to do it. Apparently, Cathy needs to know about the family."

Sarah's mouth dropped open in a look of pure astonishment, then she pulled herself together as a couple of customers came in.

"Okay, we can discuss it later," she said quietly. "There's a ton of work to do so here's what you can start on. I know this used to be your shop years ago, but we do things differently now." She handed Chris a full page list, which included prep work for herbal potions, as well as cleaning and stocking shelves.

At the incredulous look on her face, Sarah relented. "Merlin will probably drop by and take care of some of those chores, and I'll help you with the rest. It'll be alright, I promise."

CHAPTER 6
Moab, Friday, February 1, 2019, Morning

Colin Campbell was in his bathroom preparing to take a shower, reflecting on all the changes that had happened in his life since the evening he'd watched Merlin and Morry shapeshift into birds and fly over Moab. One thing in particular stood out in his mind: he'd made a decision that had changed his life forever.

It was one of the most outrageous moves he'd ever made, although he knew he'd do it again in a heartbeat. During a private conversation with Merlin back in October, he'd gotten down on the floor of the herb shop and kissed the sorcerer's feet, pledging his service and devotion to the god of magic and healing—who happened to be his ancestor Beli's brother.

And that line of reasoning led to a memory of the day he had met Beli.

It had happened several months ago. He had been hanging out at The Moab Herbalist on a Saturday morning—which he had been doing for more weekends than he could count—drinking coffee and reading a magazine, when he heard a distinctive voice greet Merlin. He glanced up and saw a large, exceptionally tall man with black hair and olive-toned skin embracing his great-uncle.

"Colin, come over here, will you? I'd like you to meet someone." Merlin grinned and waved him over.

He pushed up out of the comfortable armchair in which he'd been lounging and walked over to where the two men were leaning against the counter. He had a feeling he knew the identity of the newcomer, and was convinced when the man turned toward him.

A long black moustache adorned a craggy face that looked hauntingly familiar; he'd seen that face in the mirror countless times.

The man, wearing tattered old jeans and an ancient Grateful Dead T-shirt that stretched snuggly across his muscular chest, held his hand out and said, "Great-grandson, it's nice to meet you."

In a daze, Colin moved closer to his ancestor, who towered over him by at least six inches. As he reached out to shake that huge paw, Beli pulled him into a manly hug and pounded him on the back.

"I've looked forward to meeting you as well, uh, Great-grandfather," Colin admitted in a voice that seemed to echo Beli's but without the accent.

They stared long and hard at each other until both of them burst out laughing.

Merlin shook his head in amusement and commented that they were two peas in a pod. The three of them had chatted companionably until it was time to open the shop and Beli stated reluctantly that he had to return to the god realm. Before he vanished into thin air, he'd promised to keep in touch.

His thoughts returning to the present, Colin realized Beli had yet to keep that promise, but it was early days yet. He would be patient. After all, there was no hurry.

Colin gazed at his nakedness in the mirror and smirked at the sight. He turned this way and that, marveling yet again at the physical changes in his body. In place of a forty-something man with sagging jowls and an unsightly paunch, he saw a vigorous, muscular thirty-year-old sporting an undeniable glow of health and wellness.

His wife had confronted him months ago concerning the noticeable changes in his appearance and his attitude, suspicious he was having an affair. It didn't help that he was away from home every evening and most Saturdays, meeting with Merlin and the Knights of the Round Table. Thinking about the knights gave him a marvelous feeling of excitement regarding the future. There were four of them now, since Sir Leon had appeared in Moab at the end of October.

When Ryan—Sir Lancelot—explained that Llyr had brought Leon to Moab from fifth-century Britain, from Camelot, Colin almost fainted. The knight spoke Old British, the long-dead language that Merlin, Derek, and the other knights spoke fluently. Merlin had magically educated Leon in modern English, but since the man refused to use the language, he hadn't retained it.

Colin had tried to make friends with him, but Leon was either standoffish or not sure of himself in this modern time. In any case, he hadn't accepted Colin's overtures and continued to associate only with the other knights.

Colin reluctantly dragged his focus back to the subject he needed to concentrate on at the moment—his wife, Maggie. When he'd tried to tell her the truth, admittedly against Merlin's advice, she'd flipped out and left him, convinced he'd lost his mind. She'd taken their fourteen-year-old daughter, Rose, with her, but eighteen-year-old Josh, who had already graduated from high school and started college in January, would stay with Colin when he came home for holidays.

He wasn't sure how he felt about Maggie's departure. He still loved her, didn't he? They'd been married since 1998 and the buzz had been gone for years, but his marriage ought to be worth saving. Wasn't it? But when he delved into his innermost thoughts and feelings, he understood that he would never go back to his original state of ignorance, or give up his extraordinary association with Merlin's family, to placate her.

At last, he felt alive and proud of himself. He was assisting Merlin and would become King Arthur's personal legal advisor in the future.

Colin was thrilled at the prospect of working with the legendary king.

He took a breath, reminding himself it would be five years before the newborn Arthur matured to adulthood. He shook his head, unable to comprehend how that could happen.

But his mind was made up. He couldn't go back. Maggie would have to move on without him, as he had moved on without her. If she wanted a divorce, he wouldn't contest it. According to Merlin, his involvement with King Arthur had been foretold, and who was he to argue with destiny?

He blinked, and realized he was still standing in front of the mirror. His reflection grinned back at him as he remembered that he was descended from a god, and for that reason was more than human. He had no magical powers and he wasn't immortal, but Merlin had assured him he might live close to five hundred years, which ought to be more than enough for any man.

Life was good. No, it was more than that. It was outstanding.

* * *

"Detective, the Chief wants you in his office, pronto," a bored voice informed him from the break room door.

"What does he want?" Colin asked absently as he continued to work on a list of locations he still needed to check to see if Morgana's people had shown up yet. The evil wizards had vanished into thin air after abducting and brutalizing Jim Singleton the previous August and the whole family had been searching for them ever since.

He was oblivious to the boss's approach until he heard, "What the hell is this?"

31

Colin leaped out of his seat as the Chief barked in his ear and ripped the sheet of paper out of his hand, nearly knocking his cup of lukewarm coffee onto the floor in the process.

"Ah, a list of campgrounds I put together for, uh, a friend," he managed to say, trying to sound casual and ending up croaking like a bullfrog.

Police Chief Fred Baker, who was significantly shorter than Campbell's six one, glared up at him and jabbed a thick finger into his chest. "You're damned lucky I still need your expertise around here, because your attitude and attendance have sucked lately. You were over an hour late this morning and yet here you are, already taking a break.

"So get your ass in gear! With so many cops out sick, I need you and Smith to check out a report of a domestic disturbance over on Westwood. The neighbors claim the man's a druggie and beats on his woman, so be prepared. The guy could have weapons in the house."

"You got it, Chief. I have to grab a few things from my office and then we can take off.

"Meet you out back," Campbell barked at the officer standing indecisively in the doorway.

She gave him a curt nod and headed down the hall and out the door.

Back in his office, Colin glanced at the paper he'd managed to retrieve from his boss and picked up his phone. He entered a familiar number and Merlin answered before it rang.

"Yes, Nephew?"

"I won't have a chance to check out those locations you asked about, but I could fax the list to you—"

"No problem, Colin. Concentrate on the list and I'll see it in your mind."

"Okay, here goes," he said, trying to shut out all the background noise that threatened to distract him from focusing on the page.

Instantly, Merlin said, "Got it Colin, thanks."

"You're welcome, Uncle. Talk to you later," he said quietly. "Gotta go." He hastily ended the call, grabbed his water bottle and his kit and ran out to join his temporary partner. He was still awed by the fact that Merlin seemed to appreciate his help, although he suspected his umpteen-times-removed great-uncle gave him things to do so he'd feel like part of the family. He snorted. The guy knew everything that was going on in the entire world—at least that's what Derek claimed. Colin doubted Merlin needed anybody for anything. But he was immensely grateful to be included.

* * *

As soon as I put my phone down, a vision of Colin Campbell being shot and killed ripped through my mind, and I staggered. I felt Emily react to what I'd seen and heard her inhale sharply.

"Merlin, my God, what's happening?" Em ran out of the bedroom with Arthur in her arms.

"Colin's heading into a bad situation and he's going to die."

* * *

Detective Campbell and Officer Edda Smith drove code 10-40—silent run, no lights, no siren—to the address of the disturbance, over on Westwood off of Fifth West near what had once been the Denny's restaurant. Most of the homes on the street had been renovated, but a few were still run-down, and the address they were looking for happened to be one of them. As they pulled up in front of the property, they heard screaming and a loud muffled thud, as if something heavy had been thrown against a wall. They heard a shot, then another, and that changed the game. Smith keyed the mike. "10-23, arrived on scene. Shots fired."

They approached the house with weapons drawn.

"Go 'round back in case he tries to run," Campbell directed as he sprinted up onto the porch and pounded on the front door. "Police, open up!" He quickly stepped to the side in case the asshole with the gun decided to shoot through the door. When there was no response, he swiveled around and kicked it in. The lock broke and the door crashed into the wall with such force it splintered. In the back of his mind, he marveled it had been so easy; exterior doors were usually pretty solid. But he couldn't dwell on that at the moment.

He entered the stuffy, dim foyer cautiously, looking swiftly right and left into what appeared to be a living room on one side and a bedroom on the other, holding his Glock out in front of him with both hands. The rooms were cluttered and dirty and stank of cigarette smoke and the smell of gunpowder. There was an eerie silence, which didn't bode well for the domestic partner. He shouted again, forcefully, "Police, put your weapon down and come out with your hands up!"

Without warning, a crazy-eyed man raced out from behind a curtain and knocked the detective's weapon out of his hand with drug-enhanced strength, then aimed his own weapon at Colin's head and started to pull the trigger.

Time seemed to stop as Colin realized he was going to die. Then something inside of him reacted to the threat. Power blossomed in his chest and in one smooth motion, he pointed his hands, fingers spread, at the lunatic in front of him and blasted him with a short burst of blue fire. The man was knocked flat on his back, unconscious.

In shock, Colin stared at his hands. What the hell? Magic?

Grinning hugely, he picked his piece up off the floor, returned it to his shoulder holster, and got down to business.

When Smith came running in from the back of the house she saw her partner calmly cuffing the man who was out cold on the floor.

"Are you okay, sir?"

"I'm fine."

"I heard a weird sound and saw a blue glow. What the hell was that?"

"I don't know, I didn't see anything," he lied. "Don't just stand there, look for the woman." He couldn't possibly tell Edda the truth. She would laugh herself silly and Colin would be the butt of every office joke for years to come.

Smith quickly checked out the other bedroom and a small utility room, and ran into the filthy kitchen. She discovered a plump, battered woman in wrinkled, stained, and bloody clothing crumpled at the base of the stove, her greasy brown hair hanging across her slack face.

Smith knelt in front of her and determined she was still breathing. "I found her, Detective. She's been shot and she's unconscious, but alive."

The perp was coming around and Colin read him his rights as he hauled him to his feet and started out the front door. He paused and shouted back to his partner, "Call for an ambulance while I contact the station."

As Colin strode out to the vehicle with the prisoner in tow and shoved the dazed man into the back seat, he couldn't stop thinking about what happened. The guy had aimed his gun at him with deadly intent, and although Colin was wearing his bulletproof vest, that wouldn't have saved him from being shot in the head.

He had reacted to the threat instinctively. He'd seen both Merlin and Derek use the blue fire and remembered wishing he had that ability. But how the hell could he have used magic? He was positive Merlin had told him he had no magical abilities.

Short of confronting his uncle—which he would do later—there was only one way to find out. After he radioed the station, he leaned back against the headrest, closed his eyes and focused inside himself as he'd seen everyone in the family do at some point. And discovered something pulsing brightly in the center of his chest: Power. Magic. A gift from the gods without a doubt, but Merlin was the only god he interacted with on a regular basis, so it had to have been his doing. He didn't understand why he'd received such a gift, but he'd take it. Oh, yeah, he'd definitely take it.

* * *

I settled back in my office chair and chuckled, pleased that I'd been able to help Colin. He had expertly made use of his magic, with no training or preparation whatsoever, to defend himself—but not to kill. If by some remote chance I'd misjudged him, I would have taken over, prevented his death, and restrained the gunman.

I thought it was intriguing that Colin knew to sit quietly and look reflectively inside himself for the power that fueled the magical blue fire. But then, he'd been hanging out with my family and me regularly for over seven months and he was an observant man.

He'd actually had magic all along, a miniscule flame that had simply needed the right kindling to ignite it. I admit I had originally told him he had no magic, but at the time, he wasn't ready to handle it.

I crossed my legs and steepled my fingers on my chest. I knew Colin would be coming over to the house later—ostensibly to see the baby, but his main purpose was to confront me—and I had another surprise in store for him when he did.

In the interim, I'd check out those locations Colin had given me earlier, to see if I could find Morgana and her elusive followers. He had given me a comprehensive list of campgrounds, trailer parks, and other temporary overnight facilities in Grand County and in neighboring San Juan County. It didn't take long for me to discover most of them were still closed for the winter. Of the few that were open, none housed the group for which I was searching so assiduously. I couldn't imagine they would be staying in a hotel, although with the low winter rates they could have found one willing to take a large group. But that scenario was doubtful as I should have been able to sense their presence and I hadn't. I presumed Morgana would stay with them, but she might have separate accommodations. Since she had the ability to teleport, she could be anywhere in the world, as long as she had reliable telepathic connections within the group and was able to maintain control of them.

Using my enhanced god senses, I expanded the search to the entire country, and then worldwide, and came up with nothing. Morgana and her followers were not on the earth presently. Neither could I sense Jack Crandall or my devilish brother, but that was due to my ongoing issue of being unable to sense family.

I had to conclude Satan's followers were currently being housed in another dimension or time—or an alternate planet Earth—and I was temporarily stymied.

CHAPTER 7
Moab, Friday, February 1, 2019, Late Afternoon

Morry was busy working on an article he should have finished hours ago. He was determined to wrap it up and get out of the office at five o'clock, come hell or high water. So when his coworkers kept distracting him by chitchatting with each other, it annoyed him.

"Hey, could you quiet down? I'm working here," he said, trying to keep the irritation out of his voice.

"Morry, did you hear what happened?" Patty, the woman who had been the bane of his existence for years, asked excitedly. She'd simmered down some since he and Lainie got married, but she still knew how to push his buttons.

He gritted his teeth, took a breath, and inquired calmly, "No, what happened?"

"Detective Campbell almost got shot today."

That got his attention. "What? Is he alright?"

"Isn't he a friend of yours, or something?"

"He's a distant cousin," he stated impatiently. "So what happened?"

"They're short of people over at the police department, so Detective Campbell went out on a domestic disturbance call with Officer Smith and the homeowner pulled a gun on him." Patty fairly danced with glee. "And I got the story!" Even though she'd given up the Goth affectation and the dreads, she still used a great deal of eye makeup—which he considered unattractive—and she acted immaturely.

Morry wanted to strangle her but managed to school his expression into bland indifference. "Congrats. I'm glad Colin's okay, but I need to get back to work." He pretended he was working. In reality, he was immersed in his magic and communicating telepathically with Derek.

Hey, Dad, did you know Colin came close to being killed today?

Yeah, he described it in detail when I ran into him at the bank. He was pretty nonchalant, considerin' he used magic he didn't know he had. He'll be droppin' by Merlin's after work to see the baby, if ya want to talk to him.

Colin has magic? How could that happen? Maybe Grandpa gave it to him temporarily to save his life. In any case, I need to go straight home today; Lainie and I have a date. I'm glad he's okay, though.

Me, too. Dad's bein' pretty closemouthed about it, so I have a feelin' somethin's up, but I'm sure he'll tell us sooner or later, Derek assured him.

Talk to you tomorrow, then. Ending their silent conversation, Morry opened his eyes—he didn't even realize he'd closed them—and practically jumped out of his skin. Patty was in his face, staring at him. She'd done it before and he didn't like it any better this time.

He was livid. "What do you think you're doing? Back off!" He thought she'd finally gotten over her fascination with him, but it seemed not, and he was sick of her unwanted attention.

"Listen, Patty, you have to leave me alone," he whispered furiously. "I'm married and my wife wouldn't appreciate you focusing on me like this, so *go away.*"

She whirled around in a huff and stomped back to her desk. With his wolf's keen hearing, he heard her mutter "asshole" under her breath.

He made up his mind to do something drastic if this kind of thing happened again. He would put a spell on her that would make her avoid him. The Latin word *abscedere* flashed into his mind and he knew it would work. It was one of Merlin's old spells. Great, he'd go ahead and zap her with it now. He turned toward her to do that and saw her wiping away a tear from her eye.

He sighed and reluctantly let go of the power he'd been gathering to initiate the spell.

He wasn't in the mood to do anymore work today anyway, so he texted Gwen to let her know he was leaving early, logged off of his computer, and started out the glass door.

"Hey, Morry, wait a sec," Gwen called out.

"What is it?" he asked as he backtracked to her desk, not looking forward to being reprimanded for the altercation with Patty.

She motioned him to follow her into the relative privacy of the break room, where they both leaned casually against the counter.

"Look, I'm aware you have a history with Patty. So do I. Hell, I had sex with her once, when I was Jim."

Morry stared at her in surprise. "You did? But you were so much older than she was. Why..."

"I, uh, was going to ask Lainie out—obviously this was before you met her—and I felt uncomfortable at the disparity in our heights, so I went home with Patty instead." She looked away in embarrassment. "It didn't work out, for reasons we don't need to discuss.

"Anyway, water under the bridge. Look, you two need to call a truce —and trust me, I'll discuss this with her, too—because we can't have a scene like that happen again here in the office. And by the way, I saw you contemplating something. Were you going to put a spell on her?"

He looked at his feet. "Yes, to make her stay away from me."

"What made you change your mind?"

He glanced at Gwen and winced. "She had tears in her eyes and I couldn't do it."

"Oh, Morry," she said softly, and squeezed his shoulder briefly.

They gazed at each other and Gwen looked away first, aware that staring into a sorcerer's eyes for more than a few seconds was asking for trouble.

She checked her watch. "Go ahead and take off. I'm going to stick around until six o'clock. And Morry—have a nice weekend, okay?"

"I'll try."

"I'm sure I'll see you soon, Nephew." She winked at him and left the room.

"I have no doubt, Aunt Gwen," he muttered quietly. He loved her, but he missed the man she used to be.

As Morry drove home, he put aside the issues he needed to sort out at work, and knew that he was more than a little anxious about the situation with Lainie. The other day he'd basically given her an ultimatum: either agree to have his baby or else. He snorted. Or else what? He'd leave her? Find someone else who did want children? He doubted he'd be able to go through with it. He loved his wife, had loved her through many lifetimes, and knew he couldn't leave her. All he could do was wait, and hope she remained true to her past choices; she'd always ended up having his children before.

Other than her reluctance to get pregnant, there was one other thing that seemed to have freaked her out. Lainie's mother in this time and dimension was actually their descendent. Admittedly, it *had* been exceedingly strange, when he first met his mother-in-law, Ann, to recognize that her soul resonated with a familiar combined essence: his and Lainie's. He didn't understand it. In this, the base timeline, he and Lainie hadn't been together until they met last summer, so how could her mom be their descendent? It was definitely a conundrum, and when he could find the courage, Morry would have to ask his great-grandfather a few astute questions. Whether God would answer him was anybody's guess.

He quickly shook off those thoughts as he pulled into their driveway. They'd bought a house not far from Merlin's that was surrounded

39

by well-established trees and bushes. Morry eagerly anticipated the riotous profusion of fresh green growth and colorful flowers the realtor had promised them come spring, although he would have an outrageous water bill since the vegetation was not native to the high desert. But the truth was he missed his old backyard that had been enclosed by a thick hedge, so it would be worth it to him. Currently, however, everything was still stark and bare, like his heart had felt when he thought Lainie might refuse to have his kids. He stopped on the walkway that wound between dormant flower beds, closed his eyes, and sent out a silent, heartfelt entreaty to the gods.

A slight breeze immediately caressed him lovingly and he opened his eyes. The front door swung inward, revealing his tall, blond, shapely wife who stood there in nothing but a filmy negligee. It was abundantly clear she was cold.

"Lainie, honey, it's freezing out here, what are you doing?"

"I've been waiting for you." She beckoned to him and he slowly walked toward her. When he was close enough, she pulled him against her. He enveloped her in his warmth and she could feel the swollen evidence of his desire.

She kissed his mouth, which was turned up in a half smile, and whispered in his ear, "Let's go make a baby."

He picked her up and teleported into the bedroom.

CHAPTER 8
Moab, Friday, February 1, 2019, Early Evening

I came back to my senses. I had been standing in the middle of the living room for several minutes, answering Morry's prayer to the gods. He doubtless had no idea he was praying directly to me. My family was going about their business around me as if I was a permanent fixture, a tree that had taken root in our home. They had become so accustomed to my spontaneous mental absences they no longer stood around watching me "zone out," as Derek called it.

I observed Emily as she carried Arthur into the kitchen, putting him down in the portable crib so she could keep an eye on him while she finished up dinner preparations. Rae hurriedly dusted the furniture before our guests arrived, and Lumina teleported from one room to another with clean, folded laundry.

As the family bustled around, completely ignoring me, I felt left out, detached from the whole scene. I didn't know whether to laugh or cry. Somehow, this wasn't what I'd anticipated would happen once I attained my full potential. I thought I'd be more important in the daily scheme of things. It was obvious, however, that it had transpired as my father had intended. And, after the fact, I saw that I *couldn't* have waited any longer, since the schedule for Arthur's ascendance—and mine—had been predetermined.

It wasn't easy to function as a god while living in the human realm. I had to compartmentalize everything, to keep all the different perspectives I dealt with properly organized, so it was beneficial that I didn't need to sleep anymore—I wouldn't have time to if I did.

The doorbell rang and I knew I had been lost in contemplation. I sensed the arrival of Seth, Chris, and Cathy, a trifle early, which was fine, although Colin hadn't made an appearance yet and I still needed to tell him about his destiny with Cathy.

I crossed to the door and flung it open. "Come on in, it's good to see you. Hi, Cathy, I'm Merlin, welcome to our home."

41

Everyone seemed surprised at my effusive welcome. Perhaps I overdid it, but it took my mind off of my responsibilities temporarily.

"Thanks for inviting me," Cathy responded shyly. She stood behind Chris, who greeted us with a wave and a bubbly "Hi, everybody!"

Both Lumina and Rae returned the greeting, and Em waved back from the kitchen doorway. "We're glad you could make it."

I shook my son's hand. Seth and I eyed each other in amusement as we shared the thought that we were acting oh, so politely *human*.

Seth grinned. "Weel, Da, how's the braw, wee bairn?" His speech patterns had been gradually becoming Americanized over the past few months, but this night his Scottish burr was straight out of the Highlands.

Emily, bringing Arthur out to greet everyone, answered for me. "He's doing well, Seth, thanks for asking. Would you like to hold him?"

Without waiting for a response, she handed him the baby, who was in a light blue onesie with a unicorn on the front. Seth looked at her as if she was handing him a live grenade.

As he hesitantly took the baby, cupping his tiny head, Arthur looked up at familiar features but with bizarre, alien eyes, and started to cry.

"Arthur, I ken ye're in there—I'm yer brother, Seth. Dinna fash yersel', wee man."

"Do you think he comprehends what Seth's saying?" Chris asked doubtfully as Arthur's piercing wail tapered off and finally stopped.

I glanced at her. "Yes, he does. When Gwen and the knights were here the day he was born, he was totally cognizant of them. Just now, as Em handed him to Seth, he thought it was me until he realized it wasn't and it startled him. Remember, Arthur hasn't seen Seth in over 1500 years. And at that time, Arthur didn't know Seth was my son. I remember when the Fae delegation visited us in Edinburgh, but I can't say I recall meeting Seth. He was very young, and I wasn't even aware he was my son."

Chris's eyes widened in shock as the implications of my statement dawned on her: Seth and I had both been alive in the fifth century. She had long ago tucked this knowledge into the back of her mind and tried to forget it, because it was so difficult to grasp.

I glanced over as someone knocked and Emily opened the front door. "Hi, Colin, come on in."

He stepped into the room, saw the crowd milling around and looked taken aback. "Sorry, am I interrupting something?"

"No, not at all, we've been expecting you," Em assured him. "We hope you'll join us for dinner."

"Sure, I'd love to, thanks, Em, Merlin." He looked inordinately pleased. If he'd been wearing a hat, he'd have been humbly holding it in his hands in front of him.

Em patted his shoulder reassuringly and turned away, intent on rescuing Seth.

Colin watched her interacting with my Fae son, and glanced at me uncomfortably. "Uncle, I'm sorry, I should have called before coming over—I didn't mean to crash your party." He looked so chagrined I took pity on him.

"Don't be silly, you're part of this family and always welcome in my home. Besides, I knew you were coming over—and why," I said, giving him a wink.

He looked surprised for a moment, but when he saw my subsequent grin, he figured I had been the one to bestow his powers upon him.

I replied to his unspoken assumption. "The truth is I only helped them along a bit. You've always had magic, Colin, but you weren't ready for it last year. Now you are. It's as simple as that." I conjured a couple of glasses of Lagavulin 16-Year Islay Single Malt Scotch and handed him one.

He threw his dark head back and laughed. "*Sláinte*, or should I say *slàinte mhath*, since this is Scotch, not Irish whiskey," he said, and we toasted his new state of being.

As he sipped his drink, his eyes watered and he wheezed, "Hoo, that's potent stuff."

"I thought you'd appreciate it. Seth turned me on to it."

He didn't answer and I noticed that he'd seen Cathy. I heard his sharp, indrawn breath. "Who's that? She's gorgeous."

"Cathy Grant, Chris's sister. Would you like to meet her? She's single."

"Yeah, I would, but I'm still married to Maggie."

"Colin," I said kindly, "that ship has sailed."

"What do you mean?"

"I probably shouldn't tell you this, but she's going to serve you with divorce papers tomorrow."

Startled speechless, he jerked around and peered into my eyes until it dawned on him what he was doing. Glumly, he transferred his gaze down to the floor. He looked like he couldn't decide if he was depressed or relieved.

"You knew this was inevitable when she moved out, and you

decided just this morning that you wouldn't go back, that your destiny awaited you. It will be more rewarding than you could ever envision." My voice exuded a hint of a prophetic tone he'd never heard before and I could tell it unsettled him, as much as the fact that I knew what he'd been thinking earlier.

"Uh, is Cathy Grant a part of that destiny?" He kept his voice low and didn't look at her as he spoke.

"It's a good possibility, but take it slow, will you? She only arrived this morning and she's new to our atypical family dynamic."

"Atypical doesn't come close to describing it, Merlin," Colin muttered. "I think I need another drink."

I raised my eyebrows and inclined my head, indicating that he should do the honors by conjuring up another glass of whisky for each of us.

He was nonplussed—for a moment, he had forgotten the magic— then he smiled radiantly, white teeth gleaming, and held out his broad hands with their meticulously manicured nails. Glasses of amber liquid appeared in his palms.

I lifted one, saluted him with it, and took a sip. "You're catching on quickly," I murmured.

As Colin savored his Scotch, he glanced around the room and saw that Cathy was checking him out. He blushed, making his swarthy skin even darker, and gave her a tentative smile, which she returned in kind.

He had decided to take the initiative and go talk to her when Em announced that dinner was ready. I could feel his frustration.

"It's alright, Colin, there's no hurry."

He gave me a look. "Merlin, I'm not a teenager and you're not my father. I'll figure it out."

I chuckled as we walked over to the dining table. I sat at the head of the table, as was my custom, with Em on one side closest to the portable crib where Arthur dozed, and Lumina on the other side. Rae sat next to Em and there was an empty seat next to Lumina. Em must have invited someone else, an absent family member, presumably, since I couldn't discern who it was.

I invited Morry to drop by if his "date" with Lainie went sour, but he hasn't, so I guess everything is copacetic at their house. Em cut her eyes at me questioningly and I nodded. I did know that much.

Seth was seated across from Chris and they were already talking softly, leaning in toward each other. Colin was seated across from Cathy. Would the two of them choose to get involved with each other right away or not? Free will was still a factor, at least in the beginning. God covered all the bases, in every conceivable way.

Em's appetizing dinner of fried chicken, mashed potatoes and gravy, asparagus, and freshly baked biscuits with Irish butter was on the table in serving dishes, so everyone helped themselves. I watched the interactions of these people who were members of my family in one way or another, and was pleased to have them all here at my table. Eating together was one of the things I enjoyed most in this human life.

Colin and Cathy were silent as they started to eat their dinners, but he finally cleared his throat and introduced himself. "Hi, I'm Colin Campbell. I understand that you're Chris's sister Cathy." He paused, chuckling. "A lot of names starting with 'C.'"

"Yes, that's interesting—what a coincidence," Cathy said politely.

"My last name is still Colburn," Chris contributed, "...although my maiden name is Grant, like Cathy's."

"Okay, get this: my maiden name is Crandall, and Mom's last name is Crandall, too," Em said.

"And my maiden name is Clark," Rae reminded her.

"Unbelievable," Colin shook his head. "God must have a sense of humor."

I laughed out loud. "You have no idea."

Everyone at the table stilled, looked at each other in silence, then burst into raucous laughter—everyone except Cathy, who gazed at all of us as if we had lost our minds.

"I'll tell you later, sis," Chris promised, her eyes twinkling.

* * *

Eating commenced again and Colin finally got himself under control enough to continue the conversation. "So, Cathy, you're here in Moab on vacation?" He cringed inside at the banality, but hey, he'd never claimed to be a brilliant conversationalist and he really wanted to learn more about her.

Cathy looked up from her food and swallowed cautiously before answering. "Not exactly on vacation, but I did arrive from Denver early this morning. How did you happen to be here tonight? Are you a close friend of Merlin's?"

"A distant relation, actually. It's kind of complicated." He wasn't sure how much he should say, but if she was aware of Seth's nature—and he was sitting at the table in all his Fae glory—he assumed she knew the truth about everyone else.

"What do you mean?" Cathy tipped her head a little and looked puzzled.

"My, uh, ancestor Beli, the Welsh god of death, is Merlin's brother, so that makes Merlin my great-uncle. Sort of."

She stared uncomprehendingly at him for a moment, and then responded warily, "Sorry, I'm still not accustomed to this family. Did you say your ancestor was a god?"

"Yeah, he *is* a god, and I met him over a month ago at the herb shop. He dropped in from the god realm to say hi to Merlin." Colin had lowered his gaze to his plate and thus didn't notice the bewildered disbelief on Cathy's face. "He and I look alike, despite the fact that he's my many generations removed great-grandfather from the fifth century."

Colin looked up and saw that Cathy's mouth had dropped open in astonishment.

He grinned widely. "I get it. I've been involved with this family since last summer and I'm still not used to it. For instance, I found out today that I have magic. It's awesome, but pretty shocking as you can imagine." He didn't think he ought to add, at the dinner table, the circumstances during which he'd discovered his gift.

"M-magic? Are you serious?"

"Well...yeah." He turned to Seth, noting that all his inhuman features were on display, then looked back at Cathy. "You know Seth is Fae?"

"Oh, ah, yes, I do."

"So you know he has magic?"

"I guess you're right," she said, glancing self-consciously at Seth.

"And Merlin is, well, *Merlin*." Colin waited for her response. She looked at him as if waiting for the punchline and he felt a twinge of impatience. "As in, King Arthur's Merlin, the Sorcerer of Camelot."

"*What?*" Cathy jerked her head around to stare at me, the whites of her eyes showing. "*The* Merlin? Oh, my God, how can that be?"

Everyone heard her harsh tone of voice and stopped eating.

* * *

I could sense Cathy's blood pressure spiking. Seth gave me a concerned look. *I'll take her home, Da, if need be.*

She'll be okay once she's calmed down. Cathy's had it rough lately, but she'll adjust soon enough, and I happen to know that she is destined to become an important member of our family in the near future.

Chris put her hand on Cathy's arm soothingly. "I'm sorry, Sis. You slept most of the day, while I was at work, and after that we came here, so I haven't had a chance to bring you up to speed with, well, *everything*."

"What do you mean 'everything?'" she asked stridently.

I needed to intercede. "Cathy, all is well. You're welcome to ask me, or any one of us, any questions you might have," I said quietly, sending out gentle waves of love and peace to her heart and mind. "It's a lot to take in when you're not used to the reality of the supernatural world— or the celestial world, for that matter."

She gradually succumbed to my influence and relaxed. "You're *the* Merlin?" she asked ingenuously.

"Yes, my dear, I'm the one and only Merlin." I thought for a moment how best to reveal things in increments. "My son, Seth, is Fae, as you know, and all of us here have magic, except for you and Chris, of course. Emily is part Fae—Elf, as a matter of fact—and Lumina, our daughter, is also part Elf and a goddess in her own right. Okay so far?"

Cathy glanced at Em and Lumina, who smiled reassuringly at her. "I guess so…"

"Ladies, why don't you show her your ears?" I suggested with a smile, expecting that the simple gesture would help put her at ease.

My wife and daughter exchanged a glance, and in unison tucked their hair behind their ears, the shape of which revealed undeniable Fae ancestry.

"Oh, my gosh!" Cathy exclaimed. She glanced back and forth between the two women and Seth. The shape of their ears was similar, but not exactly the same.

Rae, who up until then had kept silent, said, "I'm sorry that someone didn't inform you of our unusual family ahead of time. It's pretty overwhelming, isn't it? As you may have guessed, I'm Em's mom and part Elf, but for some reason, the pointed ears passed me by." She shrugged and grinned at Cathy, who smiled shyly in return.

"'Tis all ma fault and I'm verra sorry, Cathy," Seth said. "I should have given ye some idea of what tae expect, but since I was using magic as weel as herbal tonics tae treat ye throughout the day, I assumed ye kent it. Did ye no' sense it?"

Cathy looked around at every one of us hesitantly, and then gazed into Seth's alien eyes with acceptance. "Yes, I guess I did. How could I miss it? I mean, you put your hands on me and healed me, so how could that be anything but magic? Sorry I've been such a ninny. Honestly, this is all remarkable and exciting."

"Alright, let's finish our meals and go from there," I said, and reheated all the food with a glance.

"Thanks, Dad," Lumina said as she added stalks of asparagus to her plate.

"Mmm, the gravy is better hot, thanks." Chris smiled at me and I winked.

It gradually sank in that I'd used magic. "That's...handy," Cathy said, relaxing and consuming her food as if she was starving. Colin decided to wait until dinner was over to talk to her.

Twenty minutes later, we all pushed back from the table, replete.

I turned to my wife and gave her a quick kiss. "Em, the meal was delicious, as usual. Thank you." *I wish Derek and Sarah had been able to make it.*

They had other plans; I'm sure they'll be here next time, Em said silently.

Chris spoke up, "Yes, thank you for inviting all three of us, and for going to all that trouble with dinner, particularly since you just had a baby."

Emily beamed. "Oh, you're most welcome. I enjoyed preparing it for you, with Mom's and Lumina's help, of course."

"I'm grateful to be here, Em. Thanks."

"Oh, Colin, you're always welcome, as Merlin mentioned earlier."

"I'd be happy to help clean up, Emily," Cathy offered.

"Thanks, but I wouldn't dream of it, you're our guest. Besides, magic, remember?" Em and Rae began to hum, and as their voices rose and blended Lumina joined in, all three directing their magic toward the kitchen. Simultaneously, the food was put away, the dishes were rinsed and stacked properly in the dishwasher, and the pots and pans were soaking in the sink.

Colin, Cathy, and Chris were all dazzled, which had been the point of the exercise. We didn't always use magic for everything around the house, especially so ostentatiously, but tonight we made an exception.

Em turned to me. *Honey, do you want to take Cathy and Colin up to the Rim, show them your favorite view?*

That's a great idea. I cut my eyes towards my son. *Seth, do you think Cathy would be able to handle a short flight?*

We can ask her. Chris and I could go, as weel. Cathy kens I fly, sae that shouldna bother her.

I agreed. "Cathy, it's obvious you're intrigued by Seth's wings. We were planning to take a quick flight up to the Rim—would you like to try that? Seth will carry Chris, and I can carry you."

"Yes, I think I would, but how…?" She looked puzzled as she glanced at my back.

I walked into the center of the living room and called forth my wings.

"Oh, God." Cathy's eyes went wide. "They're *huge*."

"Yeah, they are…" Colin whispered, all agog at the sight. He knew I had wings, but had never seen me manifest them.

"Colin, are you interested in going with us?" I hoped he wasn't disappointed that he wouldn't be able to fly by himself. He had no ability to do so that I could determine.

"I could take him, Dad," Lumina offered, manifesting her own wings.

Colin looked from me to Lumina nervously. "Uh, no thanks. I have to get going," he said hastily.

I sensed that he was telling the truth, but his statement was tinged with a strong emotion—fear. I decided to follow up with him later, but he needed to process everything that had happened to him today.

I could sense Cathy's dismay that Colin was leaving without talking to her again, so I would make sure each had the other's phone number.

"Em, do you and Arthur want to go?" The baby had been awake and in Em's arms for the last few minutes, but I was fairly sure what her answer would be.

"No, I think we'll stay here. It's time to bathe him and put him down for the night." *As you know…*

Okay, Em, I'll be back in a little while. I love you.

I love you, too, god man.

I looked over at Rae and she shook her head. "No, thanks, Merlin, not tonight. I'm going to retire to my room and read my new J.R.Ward book. Good night, everyone." A chorus of good nights followed her down the hallway.

I shook my head. For some reason, my mother-in-law loved books about vampires, despite the fact that real vampires were considerably less benign than the fictional ones.

Seth had Chris in his arms, coats on, and they both glanced over at me. *Ready, Da?*

Yes. "Cathy, are you ready?" I held out her coat and she hesitantly walked over to me, slipped her arms in and quickly zipped it up. Then she looked up at me and backed away, swallowing nervously.

"Truly, I don't bite," I murmured. She finally made up her mind and stood in front of me so I could scoop her up and hold her against my chest. She wasn't very heavy. I could have managed even without having the strength of a god.

Seth, Lumina, and I teleported out of the living room and into the air above the maze of power lines crisscrossing the subdivision, winging our way through the cold night air up to the Rim.

* * *

After everyone had gone, Colin forced himself to admire the baby and to give Em the gift he'd carried around all evening in his coat pocket. She claimed the fancy teething ring was precisely what Arthur needed, although Colin had a hunch he wouldn't be using it any time soon. Emily continued to make conversation and he felt it was only polite to respond civilly since he was a guest in her house.

Finally, having satisfied the social niceties, he took his leave and drove home as fast as he dared. As soon as his own front door closed behind him, he made a beeline for the kitchen, threw open the refrigerator door and grabbed a beer. He twisted the cap off and tipped the bottle back, sucking down swallow after swallow of the cold brew. He breathed a sigh of relief.

What was the matter with him? He wasn't a coward by any means, and wasn't afraid of heights, or he wouldn't make a habit of hanging out after work on the roof of the city building as he'd done for years. But for some reason the thought of letting Merlin, or Lumina for that matter, fly him up to the Rim had filled him with dread.

He staggered into the living room and dropped limply into his large, amply cushioned recliner, trying to get his anxiety under control. He pulled his shoes off but left his socks on, wiggling his toes in relief.

He reflected on everything that had happened during the day, and figured that the combination of having his life threatened, discovering he had magic powers, being told his wife was divorcing him, and meeting a woman who might or might not be his destiny had thrown him off balance emotionally. He relaxed, making frequent trips to the refrigerator for yet another bottle of beer until he'd finished the six-pack.

He'd get Cathy's phone number from Merlin and call her tomorrow.

CHAPTER 9
Moab, Friday, February 1, 2019, Evening

Morry padded out to the kitchen in wolf form, morphing back into his human shape as he went, so that by the time he reached the kitchen sink he could take hold of a glass and fill it with water. God, he was thirsty. They had been making love for hours, the last stint having shapeshifted into animals. And he was still hard. He glanced down at his erection and marveled at his stamina. This had never happened to him before. He hoped Lainie would be ready to go again, but he didn't count on it; he figured that she'd be sore.

The evening had been everything he'd hoped for. They hadn't used any type of contraception during their love-making marathon—Lainie promised she'd thrown away her birth control pills days ago and he hadn't used a condom—and it was Lainie's most fertile time of the month. So he must have gotten her pregnant after all that.

He thought back to the loving sensation that had flowed over him after he had prayed to the gods for Lainie to conceive, and was convinced that it was Merlin who had heard and answered his silent plea. He shook his head in astonished disbelief at how his life had turned out after his difficult years growing up as an orphan.

All of a sudden, he was overcome with the certainty that he *had* impregnated his wife.

He rushed into the bedroom and over to Lainie's side as she napped, sprawled out in unmistakable exhaustion.

"Lainie, we're having twins, a boy and a girl!"

Startled, her violet eyes opened wide as she stared up at him. "What? How do you know?"

"I'm a demigod, remember?" Morry laughed, thrilled that he would be a father in six months. Thank God, an immortal's gestation period was shorter than the regular human nine months. He leaned over to kiss her and ended up on top of her when she pulled him into her arms. She cradled him between her wide hips and he slipped inside her welcoming body.

"I love you, Lainie."

"I love you, too, Morry."

* * *

I landed in my back yard and gently set Cathy on her feet before I sent my wings back into that other dimension in which they existed when I wasn't using them. Seth landed shortly thereafter and put Chris down near her sister.

Lumina fluttered gracefully to a landing and her wings disappeared with a snap. "I don't know about the rest of you, but I'm cold. Let's go inside."

Laughing and talking, we trooped into the house, looking for something hot to drink. Even though I was able to regulate my temperature automatically—I could have been naked on that cold, windy precipice and not felt it—I still enjoyed the whole warming-up ritual.

When we were all settled in the living room with hot chocolate, Emily joined us.

"So, how was your flight?" she asked Cathy. I knew that the young woman had run the gamut of emotions from fear to elation, but it wasn't my story to tell, so I kept quiet.

"Oh, Em, it was breathtaking! I was frightened at first," Cathy admitted as she glanced at me and grinned. "But I overcame my fear and got a kick out of every minute of it after that. Merlin's wings are unbelievable."

"Yes, they are." Emily gazed eloquently into my eyes. "I'm rather fascinated by them myself."

I smiled and easily merged with my wife's mind and soul, sharing Morry's and Lainie's news, which elicited a sigh of contentment and pleasure from her. Then I looked around the room at my family.

Seth was sitting on the big, square hassock so his wings hung down the back, brushing the carpet. His black jeans and boots on one side and immaculate white wings edged with black on the other side contrasted strikingly with the forest green fabric of the hassock. Chris sat cross-legged on the floor at Seth's feet.

He put his arms around Chris's shoulders and kissed the top of her head. I'd never heard either of them express their feelings for each other verbally, but clearly, the feelings were there.

Cathy had smiled wistfully when she noticed my son touching her sister with obvious affection. I knew she was yearning for someone to hold her like that, and I decided now was the time to give her Colin's phone number.

She looked startled, thanked me, and put the piece of paper in her pocket.

"Weel, let's go, lassies," Seth said. "Cathy, ye need tae rest, and Chris, dinna ye need tae work tomorrow?"

"Yes, I do, and it is getting late," Chris responded, looking at her wristwatch.

"I need you to be alert at the shop," Em reminded her.

The three said their goodbyes and departed, and Em, Lumina, and I decided to have one more hot chocolate and chat before we called it a night.

"So Cathy will be an important addition to our family circle? How, exactly?" Lumina leaned forward in her chair, an avid look of curiosity on her face.

"I can't tell you that, Daughter. The knowing comes to me as an overwhelming sense of truth, not necessarily as specific details." I put my feet up on the green hassock and made myself comfortable.

"Not always. Earlier today you told me Colin was going to die, and you knew exactly when and how," Em said.

"Yes, that's correct, I did. But he didn't die. He more or less saved himself, but if he hadn't been able to, I would have saved him, because Colin is meant for greater things than to die in such a meaningless way."

Em and Lumina glanced at each other and shrugged.

"On that confusing note, I'm going to bed," Em stated.

"Me, too," Lumina agreed.

I just smiled mysteriously and finished my chocolate.

* * *

Cathy couldn't sleep. She relived every outlandish, impossible thing that had happened to her since she'd arrived in Moab, and decided she'd somehow been transported into an alternate universe inhabited by winged, time-traveling gods, Faeries, and Elves—and a magic-wielding police detective.

Chris had joined her for a moment after she'd crawled exhaustedly into bed, ostensibly to "tuck her in," and had explained why everyone had laughed at Merlin's comment about God's sense of humor.

"God is Merlin's father."

Cathy looked confused. "Aren't we all children of God?"

"You don't understand," Chris clarified. "Merlin is a sorcerer and a god, but he's also an angel. God is his actual father."

Cathy gaped in astonishment.

Chris grinned wryly. "Welcome to my world." She leaned over and kissed her sister's cheek. "You know, I'm glad you're here. I love you. Sweet dreams."

"I love you, too," Cathy answered faintly, her eyes following her sister as she left the room, closing the door behind her.

Holy shit, that's why I felt so peaceful after I got over being nervous. I was in the arms of an angel, Cathy thought. She started thinking about Colin, who was distantly related to Merlin. He'd acted so apprehensive about flying that he must not have wings of his own. He was an attractive, interesting guy—in law enforcement *and* he had magic. She was intrigued by him, but she was hesitant to phone a man she didn't know well; it made her look anxious. She hoped he would call her for a date.

She snuggled down under the covers, and for the first night in years went to sleep with a smile on her face.

CHAPTER 10
Moab, Saturday, February 9, 2019, Morning

D erek was dozing lazily, comfortable in the knowledge that neither he nor Sarah had to go to work this morning, when a loud retching sound startled him awake. He glanced over at his wife and saw her side of the bed was empty.

"Sarah, are ya okay, hon?" His inquiry was met by a groan of abject misery. He leaped out of bed and teleported into the bathroom, to find his wife in her pink sleep shirt on the floor hugging the white porcelain toilet bowl. Her typically shiny reddish-blond hair was dull and stringy with sweat and vomit, and she looked altogether miserable.

"Der, I feel sick," she mumbled.

He crouched down beside her and pulled her hair back from her face. Then he levitated a washcloth into the washbowl and magically turned on the tap to dampen it. "*Veniat ad me,*" he intoned, and as the washcloth came to his hand he adjusted the dampness to a comfortable warmth.

"You're okay, sweetheart," he crooned as he gently wiped her face and hair free of the nasty liquid. "Are ya done?"

"I think so—" she started to say, and proceeded to heave again.

Derek supported her forehead and kept her hair back out of the way, and hoped he could get her back in bed soon.

There's a potion at the shop that will help with the nausea, Derek, he heard in his mind.

Yeah, I'd forgotten about that. Thanks, Dad. He pictured the potion on the main shelf at the front of the store and the bottle appeared in his hand. He pulled the cork out and gave it to her. "Here, Sarah, drink this down, hon, it'll make ya feel better."

Her response was to groan and throw up again. He grabbed the bottle as the contents were about to spill and poured it down her throat as she lifted her head up.

"Ack, what *is* that awful stuff? The nausea potion?" She sputtered and coughed and continued to complain until Derek picked her up and carried her into the bedroom, laying her down on their bed.

She sat up and wiped her mouth with a tissue. "That stuff tastes terrible. I thought Merlin was supposed to fix that. But I guess it doesn't matter—it works. I feel better and my mouth doesn't taste bad anymore either. What made me so sick? Do you think I got food poisoning from something we ate last night?"

"If ya did, it wouldn't have affected me anyway, so it's hard to say." His demigod nature—and his common sense—kicked in and he knew without a doubt what had happened. "Sarah, it's mornin' sickness. You're pregnant. Didn't ya miss your period a couple of weeks ago?"

"You're right, I did. I thought it was stress; it's happened before. Pregnant! But, how did you know, Der?" As she waited for him to reply, she conjured up a tall glass of cold water and drank thirstily.

"Hey, don't drink that so fast," he admonished her. "I sensed it, Sarah, like Morry did last week when he got Lainie pregnant."

"It's not the same, though, because you didn't sense it the day I got pregnant, which must have been, oh, the end of December, around the twenty-ninth?"

He didn't answer, and Sarah noticed that his eyes had turned dark gold and unfocused as if he was communicating with someone telepathically. "Derek, what's going on? Why are your eyes a different color?"

He slowly reached out and put his hand on her belly. Sarah shivered as she felt a tingle of magic and his hand emanated a golden glow.

"What the heck?" she murmured as she saw the detached look on his face.

He blinked and seemed to come back to normal. "It's a boy and his name is Aidan."

"Really?" She brightened as it hit home they were going to have a baby boy in June. She squealed and grabbed Derek, pulling him down so she could kiss him. All six feet of his naked body landed on her awkwardly and they both laughed. They looked into each other's eyes and the laughter became murmurs of arousal. They kissed, tongues playing, and Derek made her sleep shirt disappear, revealing Sarah's perfectly formed breasts. He twirled his tongue around each nipple and she gasped as she felt the lust tug in her belly. Then he turned and slid down until his mouth was at her sweet center, while she took his hard length into her mouth. They pleasured each other until Sarah shuddered as Derek sent her over the edge. At that point, he pulled himself up so he could feast on her mouth until he was so aroused he couldn't wait any longer. He stretched out on top of her, pushing inside, where she gripped him so tightly with her inner muscles that his control vanished, causing him to climax.

Later, half asleep and relaxed, Sarah looked over at her husband, who was sprawled next to her, limbs akimbo, and quipped, "If I didn't already have a bun in the oven, that certainly would have done the job."

Derek glanced at her and grinned. "No doubt." His eyes drifted shut. "I don't think I can move yet."

Abruptly his eyes flew open as he thought of something. "Aidan'll be Morry's brother." He caressed Sarah's belly. "And Morry's kids will be Aidan's niece and nephew, despite the fact they'll be practically the same age."

"And we'll be grandparents, which is even harder to relate to."

The look on Derek's face made her laugh. "Oh, Der, I love you." Sarah kissed him soundly. "You said his name is Aidan, which is Irish. Do you know what it means?"

"No, do you?"

"Huh uh. I should since I'm part Irish, but I don't. Let's look it up." She grabbed her phone and Googled Irish baby names. "Okay, it means 'little fire.'" Looking perplexed, she kept reading. "Oh, no."

Derek read her thoughts and winced. "Oh, no, is right. Aidan is the anglicized form of the old Gaelic name—crap, I don't know how to pronounce it so I'll spell it out—A-O-D-H-A-N—and A-O-D-H in Celtic mythology was the Irish god of fire and the underworld."

He met Sarah's gaze and together they stared at her still-flat abdomen.

* * *

I could understand why Derek wouldn't know that Aodh should be pronounced "Ay." Irish Gaelic was a difficult language.

I had speculated that my father could send more gods or goddesses to the human realm, but I wasn't prepared for this. Why would he send Aodh? Did we need another god of the underworld added to the mix?

I thought about the name itself. Names were significant. They defined the character and intent of the person or object. People had always been obsessed with the meaning of names and the purpose of life, and perhaps my father had built that trait into the very essence of the human being so they would eventually find their way home, back to the source of existence.

The name Aidan, according to human interpretation at least, meant responsible, balanced, affectionate, compassionate, and trustworthy.

Those were admirable traits, but hardly representative of the god of fire and the underworld. But if the god Aodh truly exhibited such traits, perchance his presence was what was needed to balance things out here in the human realm.

I leaned against the kitchen counter and took a healthy swallow of my coffee. What could God be up to now? Could he actually expect Aodh to thwart Satan's influence? Could Aodh be here to stand at Arthur's side when we save the world? But either instance would depend on whether Derek's son grew normally, in which case he would still be a child for roughly two decades, or in spurts of growth as Lumina had done—as Arthur would be doing. If that happened, his growth would parallel Arthur's and he'd be able to assist in our efforts.

I shook my head. It had never ended well when I presumed to know my father's intentions. This was one case where all of us would have to wait to see how things played out.

CHAPTER 11
Moab, Saturday, March 9, 2019

L umina had been back to work at The Moab Herbalist for over a month and her life should have returned to normal—except for having a new baby brother at home. But she was feeling restless and dissatisfied. She was a goddess in a human body with a loving family, a fulfilling job, and plans for the future after Arthur reached his full growth, so she didn't understand why she felt that way. Was it because both her older brother and her nephew and their wives were happily married and expecting? Their babies would be born in the next few months: Aidan in June and Brady and Bonnie in August.

She got up off the floor in the reading section where she had been dusting and re-organizing the bottom shelves of the bookcase and stretched, tired of working and feeling grumpy. She was determined to shake it off; she had no reason to feel sorry for herself since she wasn't ready for a husband or children. She should take a break and go outside for a few minutes, get some fresh air.

Chris, Sarah, and Grammy Rae were all working diligently at the counter helping customers, while her mother was in the back room with Arthur making up a batch of sleeping potion. Lumina glanced at the clock on the wall and noted that it was past break time, so she felt justified in her decision. They all got so involved in their work they missed breaks and lunches and she knew that wasn't healthy for anyone. People needed to relax and recharge to maintain peak efficiency. She smiled to herself as she remembered what she'd learned through the marketing class she'd taken online. Whether or not it applied to immortals, she'd reveled in the challenge and had passed with flying colors. She'd contemplated signing up for online college courses which would help her support Arthur's future endeavors. She could even take some classes through the Utah State University extension here in town.

"Grammy, it's so late I'm going to skip my break and just go to lunch. I'll be back in an hour or so, okay?" She'd take a walk first, and grab a sandwich afterwards.

"Take your time, sweetheart. The store isn't going anywhere," Rae said. "You'll need your sweater, Lumi, it's chilly out there."

Lumina gave a little wave as she pulled her sweater on, then opened the front door and walked out into the weak sunlight. She loved her grandmother's practical nature, her sense of humor, and her thoughtfulness. And she loved that she was able to be with her every day, at home and at work.

She started south on Main Street, then changed her mind as the light turned green at the intersection. She jogged across the street in the crosswalk and headed east on Center Street instead. There was a nice landscaped area in front of the city building she liked to walk through. She might run into Detective Campbell, who was working on a case even though it was Saturday. He was considerably older than she was, at least here in the human realm, but she enjoyed talking with him anyway.

Lumina made a face. Who was she kidding? The truth was that she was hoping to run into Colin's son, Josh, who was coming home for spring break and might stop by the police department to see his dad.

Josh had been coming into The Moab Herbalist for years, picking up various products for Colin so he could send them out to be tested for illegal substances.

The family hadn't been aware of the testing until Merlin returned from his adventure in the past, and Colin burglarized the shop. After that, the man had become part of their group, and Merlin had forbidden Josh from coming into the store at all because of his habit of thinking inappropriate thoughts about her.

What her dad didn't know, since she had taken great pains to hide her thoughts from him, was that she liked Josh, but was too shy to say anything to him.

Around Thanksgiving, Lumina had run into Josh at the grocery store and they'd started talking. She discovered that she was partial to his company and he confessed that he'd been attracted to her for years. They spent a couple of minutes together every day, which wasn't enough, but Josh was happy to be with her whenever she had time to spare. The challenge was to hide her ears and her true nature from him when they began to touch and kiss each other.

She didn't want her father to know about her relationship with his great-nephew's son. Yes, she and Josh were cousins, but their connection was so distant it shouldn't matter. They'd been seeing each other secretly for five weeks when he'd had to leave Moab to start the spring semester at Utah State University.

Lumina wondered how they were going to continue their relationship when he was up north in Logan and she was stuck in Moab. He could have taken classes at the USU extension here in town, as she had considered doing, but he'd wanted to be on the main campus. She couldn't teleport or fly up to see him either, as he had no idea who, or what, she really was.

She was so lost in thought that she didn't notice where she was until she heard a masculine voice call her name.

She looked up and saw a familiar figure standing in front of the city building, a welcoming smile on his handsome face.

"Josh, you're home!" Lumina beamed. They ran to each other and she threw her arms around him as he pulled her tightly against him and kissed her thoroughly. "I missed you," she confessed as they took a breath.

"I missed you, too, honey, more than you'll ever know," he murmured.

* * *

When Lumina contacted her telepathically to say she wasn't going to be back for a couple of hours, Emily suspected that her daughter and Josh were together. However, she didn't want the details, since she wouldn't be able to hide the information from Merlin.

Lumi, why don't you take the rest of the day off?

Oh, thanks, Mom! I will.

By the way, you ought to tell your father about Josh.

How did you know I was with Josh?

Seriously?

I will soon, I promise.

By the way, don't forget our plans for tomorrow, Em admonished her.

I would never forget yours and Derek's birthday party. After all, I'm helping you set up. I love you, Mom.

And I love you, darling. Emily sighed as she finished bottling the sleeping potion. She presumed her husband was aware of Lumina's relationship with Josh Campbell, even though Merlin's god powers continued to be frustratingly intermittent when it came to family members. She plucked Arthur out of his portable crib and cuddled him

61

against her, kissing his satiny smooth cheek, wishing her children didn't have to grow up so fast.

* * *

Lumina and Josh sat on the planter seat that ringed the tall old mulberry tree in the Moonstone Gallery, an area with sculptures and a few picnic tables between the city building and the Center Street Gym. They had their arms around each other to keep warm in the chill breeze.

Finally, Josh said quietly, "This is too difficult, Lumina. I don't think I can do this anymore."

She pulled away from him and stared, a frisson of fear running down her spine. "Are you breaking up with me?" she asked in a small, tentative voice.

"What? Oh, hell, no, that's not what I meant at all. I love you! I just think you should sign up for the fall semester and move in with me. My roommate is graduating this semester so he'll be leaving when it's over.

"Besides, you need to get out of town and away from your family. Start your own life."

Lumina's heart had soared when he told her he loved her, but what he was suggesting wasn't feasible. She was confident she could figure out how to go to USU in Logan. She'd have to do some magical finagling to create a scholastic background for herself since she'd never been to school, and it would be easy for her to create a satisfactory transcript; she only had to do some research first. However, there was no way she could live with him every day without him discovering the truth about her.

"But, Josh, I was...homeschooled...and USU might not accept me since I don't have an official transcript or anything. And my mom needs me to help take care of my baby brother."

"You can make arrangements to have your home schooling records sent to the college. And as to your mother needing you to help with the baby, doesn't your grandmother live with your family?"

Lumina responded reluctantly, "Yes, she does." *Darn it, now what excuse can I come up with?* "What about my job?"

He shot her a disbelieving look. "Come on, you don't need so many people in that shop. I've been in there dozens of times and seen how efficient everybody is. The store could get by with a few less employees. And there are plenty of similar jobs available near the campus. I think you're making excuses. Do you care about me enough to try it, at least?" He hated having to plead with her—it felt demeaning.

She looked away guiltily and thought for a moment. She didn't want to lose him, and she was ready for a change in her life. She'd acknowledged it to herself this morning. She glanced back at his determined expression and relented.

"Okay. I promise I'll give it some serious thought and try to make it happen." Lumina gently pulled his head down so she could kiss him properly. "I wish there was some place we could go to be alone for a couple of hours." She had an irresistible urge to express her love for him in physical way.

Josh looked earnestly into her eyes and recognized the glow of love —and passion. "My dad won't be home until after five, so we can have some privacy at my house." His voice rose at the end of the sentence as if questioning whether she was sure she wanted to take that step.

Lumina knew she was making a major, life-altering decision by going home with him. He was her first boyfriend, and the two of them hadn't made love yet, so she was still a virgin. But it felt inevitable, and she had a lot of experience trusting her feelings. She stood up and took his hand, and making a show of pulling him to his feet, she smiled and said, "Let's go."

* * *

As he unlocked the door, Josh Campbell glanced back at the young woman he had been in love with for several years. She was stunning with her shiny, long, dark brown hair waving down her back and her clear hazel eyes looking into his brown ones with love and trust. He was afraid he'd never live up to her expectations. He knew he was reasonably attractive, tall and slender—even if he was still a little gangly—with black hair and olive-toned skin lighter than his dad's, but he had the urge to look in a mirror to make sure he looked acceptable.

He opened the door and ushered her inside, deliberately closing and locking it behind them. His parents were in the process of getting a divorce and his mom and sister had moved out a few months ago, so no one would disturb them.

"Last chance, honey. Are you sure about this?" he asked as they removed their outer garments in the warm house. "You're only seventeen, so if you want to wait, I'll understand."

He hoped she wouldn't back out. He'd been looking forward to this day for so long. His body definitely didn't want to take no for an answer, but he'd be a gentleman if she changed her mind.

Lumina, who usually respected his privacy, could read his every thought and knew exactly how nervous he was, and how urgently he wanted to make love to her. The fact that he thought she was seventeen made her giggle—in reality, she'd been born a little over five years ago. She had aged magically so she actually *was* in her teens, but the truth was, her soul was ancient.

She sobered as she thought about her own desire for him. She had a fine sense of destiny, having been in touch with her true nature ever since she was a small child, and she knew this joining was meant to be. She couldn't see if it would be forever, but it unquestionably was supposed to happen now. She just wasn't sure how much of her real self she should reveal. He wasn't aware of her family's special nature, but he'd witnessed his father looking younger and sleeker since last summer and knew something unusual was happening at The Moab Herbalist. However, he didn't know what it was.

She'd never corrected him when he'd assumed her last name was Reese; her mom had added it on after Ambrosius when she was born, but Lumina never used it. When Josh had questioned why some people thought she was Mr. and Mrs. Reese's niece, and others said she was their daughter, she'd laughed and shrugged. And when he observed that the Reeses didn't seem old enough to be her parents, she pretended she didn't hear him.

Lumina quickly let go of her thoughts when she saw how impatient he was getting for an answer. "Yes, I'm sure, Josh. I do want to make love with you." Her pulse raced in anticipation.

His face wreathed with a beatific smile, he ushered her down the hallway and into his bedroom, which he had taken great pains to clean that morning, hoping against hope that she would want to have sex with him.

Lumina knew the mechanics of the sexual act, having inadvertently barged in on her parent's uninhibited lovemaking more than once and seen exactly which parts fit together, but she knew it would be different participating in it rather than watching others do it. She felt shy, being so close to sharing her body with this man. Her heart started pounding and her breath came in gasps as she imagined how it would feel to have him inside her.

Josh stood close to her and stared, feeling awkward, and wishing he knew what she was thinking. Nervously, he bent and kissed her. Heartened by her enthusiastic response, he began unbuttoning her blouse, revealing plump breasts showcased in a lacy white underwire bra. His sigh of appreciation brought her out of her reverie and she reached back to unclasp it and toss it aside, allowing those soft globes to swing free.

Josh cupped them reverently, his big hands warming her cool, smooth skin.

"Lumina, you're so lovely," he said as he bent to tenderly kiss each of her breasts in turn. Breathing hard, he gazed into her eyes as he placed his hand between her legs, caressing her through her jeans. Lumina was so aroused her eyes fluttered closed and she moaned, "Josh, please..."

He took that for permission to continue and unbuttoned her jeans, pulling the zipper down. He pushed his hand into her panties until his fingers discovered the wet heat awaiting him there.

Lumina drew in a quavering breath as he inserted a long finger inside her.

She started as she realized they were gazing fixedly at each other and swiftly looked away, afraid of triggering the Seeing. She hadn't ever done it before and wondered what it would be like with Josh, but she wasn't sure this was the time or the place for it to happen.

When Lumina glanced away from him, he thought she was uncomfortable with him touching her and withdrew his hand, hoping he hadn't been moving too fast.

"It's okay, Josh, I liked it," she hastened to reassure him. "But let's take our clothes off," she suggested as she sat on the bed to remove her shoes.

She hurried to pull her jeans and panties off, and stood in front of her dazzled boyfriend totally naked. Her alabaster skin was flawless.

Josh ogled her beautiful body and took the hint, struggling to rid himself of his own shoes and clothing.

She watched interestedly as Josh finished stripping. When he pulled his shorts down, revealing a jutting erection, she questioned how something that size and length would ever fit inside her.

Josh saw Lumina staring at his cock and hoped that she wasn't second guessing her decision. He knew he was larger than average, and he could imagine how an innocent young woman might be intimidated by such a sight.

He could only gaze at her in admiration. She was a statuesque five feet nine inches tall, which complemented his six foot one. She was slender but had enticing curves in all the usual places. He still couldn't believe that she was finally going to be his.

He took her hand and pulled her close, his flat chest against her plump breasts, his cock pressed against her abdomen. Lumina gasped and put her arms around him, marveling at the sweet sensation of her bare flesh touching his. She reached between them and stroked his erection, astonished at the sensation of silk over steel.

Kissing frantically, they made their way to the bed and tumbled onto it, their bodies arching against each other. They caressed and murmured words of love and praise. Josh again stroked her intimately, finding her ready for him. As he gazed at her lovingly, passion swept through her and she groaned, pushing against his hand.

He quickly guided his cock to her, penetrating her slowly.

"Oh, Josh, please, I want you all the way inside me."

"You're so tight and I don't want to hurt you."

"Now, Josh!" She panted, ready to be taken completely.

He plunged into her, through the membrane of her virginity, until he was in her to the hilt. As he lay still on top of her, sheathed in her body while it adjusted to his considerable presence, he kissed her reverently. He had never felt anything more exquisite in his life than being a part of her, one being. He'd had sex before, but it wasn't like this; this was making love.

Lumina felt utterly alive, every sense engaged, her body practically giving off sparks. She felt her magic surge within her and managed to control it. The feeling of being connected to another person this way was indescribable. No wonder her father treasured lovemaking! There was nothing remotely similar to it in the god realm of spirit and energy.

Then she and Josh both responded to nature's urge toward completion and began to move in the ancient dance of love. Long, deep thrusts and rhythmic retreats created an intense lust, finally building to a climax that had them both floating on a cloud.

Afterwards they cuddled and stroked each other, kissing softly. But Lumina still wouldn't meet his gaze and he wished she would *look* at him, see into his very soul. The physical joining had been exquisite, but he longed for that spiritual union also.

Lumina felt his yearning for a more complete connection with her and made a split second decision to allow the Seeing to happen for both of them. She turned her head to look into his eyes, and felt the seamless perfection as their minds and souls merged.

Josh was ecstatic as he received his fondest desire, and saw what Lumina truly was. Her heart and soul were so pure because she was a goddess, the daughter of an angel. Their inner journey revealed that her father was the original Merlin, the god Myrddin Emrys, and Josh's own ancestor was Merlin's brother, the god Beli.

It was overwhelming, and Josh suddenly felt as if he was losing himself in her. He started to panic, mentally fighting to return to his conscious mind.

Josh, be calm, love, and I'll guide you back. I would never allow you to be lost, he heard in his mind, her voice soothing him. She returned them both to their conscious selves and smiled at him.

He pushed himself up on one elbow and gazed down at her sweet, young face. "Is it true?" he asked hesitantly, believing that he'd experienced some kind of bizarre dream or hallucination.

"Yes, it's all true. And no, it wasn't a dream or a hallucination."

His forehead wrinkled in a frown. "You can read my mind?"

"How could I have shown you who you are, who I am, unless I could merge with your mind?"

He sat up and ran his hands through his short dark hair. "Lumi, I feel like I'm going crazy. Give me a few minutes to absorb it, will you, sweetheart?"

"Sure," she responded and stroked his face, worried that she had made a mistake to initiate the Seeing after all.

He sensed her unease and hurried to explain. "It's hard to process that you're a goddess and your father is a god—and I'm descended from a god—*and* we're related." His eyes widened. "Should we have had sex if we're cousins? What if you're pregnant? We didn't use protection!"

Lumina laughed. "Josh, we're so distantly related that it's irrelevant. And I'm not going to get pregnant unless it's God's will, and I happen to know it's not, at least, not yet."

"How can you possibly know that?"

"He told me."

"*God* told you?"

"Yes, Josh, God is my grandfather."

"Fuck." He felt as if his head was going to explode. Finally, he took a long breath and relaxed. "This is insane, but I believe you." He took her in his arms, his body ready for her again. He gazed passionately into her expressive hazel eyes and kissed her softy. "I'm in love with an ancient, immortal Elf goddess whose grandfather is God. I don't know what to say."

"Don't say anything. Let's make love again and think about it later." She shifted her hips and took him inside her, the world narrowing to the two of them and their love for each other.

* * *

As Lumina and Josh bonded, I closed my eyes. It was inevitable that my daughter would take a mate and move on with her life, but there was a part of me that wished it wasn't so soon, and not with Colin's son. However, she was her own person as well as an extension of her parents, and I had to let her go. It was her destiny.

Josh would soon discover that he himself possessed a great deal of magical potential, and Lumina would be there to guide him in using his power in a suitable way. In an alternate timeline where Lumina had not been born, Josh would misuse his power and become a dark practitioner of magic much like Nimue had been.

I groaned as the knowledge of more and more alternate realities raced through my consciousness, until I actively put a stop to it and filed each one separately in my mind, which currently contained a staggering amount of information. Strangely enough, I was able to find an infinite amount of space in my brain. It was akin to increasing the size of the inside of my house as I had done when I first transitioned, the inside growing exponentially while the outside remained the same size and shape.

I leaned back in the chair in my office and gazed around the familiar space that I had made my own. Seth had occupied it briefly when he first came to Moab the previous summer, but he had quickly moved in with Chris and had ultimately left very little of his energy behind. The walls, painted a calming light blue, were covered with framed paintings and photographs by local artists. Inspired by the red rock country I loved, these works of art provided bursts of color and intriguing shapes and textures, satisfying the part of me that appreciated, and related to, the human realm.

My thoughts cycled back to Lumina's circumstances, which included her desire to go to college. I understood why she felt that way. She'd never had the opportunity to make friends with other young people, as most children did when they went to school. I couldn't truly regret that she'd missed the customary school experience, however; human children could be inexcusably cruel to each other. But on the other hand, many children formed friendships that lasted a lifetime and she didn't have that.

I could see the benefit of academically preparing for her role in helping Arthur and me in the future. I would gladly assist her in choosing the most relevant courses so she could make the best use of her time. I paused, laughing to myself. If she wanted my help, that is. She was a grown woman, making her own decisions.

It was hard for me to accept that she would be moving in with Josh.

But at least she'd still be living in my house until classes started in September. Between now and then, she'd probably teleport to Logan as often as she could to be with her mate, who seemed to have accepted the truth about her—and the rest of us—without a lot of trauma.

So many changes had happened recently. It wasn't always easy, but life in this realm was always interesting.

CHAPTER 12
Moab, Sunday, March 10, 2019

The day was cool and rainy, which was disappointing since they had planned on having a barbeque in the back yard. Emily knew Merlin could easily change the weather over Moab to suit their purposes, but he'd been extremely careful lately to do nothing out of the ordinary. She almost asked him to create a bubble of warm air in their back yard, but she supposed that would be even more suspicious than changing the weather overall.

Reconciled to having the party in the house, she'd used her magic to decorate the living room and kitchen with rainbow-colored streamers and multi-colored balloons, making the dreary day more cheerful.

After she'd finished and approved the results, she turned to watch her daughter decorating the table and realized she was feeling melancholy. Lumina was animated, glowing with happiness, and it was obvious that being with Josh had done that for her.

But she was still so *young*, too young to be mated and leaving home. Em would miss her horribly.

Lumina sensed her mother was perturbed about the rapid alterations in her life. "Mom, I'm not a child anymore, I'm a grown woman, a mated woman. And I'll still be living at home for five more months, so we'll be able to spend lots of time together before I move out." A glance told her that Em wasn't reassured in the slightest.

Lumina finished arranging the centerpiece of candles and herbs in a large flat pottery dish, then levitated the desserts they'd made the previous night—the cake and the fancy cookies and candies—from the kitchen counter to the table, leaving room for the main dishes. Napkins, plastic utensils and paper plates were next. Finally, satisfied that most of the work was done, she looked at her mother with what she hoped was a conciliatory expression.

Em sighed. "Yes, you're right, we will. I'm sorry." She wiped away an errant tear and made an effort to smile and be happy for her.

70

"Oh, Mom. This isn't just about me is it?" Lumina gazed at baby Arthur as he alternately examined his fingers and toes and reached for the musical mobile hanging over his playpen. He would be sitting up by himself within a day or two and crawling a few days after that. At not quite six weeks old, he had outgrown his newborn onesies and they'd had to buy shirts and leggings large enough for a six-month-old.

Lumina figured that the next major growth spurt would happen in a month or two and Arthur would be a baby no longer. Em didn't know it for certain but she suspected it.

"I'm sorry this is so hard on you, Mom," Lumina said sympathetically as she gathered Emily into a gentle hug. "Dad loves you, and he wouldn't put you through this if it wasn't necessary."

Em wept in Lumina's arms and allowed herself to be comforted.

After a few minutes, by a supreme effort of will, she pulled away and wiped her eyes. "I'm okay, darling. Grammy Rae will be back from the grocery store in a few minutes with the soft drinks and the beer, and everyone else should be arriving soon after that, so I'm going to wash my face and get my act together."

Lumina watched as her mother stiffened her spine and walked purposefully down the hallway, disappearing into the master bedroom. She couldn't help but admire her strength.

At that moment, the doorbell sounded. Josh had arrived early, and that was fine with her. Her heart started pounding with anticipation as she opened the door and he came in, pulling her into a full-body hug.

"Hi. I missed you," he whispered, brushing the hair away from her ears to reveal their pointed shape. He loved that outward evidence of her uniqueness.

Lumina giggled and kissed him on the cheek. "It hasn't been that long since we saw each other last, silly man. And if you appreciate my 'uniqueness,' I should show you one more thing." And she called forth her dove-gray wings.

He inhaled sharply. "How in the world do you happen to have wings?"

"My dad gave them to me last summer, so I guess you could say they were god-given." She grinned and laughed, and he was utterly charmed by her sense of humor. He was undeniably in love.

He held her face with both hands as he kissed her ravenously, delving into her sweet mouth with his tongue. She responded by pressing her hips against him, forgetting for a brief moment that they weren't alone in the house.

She pulled away after placing a quick, chaste peck on his cheek.

"Cool it, my mom's in the bedroom and my grandmother will be home any minute. We can be together later this evening." She willed her wings gone, which startled Josh.

He shook it off and continued the conversation. "Where can we go? My dad will be home tonight and your family will be here, so how are we going to, uh…"

"Make passionate love? Have hot monkey sex?" she said, intentionally explicit. "I'm sure you can spend the night with me here, Josh."

"Jeez, keep it down, will you? Your parents might not be happy that I've deflowered their daughter."

"They're both aware that we've mated. Kind of hard to have secrets in a family of telepathic sorcerers." She paused, reflecting on what else he'd said, and her lips curved up a little. "Deflowered, huh? I didn't know you were so old-fashioned."

As he started to respond, Emily came back into the room. "Hi, Josh, nice to see you. Welcome to the family."

He looked startled. "Oh, um, thanks, I guess." He glanced at Lumina questioningly.

She turned red. "I kind of forgot to mention that we're mated in the sight of the gods…permanently."

Stunned, he asked nervously, "You mean we're *married*, even without the ceremony and the license? Forever?"

Lumina nodded, chewing nervously on her bottom lip.

Josh grinned blissfully. "That's awesome. I've always wanted to be married to you! I—"

He was interrupted as Rae pushed open the front door, carrying a couple of six-packs of beer. "Sorry it took me so long. These are heavier than I thought they'd be. I guess we should have conjured up the drinks instead of shopping for them. By the way, there's more in the car, along with the ice for the cooler."

"It's alright, Mom, you're not late. I'll get the rest in a minute. By the way, do you remember when Josh Campbell, Lumina's new mate, came into the shop?" Em said.

"Oh, you mean the boy who always had such shameful thoughts about my granddaughter? Yes, I certainly do remember," she commented drily, eyeing Josh critically.

He looked away in embarrassment. "Uh, sorry, I…"

"Relax, Josh, you and Lumina are all grown up and nature has apparently taken its course."

* * *

I was aware of the conversation that had just taken place as Colin and I splashed through the water-filled gutter in my old black truck and came to a stop in my driveway.

Much to our mutual surprise, Colin and I had been enjoying each other's company like old friends, hanging out together this morning at the shop, drinking coffee. He had been spending his free time there for many months, but it had been only recently that I had deliberately joined him.

Colin had started dating Cathy a few weeks prior and I'd asked him how they'd been getting along. I was merely making conversation, since I knew exactly how close they had become. But I'd had to stop him from enthusiastically verbalizing all the inappropriate details.

"What's my son's car doing here?" I jolted out of my reverie to find him looking over his shoulder at a ten-year-old nondescript sedan parked at the curb.

I glanced at Colin as he scowled. "Josh didn't tell you?" I wasn't looking forward to the inevitable explosion of parental wrath.

"Tell me what?" he asked suspiciously.

"Why don't we go in and you can ask him?"

"Oh, shit. What's he done now?" Colin groused as we climbed out of the truck into the rain and ran to the new oak front door I'd recently installed.

Having sensed our arrival, Lumina opened the door and her face fell as she saw Colin's expression.

"Oh, hi, come on in…Dads," she said, her eyes darting agitatedly between the two of us.

It was obvious that Colin hadn't picked up on the manner in which she'd included him in her greeting, but had immediately gone to confront his son.

Don't worry, I'll deal with Colin if he loses it when Josh tells him the two of you are mated. He should know by now that he can't fight destiny.

Thanks, Dad. He already looks upset and Josh hasn't even told him yet.

Relax, Daughter, it'll be alright. I stroked her hair and leaned down to kiss her cheek.

"Merlin, could you bring the rest of the drinks in from the car, please? I was going to ask Josh to do it, but he's busy at the moment."

"Sure, Em. Easier for me to do it anyway." I moved the remaining cases of soda and beer and the bags of ice into the kitchen with a thought.

"Thank you, god man."

You're most welcome, my love.

Then I sensed Colin's temper building. *Uh, oh, here it comes.*
"You *what*? Damn it Josh, how could you? With *Lumina*? Oh, my
God! What about college? Couldn't you have waited until you graduated and had a job? Do you think I'm going to be able to support you
both? I'm barely able to afford *your* expenses. Christ on a crutch, Josh! I
thought I could trust you to keep it in your pants—" Colin's rant had
thoroughly embarrassed us all and I decided enough was enough. I
grabbed his arm, transporting the two of us to my favorite spot on the
Rim where the old chairlift used to terminate. It was cold and wet
outside, a considerable change from the warmth and comfort of my
living room. I wasn't affected by the weather, but Colin had no such
recourse.

"—and furthermore—*shit!*" Colin, shocked at the sudden change in
venue and temperature, gulped and sputtered. He turned to me, wiping
the rain from his face and moustache. "What the fuck, Merlin?"

I allowed my body to expand to my god height and stature, crossed
my arms over my chest, and looked sternly into his eyes, conveying my
extreme displeasure without saying a word.

He visibly wilted.

"Crap, I blew it, didn't I?" he muttered sheepishly.

"You could say that. Lucky for you, Derek and Morry haven't
arrived yet or they might have been tempted to beat you to a bloody
pulp for disrespecting my family that way."

"But Josh shouldn't have been messing around with your daughter,
of all people, and—"

Abruptly, I held up my hand and he immediately stopped talking.
"Lumina and Josh gave themselves to each other in a loving, respectful
way. It was destined that they See each other and to mate in the eyes of
the gods—which includes me, in case you've forgotten. They are essentially married, although they still have to abide by human law and make
it official."

"But they're so young!"

"They are, but that doesn't mean they're not ready for this step."

He looked doubtful as he tried to accept that what had occurred
was the result of destiny and not thoughtless, youthful exuberance.

"Does that mean that Josh knows everything about the family now?
I never told him because I didn't think it was appropriate."

"Yes, he does, although he's finding it difficult to accept that *he* has
magic."

"Oh, God."

My frown smoothed out as my facial muscles relaxed. "He'll get used to it and Lumina will help him. He's aware that you have magic, too, so it might be interesting to see how he reacts when you give him a demonstration. I'll let you light the barbeque." My expression returned to its previously stern lines. "I strongly suggest that you learn to control yourself, Colin. As I learned many years ago, losing your temper can have terrible consequences when magic is involved."

Colin shivered, wet to the skin and unmistakably miserable, but anxious to make amends. "I'm sorry, Uncle. Please forgive me," he said meekly.

I was hesitant to let go of my pique, but I was supposed to set an example for all as the only fully manifested god ever to live in the human realm. I asked myself, if I'd known how difficult it would be, would I have pursued this course? As I thought about Arthur and Em, and all the rest of my family and friends awaiting my return, I admitted that the answer was a resounding 'yes.' And the family, for better or worse, now included Colin and Josh Campbell.

I forgave him.

It was past time to return to the house. Derek and Sarah, Morry and Lainie, Seth, Chris, and Cathy, and Gwen Singleton and the four knights had all arrived and we needed to start the barbeque. Having heard Em's thoughts in regards to the weather, I would make an exception—a small one—and create a temporary bubble of clear, warm air right outside the back door so we could cook the meat without hindrance.

As I sensed how crowded my house had become, I made the indoor space bigger as I had done once before, enough to accommodate everyone who had been invited to Em's and Derek's joint birthday party. Since their birthdays were the eight and the tenth, respectively, we had celebrated them together ever since—and in spite of—the catastrophic barbeque out at Devils Garden in 2014 when a dragon had abducted and killed Derek and his friend Ken. Fortunately, Derek, being immortal, had come back to life. I had made the decision to resurrect Ken, which had caused problems since he'd been destined to die that day.

Reminiscing had dredged up other memories. It had been nearly six years since I awoke in the Crystal Cave, traveled by jet to Salt Lake City, met Emily and Derek, bought my shop in Moab, and started down this path to my current state of affairs.

I looked down at my brother's descendent, and thought—not for the first time—how much he resembled Beli. And I made a decision.

Beli, can you join me for Derek's and Emily's thirty-fourth birthday celebration? I would like to see you, and your descendent would enjoy that, as well. It has been awhile since you stopped by the shop, and many months since we returned from our adventure in the past. What do you say, Brother? And besides, you haven't met my youngest son, Arthur, yet.

I don't see why not, Myrddin Emrys. It would be interesting to see how everyone is doing. See you soon.

Great, we're heading back to the house now.

"Alright, Colin, let's go. There's someone coming to the party that you've been anxious to see."

I let go of my enhancements, resumed my regular height and weight, and touched Colin's arm. The instant my hand came in contact with his skin, we appeared in my living room.

"It's a god thing, isn't it?" Colin asked.

"What's that?"

"You completely bypassed teleportation."

I stared at him and it occurred to me that he was correct. I'd assumed I'd been teleporting, but in fact, I hadn't been ever since I transitioned the previous summer. Or had I ever actually teleported? I remembered when, many years ago, I had accidentally taken Em to the Crystal Cave with a mere thought and Llyr had brought us back to Moab.

He grinned. "You didn't know, did you?"

"The question is, how in the world did *you* know?"

Colin hemmed and hawed and before I could get an answer out of him, Lumina came up to us with Josh in tow. I let it go for the time being and suggested that after he said hello to Cathy, he and his son should spend a few minutes together discussing magic since everything was out in the open. As he turned to greet his girlfriend, Colin looked back at me with a bewildered look on his face, as if he had no idea why he'd said what he'd said about teleportation.

I frowned. What the hell was happening now?

* * *

Colin was so distracted he apologized to Cathy and went looking for Josh, who was chatting with Morry and Lainie. He hardly knew what to say to him. He'd hidden so much from his son since the fateful day when he'd broken into Merlin's shop—starting an unbelievable chain of events—that he didn't know where to start. He motioned to him and they stepped aside to talk privately.

"Pop, I know you're mad at me, but I can explain…"

Colin recognized that here was the way to make things right. "No,

Josh, there's no need. Merlin straightened me out. I was wrong to confront you, especially in front of everyone. It's your life; you're an adult. We'll figure out the financial stuff later, with Merlin's help." He added with a wry grin, "I'm sure he has more money than he knows what to do with. He's been hoarding gemstones since the fifth century."

Josh stared uncomprehendingly at his father, who'd never backed down from an argument before and rarely apologized for his actions. "Why didn't you tell me before? You've known the truth about Mr. Reese, uh, I mean Merlin, and his family all this time."

"Yeah. I should have told you, but Merlin wanted me to keep it a secret."

Josh shrugged. "Well, I know now, and I'm a part of it. You and I have *magic*. I can't wrap my head around it."

"Me neither. So, Merlin wants me to show you something—and I've never done it before. We'll see if it works. Come on."

Colin led the way through the kitchen and out the back door, hoping he wasn't going to get soaked again when he'd just started to dry off. He was pleasantly surprised when he noticed the area around the barbeque was dry and warm, although the rain was coming down in buckets over the rest of the back yard.

"Okay, here goes." He didn't think the blue fire would work for this, as it was way over the top; it would blast the whole barbeque across to the back wall. He had a feeling this task was so simple he could do it by a negligible effort of will, so he focused on the charcoal briquettes and pushed a small amount of power from inside his chest. They started to burn, the high temperature hardly producing a visible flame. Instead, they smoked a little and started to turn white, the intense red glow underneath indicating they were almost ready.

He glanced at Josh, who was staring at the perfectly burning bed of charcoal in amazement.

"Pop, did you…?"

"Yep."

He slowly smiled at Colin. "Awesome. Will I be able to do that?"

"And more, if you have the kind of potential Merlin seems to think you have."

"I can't get over it. It's real. And the best part is, I'm mated to Lumina," he said. "I love her so much. I can't believe my dream came true."

"Yeah, that kind of thing tends to happen around gods and angels."

* * *

77

"Dad, how could ya let that shithead Josh take Lumina's virginity?" Although he was careful to keep his voice down, Derek was outraged and not thinking clearly. And I'd had sufficient turmoil today to last for at least the next decade.

He'd gotten enough information through the telepathic links we all had to be aware of what had happened, but not why. And it was clear my own link with him was more erratic and incomplete than ever, so I clapped my hand against Derek's forehead and transmitted the truth to him directly.

"Damn it, Dad, what are ya doin'? Oh, I see. Okay, I understand. I don't like it, but I understand."

When I lowered my hand, he grabbed it and murmured, "Why is this happenin' to ya, Dad? Ya ought to contact Grandfather and find out how ya can have an intimate knowledge of, and connection to, literally everyone and everythin' else in the entire world, and such a faulty link with your own family. It makes no sense."

In his peripheral vision, Derek could see Sarah making a beeline for him. "What's wrong, Der?"

He tried for a smile and didn't quite make it. "Don't worry, Sarah, Dad and I are havin' a…discussion."

He glanced at me, concern evident in his expression.

"If you'll both excuse me, I'm going to check on Colin and Josh and get the meat on the grill. Everything's under control." I pulled out of Derek's loving yet vise-like grip and headed for the kitchen. I pulled the tray of ribs out of the 'frig, grabbed the tongs, and went out the back door with my hands full, hoping Colin and Josh were getting along.

"Hey, Uncle, let me help you with that," Colin offered, plainly in an elevated mood.

I looked at Josh, who returned my gaze shyly, exuding contentment and goodwill, and was relieved all was well with the Campbells. For now.

I responded lightly, "Sure, I'd appreciate it. Place the ribs on the grill and adjust it so it's not too close to the coals. Then turn them when they're ready. Oh, and brush on the sauce occasionally."

"Yeah, I think I can handle it, Merlin. I've barbequed before," Colin said with a wink.

"Great, of course you have." I'd forgotten the barbeque sauce, so I conjured a bottle of it along with the brush and set both on the table next to the grill. "Here you go."

It startled Josh, who still wasn't accustomed to even such simple magic as I'd been using. I gave him a nod and went back in the house. I paused as I closed the door behind me, and sighed.

Emily, sensing that something was wrong, caught me standing in the laundry room with my head bowed. "Merlin, are you alright? What's going on?"

"I think I need you to hold me for a minute or two."

I groaned as she enfolded me tenderly in her arms and kissed my cheek, loving me.

"I don't know if I can do this."

She rubbed my back. "I think you're making mountains out of molehills, god man."

I pulled back and looked at her askance. "What do you mean?"

"You've never heard that old saying before?"

"I'm from Wales, remember?" My original accent came through strongly for a moment.

"How could I forget? It simply means you're blowing things out of proportion, making a big thing out of nothing."

"Oh, of course, I knew that. I'm tired, that's all, emotionally overwhelmed," I said.

My wife looked alarmed, and well she might, for as an immortal god, I shouldn't have to rest, mentally or physically. I was supposed to be continually connected to the energy that powered the universe itself. And the universe seemed to be doing fine, so evidently my own connection to it was faltering, which was not good.

"Okay, we'll figure this out. Come into the living room with me and mingle with our guests. The mac and cheese and the coleslaw are on the table, so we're just waiting for the ribs. Let me get you a drink. Would you like beer or whisky?"

"Beer is fine, Em, thanks," I said, and returned Sir Leon's nod of greeting as I entered the room. The tall knight had never adapted to the twenty-first century and was moody and taciturn. At some point, I would have to address his issues, but I could scarcely deal with my own at the moment. It was depressing to think I might have to return him to the fifth century.

Gwen approached and gave me a one-armed hug, her other arm securely around the chubby form of my son. "Merlin, thanks for inviting me. Arthur has grown so much already! He'll be a man before you know it."

I couldn't help but laugh. "Guinevere, it's going to be years before he's old enough to marry you again, so don't hold your breath."

"Oh, I know, but I'm so excited he's here." She grinned at me and turned away as Lainie came up to admire Arthur and they started chatting. I smiled at the picture they made as they both played with my son.

"Here you go, big guy," Em said as she handed me a bottle of beer from our local brewery. She hadn't called me that in years and I almost said something facetious until I caught the troubled expression on her face. I sobered at once.

Thanks. Sorry, I'm not myself at present.

It's okay, we'll sort it out, my love, Em replied silently.

Then I sensed something else was amiss—Beli wasn't here. There was no reason for him to be late, unless something calamitous had occurred in the god realm, and that seemed far-fetched.

Beli, Brother, where are you? I thought you were coming to the party.

What party?

Why, Em's and Derek's party. We spoke an hour ago and you said you were anxious to see everyone.

No, we haven't spoken for many weeks, Brother. But I'd be happy to come.

He materialized suddenly in the middle of the room, startling everyone.

I overheard Cathy whisper, "Who is that? He looks like Colin, only bigger."

Chris whispered back, "It's Beli, Merlin's brother."

As he stepped in front of me, he noticed my uncharacteristic pallor and lack of energy and scowled. "What the hell is going on? What's wrong with you?"

"That's what I want to know," I said quietly. "And furthermore, who answered me earlier if it wasn't you?"

I have an idea who it was, Merlin, and you're not going to like it.

It hit me like a ton of bricks. *It was Sam, wasn't it? Bollocks.*

I'm afraid so. He's been raising hell—pardon the pun—in the god realm, giving me and Llyr and some of the minor gods and goddesses a difficult time. You're lucky he didn't show up here in disguise. We should have checked in with you before this.

It's alright. But it could be the reason I've been having more and more trouble sensing my family members, their thoughts and feelings, their needs. And I've been allowing myself to get distracted. In fact, I've been feeling all too human lately, tired and depressed at my failings, I admitted.

Damn it, it's not you, Myrddin Emrys! It's Sam's doing, and…bollocks, something's coming, something big!

I felt it, too, an imminent threat, traveling towards the house from above at a high rate of speed. I mentally reached out to Beli, and with his help I was finally able to break free of the pall of dark energy inhibiting my connection with the universe and my higher god powers. And I sensed a huge meteorite streaking through the atmosphere, headed directly for us. Even though the bulk of it would be burned away before it entered the skies over Moab, the impact would vaporize everything and everyone in the county, perhaps even the state.

I slowed the passage of time to alert my guests and assure that everyone was able to evacuate—teleport or be teleported by those with the ability to do so—to Wales, to the Crystal Cave. My family, Derek and Seth in particular, objected strenuously to leaving me but I insisted, and within scant minutes, the house was empty.

Beli and I gazed at each other, and in perfect accord appeared in the sky high above Moab, transforming into a solid shield of pure energy which covered the valley in a brilliant golden light. When the meteorite collided with us, we wrapped ourselves around it and absorbed the explosion, but we failed to contain all the light and sound it produced.

As soon as I regained human form, I sensed the fear, confusion, and amazement in the minds of the people of Moab. No one had seen our physical forms, but they had experienced an inexplicable event, the repercussions from which could be an issue.

Beli materialized next to me in the back yard. "How do you want to handle this, Brother?"

For a moment, I was many thousands of years in the past, hovering in the sky over a vast desert filled with human beings on their knees, staring up at the angels above them, praying, fearful—

"Myrddin Emrys, it's not the same as it was then," Beli said. "These humans didn't see us, nor are they the simple folk you're remembering. Let's make everyone in the area who could have witnessed this event forget. That's all. Their own minds will fill in details that make sense to them about the time they've lost."

"That will work. Let's do it."

* * *

"Grandpa, how did it feel when the meteorite hit you? I mean your joint energy shield?" Morry asked.

It had been a simple matter to let everyone know it was safe to return, and they had done so with alacrity.

I was surrounded by curious gazes and expressions of amazement, even from my closest family members. Josh and Cathy in particular, who were new to the magical, supernatural world, couldn't contain their enthusiasm as they watched me field questions. Beli leaned against the wall with a half-grin on his dark face.

"It's hard to describe since I wasn't in human form or consciousness. I do know that it was incandescently hot and bright, like being inside the sun itself." I glanced at Beli. "I believe you experienced something comparable?"

He tipped his head in acknowledgement and I continued. "It didn't hurt, if that's what you're asking. It was…exhilarating."

"But how were you able to come back to human form from something like that? Doesn't it feel confining and anticlimactic?" Chris looked thoughtful as she waited for my response.

I smiled kindly at my son's lover. She was an intelligent woman, but a mortal could never comprehend what it felt like.

"Chris, I was originally created 14 billion years ago." Indrawn breath and looks of shock and astonishment rippled through the group assembled in my living room as I revealed something I'd told Derek and no one else. Even my wife looked stunned.

"You can't imagine what I've experienced. I existed incorporeally as spirit, energy and Light, for eons. And then I, and my brothers and sisters, took the form that humans call angels." I stole a quick look at my brother, who winked at me. "All of us have kept the same human appearance that we created for ourselves back in the early days. All my experiences, great and small, have been precious to me, but experiencing a human life has by far been the most significant, and therefore I will never consider it confining or anticlimactic."

Chris was rendered speechless by my admission. I noticed that everyone else glanced back and forth between Beli and me as if they were picturing us as angels in the way they are always portrayed: wings outspread and long robes flowing gracefully around our bare feet.

I waited to see if there were any other comments or questions forthcoming, and when everyone remained silent, I suggested that we eat. Personally, I was starving.

We all converged on the table laden with the food we had abandoned less than an hour ago. Before we filled our plates, I adjusted the temperature of all the dishes and fixed the charred ribs. It seemed we were always diverted by one thing or another on every occasion when we were about to sit down to a meal. I shook my head.

I noticed Beli chatting with Colin and eating prodigious amounts of ribs, slaw, and macaroni and cheese, and grinned. It reminded me of the relatively few occasions Llyr had joined us for a meal. Since a god who generally dwelt in the god realm had no need for food, it was a personal choice to actually eat. I'd mentioned to Beli that I should have invited Llyr to the party, and he reminded me that our brother was busy dealing with problems "at home."

Josh was rather intimidated to be face-to-face with his larger-than-life ancestor, and sat close to Lumina trying to be inconspicuous. My daughter and I exchanged amused glances until Emily decided we were being rude and insisted telepathically that we stop.

I had finished eating and taken my plate to the kitchen when Sir Leon approached me with a somber look on his face. Although I had provided him with awareness of modern English when he first arrived in Moab, he addressed me in the old language.

"Lord Merlin, I would speak with you." He dipped his head subserviently.

"What is it, Leon?" I reluctantly replied.

He made eye contact with me briefly, scanned my body from my long black hair tied back in a tail, down my jeans-clad legs to the athletic shoes on my feet, and hastily looked away. I had always considered him a friend, but he had never been comfortable addressing me in familiar terms.

"I do not know how to say this to you, my lord." Again, he glanced away nervously. "I…am not able to fit into this…twenty-first-century life. This time is very confusing and this place is not at all to my liking —it is too hot and there are few horses; everyone rides around in noisy metal boxes. My fellow knights have changed and I can no longer relate to them. And you—no offense to you, my lord—you are not the same man I served back in Camelot." His eyes drifted over to the sleeping form of Arthur in his portable crib. "And Arthur…I find it difficult to comprehend that he has returned as your son. I am mightily confused."

"And you're unhappy?" I cut to the heart of his confession.

He looked down at his feet. "Yes. I am sorry, Lord Merlin."

I knew that he wanted me to send him home, back to the fifth century, and I had considered it earlier. But I couldn't give in to his plea.

"Sir Leon, I have need of you here, in this time and place, whether it's to your liking or not. And in the next few years, Arthur will be grown to manhood again and will have need of you. Did you not pledge your allegiance to Uther Pendragon when he knighted you? And did you not do the same when Arthur came to be your sovereign lord?"

He straightened his posture and replied stiffly, "Yes, Lord Merlin."

"You will remain here in the twenty-first century and serve King Arthur, and me, again. Do you understand?" The imperious authority in my voice sliced through the undercurrent of conversations in the room until there was absolute silence.

"Yes, Lord Merlin," Leon muttered before bowing to my command.

* * *

Unlike everyone else present except Beli and the knights, Derek understood every word spoken between his father and Sir Leon, so he knew what had transpired. Sir Leon had been reprimanded by the god Myrddin Emrys, not Merlin. It was no surprise Leon claimed Merlin wasn't the same man he knew in Camelot—he definitely was not.

For the second time since he'd known he was Merlin's son, Derek was somewhat leery of his father. The first time this occurred was years ago when he'd shared their family secrets with his friend and fellow Park Service employee, Ken Wilson.

Nephew, there is no need to fear him; he would never hurt you or anyone else he loves. And he does love you, deeply.

Derek was startled as he heard Beli's strongly accented voice in his mind. It wasn't very long ago that Beli was a ruthless enemy, so it took some getting used to that the god was now his friend.

Yes, I'm on your side and shall be forevermore. And I tell you truly, that Sir Leon has resisted all attempts to help him adjust to your century. He's been most uncooperative when asked to participate in training exercises and in other activities. Myrddin Emrys had to take a stance that Sir Leon, as an ancient knight, would understand and accept.

Thanks for explainin' that to me, Uncle. Derek threw a shuttered look at Beli, who nodded unobtrusively.

* * *

I felt the unease and a trace of fear in the room after I finished chastising Sir Leon. I hadn't meant to do so in front of everyone at the party, but it had been necessary to put the knight in his place. I couldn't afford to lose his respect by allowing him to continue with his insolent behavior. It had not been his decision to come to this century, but it had been his decision many years ago to serve his king in any and all ways.

As Merlin, I most often presented an easy-going human nature, but my god self was neither easy-going nor human. Myrddin Emrys could be high-handed and unbending and had no qualms about conveying the appropriate authority to discipline Sir Leon.

84

So which part of me was Merlin, and which part was Myrddin Emrys? The question had been plaguing me since long before I transitioned. Logically, if I had transitioned, I was no longer Merlin, I was my god self, irrevocably. But in my heart, I knew I was both and always had been, despite the centuries I'd been unaware of my real nature, and that might be the problem. I needed to accept, once and forever, that *all* parts of me could function seamlessly as one.

I merely had to figure out how to do so.

For the time being, the party was at a standstill, friends and family members standing around quietly, wary of what I would do or say next.

So I made sure I appeared harmless. "The party's not over yet, we still have cake and other desserts to partake of and gifts to be opened. But first, I propose a toast to Derek and Emily for their thirty-fourth birthdays."

Beer, liquor and champagne were distributed, everyone gladly getting back into party mode, and I toasted first my son and then my wife, praising their loving support of my efforts over the years, which had culminated in my transition to wholly actualized god.

Beli surprised me by proposing a toast—to me.

Towering over everyone, he made brief eye contact with every individual until the focus was completely on him. "My brother, the god Myrddin Emrys, better known to all of you as Merlin Ambrosius, has always striven to do the right thing, to be the best, to do our father's bidding, and since he and I have settled our differences, I am prepared to stand by him for all of eternity. Join me in a toast to the one who is the real reason you are all here today."

As all glasses were raised amid murmurs of love and encouragement, I felt an overwhelming sense of completeness and joy that heartened me to put aside my troubles and trust that tomorrow would take care of itself—with my family's help.

CHAPTER 13
Moab, Early June, 2019

The heady feeling I had experienced at the party in March continued unabated for several months, as I worked in my office on the plans for our twenty-first-century version of Camelot. It would be our center for living, working, and administration for the new State of Albion. I left the running of The Moab Herbalist in the capable hands of the women in my life while I attended to my true purpose—preparing for Arthur's comeback. His adulthood was still years away, but I couldn't be sure exactly when it would occur and there was a great deal to do.

Early one morning, around six, I thought I heard my daughter talking to someone in the kitchen. I assumed it was Arthur, because Emily and Rae were still in bed, and Lumina often fixed breakfast for him. I had been focusing so completely on Arthur's future that I was losing track of the present again.

It hadn't occurred to me that he might have experienced a major growth spurt until I walked into the room and a two-year-old child peered up at me. He was dressed in clothing of the appropriate size, so Lumina must have conjured it for him.

"Daddy!" he shouted and ran towards me exuberantly, as only a young child can do. A radiant smile lit up his face.

I scooped him up into my arms. "Hello, Arthur." I kissed his round, baby-soft cheeks and he kissed my rougher ones right back. My heart quickened with love for my son.

"*My* daddy." He flung his pudgy little arms around my neck and clung possessively for all he was worth.

"Yes, I'm your daddy and I love you so very much." The weight of his warm body in my arms gave me a thrill, reminding me Arthur was back in my life.

The boy sighed with pleasure and rested his sandy-blond head on my shoulder. *I wanted you to be my father before, Merlin.*

I responded to the older voice in my head, "I know. I'm sorry."

I resemble you this time, do I not?

"Yes, you do, except your hair is the same color it was in your previous life."

He grinned and touched his hair. I blew a raspberry on his cheek and he giggled.

"Mornin', Dad."

"Morning, Derek." I glanced inquiringly at my oldest son as he sauntered into the kitchen. "When did you arrive? Where's Lumina?"

"I teleported into the livin' room a few seconds ago and I didn't see her. I suppose she went in to work early. I think there's a delivery comin' in." A worried frown creased his forehead as he noticed my lack of prescience. It was clear that this nagging problem had returned, if it had been gone at all or had only subsided temporarily.

I shrugged. "It's worse than ever. I'm not at all aware of what's happening—or going to happen—with the family and I don't think Sam's causing it."

When Derek didn't respond, I noticed that he was staring at his brother, perhaps remembering Arthur as he had been in his previous life.

Arthur turned his head and stared back at him. *Hello, Derek*, he said telepathically in Old British.

"Hello, Arthur," he responded aloud in the same language.

Arthur held his arms out to Derek, who took him from me and hugged him close.

Derek looked over the child's shoulder and grinned at me. "I have to get used to this. Once Aidan is born at the end of the month, I'll be holdin' a kid pretty frequently."

"Yes. And you'll be feeding and bathing him, changing his diapers—it's a package deal when you're a parent. Something I experienced only twice when *you* were a baby, before Llyr caused me to forget you existed."

Derek noticed that I looked a little sad and pulled me into a hug with Arthur between us.

A few seconds of that was all Arthur could take. He squirmed until Derek pulled free and set him on his feet, whereupon he ran into the bedroom calling for his mother.

Derek watched him go, shaking his head in disbelief. "Did ya expect him to grow so fast? He's not even five months old."

"I knew he would, in general, but it's still startling, isn't it?"

"How's Em takin' it?" he asked apprehensively.

"She was doing surprisingly well until Lumina mated with Josh. Now any change Arthur experiences upsets her. She knew about Lumina's relationship with Josh long before I did, but apparently never thought it would go so far. And for some reason, Lumina hadn't wanted me to know she was seeing Josh. Perhaps she was afraid I'd react badly." Somehow, we'd gotten off the subject of Arthur's rapid growth, but I sensed Derek needed to talk about his sister.

"But ya didn't react the way she expected," Derek said.

"No, of course not. Their relationship was destined, pure and simple. I sensed it when she mated with Josh. I got a surge of information about Josh's life in this and several other realities concurrently. Came close to overloading my circuits." Derek looked at me blankly as my attempt at humor fell flat.

"Dad, I can't imagine what's it's been like for ya. But it was kinda disturbin' for me to find out my baby sister was havin' sex. And I still don't like that it was with Josh Campbell. Christ, couldn't she have found someone better than him? He's a damned pervert."

"He's actually pretty normal, and a nice, intelligent young man, Derek."

He continued to give me a disbelieving look.

"And as I said, the two of them are destined to be together. They will produce a child who will be instrumental in aiding Arthur in the future, but the details aren't totally clear to me yet."

When Beli showed up at the birthday party in March and we destroyed the meteorite Sam had sent, I thought that all my issues had been resolved, but that didn't turn out to be the case.

"I'm surprised ya know that much, considerin' your problem sensin' family business."

I gave him a pained half-smile. "True. I may have to bite the bullet and have a talk with my father, but it's hard to get a concise answer out of him."

Derek looked at me thoughtfully. "Hmm, I have an idea. This might sound peculiar, but I think the reason this is happenin' is you're not all together."

"Whatever are you talking about?"

"Remember when the other Merlin's personality came through unexpectedly?"

"Yes, and later it happened again—briefly—when I doctored my coffee with cream and sugar. And you know I always drink it black, no sugar."

"What? Ya didn't mention that!"

"It didn't seem important. But you may have a point. I need to bring all of my alternate selves back together before Merlin, and Myrddin Emrys, can truly be complete. And it could be the answer I've been looking for my entire life. That's brilliant, Derek. Perhaps I won't need to talk to my father about it after all."

He looked embarrassed for a moment, then said gravely, "I've told ya before, Dad, I'd do anythin' for ya. *Anythin'.*"

CHAPTER 14
Moab, Saturday, June 29, 2019

As the month of June drew to a close, I hadn't accomplished as much as I had hoped, and it appeared I'd have to have a chat with my father whether I wanted to or not. But a noteworthy event was imminent—the birth of Derek and Sarah's son, Aidan. I could sense him preparing to leave that safe warm haven of his mother's womb and enter this physical world.

Dad, Sarah's goin' into labor.

Yes, I can feel Aidan getting into position. He's very excited.

He is?

Oh, yes. Tell Sarah he's anxious to meet both of you.

We're lookin' forward to finally meetin' him, too.

It should be a quick delivery, so Em and I will be there shortly.

Okay, Dad, see ya soon.

Em and I appeared in Derek's home straight away, where my son was nervously pacing back and forth in the living room.

We watched him for a moment, glancing at each other with wry amusement, and I felt compelled to comment. "Derek, you have to be aware that your nervousness isn't necessary. Sarah will be fine."

He looked sheepish. "I guess I should go meditate."

"That would be best. We're here, so there's no need to worry." I smiled and clasped his shoulder affectionately. We joined Sarah in the master bedroom where she was calmly putting a rubber pad over the mattress to protect it from the birthing fluids. She glanced at us and smiled shyly. At the risk of hurting the other women's feelings, she'd asked that we be the only ones present when she gave birth. Understanding and accepting Sarah's wishes, Lumina and Chris ran the shop while Rae stayed home to watch Arthur, and pregnant Lainie stayed home with her feet up. All of them were content to let us handle Aidan's arrival.

"Are you ready, Daughter?"

"Oh, yes, and if I'm honest, a little nervous."

"We'll be right here with you. Everything will be fine," Em assured her warmly.

"Of course, and thank you both." She stood on tiptoe and kissed my cheek, then turned and hugged Emily. "I feel pretty good—" And she promptly doubled over in pain.

* * *

Labor progressed relatively quickly, given that this was her first child. But when the hours went by and she had still not delivered the baby, it became evident she was having some unforeseen trouble. I entered Sarah's womb with my god senses and discovered that Aidan had gotten tangled up in the umbilical cord, and it was perilously close to strangling him. I took care of it with a quick touch of magic, giving him enough assistance to finish his journey, and he was born at six twenty-six in the evening, seven pounds two ounces and twenty inches long.

I had known since early February that my father was sending another one of the gods to be born into my family. Aidan was an old soul, the god Aodh, of the ancient Celtic pantheon.

I had rarely associated with any of the Celtic gods except for Aodh, and I wondered if that was the reason the Irish god of fire and the underworld had been sent to this realm. But it didn't matter in the long run, he was my grandson and the newest member of my growing family.

Derek, Aidan is here and Sarah needs you.

Without delay, he teleported into the bedroom and hovered over the bed anxiously. "Hey, Sarah, how are ya doin', honey?"

Sarah smiled proudly and held Aidan, wrapped snugly in a receiving blanket, out to Derek. Gingerly, he took the baby from her and held him close, marveling at the delicate features and thatch of red hair. "Hi there, Aidan," he murmured, gently tracing the edge of a tiny ear.

Em and I glanced at each other lovingly, remembering the births of our own children.

Let's give them some privacy, Em suggested.

I concurred, and with a slight gesture all the soiled towels and sheets were clean, folded and stacked on the dresser. A carafe of water and a glass appeared on the bedside table along with a vase of roses. Em had already gotten Sarah cleaned up and into a new gown and the room had been restored to its typical, tidy condition.

We let Derek and Sarah know that we would be available day and night to help if they needed it, but they didn't call on us for a few days, preferring to adjust to the change in their household in their own way.

"Dad, when can I see Aidan?" Arthur asked shortly after we had returned home. He had met us at the door, practically dancing in place.

"I think it would be okay to go see him on Monday." I smiled at Arthur's excitement. "You do know that Aidan isn't one of the knights reincarnated?"

"Yes, Dad, I'm aware of that. It will be gratifying to speak to Aodh again."

My eyebrows rose in surprise. "You met Aodh before, while you were King of Camelot? How did I not know that?"

"No, I met him after I died, while I was in the Other World," Arthur said nonchalantly, trotting back toward the kitchen where Rae was busy cooking dinner.

"Ah, I see." I gave Em a quick, wry look. *Every so often he amazes me.*

She smiled. *Yes, me, too.*

CHAPTER 15
Moab, Early August, 2019

It seemed but a few short weeks between Aidan's arrival and the twins' birth. I was positive those two were not gods. They came into the world complaining loudly about being evicted from the calm, safe environment of their mother's womb. And they continued to squall whenever either of them was too hot, too cold, too hungry, too tired or, it seemed, too bored.

It didn't take long for Morry and Lainie to beg for help. Two human babies at the same time are a lot of work. With two shapeshifter babies in the house, normal daily living was virtually impossible.

With an infant of their own to take care of, Derek and Sarah weren't able to help, though as the twins' grandparents, they regretted it.

Arthur was still a young child, but didn't require all four of us to care for him at once. We took turns helping with the twins until Lumina moved in with Josh before classes started at Utah State University later in the month. After that, it was just the three of us. At least focusing on Arthur and the babies took Em's mind off of Lumina's departure.

It appeared that Seth, Chris, and Cathy had no desire to help care for newborn babies. They had diplomatically given baby gifts but stayed away from the abodes of both Colburn families.

My great-grandchildren were a handful, and I sympathized with Morry. But he had begged for divine intervention to assure the conception of the tiny fiends, and I had supplied that intervention. So now, he had to live with the consequences.

I had to admit, they were beautiful children. Brady looked like Morry, with his father's original brown hair and his grandfather's warm brown eyes. Bonnie was a miniature of her mother, with curly blond hair and violet eyes. Both children had inherited the slant of their eyes from their father, their grandfather, and me. I loved them, but I didn't envy their parents the task of raising them. I knew Morry was hoping they'd have growth spurts like Arthur did, but it wasn't probable.

* * *

As young as they were, Brady and Bonnie had to be watched constantly and were confined to crib or playpen, whether during the day or in the evening hours. The two babies had virtually no control over their shapeshifting abilities. They spent hours as wolf pups and even lynx kits, and in animal form they had way more agility than human infants. Fortunately, Morry had been able to take the month of August off from work, and at first, he was able to contend with the babies' shifting.

However, one day when the twins were three weeks old, they had both been extremely fussy. When nothing else calmed them, Morry had picked them up and cradled them in his arms. He walked around the house singing to them in a surprisingly skilled voice, according to his wife. The babies continued to fuss, gradually quieting until they were asleep, whereupon they both shifted to pups.

"Honey," Morry called softly. "Come and look at this."

"What is it?" She walked out of the kitchen and saw what was in his arms. "Aw, how cute is that?" It had happened before, but neither one of them could resist admiring their children in animal form. Brady had brown fur and Bonnie's was a creamy white; they were adorable. It was difficult to resist petting them, but Lainie didn't want to wake them up.

As Morry started to reply, there was a loud knock at the door. "Damn it," he muttered, as the pups started whimpering.

Lainie hurried to open the door.

Morry realized that they shouldn't be showing the wolf pups—their *kids*—to whoever was at the door. "Lainie, don't—"

It was too late. As the neighbor peered around the partially open door, her kind, wrinkled face brightened as she saw the little animals in Morry's arms. "Oh, I didn't know your dog already had her puppies! That's a lot to handle considering you have new babies in the house, isn't it? They're so sweet—may I pet them?"

Lainie said rapidly, "I'm sorry, Mrs. O'Kelly, we'd rather you didn't, they're still awfully young. Morry, why don't you give them back to—" Her face went blank for a moment as she improvised, "—Mama Dog, so she doesn't get worried about them."

Morry leaped to take advantage of the excuse to get the kids out of sight before they shifted back to human in front of their inquisitive neighbor.

In the kids' room, he was just laying them down in their bed—they did better curled up next to each other than in separate cribs—when they both spontaneously regained human form.

"Crap, that was close," he said as Lainie came running into the bedroom with a concerned expression on her attractive face.

"She must have seen me in wolf form when we were out in the back yard, before they were born."

He scowled. "Yeah, peaking through the bushes, the nosy bitch."

"Morry, watch your language around the kids!"

"Sorry, honey," he said, properly chastened. The next eighteen years, until the kids were grown and left home, loomed as an insurmountable challenge.

* * *

I couldn't help but notice the contrast between what Morry was feeling and Em's fervent desire to have a longer period of time with Arthur.

Humans always seemed to want what they couldn't have, but were we immortals any different? In some ways, it seemed not.

CHAPTER 16
Moab, Saturday, August 24, 2019

Perhaps it was the birth of Derek's son Aidan in late June or the arrival of Morry's children earlier this month that stimulated Arthur's growth again, or it was simply a part of my father's plan. In any case, my son was the size of a three-year-old. He had been born at the end of January, and he'd been alive in his new body for scarcely seven months, so it was a huge step for him to take towards his goal all at once.

It didn't surprise me that Arthur didn't usually sound or act like a child. He was an old soul after all. But it unquestionably stunned a few members of our group when he first spoke to them from that adult part of his psyche.

I had spent many an hour with him in the past few months, helping him to become accustomed to living in this time and place, but I'd never included any instruction other than basic life skills in the twenty-first century.

Now, I decided that he needed to experience some of the magic that was an integral part of our family. I was aware that Derek had previously revealed a few of our magical secrets, but as Arthur's father and mentor, I felt it was my responsibility to teach him the bulk of what he needed to know. And this was the day I'd begin to do that.

We stood together in the living room of our home on Doc Allen Drive and I told him I had something to show him.

"Certainly, Dad, what is it?" Arthur responded excitedly in his high-pitched child's voice as he looked up into my face.

I smiled at him and called forth my great, black wings. Arthur's eyes widened. "Ohhh!"

"Someday, you'll have wings, too. You're my son, so you are a demigod and have inherited magic from me."

Arthur smiled widely and said matter-of-factly, "Yes, I know, Merlin. How could I not? You're my father *and* my god. I have felt the magic ever since I was conceived. You'll teach me how to use it, and when I'm old enough, you and I will save the world."

His articulate, emotion-laden speech triggered a surge in my own emotions and I could feel my eyes start to water. I blinked rapidly. "Yes, we will. Come, let's fly."

I picked up my disconcertingly mature child and was instantly outside in our dark back yard, which was surrounded by a high wall built for maximum privacy. From there I took wing for my favorite spot at the top of the Rim. As we approached that vantage point approximately a thousand feet above the city of Moab, I could see a faint glow of reflected light on the sandstone cliffs towering above the valley. Although it was dark enough to hide my celestial form, I had activated an invisibility spell before we left home, to be on the safe side. As soon as I landed I put Arthur down beside me.

He was silent as we stood gazing down over the brightly lit cityscape, and I knew he was remembering ancient times and places. I imagined he was seeing immense old trees of oak, alder and ash, and gray stone castle walls over which a banner of a red dragon fluttered in an intermittent breeze.

I pulled my attention away from that vision of the past and looked down at my son. "Are you alright?"

"I miss Camelot." Arthur sighed. "This…" He gestured with a wave of his hand towards Moab and beyond. "This is all so new and strange to me."

"It is, but you'll become accustomed to it eventually." I stroked his sandy-blond hair comfortingly. "And the truth is if you weren't here, you'd still be in spirit-form, forever apart from the human realm."

Arthur looked up into my eyes and said solemnly, "That's undeniably correct. And it *is* a wondrous thing, to be alive again and here with you." He slipped his small hand into my large one.

I couldn't speak as love welled up in me.

"Oh, Merlin," Arthur said, looking up at me adoringly. "You mean the world to me." He knelt and kissed my feet.

For an endless moment, I gazed down at my king and had a vision of my much-younger self on *my* knees at *Arthur's* feet. A detached part of me felt it was horribly wrong for Arthur to humble himself before me, but in a flash of insight, I saw that I was not his servant—he was mine. I closed my eyes, overcome by the realization.

Arthur got up and tugged on my hand. "Dad? What's wrong? What happened?"

"I…had a rather staggering epiphany."

He tilted his head and looked puzzled. "I don't understand."

"It's alright, Son. I'll tell you about it later. Let's go home—your mom's waiting for us." I picked up my son, held him securely against my chest, and spread my wings.

* * *

Emily watched as Merlin dropped down from the Rim like a gigantic bird, his wings catching the air to slow his descent. She knew he had used an invisibility spell so that the general populace of Moab couldn't perceive him. But she could.

As he approached her, she heard a high-pitched giggle echo off the cliff face. Arthur was having the time of his young life. The bright head was tucked snugly against his father's neck, and Merlin's long, silky black hair blew out behind them.

She saw the silver circlet on his head that he'd retrieved from long-ago Camelot. Merlin wore it regularly now. One day when he had decided to wear the ancient symbol of his exalted status, their customers at The Moab Herbalist and his acquaintances around town had started calling him "Prince Michael" as a joke. They didn't realize, first of all, that Merlin wasn't really Michael Reese, even though he had used the name since coming to Moab in 2013. Secondly, they didn't know that the sobriquet was correct: his great-grandfather had been the King of Dyfed in fifth-century Wales, so, stretching the truth some, he *was* a prince.

Emily's eyes continued to follow the descent of her husband and unique son. Her heart ached with love for them both, but at the moment for Arthur in particular, as she'd been given so little time to embrace his childhood. The boy in Merlin's arms would be a full-grown man in four and a half years. She'd known it since Merlin had informed her who was growing inside her. She knew she had no choice but to accept the situation since it was her destiny to be the mother of the reincarnated King Arthur, but that didn't make it any easier to bear.

She had never met the original Arthur, but apparently, he and Derek had closely resembled each other. Now, Arthur looked like Merlin. And despite his new outward appearance, she was aware Arthur's mind and soul were those of a thirty-five-year-old man, as they had been at his death centuries ago. Nevertheless, in many ways, he was just a young child.

It must be difficult for him to be both, Em thought.

"Mom! Dad flew me up to the Rim!" Arthur yelled excitedly when he spied her watching them. She smiled and waved, but inside she cringed, hoping the neighbors hadn't heard his voice emanating from high in the air.

When Merlin landed in their back yard, he retracted his wings and set their son down lightly on the grass. The child immediately ran to his mother, who scooped him up and kissed his warm cheek.

"Yes, I saw you, darling. Did you enjoy flying with your dad?"

Arthur wound his arms around her neck and hugged her tightly. "Indeed I did! I can't wait until *I* have wings. Dad promised I could have them in a few years, as soon as I'm a man again."

"He did? Then you shall have them. Did he tell you what color they'll be?"

"No, Mom, he didn't. Does it matter?" Arthur asked her quizzically.

"Of course not," she murmured. "I was simply curious. They could be white like Seth's."

Arthur contemplated his future wing color for a moment. He shook his head and replied, "No, they will be more like Derek's."

Emily's eyebrows lifted in surprise. "You've seen Derek's wings?"

"Why, yes," Arthur replied self-assuredly. "He showed them to me months ago."

She stared silently at her son for a moment then said, "Okay, let's go in and get you ready for bed, sweetheart." She reached for his hand and he held it out to her trustingly.

"I love you, Mom."

Em glanced at Merlin and back at Arthur, her eyes blurring with hot tears. "I love you, too, my darling." When the tears lasted a little too long and became more about missing her daughter, she hoped that Merlin wouldn't notice.

* * *

Pretending I didn't see her tears, I followed them into the house and walked into Arthur's room to tidy it up while Em helped him in the bathroom. I thoroughly enjoyed listening to the dialog between them as Arthur objected strenuously—and predictably—to his nightly ritual.

"But Mom, I don't *want* to bathe every day!"

"Arthur, you're dirty, so you need to take a bath. Besides, I changed your sheets today and your pajamas are clean."

"Aww, Mom, what does it matter?"

"Arthur, please stop arguing with me."

"But Mom…"

"Get in the tub!"

Much splashing ensued after he finally capitulated and climbed into the bathtub. Em talked to him as she scrubbed his body and he played with his tub toys. I grinned. It was difficult to reconcile this small, rambunctious boy with the fearsome warrior and ruler of all Britain he once was.

Finally, I heard the water draining from the tub, and the two conversed quietly while Em dried him off and helped him into his pajamas. Then came the inevitable discussion about his teeth.

"Do I have to?" Arthur whined.

"Yes, you have to brush your teeth after meals and before going to bed."

"But why? I cleaned my teeth once a day in Camelot."

"Because your mouth is healthier and your breath smells better when you brush frequently."

"I do *not* have bad breath."

"That's because you brush your teeth often." Em was beginning to lose patience and I could tell she was gritting her teeth in frustration.

I stood in the doorway, observing as Arthur obstinately refused to take the toothbrush from Em. Ah, the joys of parenthood.

I stepped forward, took the paste-laden toothbrush from Em and put it in Arthur's hand. "Brush, Arthur. Now. It's bedtime," I said sternly.

He glanced up into my eyes, accepted that he couldn't win this particular battle, and sighed piteously. His little face scrunched up in distaste as he reluctantly put the brush in his mouth and half-heartedly ran it over his teeth.

After he had done a decent job, I allowed him to rinse. "There, was that so bad?"

"Yes," he said haughtily and stomped out.

I glanced at Em, who was cleaning up the after-bath mess, and we shared a wry look and a hastily squelched laugh.

CHAPTER 17
Moab, December, 2019

Without question, Rae loved all her grandchildren and step-grandchildren, but Lumina and Arthur held a special place in her heart since they were her daughter's children. With Lumina gone from home and starting her own life, Arthur received an abundance of Rae's love and attention.

She adored her son-in-law, worshiped him, if truth be told. She had declared her devotion years ago to the god of magic and healing, but she also loved Merlin, the man, and was grateful for his protection and generosity. When she had been fleeing her abusive husband Jack, Merlin and Emily had taken her in and she had known she was safe.

For months after she'd moved to Moab, she'd had disturbing dreams about her husband stalking her. After a while—and to her vast relief—they'd slacked off. Unfortunately, those unpleasant dreams had returned with a vengeance during the four years Merlin was lost in the past.

She had dreamed of her husband with Satan's face for over a year, and she knew it wasn't her husband she was afraid of, it was the evil that inhabited his body. She was convinced the soul of Jack Crandall, the man she'd once known and loved—Em's father—was gone, absorbed into the evil presence inside him. Her fear had abated to some extent since Merlin's return. The dreams had slackened, not stopped, but at least she felt safe again.

Now that Arthur had been born, the offer she had made to Merlin to help him rediscover the route to Avalon was no longer necessary. Once it was clear that Emily was the portal through which Arthur would return to the land of the living, Rae was no longer needed to lead anyone anywhere and her self-esteem had suffered.

But she worked hard at The Moab Herbalist to earn her keep, even though Merlin had insisted she needn't do so. And she worked hard at home to help take care of the household and her young grandson. She

101

had felt especially obliged to do so in the months since Lumina's departure.

By December, she was mentally and physically exhausted, but she was determined to get through the holidays with good cheer. So she dredged up the energy and the fortitude and kept going.

She found intriguing new recipes and prepared culinary master-pieces, to the family's gustatory delight, and baked a dozen different varieties of Christmas cookies, which she packed in fancy tins and distributed to everyone in the group. She helped Em and Merlin put up a large Christmas tree and decorate it and the house in the most festive manner she could contrive. Since it was Arthur's first Christmas, she shared Em's desire to make it particularly memorable for him. Although he was eleven months old, he was already the size of a four-year-old, with the mental acuity of a man in his prime, so he would remember this holiday fondly for the rest of his life.

A week before Christmas Rae was beyond tired, but she hid it well and went to bed early, falling asleep as soon as her head hit the pillow. She had vivid dreams but couldn't remember a single one.

On December twenty-fourth, in the predawn hours, she dreamed about her grandfather, Oengus, whom she hadn't seen since she was a small child. In her dream, he spoke to her in an ancient language she recognized from her childhood. As she slowly awoke, she was surprised to find she remembered everything, including the fact that she had dearly loved her grandfather—and he had loved her.

Rae was confounded by this realization, since Grandfather Oengus had disappeared when she was four years old, never to be seen again. She thought about the beautiful ring he had left behind, made of silver and gold worked in an intricate design. No one in her family had been able to wear it, as if the ring itself had rejected each and every person who'd tried it on. She had subsequently given it to her daughter as a keepsake when she was a teenager. It hadn't fit Emily either, and since it had made her feel uncomfortable she'd put it away in her jewelry box and forgotten about it until Merlin came along.

Rae lay in bed and smiled hugely as the rays of the rising sun broke through the clouds and shone on the walls of her bedroom. It was Oengus's ring Merlin wore as his wedding ring.

* * *

He arrived on Christmas Morning. I must have had an odd look on my face as I responded to the knock on the front door by opening it with magic, something I never did unless I was absolutely sure of the visitor's identity. I could sense the curiosity in the room as everyone looked around, wondering who it was since all were present and accounted for. Our numbers overflowed into the dining area from the living room, the interior dimensions of which I had expanded earlier this morning.

"Please come in, sir," I said politely in the Elven language as my ring chimed a greeting and shone with an eldritch light.

I saw Rae and Em turn to stare at each other speculatively, then stand to greet their unexpected guest, each holding one of Arthur's hands. He was uncommonly quiet as he stared at the doorway.

The man who entered was abnormally tall and slender, even more so than Seth, who leaped to his feet in surprise and with his wings tucked close to his body, bowed stiffly and somewhat submissively.

"*Madainn mhath, ciamar a tha thu?*" Seth asked in a formal tone of voice.

"*Tha gu math, tapadh leat,*" the man replied, as he bowed low in turn, conceding Seth's royal status.

Chris's expression as well as her thoughts told me she was surprised at Seth's reaction to the Elf's visit. Apparently, Seth hadn't shared with her what the real reason had been for his appearance in Moab the previous year. I had known that he'd been at the Council's beck and call but hadn't been able to identify any of its members. Until now.

What did they say? Is that Gaelic?

I glanced at Em. *Scottish Gaelic, yes. Seth said, "Good morning, how are you?" and our guest replied, "I am fine, thank you."*

"Merry Christmas tae ye all. I am Oengus," the Elf announced in English with a distinct Scottish accent. He looked to be no more than in his midthirties, yet he gave the impression of great age. His pointed ears were the identical shape of Em's and Lumina's and the pupils of his reddish-brown eyes were more like a human's than a reptile's, round not vertical.

Seth, who had returned to his seat next to Chris, looked apprehensive.

"Merry Christmas to you also, Oengus. Won't you have a seat?" I offered. I conjured another comfortable chair, placing it next to the tree after expanding the room even more.

"Aye, thank ye," he said with a courtly bow. "But first, I wish tae greet ma granddaughter." He held his arms out in invitation. Rae pulled away from Em and Arthur, rushing to Oengus with a jubilant cry.

Arthur stood quietly and studied him with a puzzled frown.

Oengus held Rae tenderly, murmuring phrases of affection in the

Elven tongue, as all eyes watched the two get reacquainted. He appeared to be half her age, but no one could mistake that he was centuries older than Rae.

"Grandfather, you're really here! Why did you leave without saying goodbye all those years ago?"

"I thought 'twould be for the best, lass."

"The best for whom? I've had an empty place in my heart for sixty years and didn't know why. Now I know it was you I was yearning for." Tears welled in her eyes.

"I'm sorry, Granddaughter. We Elven Fae dinna feel aboot things the way humans do, and time flows differently in the Fae realm. I didna realize ye would miss me."

As Oengus and Rae continued to converse, I crossed my arms over my chest and frowned. The appearance of this high-ranking Elf within a year of Arthur's birth, and Arthur's apparent lack of recognition of someone who had been instrumental in protecting his soul for centuries, seemed suspicious to me. I sent a quick silent message to Derek and Morry, who surreptitiously moved closer to their wives and children and Morry's mother-in-law, Ann. I did the same with the knights, who shifted to surround Emily and Arthur.

Seth's eyes were wide, his wary gaze shifting back and forth between his step-grandmother and her ancestor, but he made sure he had his arm around Chris. Colin guarded Cathy protectively on one side and Josh kept Lumina close on the other side, with Gwen between the two men. Excellent, everyone was covered. All these security precautions had taken only seconds due to our previous drills. Oengus seemed unaware of our preparations and his attention remained on Rae.

Em, did ye ken yer great-grandfather would come for Christmas? I heard Seth ask telepathically.

No, I didn't, and apparently, your father wasn't aware of it either. I wasn't, but I didn't comment.

Oengus is the head of the High Council of Elders. He's the one who sent me here tae spy on Da.

I grinned humorlessly. Well, that explained Seth's initial reaction.

What? Are you serious? Em asked Seth silently.

Aye.

I watched as Emily turned to stare at Oengus, noticeably unhappy that he had done such a thing, yet reluctantly fascinated at the family resemblance. It was evident she and her mother both had inherited the shape of his nose, and although his hair was dark auburn, it was long and wavy like Em's. He was dressed in a floor-length woolen robe reminiscent of the type I had worn in the fifth century, in a rich dark green edged with fine brown fur. And it was apparent by the way he carried himself that his position on the Council of Elders afforded him a measure of distinction in the Fae realm.

As if feeling Em's gaze on him, Oengus glanced at her over the top of Rae's head, and noticed the defensive groupings in the room. Finally, he turned to me with a wry grin. "I havena come tae hurt ye or yer family and friends, Myrddin Emrys." He gestured at my wedding ring, which was still reacting to the Elf's presence, throbbing warmly and chiming faintly, as if overcome with happiness. "Do ye suppose yon ring ye wear, that once belonged tae me, would be reacting in such a way if I'd come tae harm ye? Nay, lad. Freezing cold it would be and screaming like a banshee." The term he actually used was the Gaelic, *bean sidhe*.

He focused on Seth and gave him a faint smile. "Ye can relax, Yer Highness. Ye fulfilled yer quest and passed the test we'd set for ye." Seth glanced at me, mystified, and although I returned his look with raised eyebrows and a brief shrug of my shoulders, I didn't let on I'd suspected something of the sort.

Oengus looked around and continued with a smile, "Let us celebrate the noo, with food and drink and gifts." As he lifted his arms, powerful magic filled the room and I stiffened, prepared to respond with like power. I needn't have worried.

The tables were suddenly piled high with platters of sweet rolls and sausages, and carafes of hot cider, hot chocolate, coffee, and tea appeared next to a stack of coffee cups and plates sporting a holiday motif. Brightly wrapped gifts were piled next to, and on top of, the existing ones under and around the Christmas tree. Everyone was a bit dazzled and the children, although too young to understand what was going on, responded excitedly. Only Arthur was unaffected by the largesse as he continued to stare at Oengus with a perplexed look on his young face.

What's wrong, Arthur? What do you sense? I asked, discreetly shielding our communication.

I feel as if I should know him. I may have met him before, but I can't remember. I don't sense he's evil, and yet he makes me uneasy...

I completely understand. Whatever was causing this feeling of apprehension didn't seem indicative of any particular danger, so I let everyone know silently that it was safe to relax and enjoy the festivities.

* * *

Despite the fact that we'd already had breakfast, the food and beverages were consumed with a hearty appetite. Oengus was busy handing out gifts when Derek, Morry and Seth all sent their silent concerns my way regarding the behavior of our uninvited guest. Colin sidled up to me and quietly said, "Something feels off."

I glanced at him, impressed that he had perceived the feeling of trepidation we'd all had.

I agree with all of you, however, I have no idea what the problem is, I sent out telepathically to my family members in such a way Oengus could not intercept my thoughts, even if he had the ability to do so.

Rae was happier than I'd ever seen her, and it pained me to think Oengus might not be who he appeared to be, or that he had ill-intentions toward us. For her sake and ours, I hoped we were all misinterpreting the circumstances.

After all the gifts had been opened and the resulting abundance of torn wrapping paper and ribbon disposed of, the babies started to get fussy and the families prepared to head home. The knights thanked us and took off, intending to spend the afternoon at Moody's drinking beer and playing pool.

Colin gave me a look as he departed and I sent him a quick message he alone could hear. *I'll notify you if I need you. Merry Christmas.*

He bobbed his head, his swarthy face flushed with pleasure. Josh and Lumina went with him, planning on spending a few days at Colin's before they went home to Logan. Lumina looked back at me before she went out the door. *Everything will be okay, Dad. I think you can trust Oengus.*

Did she truly know something I didn't? I doubted it. She most likely had analyzed the situation and decided we were all being excessively cautious. I stood on the front step with Emily and Arthur and waved goodbye as everyone drove away, then turned to confront our Elven visitor.

* * *

Oengus and Rae were chatting quietly as I came back into the living room, preceded by my wife and son. To his disappointment, Em hustled Arthur off to his bedroom to give me a chance to speak with Oengus, since I didn't know what to expect. My intermittent problem reading family members applied to extended family, and those closely associated with the family, as well.

He must have sensed my objective and my body language, if

nothing else, and convinced Rae to give us a few minutes alone; she got up from her seat and hesitantly left the room. I knew beyond a doubt she loved and trusted me as her son-in-law, and she was undeniably devoted to my god self, but she seemed reluctant to leave us. I couldn't imagine she thought I would harm him, but stranger things have happened.

"No, Myrddin Emrys, she has nay doubt yer intentions are pure and neither do I."

My eyebrows rose in surprise when he seemed to hear my thoughts.

"Nay, I dinna have the ability to read yer thoughts, but I do have a wee touch of empathy, and yer facial expressions make it clear tae me what ye're thinking." He paused as if to give me time to comment and I inclined my head to signify that I understood.

"I failed tae handle this weel, I admit it tae ye. And I'm as sorry as I can be tae have caused such a stramash. But coming tae yer household at Christmas was a risk I was willing tae take. I needed tae see all of ye together tae make sure Arthur was surrounded by those who would feel bound tae protect him."

"Oengus, while I can understand your desire to protect my son, what I've felt throughout this visit of yours is a sense of unease, unrest, and suspicion, and my family members—including my Fae son—have also felt it. Even my distant relation, Colin Campbell, who, although he is the descendant of a god, is mostly human, felt the apprehension the rest of us did. I would appreciate it if you would give me more of an explanation than the fact that you wanted to check on Arthur. After all, the High Council must have a powerful scrying tool for such a purpose, so that leaves but one other reason for you to have come here, and that is to see Rae. I have to warn you, I will not tolerate it if you plan to mistreat her in any way. She loves you and hopes to have you in her life henceforth. I sincerely hope you have not misled her in that regard."

Oengus slanted his head and smiled as he looked at me thoughtfully. "Ye have allayed ma fears in regards tae my granddaughter, as weel. Ye are more than I anticipated, much more: A god, but one who cares for and respects others."

He had been testing me all along. I wanted to be incensed that he dared to come into my home and test me thus, but I decided to let it go, because now I realized why all of us had felt such agitation. Despite his great age and his magic and his high standing among the Fae, Oengus had been afraid. It was hard to fathom, but I was convinced it was the truth.

I did not allow my thoughts to be reflected in my facial expressions or mannerisms again, and I decided to let go of all the uncertainty I had been experiencing. I could easily have chosen to intimidate him by reverting to my god stature, but fortunately, I restrained myself. The result would have been to frighten him even more.

"Let us put aside our suspicions of each other, Oengus, and come to some understanding."

I could see him start to relax and knew I'd made the right decision. I contacted Arthur telepathically to let him know what was going on.

It's safe for you, if you wish to talk to Oengus now.

I finally remembered him, Dad. He was one of the Elves who protected my spirit, but all those centuries ago when I died, he wasn't the leader of the High Council and that's why I couldn't place him. He was kind to me; they all were. And he's truly my great-great-grandfather?

Yes, he is. Come and see him, Arthur. I think he'll be pleased to talk to you.

As I watched my son and the Elf greet each other, I wondered how I could have been so suspicious of him. Relaxed and feeling pleased with the results of his endeavor, he exuded nothing but benevolence and friendliness.

I must admit, I was relieved. The day had gone reasonably smoothly, all things considered, but I would be glad when it was over.

Em and Rae were chatting in our bedroom, so I decided to go outside and enjoy a moment alone. I closed the door behind me and looked up towards the Rim, admiring the snow-topped ridge of red rock glinting in the late afternoon sun.

I slowly inhaled the fresh, chill air and happened to glance across the street—and saw a familiar-looking black cat run up the sidewalk to my neighbor Rod's house. It resembled the one that had visited Em and me at her place when I first came to Moab.

The front door opened and Rod's wife—at least I presumed that was who it was since I had never met her—let the cat in. As she started to close the door, I could see the animal change into a person who looked like Rod. He was a shapeshifter? As the cat that had declared his loyalty to me, he had been instrumental in providing assistance during the battle with Nimue in 2013.

All these years, he'd lived across the street from me and I'd never sensed what he was. It couldn't be a coincidence. I'd be willing to bet my father had something to do with it. Perhaps I should stir things up.

I appeared at my neighbor's front door, which was still standing open a crack, and said, "Rod, I think it's time you and I had a chat."

He jerked the door open and gawked. "Uh, Myr..Michael! Merry Christmas to you! Won't you come in? This is certainly a surprise."

I strode in without further ado. "I'm sure it is. You're getting sloppy, Rod. I saw you shift from cat to man. And I doubt Rod is your real name."

"I told you not to shift until the door was shut, didn't I? Imbecile." His wife hissed impatiently and stomped out of the room shaking her head.

"Great. I'm in trouble now," he muttered, his eyes following her retreat.

The more I stared at Rod the more familiar he looked, until it occurred to me who he truly was. He had dark brown hair, gray-blue eyes, and a hawk-like nose. "I haven't seen you for millennia... Portunus. What in the world is the Roman god of keys, doors, and ports doing here playing shapeshifter?"

"You forgot livestock. I'm also the god of livestock, don't ask me why." He grimaced. "People don't seem to need a god with my particular job description anymore, so God assigned me to you." He was quiet for a minute as if deciding how to deal with the fact that I'd blown his cover. "Well, crap, Myrddin Emrys, I told Father you'd eventually find me out." He allowed himself to expand to his god height.

I did the same and folded my arms across my enhanced chest. "So, God has had you, what, guarding my house? Watching out for me and my family?" I wasn't sure how I felt about that.

He looked embarrassed, and cleared his throat nervously before he spoke. "Yeah, that's exactly what I've been doing ever since you came to Moab. Remember when I came to see you at Emily's old place years ago? I thought I handled it rather smoothly."

"Yes, you did," I admitted. "I even wondered if the cat was actually one of my clones from an alternate reality, here to help me find a portal back to Avalon and Arthur. As it was, you and your friends were instrumental in defeating my nemesis during the Battle of Matheson Preserve."

"Aw, you could have done it without my help." He gave me an easygoing grin, but I got the feeling he was hiding something...unless it was leftover uneasiness from dealing with Oengus. I decided that must be it and grinned back.

"By the way, I've never seen or heard from the other shapeshifters since that night."

Portunus chuckled. "They were a bunch of minor gods and

goddesses who didn't have anything better to do, and they all returned to the god realm after the battle."

"That explains it." I paused, wondering why I hadn't sensed they were gods. "I'd better get home. We still have a guest and I need to find out if he's staying with us or intends to depart tonight."

"You mean Oengus? He'll teleport back to Inverness. He only came over for the day." His face fell as he saw my expression. "Ah…"

I glared at him. "Portunus, what the hell is going on?"

"Look, it's not what you think. My function here is to be aware of what occurs in and around your house and help guard you and your family. So, to that end I'm able to discern everything that goes on in your home except for, you know, intimate moments, and things that are irrelevant to ensuring your safety."

"I certainly hope that's true. I'm feeling very disconcerted about this."

He looked apologetic. "Sorry, but I'm afraid you'll have to talk to Father. I'm doing what he specifically assigned me to do. If you'll excuse me, I have to go smooth some ruffled feathers, so to speak."

I resumed my normal height and started out the door.

"Oh, Myrddin Emrys?"

I paused on the doorstep and turned back to him. "Yes?"

"It's good to talk to you again."

I searched his eyes for duplicity and found none. He was sincere. "You, too, Portunus."

* * *

Arthur and Oengus were still engrossed in conversation when I walked back into the house, so I sought out my wife to tell her what I had discovered across the street. As I went down the hallway, following her scent into the master bedroom, I wondered how I had been kept in the dark so long about my friendly neighborhood god-turned-shapeshifter and watchdog. Or should I say watchcat.

"Oh, there you are," Em said as she came out of the bathroom. "What did Rod have to say?"

"You won't believe this, but…" I said, and filled her in on my discovery.

"You have to be kidding me! He's been there since before we moved into this house? That means your father manipulated things so we'd buy it. And Rod was the cat that came over to my place?"

"Correct. Hmmm…I have an idea." I turned into a black cat with intensely green eyes.

Em looked shocked. "Wow, I didn't expect that. You're a larger version of the black cat in my dream; the one that turned into a panther and morphed into…you."

Yes, but do I look like Rod did when he came to our place as a cat?

She tilted her head and stared at me, her eyes slitted in concentration. "No, not the same at all. You're bigger, for one thing, taller, and your nose is different, long and straight like your nose in human form. To tell you the truth, you look the size of a bobcat but with a long tail."

I sat on the floor looking up at her, my tail switching back and forth in a credible imitation of feline irritability.

She grinned and bent down to pick me up. "Oof, you're heavy, but you're so cute!" She sat on the edge of the bed and held me on her lap, petting me in long strokes from head to tail. I couldn't help it, I started to purr, arching my back under Em's hand.

This is most enjoyable. Why have I never thought about doing this before? I purred louder. *That feels amazing.*

"Oh, Em, I forgot to ask you if—whoa! Where in the world did that huge cat come from?" Rae stood in the doorway, gaping in astonishment.

Emily laughed, scratching behind my ears. "It's alright, Mom, it's Merlin. We were doing an experiment."

Rae watched wide-eyed as I leaped down onto the floor and morphed back into my human form. Fortunately, my clothes came with me. I smiled at Rae and Em. "That was fun. I'll have to do it again soon."

"You make an awesome cat, but definitely not like Rod."

"Rod? Our neighbor? What does he have to do with it?" Rae glanced between us, bewildered.

"We found out he's a shapeshifter we met as a cat years ago," Em responded.

"In truth, I know Rod from the god realm. He's an ancient Roman god named Portunus." And I went on to describe what I learned.

Rae shook her head. "A cat that's a Roman god? And he's our neighbor? What next?"

I didn't share with her the detail that Rod had been aware of Oengus's visit all along. And speaking of Oengus… "I'm going to check on Arthur."

"And we're going to start dinner since the ham will take time to heat, and we need to get the yams in the oven and the Brussels sprouts started," Em explained.

"Don't forget the rolls," Rae said.

"Right, and the rolls," Em added, then turned back to me. "Do you want to invite Rod and his wife to have Christmas dinner with us?"

"That's kind of you, Em, but no. I have no desire to socialize with him, to tell you the truth. And I doubt the woman is his wife—she's probably a minor goddess on assignment with him."

We all traipsed out into the living room and discovered that Arthur and Oengus were nowhere to be seen. I sensed them right away and spoke calmly to Em, who had immediately assumed the worst. "They're both okay—they're out in the back yard."

My wife's heart was beating unusually fast and I put my arm around her, holding her close until she took a deep breath and relaxed. "Sorry, I responded like a mother instead of an immortal with magic, but oh, my God, it scared me!"

"It's alright, I understand. And according to Portunus, Oengus will teleport back to the Fae realm rather than spend the night with us."

"I can't get used to the fact that Rod—Portunus, that is—has been watching us all along. It should make me feel safe, but it doesn't, it's just creepy."

At that moment, Arthur and Oengus came in the back door, both of them glowing with the cold and the pleasure of each other's company, and I decided to continue giving Rae's grandfather the benefit of the doubt until such time as he proved me wrong.

CHAPTER 18
Moab, Pandemic 2020: The World Changes

The year began with the knowledge of a potent new virus, but it wasn't until March of my seventh year in Utah that life in the human realm changed irrevocably. A pandemic of massive proportions swept through the populations of every country in the world, causing devastating illness and loss of life.

This catastrophe proved to be a major distraction to my ongoing work, but ended up being a catalyst in making it a priority.

And my father instructed me, in no uncertain terms, to do nothing. This particularly went against the grain, as it would have been easy for me to go back in time and prevent the virus from mutating (or from being manipulated by human hands as some people contended) or to utilize powerful magic to eradicate it after the fact. I knew I, acting alone or in concert with my brothers, could easily remove every trace of illness on the face of this earth. Not only COVID-19, but *all* diseases. All of humanity could be safe and healthy. Forever.

But as I had experienced before, the fact that I could change things, fix things, heal things, didn't mean I should do so.

When I questioned his decision, God informed me he had a reason for introducing this kind of challenge to the human race. He wanted his human children to learn and grow and make crucial decisions on their own, to unify as a race against a common threat. And having everything locked down to prevent or slow the transmission of the virus would also slow people down and force them to examine their own lives, their actions regarding pollution, environmental degradation, and global warming, and ultimately, the fate of the planet itself.

I understood, but it pained me to watch millions of people die. I felt every one of them leave their bodies, most heading for Heaven and the evil ones heading for the Hell realm. I would mourn those individuals above all because they had taken the wrong paths, made the wrong decisions, and would spend an eternity regretting their actions, or lack thereof.

During the lockdown, it was sometimes difficult for my family to blend in since we were literally incapable of catching the virus; it was specific to mortals. Arthur was physically a child, and Derek's son and Morry's twins were babies, so we had to maintain a pretense of concern for their health, but since they were the offspring of a god and of demigods they were immortal and therefore immune to all viruses, including COVID.

Unbeknownst to Derek and Morry, I had made Sarah and Lainie immortal prior to them conceiving, thus they were immune to the virus. Since the spouses of demigods were not automatically immortal I should have granted them their immortality as soon as they wed. But in Sarah's case, I had still been lost in the past at the time of their marriage, and around the time Morry and Lainie had gone to Reno to get married I was focused on Jim Singleton's abduction and death, and Gwen's rebirth.

I was allowed to place a powerful protection spell on those individuals specifically under my care who weren't immortal, so they wouldn't catch the virus or be carriers of it.

We all wore our masks in public even though we didn't need them, because we wanted to present a cooperative front during the crisis. I had magically modified our masks so we could breathe comfortably, since that seemed to be the major complaint about them, not to mention that they were a nuisance if one wore glasses, which were always fogging up.

Eventually the lockdown ended and businesses opened back up again, but it turned out to be way too soon, as numbers of COVID cases rose dramatically with the influx of visitors determined to ignore the fact that the crisis wasn't over.

We sold the potent, chemical-free hand sanitizer we had created in The Moab Herbalist for a reasonable price and regularly donated bottles of it to the hospitals and nursing homes in Grand and San Juan Counties. In addition, we supplied it to other retail stores in the area. I had, when the pandemic started, explained to everyone in our group why we couldn't stock a potion in the shop that would cure the virus. It was galling, but I had to follow my father's mandates first and foremost. Customers used the hand sanitizer, wore masks, and maintained social distancing while in our store, as required by Grand County and later in the year by the State of Utah, and by our own concern for others. Regrettably, many people ignored logic and made a political issue out of a medical one, by eschewing the use of masks and continuing to congregate in crowds, thus causing an even more drastic spread of the disease.

The year 2020 was also memorable for being a singularly critical election year, and the tension caused by election issues added to the stress of having to cope with the COVID crisis. By the time the election was over and a new administration claiming commitment to social, political, and economic reform had been voted in, the year was waning and I wondered what was going to happen next. The fight for decency and fairness had only just begun and I knew better than anyone how many years it would take to make a substantial difference. And that the real battle had yet to be waged.

* * *

We planned to celebrate Arthur's second Christmas with the usual get together at our place, and anticipating it to be well-attended by friends and family I again moved the inner walls of the house to accommodate everyone. I was glad to do it in order to have all of our guests here under my roof, and at my present level of power, it was easily accomplished.

Emily reminded me that it would seem irresponsible during this time of virus paranoia to be having a big gathering when most people were staying at home for fear of spreading the disease. The fact that it couldn't happen in our family was irrelevant since no one knew the truth about us. We finally decided to have everyone that could do so teleport to the house and the rest would have to arrive by car. I would create a magical shield around our property to prevent people from seeing or hearing us.

It seemed appropriate to go ahead with the celebration. Everyone, but especially the kids, would have been very disappointed if we had cancelled the traditional festivities.

Approaching his second birthday Arthur had grown again—he was the size of a six year-old—and it was possible he might be even larger by the end of January. He was a typical boy, always into mischief, but that child's body couldn't hide his adult intellect, which became increasingly clear one morning a week before our get-together.

We were starting to eat breakfast when Arthur put his fork down and looked at me earnestly. "I was thinking of reciting *The Night Before Christmas* at our party, Dad. Is that okay?"

"Of course, but what made you think of doing so?"

"I thought it would be advantageous for me to get used to public speaking again, and reciting something I'd memorized in front of people I know might be an easy way to get back in the game." I fought to keep a straight face. "What an excellent idea, Arthur. Yes indeed, I'm sure that everyone would enjoy hearing you recite such an enduring classic."

I glanced furtively at my wife. *Em, stop grinning, or I won't be able to contain myself. If Arthur was paying attention you'd hurt his feelings.*

You're right, sorry. She made a valiant effort to control her reaction and must have succeeded, because Arthur never mentioned it.

* * *

On Christmas Day, as we all gathered to celebrate the holiday, something happened that made me realize I had been wrong to assume we could carry on as we had in the past.

As usual, the knights were all present and I noticed Sir Leon seemed more or less content. I was pleased he had finally resigned himself to living the rest of his life in the twenty-first century. Since my ultimatum in March, he had applied himself to learning the nuances of modern English and speaking it exclusively, and he had gotten involved in weapons training as well as the fitness program Ryan had developed to keep the men in shape. I anticipated that he would keep up the good work.

Arthur had carried through with his plan to recite *The Night Before Christmas*, and his calm and mature delivery of the tale was applauded by all.

The presents had been opened and everyone was relaxing with his or her favorite hot beverage, the adults congregating in small groups chatting happily. I was standing alone for the moment, appreciating the company of my family and friends, assuming all was well, when the tone of our gathering changed radically.

Leon raised his voice as he began arguing with Ryan about a minor point of protocol they had been discussing, and the situation quickly escalated into a brawl between my usually quiet and courteous knights.

Colin, Morry, and my two adult sons jumped into the fray, separating the battling knights and restraining them. Meanwhile Em, Lumina, and Sarah brought their own powers into play to quickly corral the children and the rest of the women and hustle them into the bedrooms.

I focused my god powers on the combatants and released a burst of power that effectively had all of them sinking unconscious to the floor.

"Jesus H. Christ! What was that all about?" Colin exclaimed as he stepped back from the inert bodies of the four knights.

Derek, Seth and I gazed at each other while Morry went to check on the kids.

Sam must have gotten to them.

Aye, it would seem sae.

And where was Portunus when we needed him? I generally succeeded in managing my temper and I seldom had to deal with it anymore, but I was utterly enraged. I reacted without thinking, which was an unfortunate choice. I directed my rage, not at my evil brother where it belonged, but at our supposed guardian.

"Portunus, what kind of protector are you, that you have allowed Satan to infiltrate my knights, endangering my family in my own home?" I thundered as I burst without warning into our neighbor's home across the street.

Rod, or the Roman god Portunus, reacted swiftly by reverting to his god height and power, calling on his own magical resources to surround himself with a defensive shield of Light.

"Merlin, what the bloody hell is wrong with you?" he snapped. "Stand down!"

His command was laced with the strength that God had bestowed on him and I backed off forthwith, the red haze of my anger dissipating as I realized how out-of-control I was.

He and I had been practically nose to nose when I'd confronted him, and I had never seen this innocuous god so incensed.

"I can't be everywhere at once, Myrddin Emrys, and I have obeyed Father's instructions to the letter. I never get a vacation, a weekend off, or a break from this assignment, and if you think I particularly fancy overseeing every damn move your entire family makes, *think again*." He turned and started pacing back and forth. "Look, I'm sorry that Satan somehow infiltrated your knights, and I'll be sure to keep that in mind for the future and try to guard against it. But I strongly suggest that you enlist God's help, because I can't do it all."

Even though I wanted to continue blaming him for his failure to protect my men, I couldn't fault Portunus's logic, nor could I hold him responsible for Sam's devious behavior—or for my own failings, for that matter.

I returned to the house and purged the knights' beings of the thin layer of black magic they had been carrying around, unwittingly waiting for Sam to activate it and cause a disturbance. I was glad that it hadn't been worse, and I swore that I wouldn't let my guard down again. In reality, none of us could afford to do so. Consequently, we spent the remainder of the year expanding wards and protocols against future incursion by my brother. Little did we know that it wouldn't be nearly enough.

CHAPTER 19
Moab, 2021

As the New Year commenced, no one could bear the thought of continuing to be consumed by anxiety, sickness, and death, so the news of a vaccine seemed to be a light shining through the darkness of the past year.

The political climate continued to improve, but beneath the outward show of cooperation, there existed a great deal of unrest and violence, no doubt fomented by Satan and his followers. Logically this included Morgana and the renegade wizards, although I couldn't prove it since they continued to elude me.

There was a long way to go to return to normal life, and I feared it would have to be a different normal, not the one we had been used to. How I wished to shout the truth to the city, the state, the country, and the world, that King Arthur and I were here to create a new way of living, for all people, for all time.

I found it difficult to remain aloof from the world's problems, but the truth was that the time to act was still some years in the future. Arthur was still a child, and while he was making incredible progress, he needed at least three more years to grow to adulthood before we could even begin our actual work.

On his birthday in late January, he ran into our bedroom early in the morning to show his mother that he had grown again. He was the size of an eight-year-old. I had been lounging on the bed, waiting for Em to wake up, and he leaped eagerly into my lap. It was his smallest growth increment yet, but his body was solid and heavy and I confess I made a sound of surprise and a grunt of discomfort as his knees connected with my groin. A god in a human body was as susceptible to pain in the private bits as a mortal male.

"Good Morning, Arthur! Happy Birthday!" Em exclaimed as she swiftly awoke, sat up and scooped him off of me. *Are you okay, god man?*

I think so, although lovemaking may be out of the question today, I wheezed silently.

Haven't you ever heard of the old adage, physician, heal thyself?

Hmm, I can't get away with anything, can I?

Nope.

We turned to focus on Arthur, who was jittering with energy and excitement.

"I'm bigger, I just know it! Can I get new clothes, Mom? Please?"

"We can go shopping after we sort through your clothes, okay? You can help me put a few of the smaller things away for Brady."

"Sure, Mom, thanks." Dropping his childish behavior, Arthur turned to look at me with a decidedly adult intensity. "Dad."

"Yes?"

"I know you have Excalibur. You've always had it." His voice seemed deeper as he calmly confronted me. "And I want to see it."

I was taken aback. That was the last thing I'd expected him to say, and I had no idea he knew that I'd never thrown it into the lake at Avalon. After his death in AD 474, I had been understandably grief-stricken and hadn't been able to part with the legendary sword he had so prophetically pulled from the stone.

I had lied to everyone, and had promulgated the stories and legends that Excalibur was lost to the realm of men long ago, and no one had ever known or said anything to the contrary. I had even lied to Derek when he'd asked about it early in our relationship. I should never have become so nonchalant about my possession of Arthur's sword, but I'd had a multitude of other things to sort out, and revealing the sword's true hiding place hadn't been a priority—or a necessity.

"You have Excalibur? Why didn't you tell me? Where is it?" Em asked, exasperated.

"It didn't seem important at the time and I never thought to tell you. It's concealed in the wall in the back room of the herb shop."

I returned my attention to my son, who awaited my response with ill-concealed impatience. "Yes, of course you may see it, Arthur. It's yours, after all."

Thirty minutes later, with Em and Arthur bundled up in warm clothing, the three of us stood in the chilly back room of The Moab Herbalist facing the wall in which I had secreted the most famous sword in history. As I released the powerful spell, the inner wall disappeared, revealing my own sword and all of the ancient possessions my old care-taker, Tom Reese, had shipped to me from Wales when I first came to Moab.

"I don't see Excalibur, where is it?" Arthur asked anxiously.

"Have patience," I murmured.

I cautiously withdrew Arthur's sword from its hiding place and removed the glamour of a rune-covered staff that I had long ago applied to it. The sharp edge of the blade was protected by a well-maintained leather scabbard I had obtained many centuries past, after the canvas it had originally been wrapped in had disintegrated with age. I held the grip and pulled the scabbard off, and the blade shone with an other-worldly light as it responded to Arthur's presence. The jewels embedded in the golden hilt sparkled, and I could hear the sword sing to him.

Arthur's countenance lit up with joy. As he took the sword from me, I wanted to admonish him to be careful, but managed to restrain myself. He might be in a child's body, but he knew instinctively how to handle that beautiful instrument of death.

As Em started to protest that it was too heavy for him, I glanced at her. *It's alright. Let him hold it. He'll know what his limitations are.*

She held her breath when his small arms began to shake with the effort of holding up the heavy weapon. But Arthur simply chuckled and handed it back to me with a wry look.

"I guess I'm not ready for it yet, am I?" he asked in his child's voice.

"No, but you will be," I assured him. "Until then, it will be waiting for you, here where it's safe." I returned it to its hiding place and rein-stated the glamour and the spell.

The three of us shared a look of wordless understanding, and we returned to the house.

* * *

In May, Lumina informed us that she and Josh weren't going to wait until after graduation to get married. They planned to wed before the fall semester started. Josh had been in college over two years at that point, majoring in business administration, and Lumina for less than two years. She had decided to major in marketing, with a minor in psychology, which could prove invaluable for our future endeavors. I was proud of both of them for persevering with their studies in these difficult times, studying remotely on their home computers the previous year, and I was aware they both needed an official acknowledgment of their commitment to each other. When Colin objected to scheduling their nuptials in August, I reminded him that they were already mated, and there was no reason they shouldn't fulfill their destiny. He reluc-tantly agreed and they started planning their wedding in earnest, with the enthusiastic assistance of all the women in the family. Josh wanted to include his mother and sister, but they declined to participate. I suspected Sam had interfered with them—apparently, anything was fair game to disrupt our lives.

In June, my grandson Aidan Colburn was two years old. He was the most gentle, loving child you could ever hope to meet, and not what I'd expected knowing he had the soul of the Irish god of fire. He and I had developed a strong bond, not between gods, but between grandson and grandfather. He had never exhibited a magical nature, but he was certainly aware magic existed since he was surrounded by it constantly. It was clear to me that his connection with the gods and his own proficiency would be revealed in time.

Morry's children were another story entirely. They turned two on August third, and every move they made was filled with barely controlled chaos. They still shifted unpredictably, making it virtually impossible to take them out in public. Any attempt to teach them how to control their abilities was met with obstinacy and deliberate incomprehension. Occasionally, Brady would levitate in his sleep, which concerned his parents greatly. So far, Bonnie hadn't done so, but at some point she would learn that particular skill. I told my grandson that he should be grateful the children weren't teleporting in their sleep into their parents' bedroom, as Lumina had done.

Morry returned to work when the kids were a month old, so Lainie stayed home with them. As luck would have it, her mother, Ann, was able to spend many hours caring for them when Lainie needed a break from the pint-sized fiends. Em helped out sporadically, but she was deeply involved managing The Moab Herbalist and didn't have more than a spare moment here and there.

I loved the twins, but the frenetic atmosphere in that household was not conducive to maintaining my focus, and therefore I didn't participate in their upbringing as much as I would have liked. And perhaps, as much as I should have done.

* * *

It was a spectacular Saturday in mid-August when Lumina and Josh were married outdoors at Warner Lake, surrounded by friends and family and the natural beauty of the La Sal Mountains.

Having been raised in the Catholic Church, Josh had originally insisted on a traditional ceremony. Frankly, I was relieved when Lumina convinced him otherwise. None of my group, except Colin, would have been comfortable attending Catholic services. Not that there was anything wrong with religious observances, but it would have been the height of irony for me—an ancient god who was also an angel—to attend a wedding ceremony in a place devoted to the worship of my father and my brother.

Perhaps I was being unreasonable, but I didn't see the point in a church wedding for Lumina and Josh. They were married in the eyes of the gods, and a simple ceremony was all that was necessary to satisfy human laws.

Although I was initially hesitant to do so, Em persuaded me that I was eminently qualified to conduct the service, and she urged me to magically take care of the marriage license as well.

The morning of the wedding, Derek and Seth jointly cast a spell around the area, including the intersection of the road to Warner Lake with the La Sal Loop Road, so people who didn't belong there wouldn't be tempted to visit the lake that day. Colin and Morry magically persuaded campers to depart, and the knights made sure the grounds and picnic tables were clean and trash-free and the grassy lakeside site mowed for the ceremony.

Everyone volunteered to bring food and beverages for the reception, while my wife and my mother-in-law were in charge of decorations and tableware, and Chris and Sarah were in charge of flowers.

Those who owned four-wheel drive vehicles and chose to drive did so, but since it was a rough, steep, gravel road, most of us teleported in.

The day dawned clear and breezy, and by noon, the temperature was about eighty—on the warm side, but tolerable. The bride was radiant in a vintage 1990s ivory brocade gown with short sleeves and a sweetheart neckline, which she had found in a shop in Salt Lake City. The groom had decided on an ivory tuxedo with a gold tie and according to my wife, he looked especially handsome. I wore a summer-weight gray bespoke suit and pale gray dress shirt and called it done. I had never liked wearing a tie and had no intention of starting now. My long hair was pulled back in a tail and clubbed, as Seth would have done when he had been a Scottish warrior, and I received several admiring looks from the ladies attending the event.

As I stood in front of my daughter and her mate, and looking past them to the familiar faces of my friends and family, I allowed my god power to flow out of me until we were all surrounded by golden Light.

* * *

Colin found his eyes filling with tears as he watched his son and Merlin's daughter prepare to join their lives before the people that mattered to him. Most of them anyway. His daughter Rose wasn't there, which was a shame, but she and her mom had chosen not to attend. Even though he missed her, he couldn't do anything about it. He looked around at these magical individuals with whom he had allied himself, and felt proud and grateful to be a part of it all.

As his gaze was drawn inexorably to the golden presence in front of them, he felt a surge of familial love and potent magic envelope him, and he had an epiphany. Joy filled his heart as he recalled that Merlin was actually—

Colin's brain shut down, and when he came to a moment later, he couldn't remember the unimaginable insight he'd had. He shrugged and decided it must not have been anything critical and returned his attention to the scene in front of him.

* * *

I closed my eyes and allowed the feeling in my heart to inspire me, since I hadn't prepared a speech for this momentous occasion, nor did I want to use someone else's prewritten version of such sacred vows. I opened my eyes and began speaking in a voice that resonated throughout the valley.

"Lumina and Josh, we are all gathered here today in love, to acknowledge your heartfelt desire to officially bond with each other for all time. In this realm of flesh and blood, we are drawn to the opposite sex not only to have children, but for the joy and pleasure of lovemaking, to comfort and support each other, to laugh and play together, and to enrich each other's lives...

"The rings that you exchange are the outward sign of the commitment you have made to each other in your hearts...

"Your bodies, your minds, and your souls are united in the sight of the gods, and most importantly, before the one God. As his representative, and with his blessing, I proclaim that you, Lumina, and you, Josh, are now wed. You may kiss each other before this assemblage to seal your pledge, as wife and husband."

A resounding cheer arose as my daughter and Colin's son embraced each other and indulged in a deeply satisfying kiss, and Emily and I shared an intimate moment in our hearts as we remembered our own marriage ceremony.

* * *

The wedding proved to be a positive and inspiring event that buoyed our spirits for some time. All of us continued with our personal projects and enjoyed our separate family lives, while we made a collective effort to focus once more on our long term goals.

Protecting and teaching Arthur was a priority for me, and with that in mind, I vowed to redouble my efforts to find Morgana and her renegade practitioners of dark magic. As long as they were unaccounted for, our families weren't safe.

Time passed, and I was no closer to finding Sam or his sinister crew. I hoped that the wizards who had once been willing to lay down their lives for me could be saved from Satan's deadly influence, but more than likely it was too late. What a shame that those brave souls, who had sacrificed so much at the Battle of Matheson Preserve when we defeated Nimue, had been swayed by my brother's insidious nature.

The numerous efforts we had all made to find my brother's followers had been in vain. I had conferred with my family members, Gwen and the knights, my brothers and other gods, my father (*that* meeting had proved to be filled with his evasions and vague reassurances), and I had made fruitless expeditions into alternate timelines and realities. As we approached year's end, I was no closer to finding them then I had been in January.

Finally, I conceded a temporary defeat, and we celebrated New Year's Eve in a subdued fashion with an earnest toast to success in the future.

CHAPTER 20
Moab, 2022

Another year under our belts, and I was feeling exceedingly restless. I hadn't accomplished everything that I should have in recent years. And I couldn't in all honesty use the pandemic as an excuse since, as an immortal, I wasn't affected by it except peripherally.

My wife, who had always seen through my preoccupation with things I couldn't control, firmly reminded me that my father's plans superseded my own. I had always appreciated Em's advice, but this time I couldn't ignore the sense that there was something decidedly off kilter.

Arthur had grown again, but at three years from the date of his birth, he was still ten years old. The intent had always been for him to be a mature adult by 2024, which meant that he would have to go through even more dramatic growth spurts in the next two years to adhere to that schedule.

I had to keep reminding myself that it wasn't up to me; I was merely anxious to take the next step toward our ultimate goal.

At this point, Em and I decided to reinstate the storytelling sessions, which had been discontinued early in 2020. I felt reasonably certain we could have small gatherings in the store again, as long as we required people to wear masks and to observe social distancing. I often told tales about King Arthur, wanting to remind myself and my son—who often sat with the attendees—of what he had accomplished during his reign, and what he would strive to accomplish once he returned.

One day, my son and I went to the Aquatic Center gym to work out, and as I watched him exercise, I finally caught a glimpse of the man he would eventually become. He wasn't that tall yet, around four foot nine, and he weighed seventy pounds, but he was strong and determined and was starting to develop some impressive muscles for his age. His hair was shoulder length and a little shaggy, but he liked it that way and I saw no reason to insist he cut it short. It helped to connect him to his old persona.

Arthur and I ran next to each other on treadmills facing westerly out the large front window, which gave us a partial view of the hills. It was better than looking at the interior wall or watching ongoing news programs on the flat screen televisions.

I glanced sideways at my son. I could have read his thoughts easily, but I had taught him to honor other people's privacy, so I didn't dive into his head and take the information I wanted.

"Mind telling me what you're thinking about?"

Arthur quickly glanced at me and then away, those familiar green eyes twinkling. *Are you sure you want to know, Dad?* He nodded toward a shapely young woman in spandex workout attire on a recumbent bike near him.

You're ten years old, Son.

Physically, yes, but mentally I'm thirty-five.

Of course. Once in a while, I get caught up in being your father and forget who you really are.

No problem. Every now and then I get caught up in being your son and forget who I am. And who you *really are.*

I guess we're even.

I'd say so.

We grinned at each other, and slowed our pace gradually until the treadmills came to a stop.

It wasn't until later in the year that I looked back on this day as one of the few normal times we'd ever spend together.

* * *

The days, weeks and months continued to speed by at an alarming rate. I honestly had expected Arthur to grow again during that time and was surprised and disappointed when it didn't happen.

At Brady and Bonnie's third birthday party in August, the kids were all playing hide-and-seek in Morry's densely landscaped back yard, when I heard Arthur trip, fall and groan as if he'd been injured. All of us who had been reclining on the patio furniture chatting responded by leaping up and running to Arthur's side. He was sprawled on the ground, the seams of his jeans ripped out and his shirt too tight on his larger torso. He'd grown at least three inches in height and put on thirty pounds between one second and the next.

He sat up, looked at all of us hovering over him, and winced. "Ow, that hurt. I usually grow in my sleep, and this time, it got me midstep.

Dad, could you conjure some clothes for me? I haven't got the hang of it yet."

I grinned. "I'd be glad to." I changed the clothing he'd outgrown to new jeans, shirt and shoes that fit his larger body. "I'd say you're thirteen, correct?"

He deliberated for a few seconds. "Yes, and I think I'm entering puberty."

"Are you, indeed?" I raised one eyebrow.

He glanced around surreptitiously, and discovering that everyone's attention was elsewhere now that they knew he was okay, he self-consciously adjusted himself in his pants and whispered, "Yes, I'm sure of it. I can't stop thinking about sex."

Abruptly, I was thrown into an unwelcome memory from hundreds of years in the past. When I was a couple of years older than Arthur's current age and had sex with an older woman, it had turned out that she was unrepentantly evil and had harassed me for centuries afterward.

"Dad, what's the matter?" my son asked.

Impatiently I dragged myself out of thoughts that were ancient history. The here and now with Arthur was what counted. "Nothing, just some old baggage I've been meaning to deal with."

"That's good, because you had an awfully bleak look on your face." He got up and brushed the dust off the seat of his new pants. "I was thinking. Maybe the two of us could go hiking together out at Arches tomorrow." He raised his own eyebrows in a familiar look of inquiry.

I had to chuckle. Except for the difference in hair color, looking at him was like looking at a younger version of...me. "Sure, why not?"

* * *

We arose fairly early the next morning, before the sun came up, since August could still be blistering hot during the day. We had a quick bowl of cold cereal for breakfast and put water and snacks in our day packs. It had been a long while since we'd planned an outing together, and I found myself as excited as Arthur was.

Parking was at a premium in Arches National Park during the summer months, so driving out there was not an option. The National Park Service had recently set up a metering and reservation system to regulate the number of visitors in the park, but time would tell if it truly took care of the problems or merely created more.

I transported us from our living room to the trailhead at Devils Garden and we stepped directly onto the trail as if we had walked over from the parking lot. No one noticed our sudden presence. It was early enough in the day that visitor foot traffic was light and the people that were present were busy taking in the scenery.

I was pleased Arthur had suggested a hike. I'd wanted to get out to the park for I don't know how long; it had been ages since I'd visited Derek on the job, or driven out for the fun of it.

During my first summer in Moab, I had made numerous exploratory trips into the park, searching for portals through which I could enter Avalon in order to reunite with Arthur's spirit.

Months later, on a frigid night in January of 2014, Em and I had braved the cold and visited the Windows section of the park to admire the star-filled winter sky. It was before Lumina was born, and we'd had to cut our walk short when Em had gone into labor. In March of the same year, we'd had a birthday picnic at Devils Garden for Em and Derek, which had ended tragically in death and resurrection for Derek and his lover.

Apparently, it had been more than eight years since I'd been in the park. Where had the time gone? Being immortal did affect how I thought about the phenomenon of time, but the last few years had seemed to fly by. Of course, four of those years I'd been gone from Moab, lost in the past with no memory of who I was, or where I belonged.

I'd been standing next to my son, unmoving for several minutes lost in thought, my arm still wrapped around his shoulders. I glanced at him to find him staring up at me with such a rapt expression of love on his face that it startled me.

"Are you alright?" I asked.

He nodded shyly and put his arms around me, hugging me tightly. "I love you, Merlin." With an ironic grin he added, "I mean, Dad."

"I love you too, Arthur, more than you could ever imagine." I kissed the top of his head.

As we started walking out the trail toward Landscape Arch, Arthur said, "You don't know how many times when I was King that I wanted to tell you how important you are to me."

"And I wanted to tell you the same thing, but it wasn't proper for me, as your servant, to do so."

He snorted inelegantly. "Oh, come on, you were hardly my servant. You practically ran the whole place. You were the glue that held Camelot together. I would have been lost without you."

"I doubt that. I couldn't have kept up with you in battle."

We heard a group of hikers coming up the trail behind us and stepped off to the side to let them go past. Several of them gave us odd, inquisitive looks as they overheard our conversation. Arthur and I shared a glance and a brief smile. They'd never believe who we were even if we admitted it to them.

We resumed our hike in companionable silence. It took us roughly twenty minutes to reach the Landscape Arch viewpoint. We stood there drinking from our stainless steel water bottles and munching on granola bars, admiring the 290-foot span of the largest arch in the world. The morning was still relatively cool, and a light breeze promised to mitigate some of the heat that was beginning to radiate off the red rock structures. The sky was that clear, cerulean blue unique to the Utah high desert, and it was so quiet I relaxed and breathed in the pure air. I rarely allowed myself to take a break and I was basking in it.

I turned to Arthur. "Do you want to go all the way out to Dark Angel? We can take the primitive loop." The primitive trail contained steep sections and narrow ledges, and some scrambling across slickrock fins was necessary, but it was fun and challenging.

To my surprise, he looked hesitant. "I don't know, Dad. Remember, Derek brought me out here last year, when I was eight. To tell you the truth, being near Dark Angel gave me the willies."

"It did? It's merely a red rock pillar coated with desert varnish, which makes it look like a dark-cloaked figure."

"I know, but I had nightmares for weeks after seeing it. I don't know why."

"You never told me about that."

He shrugged in embarrassment.

I viewed the unexpected emotion on Arthur's face with some concern. He had been a fearless warrior in his previous life and I couldn't imagine that a geological feature, even a 150-foot tall one that appeared forbidding, would have such a negative effect on him.

"I tell you what. Let's hike out the primitive trail until we get to the first steep downhill stretch. Then we can dematerialize and head over to Delicate Arch, or we can go home. Will that work?"

Arthur flashed a relieved grin. "Yes. Thanks, Dad."

I grinned back and ruffled his hair, and we started walking. My grin faded as I considered what could have frightened him so badly, and the answer that came to me wasn't reassuring. I knew of only one being that was a true dark angel, and I had a sinking feeling that we would be hearing more from him in the near future.

* * *

As they continued their hike, they didn't talk much and Arthur mulled over their conversation. What possessed him to admit his fear to Merlin? He could sense how puzzled his father was.

As the King of Camelot, Arthur had leaped into many a battle without hesitation, fierce and skilled in combat. His reputation was such that his enemies had been known to throw down their arms and surrender at the first sight of him on a battlefield.

Now, as the teenage son of Merlin, he had magic, but he was inexperienced and it was often unclear to him how to handle certain scenarios.

Keeping the awareness of his two lives active, yet separate, in his mind wasn't always feasible, despite the fact that he had prepared himself for doing so while he was still in the Other World.

This irrational fear that seemed to overwhelm him was unwelcome, to say the least.

As Arthur looked deeper, he realized there was a place inside of him that resonated with the darkness he'd sensed when he'd seen the stone monolith, Dark Angel, for the first time. It scared the hell out of him and he was inclined to tell Merlin about his inner darkness without delay. But he sensed that it would ultimately be up to him, not Merlin, to deal with it.

CHAPTER 21
Moab to the Crystal Cave and back, September, 2022

I received a phone call toward the end of the month from Ben Reese in Wales, concerned that he hadn't heard from me recently. I had assigned Lumina the task of keeping in touch with my young caretaker on a regular basis, to make sure he and his family had everything they needed to live comfortably and to take care of my property. Evidently, she hadn't done so in several years, due to the COVID crisis or because of the changes in her personal life. I was disappointed she'd dropped the ball, but all I could do was to keep abreast of my responsibility from here on out. It was another reminder that gods and goddesses living in the human realm could be as prone to make mistakes as mortals.

I apologized to Ben and promised to make amends. I decided to go see him in person.

Colin and I had been close friends for so many years that I wanted to show him my cave and share some of my experiences with him. I mentioned it when he dropped by after work that evening.

"You want to take me *where?*" he asked.

"To Wales, to see the Crystal Cave. I need to give my caretaker some funds. I haven't been there in way too long, and he finally called the other night, wondering what was going on."

"You own property in Wales?"

I raised an eyebrow. "Colin, I'm *from* Wales, and I slept off and on under an enchantment in the Crystal Cave for more than 1500 years, remember? I own the hill and thousands of acres around it. I arranged for a caretaker to manage my holdings when I decided to sleep for centuries after Arthur died. My current caretaker is descended from the man I hired in the fifth century."

Colin looked stunned for a moment, and considered the unique opportunity he was being offered. "How long will it take? Do I need to take a day off from work?"

"Tomorrow's Saturday, and I presume you're not working. Let's go early in the morning and we can be back by afternoon."

He laughed. "I forgot we can be there instantaneously. Sure, I'll go with you, Merlin."

I appeared in his kitchen at seven the next morning and he jumped back in surprise, spilling coffee down the front of his shirt. "Shit, you could give a guy a heart attack doing that!"

I rolled my eyes. It was doubtful that a man as healthy as he was, a man with magic at his disposal, would have a heart attack.

He put the mug down and half-heartedly wiped at the dark brown liquid. "Crap, this was a clean shirt."

"You could use magic," I reminded him.

"Oh, yeah." He looked down at the stain and concentrated, and it disappeared without a trace. He raised his eyes to mine and grinned.

"Ready? Let's go." I touched his arm and we disappeared.

* * *

I watched while Colin took a moment to orient himself. One second we had been standing in his warm kitchen in Moab and the next we were on top of a cloud-shrouded hill in the wind and rain. It was early afternoon here in Wales and the weather was cool, which was typical for this season of the year. It didn't bother me, but Colin quickly conjured a lined rain jacket and put it on. We were surrounded by bushes and trees that had covered the hilltop in the centuries since I lived there. They were starting to hint at the flaming colors of autumn slated to arrive in the next couple of weeks.

Through gaps in the vegetation, I could see sheep grazing in a meadow down in the valley, and on the other side, I had a partial view of the Tywy River, flowing along as placidly as it always had, time out of mind.

"This is the greenest place I've ever seen. It must rain constantly," Colin said.

"No, but it does rain frequently," I said. "In the summer, which can be quite warm, the humidity is usually high. I never minded it when I lived here, because I didn't know any different. But after living in the high desert for nine years, I'm not particularly fond of the dampness."

Even so, when I closed my eyes and reveled in the fresh cool air of southwest Wales, I was assailed by poignant memories of my childhood explorations of these hills and valleys, on foot and on the back of my sturdy pony.

"Let's go into the cave first, and I'll show you around. After that, we'll head down to the house. I wanted to ride the horses, but they won't be happy to leave their warm, dry stalls, so I'll take us there instead."

"It's just as well. I don't know how to ride," Colin said as his eyes followed the flight of a flock of birds overhead.

I looked at him askance. For a fleeting moment, I knew that in the distant past, he had ridden horses as a matter of course, but before I could pursue the thought it dissipated like smoke in the wind.

I turned towards a certain spot on the brushy hillside and whispered, "*Aperi.*" An opening magically appeared and the two of us pushed through the rain-soaked brush and entered my cave.

Colin glanced at me quizzically. "Since when do you verbalize a spell?"

I smiled as I perused the familiar interior space. "I don't need to, but I feel rather nostalgic for the past when I come here."

It was dim, a thin stream of diffuse light filtering in from the entrance. I flicked my hand and a soft glow illuminated the interior of the cave, reflecting off the thousands of tiny quartz crystals embedded in the cave walls and crevices. When I had awakened from my centuries-long sleep in 2013, those crystals had shone with an inner light, the result of a spell that I had since deactivated. "I don't need to use hand gestures either."

I strode forward into the main room, where a few items of simple furniture remained: a bed, and a chest in which I had stored my garments, several large crystals on a workbench against one wall, and a row of old jars, some of them still containing herbs. Next to them was the astrolabe I'd acquired during one of my early ventures out into the changing world. There was no dust, and the temperature in the cave was comfortable, slightly warmer than outside and without the wind.

Colin removed his jacket and tossed it over one shoulder. "This is pretty sparse—was it like this when you lived here, before you slept for hundreds of years?"

"No, I had a desk of sorts, and a chair, and a rug I'd brought back from my travels during one period of waking. A few years ago I gave Ben permission to sell them when he needed extra funds to repair the manor house. As old as they were, they brought a goodly price at auction.

"During my enchanted sleep, I awakened every three hundred years or so to see if the portal to Avalon—a back door to the Other World, if you will—was available, but it had closed and never opened again.

That's the main reason I traveled to Moab in 2013. I was instructed to search for a new portal through which to reach Arthur. Now we know it wasn't destined to happen that way and—"

"Hello the cave!"

I recognized Ben's voice and called out, "Come on in."

A man in his twenties with a familiar face and wavy brown hair entered. He bowed obsequiously and gave me a tentative smile. "Lord Merlin! I came up to check on the horses and heard voices. I hoped it was you and not someone who shouldn't be here." He'd forgotten, or might not have known, that no one could enter the cave without using magic.

"Oh!" He was startled when he noticed Colin standing behind me.

"Ben, I'd like you to meet my friend, Colin Campbell. Colin, this is Ben Reese, my caretaker, although property manager is a more accurate description these days."

"*Croeso i Gymru*, Mr. Campbell. Welcome to Wales," Ben said. "I'm pleased to meet you."

I could tell that he was somewhat taken aback, as I had never brought anyone here besides immediate family members.

"It's alright, Ben, he's a distant relation, and he's aware of my true identity."

"Whatever you say, Lord Merlin," he said with a bob of his head. He turned expectantly toward Colin.

"Nice to meet you, Ben. And it's actually Detective Campbell, but you can call me Colin."

"You're a detective?" Ben glanced between Colin and me, perplexed. "Anything amiss?"

"No, not at all. I wanted Colin to see where I had lived—and then slept for all those centuries—after I left Camelot."

Ben and Colin shared an amused look. "Do you ever get used to this?" Colin asked.

"No, never. When he awoke in 2013 and came down to the house, I didn't recognize him; I thought he'd be an old man and instead he was so *young*. I was born here, expecting to serve the Sorcerer of Camelot for the rest of my life, but it's still a shock when he decides to pop in for the day."

Colin laughed. "I know exactly what you mean."

Ben turned back to me, started to speak, then hemmed and hawed uncomfortably.

"What's wrong, Ben?" I asked. His hesitation concerned me. He had always been self-sufficient and I'd never known him to be unsure about anything. His parents, Tom and Sandy Reese, had trained him painstakingly, despite his brief, rebellious episode when I'd encountered the family upon my awakening ten years ago. With a wife and young family of his own, he was settled and dependable.

"Would you be able to come down to the house, sir? My parents are visiting, and I'm worried about them—they haven't been themselves lately and they won't tell me what's wrong. Can you find out what's troubling them?"

"Yes, I'd be happy to help." I glanced at Colin, who shrugged and said, "Fine with me, I'm not in a hurry to go back."

"Alright, Ben, I'll get the funds you require, and we'll all go to the house together."

I accessed my cache of gemstones and precious metals, which was in a separate alcove so full of crystals that I had named the Crystal Cave for them. The gemstones, gold, and silver that I'd squirreled away when I'd chosen to sleep through the years after Arthur's death, had been the method by which I had paid my caretakers over the centuries.

I removed a specific quantity of silver and gold that would provide funds to sustain the family—and my property—for a year. My caretakers had always accepted what I'd given them and exchanged the gemstones or metals for currency or services. Over the centuries, and particularly in the past decade, it had become more and more difficult to find merchants or brokers who were willing, or able, to provide this service. At some point in the near future I would have to convert the rest of my cache to currency and invest it. But not today.

I presented the bag of valuable metals, including some ancient coins, to Ben and he bowed, accepting the offering. "Thank you, Lord Merlin, I appreciate it."

"No, thank *you* for being so loyal. Now, let's get down to the house and determine what the problem is with your parents." I touched the arms of both men and we were instantaneously in the courtyard of the old manor house.

Ben looked green and he gulped, "Ah, I, I didn't expect that."

"Sorry. I can take care of it." Since I wasn't teleporting, I'd assumed that there would be no issue with nausea, but the mere fact of traveling by supernatural means affected some humans adversely. I magically adjusted his metabolism to eliminate the nausea forever, and headed toward the front door.

As we entered the manor house, I sensed the wrongness even before I saw the older couple. Colin looked uneasy, sensing it also.

Ben ran ahead of us into another room and we heard his shout of horror. "Merlin! They're in here!" His voice was high-pitched with fear.

We followed his voice into a nicely furnished sitting room and discovered his parents groaning and straining on the floor, their hands around each other's throats, focused on strangling each other.

"Jesus, Mary and Joseph," Colin muttered.

I sensed that Tom, being the larger and heavier of the two, had instigated the attack and Sandy was trying to prevent him from killing her. I instantly rendered them both unconscious and after using magic to separate them, I placed her gently on the sofa. Colin bent down and put a couch pillow under Tom's head as he lay on the carpeted floor of the sitting room.

He had all but crushed his wife's windpipe. The hyoid bone was fractured and she was in severe pain and struggling to breathe. As I directed healing Light to the injury, I saw the darkness in her soul that had not been there before. It had a disturbingly familiar signature. Disgusted and dismayed, I recognized that my brother was way ahead of me here in Wales, as well.

Sandy coughed and blinked her eyes, startled to see me sitting next to her. We hadn't seen each other for years, and though her physical appearance had changed, mine had stayed the same. Her hair was gray and she was a few pounds heavier, but she seemed to be the same sweet person I remembered. "Lord Merlin, how lovely to see you again. What's happened, did I faint?"

"Tom was attacking you. Why he would do such a thing?"

For a moment, she had forgotten, and I regretted having to remind her.

Sandy's eyes filled with tears. "I don't know. One minute we were having a quiet conversation and the next he had his hands around my neck, squeezing as hard as he could. I tried to stop him, but he was too strong." She saw Tom lying still on the floor and clapped her hand over her mouth. "*O fy Duw*, is he dead?"

"No, he's only unconscious. I wanted to talk with you before I bring him out of it."

"I can't imagine what's gotten into him." Her accent became more noticeable as her emotions surged. "We've been quarrelling recently, which isn't normal. We were married thirty-six years ago, when we were eighteen, and in all that time, we've never been physically violent with each other. I don't understand what's happening." She started sobbing.

At that moment, I experienced such hatred for my brother that I wanted to find Sam and destroy him. I got my emotions under control with considerable difficulty, and went over to take care of Tom. I glanced at Colin, who sat down next to the distraught woman and slipped an arm around her shoulders to comfort her, and our eyes met. In that split second we were totally in accord and would have hunted the bastard down, but we were both aware that we would have to put aside our wrath. It would be a mistake for either of us to become as steeped in hatred as my brother was, since it was exactly what he wanted. It was not easy, under the circumstances, to remember that Sam had to be utterly miserable, and misery loved company. But that was the truth of it. For as long as I could remember, Sam had fomented grief, anger, frustration, hatred and misery.

I bent over Tom and used my god senses to discover what had transpired to trigger this uncharacteristic behavior. I found a pervading inner darkness in his being that was even more profound than within Sandy's spirit. It seemed to have no source, and no specific trigger.

I sent a powerful wave of Light, love and energy into Tom's being, which cleansed his soul and his mind. As soon as I determined that all the darkness had been removed, I did the same for his wife.

I stood up and stretched and noticed Ben huddled in a large chair in the corner of the room. "*Sut wyt ti?*"

"I think I'm okay. What about my parents? Will they be alright?"

I smiled. "Yes, they will. Don't worry. Let them sleep until they wake up naturally."

"What could have caused this?"

I deliberated on the best way to explain it. Telling him that an evil darkness had been placed inside them by Satan wouldn't help matters. Hence, I told him they'd been infected by a rare organism that caused a change in their behavior, and that I'd cured them and they would be fine.

"*Diolch i Dduw*, I'm so relieved! Thank you, Merlin. I'm grateful my wife and children didn't have to witness this."

"You're most welcome, Ben," I said, and transported both Colin and myself instantaneously back to my living room in Moab.

* * *

"That was *not* the journey I'd planned," I said wryly, dropping into my favorite overstuffed chair. I motioned to Colin to sit in the one next to me.

He settled into the plush cushions and shrugged. "It's okay. But that was a real wake-up call about the extent of Sam's influence. Are Tom and Sandy going to remember what happened?"

"No, they'll think it was an illness, the same story I told Ben. They're not attuned to the mystical world of which we are a part, despite the fact that they used to work for me.

"I think we need a drink. Would you care to do the honors?"

Colin didn't bother to remind me it was still morning here, but gave me a perceptive look and conjured two tumblers of Lagavulin. He handed me one and tossed his own whisky down as if it was water. He coughed a little and magically refilled his glass. "I know it's not politically correct to drink good Scotch this way, but there's an exception to every rule. And this is one of them."

I agreed with him and touched my glass to his. The problem was, how far and how fast was this state of affairs going to escalate, and what was I going to do about it?

"I have a suggestion. Let's muddle through and celebrate the holidays as usual, taking one step at a time while keeping alert. I'll be at your side to help you, Merlin, no matter what happens."

"I know you will, Colin, and I'll hold you to that."

We sat in silence for a few minutes, sipping our drinks, until Colin grinned and said, "I know, let's plan a Halloween party and have it at the herb shop. Won't even need costumes—just let everything show: wings, ears, eyes—everything."

My eyebrows shot up to my hairline. "Seriously? After all these years hiding our...assets, I guess you could call them?"

"Hey, on Halloween, the most extreme costumes are the best, and no one will suspect we're the real deal, trust me."

I kept silent while he realized what was missing from his scenario. His forehead wrinkled up in a frown. "Huh, I don't have any special 'asset' to use as a costume, do I? Well, hell."

"I suspect you can come up with something, Colin. After all, we have over a month until Halloween."

He tossed back the remainder of his drink and stood up. "I know just what costume I'm going to wear. Gotta go and start working on it."

CHAPTER 22
Moab, Monday, October 31, 2022, Evening

The Moab Herbalist looked fabulous decorated for Halloween. In all the years I had owned the store, I had never thought of having a party here. I glanced around, admiring our efforts. We had lowered the lights, hung long stringers that looked like spider webs, and placed fake spiders, big, black, and furry, liberally throughout the "webs." Glowing jack-o'-lanterns with grotesque grins were strategically placed around the store and realistic-looking bats hung from the ceiling. We had a table against one wall draped with Halloween-print fabric and loaded with bowls of orange fruit punch, trays of black-and-orange-frosted sugar cookies, and baskets of individually wrapped Halloween candy.

We had closed the store earlier this afternoon to give us the time we needed to decorate and change into our costumes—or, in my case, manifest the changes in my appearance.

I confirmed that all preparations were completed and we were ready for the evening. I was glad Colin had suggested holding our party here at the shop so that we could share the experience with our customers. We had even invented several products to sell that were especially labeled to reflect the season: "Vampire Fangs" (white candy corn shaped liked teeth), "Blood Tonic" (non-alcoholic Bloody Marys), and "Dead Body Lotion" (our gardenia lotion colored gray). Cathy had suggested that the lotion be unscented, but I vetoed that idea. No one would buy it if it didn't smell nice.

As Em was unlocking the door at six o'clock to let everyone in, I glanced at my reflection in the mirror and approved of what I saw. I had chosen to appear as the Merlin of legend was always portrayed, wearing a long robe covered with magic symbols and a pointy hat with stars on it. I carried a "magic wand" and sported a wispy gray beard. My long hair was loose on my shoulders, the black threaded liberally with gray. I had aged myself to about sixty-five years old, creating a generous assortment of wrinkles and age spots on my face, neck, and hands.

I had to suppress a few twinges of anxiety when Seth showed up with his wings, pointed ears, and reptilian eyes blatantly on display, and when Lumina dropped in with her dove gray wings and Elf ears showing. As far as I knew, the Elven Fae didn't have wings, but it didn't really matter—it was supposed to be a costume. Josh was apparently cramming for a test and had decided not to come.

"He could have used magic to help him learn the material," I mentioned.

"I know, but he thinks it's cheating," Lumina confided. "Besides, he wanted to give out candy to trick-or-treaters. There are a lot of kids in our apartment complex." She glanced around, noting that at least half the customers in the store wore elaborate costumes. "I thought Derek and Morry would be here by now…"

Originally, Derek and I had planned on calling forth our wings as well, but we changed our minds. Too many wings might be a little suspicious, and we were already pushing the envelope. My son had kept his costume a secret and had yet to put in an appearance, so I was curious what he had chosen to wear.

Lumina continued, "…with Sarah and Lainie and the kids. Oh, never mind, they're on their way."

"I'm glad someone can sense what's happening with the rest of the family," I said wryly. As we stood quietly checking out the customers' costumes, I caught sight of my wife, who was dressed as an Elf, of course, her wavy golden-brown hair pulled back in a tail to best show off her ears. Rae and Chris were witches, theatrical makeup artfully applied, broomsticks leaning against the wall behind the counter.

I had to laugh when Colin arrived disguised as a pirate, his hair and moustache magically enhanced so both were even longer and thicker than usual and looking very authentic. He had procured a custom-made costume: velvet frock coat, knee length breeches, shoes with high square heels and large buckles, oversized plumed hat, and gold hoop earrings in his ears. I doubted that real pirates during the era known as the Golden Age of Piracy wore anything so ostentatious and impractical as they sailed the turbulent seas. I had never met any pirates when I was in England in 1700, so I wouldn't know from personal experience, but Colin certainly matched the descriptions in Robert Louis Stevenson's novel, *Treasure Island*.

"Ahoy, matey, shiver me timbers! You'll walk the plank, ye rascal!

Arrgh!" he bellowed as he swaggered around the store, alternating with a deep, evil-sounding laugh.

After his second walk-through I hauled him off his path and introduced him to the refreshment table, where we surreptitiously conjured liquor and ignored the punch.

"I saw that, Dads," Lumina called from across the room.

We both looked a little sheepish at having been caught in the act, but vowed to relish our drinks anyway. Colin went ahead and tossed his Lagavulin down, then conjured another. "Ah, that hit the spot. Pirating sure works up a thirst, let me tell you."

I chuckled. "I like your costume and persona very much. Whoever made your costume did a terrific job."

"Thanks, I think so, too." Colin eyed me up and down. "Whoa. You look old. Is that what most people think you look like?"

"Yes, the original versions of my legend and some of the stories describe me thus, although my favorite was written in the seventies as a series of books by the author Mary Stewart. I suspect she was truly able to part the curtains of time with her mind and see me. When she was writing the books about me she lived at a guest house in Carmarthen, not far from my land. She undoubtedly had walked up to my cave. She might have boldly entered if I hadn't hidden the entrance with a robust spell. I couldn't use her version of me as a costume, though, because I would look like I actually did in the past, and do now." I must have gotten too convoluted in my explanation, because Colin's eyes had glazed over. "Anyway, this is my 'costume' tonight, for better or for worse. I have to say, it's refreshing to clothe myself in the old way."

Colin blinked and refocused on me. "You look relaxed, I'm happy to say. You've been stressed out for a long while."

"Yes, I'm feeling quite well tonight." I looked around for Colin's date. "I thought you were bringing someone?"

"I was hoping Cathy would come with me, but she turned me down, as usual. I'm sure she'll be here, just not with me," he shrugged, trying to make light of his disappointment and failing miserably.

"You could've invited someone else."

"I know, but—"

A minor disturbance at the door had us both looking up.

"That can't be," I murmured. I shook off a momentary thrill of recognition. "No, it must be Derek."

"Can't be who?"

"For a minute there, I thought it was another one of my brothers from the god realm, whom I haven't seen since before I was born in this world."

Colin gazed at the newcomer and turned back to me. "Don't make a liar out of me and get all anxious, it's only Derek dressed up like Darth Vader. I don't know how you could mistake a Star Wars character for one of the gods. He must have enhanced himself—he looks bigger and taller than he normally does."

Derek's costume became relatively inconsequential as Morry, Lainie, and the twins surged into the shop in their wolf forms.

I could foresee this becoming a disastrous situation if the kids decided to shift back to human right in front of our customers. As it was, people were staring at them with suspicion and a trace of fear since they looked like—and were—real wolves. And most people sensed it.

Morry, I think your family being here in wolf form is a bad idea. Please go home and figure out something else as costumes for your family.

I thought you said it was okay to come as we are?

I'm sorry, Morry, but in your case, I've changed my mind.

Okay, Grandpa, we'll be back soon. I hated that he sounded so disappointed.

As he led his family out the door I felt it as he cloaked them in an invisibility spell. He had done the same thing when they arrived, as they got out of the car and shifted to their canid forms.

Our customers were still milling around, questioning the appearance of real wolves, even werewolves, so I whispered, "It was a Halloween trick. Of course there is no such things as werewolves," and flicked my hand in front of my mouth to disperse the suggestion throughout the store. I could have instantly removed the memories from their minds, but I wanted to use one of my old techniques, which was more in keeping with my current appearance as the legendary version of myself.

I chuckled as I remembered that Uther Pendragon had called me Merlin the Magician when he had first introduced me to his court. It had been a chore to change that title to Merlin the Sorcerer in the minds of his men.

Things seemed to get back to normal at the party. I felt bad about ruining Morry's family's fun, but we couldn't afford to truly reveal ourselves too soon.

I turned to Colin and smiled.

"That's better," he said. "Oh, by the way, where's Arthur? And I don't see Sarah or Aidan, either—oh, wait, there they are, they came in after Darth Vader. Should have known Sarah would be Princess Leia. And Aidan is R2-D2. Cute.

"Well, I'd better get back to my pirating." Colin strode off repeating, "Ahoy, matey, shiver me timbers…"

Honey, could you go pick up Arthur? He's ready, Em said to me telepathically. Arthur had wanted to put together his own costume, but I suspected he'd needed to use more sophisticated magic than he knew, so he had asked Derek for his help conjuring props or to alter his appearance.

Alright, I'll—

At that moment, Cathy Grant walked in swaying in her version of a hula, accompanied by Hawaiian music playing on her phone, which she'd placed in a hidden pocket in the skirt. She looked cute as a bug but a little cold in the outfit, which left most of her torso and her arms and legs bare. I gave her a thumbs up and an encouraging smile as she danced past me. She grinned and her face turned red as the coconuts shells covering her breasts wobbled loosely.

Then, Gwen and the knights walked in, dressed as they would have been in Camelot. I have to admit, I was impressed, and for a moment, I was overcome with nostalgia. I managed to extricate myself from my emotional reaction as I remembered Arthur was waiting for me at home.

I appeared in the living room in front of my son, who was dressed as King Arthur. How could he be anyone else?

He looked magnificent, his crown shining upon his fair, shoulder-length hair and his cloak sporting a red dragon. He wore a tunic, loose trousers and boots—not quite the style appropriate for the era, but close enough—and carried a reasonable facsimile of Excaliber.

Derek had done an impressive job of turning a thirteen-year-old boy into a king.

I transported him into the back room of the shop and watched as he stepped proudly through the door into the midst of the party. A hush fell over the crowd. Then everyone roared, "Long live the King!"

Late that night, Arthur called to me from his bedroom as he was climbing into bed.

"Yes? What did you need, Son?"

"I just wanted to thank you, Merlin."

His voice sounded odd, stiff and formal, and I wondered what was wrong. Everything had gone so well, so smoothly, at our party that I must have been waiting for the other shoe to drop.

I looked closer and realized that he was weeping. I had been so caught up in dealing with my own problems lately that I hadn't even considered the amount of stress Arthur was under.

I sat down on the bed beside him and pulled him into my arms. He burrowed against my chest as if he were a small child again and then relaxed with a sigh. "I love you, Dad."

"I love you, too, Arthur. It's okay, everything really is going to plan, I promise, and before long, you'll be a man again, standing before us tall and proud: King Arthur in the twenty-first century."

"Sounds like the title of a movie," he said drowsily.

"Oh, I guarantee that your presence will have way more impact on the world than the biggest blockbuster movie in history," I said quietly to my son, who had fallen asleep in my arms.

CHAPTER 23
Moab to the United Kingdom and back, Monday, January 30, 2023

I stood in the doorway of Arthur's bedroom and watched him sleep. It was just shy of dawn and the light creeping in beneath his bedroom curtains was very faint. I could see his tousled hair on the pillow, his face half hidden under the covers.

It was his fourth birthday today. However, his body still reflected the growth he'd experienced the previous August, and no more.

Impatience welled up in me and I took a slow breath, calming my unwelcome emotions. I could sense the relentless passage of time and I worried that Arthur was progressing too slowly. I needed to remember what I'd said to him on Halloween: 'Everything really is going to plan,' and Em and I both needed to have faith that it was true. If Em had her way, our son wouldn't have any more sudden growth spurts, and would progress at the normal human pace from here on out. My heart went out to my sweet wife who had borne two of my children and hadn't had enough time with either one of them. It was destined that Arthur would be a grown man within the next twelve months, and destiny would prevail.

I thought for a moment how much I appreciated Colin's presence in my life. Ever since September, when he had sworn to support me through another busy holiday season, he had done his best to help keep my spirits up and my perspective straight, despite Arthur's lack of progress. Admittedly, our Halloween festivities helped a great deal to get my mind off my worries and remind me of our ultimate goal. Our Christmas and New Year's Eve celebrations, however, had lacked their usual luster and optimism.

I shook off my introspective mood. I needed to get out of the house and take a few minutes for myself.

I thought of my favorite spot on the Rim, where the long-gone chairlift once terminated, and instantly I found myself standing there on a ledge of sandstone. I had always loved the view of Moab from this vantage point, but I wished the uncontrolled urban sprawl hadn't filled the landscape with unsightly buildings. I imagined transporting all the superfluous construction to some other area of the state that was less populated—and the shock, disbelief, and hysteria that would result from such an action.

Of course, I would never do something so irresponsible. But I couldn't help thinking how liberating it would feel to step outside the boundaries God had set for me, as well as the ones I had set for myself.

I shook my head at my unrealistic thoughts. Someone as powerful as I could never have free rein, or I might wreak the kind of havoc at which my damnable brother excelled. Or worse.

I couldn't live with that.

The sun chose that moment to break through the early morning clouds in the eastern sky and turn the surrounding cliffs a soft, glowing orange-red.

It reminded me why I loved it here, and I reflected on what the future held for all of us once Arthur's reign brought a badly needed balance back to the world. I was more than ready for it.

Restless, I made myself invisible and shot upward, calling forth my wings as I went, and soon those enormous appendages were pumping the air and sending me even higher. I forced myself to top speed, wanting to tire myself out, though it was pointless since I never needed to rest. Now and then I missed feeling human, even though my "humanity" had always been an elaborate illusion.

I continued to push myself, but I decided to level out rather than travel beyond the atmosphere. I dispensed with my wings since I wasn't using them to increase my speed on the horizontal plane.

A vapor cloud erupted around me as I moved so fast I broke the sound barrier. I knew that people on the ground would hear the sonic boom and assume I was a jet.

I grinned. Fortunately, I was invisible.

I slowed my speed and noticed that I was approaching the British Isles. At some point, I must have utilized my ability to move instantaneously through time and space, because I'd been flying for no more than five minutes, and it was almost 5000 miles between Moab and London. I'd exceeded the speed of sound, which was about 767 miles per hour, but it should have taken me at least six hours to cover that distance. Derek used to tease me that I was the real Superman and I had scoffed at him. He might be correct, but I would never flaunt my presence by wearing a brightly colored costume with a red cape.

Needless to say, I had dispelled my edginess. I hung in the frigid air over

London, the Thames flowing dark and sluggish below me, and considered stopping in Wales at the Crystal Cave before going home. I rejected that idea straightaway as I felt the draw to return to Moab to be with Arthur on his birthday. But I did have one quick stop to make before I headed home.

As soon as I had accomplished my errand, I pictured myself standing in my living room and then I was. Good thing I was a god. It saved me a lot of traveling time.

* * *

Arthur yawned as he trudged in his pajamas and slippers into the front room to find his father vigorously brushing his long black hair. "Dad, why do you have ice crystals in your hair?"

Merlin swung around and greeted him with a wide smile. "I went flying for a few minutes and ended up in England. The weather is most disagreeable there today." He walked into the kitchen, starting the coffeemaker with a glance. "Happy birthday, by the way. Would you prefer hot chocolate or coffee this morning?"

"Hot chocolate, please." Arthur climbed onto a high stool next to the counter and watched his father as he conjured a perfect mug of chocolate.

"Thanks, Dad," Arthur said as he scooped the whipped cream off with his tongue.

"You're welcome, Son." Merlin poured himself a mug of coffee, black as usual, and sipped it slowly, obviously savoring the flavor of the dark French Roast.

"Uh, Dad—Merlin—since it's my birthday, I have a request."

"What is it?"

"Well, this is going to sound crazy, but I'd like you to take me back to the fifth century to see Camelot again. Not to interact with anyone, but merely to...see it." He held his breath as Merlin stilled and closed his eyes. Several minutes went by, and Arthur comprehended that his father was communicating with a higher authority.

Finally, Merlin opened his eyes and spoke. "I'm sorry, Son, but that cannot happen. You and I have been given more leeway in this life than anyone else in history, so there are only a few lines we can't cross, and that's one of them."

"But you and Derek went back—"

"Arthur, two of you can't be in the same place at the same time, even if you don't look like you did then."

His shoulders slumped in disappointment. "I miss it so much."

"I know. Believe me, I know." Merlin clasped his son's bony shoulder, conveying love and understanding with his touch.

"I feel like I'm never going to grow up!" The young voice took on a deeper tone as Arthur's memories of his past life surged to the forefront. "I need to get to work and make Albion a reality. I need to accomplish what I was not able to achieve in my past life and unify this world before the evil forces in this current time destroy it."

* * *

As the urgency in Arthur's voice rang through the house like the prophetic tolling of a bell, Em and Rae came running into the kitchen in their night clothes.

"What's going on? I heard a loud voice and thought Arthur had suddenly become an adult." Emily sounded fearful, since she had been dreading his final growth spurt for months.

I had been standing in front of Arthur when Em appeared in the kitchen, and Arthur peered around me. "I'm right here, Mom, the same age I've been since last August," he said with disgust.

"Perfect," Em said, relieved. "I know you're anxious to get on with your quest, but I just want my little boy to stick around for as long as possible."

I could tell from the expression on Arthur's face that he heartily disagreed with her and was about to make a comment to that effect, so I suggested that we go out to breakfast to celebrate his birthday. I had already spoken to the family several weeks ago and arranged for everyone to meet at a special breakfast place that Seth recommended, knowing what Arthur would invariably want to order.

"Can I have pancakes?"

"Yes, you can, and I have just the place in mind." I turned to Em and Rae and winked.

"Better get dressed quickly—and warmly—it's pretty cold out there."

As soon as we were ready to go, I encouraged the three of them to get as close to me as possible.

"Why aren't we going in the car?"

"Well, Arthur, it would be rather difficult to get to where we need to go by car." My eyes twinkled as I transported us to Church Street in Seth's hometown of Inverness, Scotland.

Of course, it was early afternoon in Scotland, but the place I had in mind served mainly pancakes, all day long.

"Seth, what are you doing here?" Arthur asked as his brother walked out the door of the Black Isle Bar—which we were standing in front of —at the intersection of Church Street and Post Office Avenue.

"I live here when I'm no' in Moab, lad. I dropped in tae say hello tae a friend who works at the Black Isle while I was waiting for ye. Anyway, the restaurant we're going tae is right down the street, sae let's walk there the noo."

Seth led us along the sidewalk on the northerly side of Church Street, and it took us only a few minutes to reach the small restaurant.

"But the sign says it's closed!" The depth of disappointment in his voice would have been heartbreaking if I hadn't known the reason the sign was there.

I reached for the handle and opened the door for my son. As soon as he was inside, excited voices shouted, "Surprise! Happy birthday, Arthur!"

His face lit up with pleasure. "The whole family is here—even Lumina and Josh! And Oengus is here, too."

"I arranged for Wild Pancakes to be reserved only for us today, for your birthday breakfast, Arthur."

He started to turn to me, his eyes expressing his gratitude, until he was enveloped in hugs and sweet kisses from the rest of the family.

I would hold his joy in my mind and heart and remember it whenever I felt blue. I trusted that this happy occasion at the beginning of the year foretold great things for the near future.

CHAPTER 24
Moab, Wednesday, March 8, 2023

E mily Reese was restless. She knew she had no excuse to be unhappy or dissatisfied. After all, she was married to the love of her life, and after almost ten years of marriage she could honestly say that the bloom was still on the rose. Her husband adored her and the sex was mindblowing.

She loved her children, stepchildren, and grandchildren to distraction and they all doted on her.

She literally had everything she'd ever wanted, except a little privacy and a night out with the girls every now and then. She tried to recall when she'd last gone out with friends for drinks and dinner and wasn't surprised to find that she couldn't. However, she suspected that it was prior to her trip to England in early 2013 and meeting Merlin, in the guise of "Michael Reese," on the flight home. At that point, her life changed, irrevocably.

She had no women friends besides the ones in their circle of close friends and family; in other words, everyone in the know about their supernatural and celestial natures. Anyone she had known prior to 2013 had either gotten married and had new friends, moved away, or moved on, finding others who were actually available for "girlfriend time."

She had decided to take her birthday off, and she made sure everyone knew she wanted to spend the day by herself. No phone calls, no texts, no emails, no telepathic messages. Privacy was a priceless commodity these days and she desperately needed to spend the day pondering what exactly she needed and wanted, and how to achieve it —including more time with her female friends.

So she was taking an extended hike in Arches National Park, out through Salt Valley, and had told Derek (who was working that day) specifically to stay away.

She suspected that the root cause of her restlessness was Arthur's growth, or at the moment, lack thereof, which kept her in a perpetual state of distress. She'd been aware right from the start of the pregnancy that her sole function was to be a portal for the King of Camelot to return to the human realm; for his new body to grow inside of her until he was born, and to protect and nurture him until the magic caused his body to mature in a mere five years. So he could become the leader destiny required to save humanity.

She just had to convince herself that it was enough for her peace of mind and sense of self-worth.

* * *

I was aware of Emily's thoughts and feelings and I wanted her to be able to reconcile the facts with her desires, so I didn't attempt to dissuade her course of action. However, I did suggest to Derek that while she was on her own version of a "vision quest" that we should get together and determine what would suit her most for a combination girl's night out and birthday celebration that night. I had already forewarned all the women in the group to be ready to go at a moments' notice.

"I thought ya were gonna honor her request to leave her alone for the day, Dad?"

"Trust me, after hiking by herself all day—on her birthday—she's going to want that night out."

"We should find a place in town where she could go out with the girls, then. How about Moody's Tavern?"

"I have a better idea. There's a pub and restaurant I know of that would be perfect. They're in a charming old two-story building on a riverfront and I definitely approve of the ambience."

Derek's tawny eyebrows drew together as he frowned slightly, trying to figure out where that business could be—and when I would have been there. "I can't think of a pub like that anywhere near here."

I chuckled. "Oh, it's not here, Derek, it's in Dublin."

"When were ya in Dublin, Pennsylvania?"

"I wasn't. But when I didn't remember who I was, I spent some weeks in Dublin, Ireland in 2007. A particular favorite of mine for drinks and dinner was called The Merchant's Arch, on Wellington Quay in the Temple Bar District. It's on the south bank of the River Liffey near Ha'penny Bridge and certainly would be a nice change from the bars and restaurants in downtown Moab. "

"Sounds interestin'. And you'll transport all the women there for a 'girl's night out' they'll never forget."

"Yes, I think she'll find it a good choice. What's the matter, Derek?"

He hesitated for a moment, then said, "Ya know that this lack of a 'girlfriend night' is just an excuse. Em is actually goin' through some kind of identity crisis."

"I know. She feels like the only reason for her existence has been to provide a vessel to deliver the savior of mankind, so to speak."

"She's gotta know that's not true," Derek protested.

"Deep in her soul, and in her mind, she's aware of that, but the pressure she's been under is forcing her to rebel, to ensure that she doesn't lose sight of her own goals, her own nature."

"We've all gone through somethin' similar over the years."

I nodded. I'd certainly had my share of issues, despite the fact that I knew better.

"After she's had a few drinks and enjoyed a good meal in the company of the women she loves, I have an additional birthday surprise for her."

Derek's eyes lit up. "Oh, yeah?"

"I'm not going to tell you what it is. It's only for Em, and she can tell you about it after the fact."

* * *

"Get dressed up, wife of mine, I'm taking you to a special place for dinner tonight." I kissed her and stroked her back.

She had arrived home around three from her hike out at Arches National Park and immediately climbed in the shower. Now she was drying her long, golden-brown mane of hair in front of the bathroom mirror and looking annoyed.

"I came home a little earlier than I'd planned, but I still want some time to myself for the remainder of the day, god man," she said with a slight edge to her voice.

"Perhaps you can forgive me if I steal you away for a few hours. After all, it's your birthday. I promise it'll be worth it."

She closed her eyes and drew in a breath, trying to be patient. "Okay, you win. I can't seem to deny you anything, but isn't it early to be going out to dinner?"

I shrugged and kept silent.

Em sighed and opened the closet, looking for the dress she recently purchased. It was green, a shade guaranteed to make her hazel eyes shift to match. Being short-sleeved and a lightweight material, the dress might not be appropriate for the cooler weather in Ireland, but I would assure she'd be warm enough.

153

"I suppose you want me to wear my heels?"

"Sure, they'll go well with your dress."

She didn't often wear heels as she was already fairly tall at five nine, but her legs looked spectacular when she wore the sleek white shoes. She looked up at me as she slipped them on and narrowed her eyes. "You have something planned, haven't you? Your mind is completely closed to me."

"Actually I do."

"And you're not going to tell me, I get it."

"We'll leave as soon as you've applied your makeup."

"What about you?"

I grinned and snapped my fingers—an unnecessary gesture but fine drama—and I was clothed in a superbly tailored gray suit with which I had paired a pale green shirt and a tie in a dark green and gray swirled pattern.

"You're wearing a suit? And a tie? You never do that! Hell must have frozen over." Her eyes were practically popping out of her head.

"For you, for the occasion, I'll make an exception."

A few minutes later she was ready. I put my arm around her, extending my warmth to her, and we disappeared.

* * *

Emily's heart was ready to burst with happiness. Her husband had delivered them to a unique establishment, in Ireland, no less, and when they had entered the pub to have a drink before dinner, the bartender had greeted Merlin like an old friend, calling him Emrys. After they had taken a seat at a rather large table and ordered their drinks, a group of woman suddenly leaped out of a snug across the room and yelled, "Surprise!"

In disbelief, she saw her mother, her daughter, Sarah, Chris, Cathy, Gwen, and Lainie, grinning from ear to ear. They pulled her up and into their arms, surrounding her with their enthusiastic expressions of love.

Em burst into tears of joy, which spurred another round of hugs, kisses and pats on the back. She glanced over at her husband, who had stood up and seemed ready to leave. "Whoa, wait, where are you going?"

"I'm the odd man out at a gathering of females. I wanted you to have your 'girl's night out' and birthday celebration all in one, my dear. I'll be back whenever you're ready to go home."

* * *

Several hours later, I heard Em in my mind, telling me everyone had enjoyed their time in Ireland thoroughly and were ready to call it a night. I appeared in a dark corner of the pub and walked into an enthusiastic crowd of inebriated individuals. The ladies were all dancing with each other to the Irish tunes on an old-fashioned jukebox and having a great time, until they saw me and rushed over to surround me with lovely smiling faces and sweet-smelling hugs. I suggested we go outside, as the sight of a group of people vanishing into thin air might be shocking to some of the Irish patrons.

We appeared in my living room and the ladies departed from there, some accompanied by spouses who had been alerted to their arrival.

Finally, we were alone, and I gave Em her final birthday gift. It wasn't something I would normally do, but I had received special permission from my father. He and I both knew that she would keep the information to herself.

"Close your eyes, Em."

She did so and I took us to the future.

A small child ran and played in Swanny Park, his sandy-blond curls bouncing as he was lifted in loving arms and held high, then passed from one parent to the other with tender care. Em's breath caught as she saw Arthur and Gwen put their arms around each other with their son in the middle.

I brought her back to the present and we smiled at each other.

"Thank you, Merlin," she whispered. "This was this best girl's night out ever."

CHAPTER 25
Moab, Tuesday, August 15, 2023, Morning

A rthur Pendragon Ambrosius awoke with a start in the pale, pre-dawn light and knew something was different. He'd been restless and on edge the previous night, pacing back and forth in his bedroom until boredom rather than fatigue had driven him to bed.

He had barely slept yet he felt a jolt of energy so powerful that he leapt out of bed, needing to move, to run, to *do* something.

He started to dress and found he couldn't pull his jeans up past his ankles. They were way too small. Puzzled, he stared at them uncomprehendingly until it dawned on him what must have happened—he had grown again. And from the discrepancy in the size of the jeans he had worn only last night, it was apparent that he had finally achieved his goal: adulthood.

Heart pounding in excitement, he teleported into the bathroom, magically turned the light on, and stared wide-eyed at his reflection in the mirror.

A grown man stared back at him. Oh, he knew what he looked like in this new life, but it always startled him to see Merlin's face and eyes topped by his own sandy-blond hair.

He looked closer at his reflection. He was noticeably taller, perhaps six three like his brother, Seth. He was bulkier though. Seth had that abnormally slender, willowy, Fae build and Arthur was broad-shouldered and muscular, like Derek.

Last night when he had bid his parents good night, he had been a puny thirteen-year-old boy. This morning he was a well-built twenty-two-year-old man. At last. Gods, he couldn't wait to talk to Gwen, to make plans to get married again. Intense sexual arousal assaulted him at the thought of her. He glanced down at his impressive erection. He closed his eyes and willed himself calm—as much as he wanted her, it was not yet time for that.

And another thing—Merlin had promised that when he matured he

THE WINDS OF CHANGE

would have his wings. He'd longed to fly, ever since he was two years old and watched his sister and brothers fly away, up to the Rim, leaving him behind.

He closed his eyes, tentatively focused inside himself, and found and triggered the specific magic that called forth his wings from that other dimension—and felt them manifest.

Arthur laughed out loud, eager to see what came next.

* * *

I sensed Arthur's excitement and appeared in his bedroom. I could see him through the door we had recently installed into the hall bathroom, standing naked in front of the mirror. He was admiring his sculpted body and elegant wings, which were extended as far as possible in the cramped confines of the bathroom. Arthur now had Seth's height and Derek's build, and cut an impressive figure.

My son, who should have sensed my presence but was distracted by his new body, caught sight of me out of the corner of his eye and grinned.

"Dad, I finally did it! Full-grown and winged at last." His voice was that of a mature man.

I smiled at his enthusiasm. "I see that. Congratulations." Why did I sound so sad? This was what I'd wanted, wasn't it? For Arthur to bypass the normal growth process and mature in five years—or less, as it turned out? Maybe I wasn't any different than Em in wishing he could stay a child longer.

Arthur retracted his wings and turned to face me, his expression one of loving concern.

"Merlin. *Dad.* I will never leave you, if that's what you're worried about. I came back from death...for *you*. I left my original body behind with the Elves in the Other World so I could be born again as your son."

Was my sadness so obvious? "I know." My heart ached with love for this remarkable young man, but I also felt both trepidation and antici-pation at what the future held for us. "My brother Sam—Satan—and his cohorts are still out there. I was so sure they would attempt to kidnap or harm you as you were growing up. But they didn't." A fleeting thought that I was wrong about that came and went before I could examine it.

"The entire family, including Grammy Rae, saw to that," Arthur said. He stood in front of me and put his big hands on my shoulders. "Don't you know that I would protect and defend *you*? I love you."

I struggled to get my emotions under control. "I know. I love you, too. Always have."

We stared into each other's eyes, sharing a close moment.

Arthur moved restlessly. "I, uh, hate to leave you right now, but I want to surprise Gwen at the newspaper office."

He had been visiting her at her workplace for the past few years as he grew up, and I knew he was anxious to show her his new physique.

"And I need to stop at the jeweler's and pick up an engagement ring for her."

I smiled widely, with sincerity. "You've waited over a thousand years for this moment. I understand and I'm pleased for you both. But there's no need to buy a ring."

Arthur looked puzzled. "Why is that?"

My god Light flared brightly for a moment then subsided. I held out my hand. In my palm was a dainty, filigreed gold ring with a faceted blood-red ruby.

Arthur gasped and took it gently between his thumb and forefinger, holding it up in front of him. "By the gods, it's Guinevere's ring. The one I gave her when we became engaged in the fifth century. How...?"

I shrugged. "I simply reached back in time, to the moment after her death, and brought it here."

He stared for a moment. "At the risk of repeating myself, I often forget what you are..."

I chuckled. "Emily says the same thing. Never mind that. Go and see your lady." My eyes traveled down the length of his body. "But be sure to get dressed first." I winked and disappeared, leaving him blushing as he remembered he was stark naked.

* * *

Gwen Singleton was absorbed in her work at the newspaper when she heard a man clear his throat noisily in the vicinity of her desk.

She kept her eyes on her screen and wondered impatiently why someone hadn't intercepted the guy at the reception desk. He'd have to wait while she finished typing her article.

Eventually, she came to a stopping point and realized that the man was still waiting patiently for her to look up at him.

She swallowed an angry retort, and calmed herself.

When she had her professional smile firmly in place, she looked up.

And inhaled sharply. A tall, handsome man stood in front of her dressed in tight jeans that emphasized his athletic body, his startlingly green eyes filled with longing. There was something so familiar about him, if she could only remember where she'd seen him before—

"Arthur?" Gwen stood up so quickly that her chair toppled over backward with a resounding crash.

"Yes, I—" He never had the chance to finish the sentence as she threw herself into his arms. He held her slender frame tightly against him and kissed the top of her head. "Gwen. Gwen, my love."

Oblivious to the fascinated gazes turned in their direction, Gwen clung to Arthur's magnificent twenty-two-year-old body. She'd waited so long for this. She hadn't dated anyone, hadn't even gone out with female friends besides the women in Merlin's family since she had taken over Jim Singleton's job five years ago, shortly after his death. Oh, God, she still felt peculiar when she remembered that *she* had been Jim, and had died—and had been restored to a close-to-perfect replica of her original female body. No one in the office except Morry knew the truth, so hugging a stranger at her desk was an abnormal and noteworthy occurrence. She deliberately ignored her coworkers' avid interest.

* * *

Arthur hadn't held Gwen in his adult arms for over 1500 years, but he hadn't forgotten the feel of her—warm, lithe and very, very female. He was afraid his body would react in a way that was utterly inappropriate. After all, they were standing in her place of business and they weren't currently married. Even though Derek had informed him that sexual relations between unmarried couples were common in the twenty-first century, a part of him was old-fashioned enough to feel uncomfortable even contemplating it.

Gwen apparently had no such inhibitions regarding premarital sex.

"We need to go to my place, Arthur," she whispered urgently. He'd always been able to tell when she was aroused, but now he could also hear her thoughts. And she was irrefutably frantic to have him inside her.

"Why, Gwen, you naughty little thing," Arthur murmured quietly as he stroked her hair and felt her breasts press against him. "I think I like it. By all means, let's go."

"Let me clock out and grab my purse—it'll only take a second."

"Okay." Arthur couldn't help grinning from ear to ear, happiness and anticipation flooding his being. He watched Gwen as she raced back and forth, saving her work, shutting down her computer, and informing her coworkers that she would be gone the rest of the day. She was wearing formfitting designer jeans and a stretchy yellow long-sleeved top that showed off all her assets—trim waist, shapely hips, round bottom, and high, firm breasts. He knew he shouldn't stare, but he couldn't stop himself, and as a consequence, he was getting aroused —which was uncomfortable since his jeans were pretty snug. When he'd conjured new garments to fit his brawny adult form, he'd misjudged the size and had been in too much of a hurry to make any adjustments.

Finally ready to go, she grasped his hand and literally dragged him out the door and down the street to where her car was parked.

As they jumped into her vehicle, Arthur reflected upon all the advanced technology this century had to offer —the cars, the electronics, everything—and marveled at his acceptance of them. He supposed the reason for it was that he had been born in this miraculous era, so he took it for granted like everyone else here.

Of course, there was a continual clash of his past memories with the experiences of his new life. He'd known from the moment of his conception that this would happen and had learned how to compartmentalize all the conflicting information—well, mostly. And that made him think of Merlin—once his servant, his mentor, and his best friend, and now, his father and his god. That last part still seemed surreal.

When he'd been killed at the Battle of Camlann, the Elven Fae had kept his body in stasis, awaiting the time of his resurrection. But in 2013, after Merlin had awakened and been directed to seek a new portal to Avalon due to unrest and conflict between the gods in the Other World, it had apparently become clear to the Elves that there was a better way to resurrect Arthur. He would return in the form that made the most sense in the twenty-first century, as the son of the one who was destined to save the planet.

He hurriedly put aside every thought but the current one. He was going to have sex for the first time in over a millennium with the woman who had once been his wife.

He'd had many centuries in his incorporeal state to come to terms with her past infidelity—and his old friend's betrayal. Lancelot had had sex with his queen. But Arthur knew that ultimately it had been his own fault for leaving her in Lancelot's care when he went to war, which was frequently. The two of them had commiserated together about the pain and loneliness resulting from his continual absence, until one day, they had sought solace, and love, in each other's arms—in *his* marriage bed.

But that was in another life, and though Lancelot had been reborn in this century, Gwen had not encouraged her old lover's attentions in any way. She'd been celibate, waiting for Arthur to reach maturity once again. Not that she had told him that, but he had known, nevertheless. He knew he would eventually have to confront Lancelot—Ryan Jones, that is—and resolve their differences.

Arthur surfaced from his reflections as they pulled up in front of a small, neat house. Gwen had lived here with his nephew Morry when she was Jim Singleton. She'd had the place to herself since Morry moved out and married Lainie, and Arthur could sense how well it suited her. He took a closer look. The house was painted a cheerful sunflower yellow with white trim, and the front door was the same deep red as the dragon emblem on the Royal Standard of Camelot.

They turned to each other and grinned as they bounded out of the car and raced up to the door, which quickly swung open in response to Arthur's subverbal spell.

Gwen laughed gaily. "I keep forgetting that you have magic! I love it."

As they entered the house he swept her up into his arms and teleported them into her bedroom, dispensing with their clothing with a thought. He was glad that he had practiced his magic enough to perform those actions flawlessly.

"Oh, my, aren't you talented—and impatient. One would think you haven't had sex in centuries," she teased him as she reclined on the bed, her rich brown curls contrasting nicely with the orange, turquoise, and white geometric pattern in her bedspread.

Arthur felt a sharp spike of desire. "I'm sorry, my love, but this first time, I can't wait."

"And I don't want you to," she murmured as she pulled him down on top of her.

The sensation of his warm skin sliding against her soft, sleek naked body caused them to simultaneously groan and clutch each other tightly.

Need caused her to spread her legs wide in invitation and need caused him to respond by sheathing his hardness to the root inside her wet heat.

Although aroused, she hadn't had sex for many years, and his hasty penetration was a shock. "Oh, my God," she panted, "you're so much bigger now. And you weren't small before."

He couldn't answer, could only react by pumping frantically, pausing only to suck lustily on her erect nipples. It didn't take long for him to come with a roar of masculine satisfaction as she experienced her own climax with a shriek.

* * *

Derek and Seth were flying high above Moab, enjoying each other's company on Derek's day off, when they both felt a surge of sexual energy so powerful they faltered, their bodies aching for sex.

"What the hell! Did ya feel that?" Derek exclaimed.

"Aye!" Seth responded, overcorrecting his trajectory.

They glanced at each other in astonishment as they recognized the magical signature.

"It's Arthur! He's a man now."

"Nay doubt aboot that," said Seth in a dry tone of voice. "Do ye think we should, ah, do anything?"

"I don't think either of them would appreciate it."

"Nay, Brother, I dinna think they would." Seth laughed out loud.

* * *

After Gwen had left the office with her hunky new guy in tow, Beth Douglas had found it difficult to concentrate on her work. She was busy staring stealthily at Gwen's former roommate, Morry, who was grinning as if he'd had a hand in setting them up. As Beth pondered Morry's possible role in this unexpected turn of events, she remembered a certain shopkeeper and storyteller whose green, slanted eyes were identical to Gwen's friend. The same slant to Morry's eyes could indicate he was a part of that family, as well.

Something was rattling around in her head, a memory she couldn't quite pin down. It was frustrating since on the whole she had excellent recall. Then she had it. Back in 2013, when she and her best friend Chloe had started attending storytelling sessions at The Moab Herbalist, the owner, Michael Reese, had often gotten carried away and would speak in a foreign language he claimed was Old British. He would explain away his use of a dead language as something he had studied at the university he'd attended in Wales, but she and Chloe often conjectured, laughingly, that he had been born in the fifth century and was really Merlin. It seemed so far-fetched and ridiculous that they both eventually let it go. Now, she wasn't so sure they'd been wrong.

* * *

"Arthur? Are you awake?"

"Hmm?"

"I…I'm so sorry." Gwen's voice was rough with tears.

Sated and happy after making love off and on for most of the day, Arthur blinked sleepily in confusion. He rose up on one elbow and stared at her in the slanted light of early evening. "Sweetheart, what in the god's name are you talking about?"

"My affair with Lancelot. All those years, when you were gone, I was lonesome and so was he. We both loved you and you were never there for either of us," Gwen sobbed. She sat up and reached for the box of tissues.

He wanted to draw her into his arms, taking away her pain and regret by making love to her again, but he didn't. She needed this chance to express her guilt and sorrow in her own way.

He should have known this would happen. During the centuries he was in the Other World, he'd come to an understanding and acceptance of the events that had preceded his death.

In his previous life, he'd had no choice but to be what he'd been born to be: king, warrior, leader, battling his enemies to keep the kingdom safe. In the end, it hadn't made any difference. He'd died and his queen had taken his place on the throne. Sir Lancelot had died as well, so Guinevere had done her best, with only Merlin's help, to hold the kingdom together. But once she was gone and Merlin had retreated to the Crystal Cave, all Arthur had fought and died for had eventually crumbled into dust.

Now he knew that he'd never been forgotten, tales of his exploits with his knights having been told and retold until they became myth and legend.

But Gwen had never had the chance to reconcile what she and Lancelot had done and it had haunted her throughout untold lifetimes, until her incarnation as Jim Singleton, when she had met Merlin again.

"Arthur, can you ever forgive me?" She turned to him, her beautiful brown eyes, brimming with tears, beseeched him.

Arthur lovingly stroked her face. "Guinevere, my darling, I forgave you and Lancelot long ago. I had many centuries after my death to contemplate my successes and failures, and I would never hold that against either of you.

"At some point I'll speak to him privately, but in all honesty, I can only thank him for taking care of you, past and present."

She bristled. "I haven't needed him to take care of me in this life. And I was a man in quite a few lifetimes since Camelot, so I can take care of myself. "

Arthur laughed. "Yes, you're certainly ferocious."

His laughter was infectious, and Gwen had to grin. She gazed at him appreciatively. The man was amazing and gorgeous and he was hers. He reclined on her bed like a big golden lion, his sandy-blond hair brushing his muscular shoulders, and the smattering of silky, light-brown hair on his chest inviting her to stroke him. His brilliantly green eyes, so different from his original warm brown ones, sparkled with love for her.

This was her second chance, *their* second chance, at a lifetime of loving each other, and with any luck, having children, and she was going to take full advantage of it.

She leaned into him and kissed him, running her hand down his chest and across his taut belly, then lower, and lower still, until she found him, hard, ready for her again.

"Love me, my lord."

"Gladly, my lady. But first…" Arthur leaped up and dug into the pocket of his jeans, pulling out a small box. He kneeled down next to the bed.

"What are you doing?"

Arthur looked expectantly into Gwen's loving eyes and said, "Will you be my wife? Again?"

As she tearfully agreed, he slipped the ruby ring on her finger and kissed her.

She did a double take when she looked closely at the ring. "Is this—"

"Yes, it is."

She started to ask how in the world he'd retrieved it, but he simply said, "Merlin."

* * *

That evening, after they'd put together and eaten a simple supper, they decided that Arthur should return home to pack his things and spend one more night with his parents.

As he left Gwen's house, he decided it might be opportune to drop in on Ryan and let him know that all was well between them. Arthur was aware the man might find it difficult to accept that he and Gwen were back together again. He suspected Ryan still hoped to rekindle the love he'd shared with Guinevere centuries ago, when he'd been Sir Lancelot.

Arthur had no desire to hurt him any more than was inevitable; after all, they had been as close as brothers in Camelot. But he knew that this step was necessary for both of them to attain closure.

Before he could talk himself out of it, he teleported to the knights' home on 400 East, but he stood on their porch debating whether he wanted to go through with it after all. He had half turned away, ready to teleport home, when the door opened and a burly man stood in the doorway. "Can I help you?" he asked, not recognizing the one in front of him.

Arthur turned back and stepped into the illumination given off by the porch light next to the front door. "It's me, Lancelot, it's Arthur."

Ryan stared in disbelief at the tall, regal figure. Suddenly his face crumpled and tears poured silently down his rugged cheeks.

The two men stepped forward and threw their arms around each other. "Oh, God, it *is* you," Ryan said with a catch in his voice.

"Yes, and who would have thought that we would be reunited again, eh?" Arthur's voice was thick with emotion.

Ryan gave a half-hearted chuckle. "And neither of us looks anything like our fifth-century selves. Your hair is the same color, but you look like Merlin, and now I'm big and muscular, whereas I used to be shorter and slighter of build."

"Our souls are the same as they were so long ago, Lancelot, and it is our souls that recognize each other."

"True. Why don't you come in and we can continue this conversation privately. I know what you want to talk about, and while I'm not anxious to dredge up old wounds, it needs to be done, for both of our sakes."

"Where are the rest of the men tonight?" Arthur asked as he followed Ryan into the house.

"Percival is out with his girlfriend and Gary and Leon are playing pool at Moody's. I felt like staying home."

"I'm glad, old friend."

"Are we really still friends after what I did?" Ryan's voice sounded strained and apprehensive. He stood in the middle of the living room facing away from Arthur, as if he couldn't bear to see the look of disgust and anger that by rights should be on the face of the man he still considered his king. "I cuckolded you. I made love to your wife, your queen, in your bed. And I love her still. How can that ever be forgiven or forgotten?" The timbre of Ryan's voice reflected that of Lancelot of old.

Contemplating the best way to answer him, Arthur wandered over to look at a large painting on the wall. It was of an ancient castle that looked remarkably familiar. "I had many long centuries after my death to think about it. After all, what else was there to do, but think and regret and wonder if I could have done things differently?" He swung around. "The conclusion I finally came to was that I *couldn't* have done anything differently. I was a warrior and so were you. I was the King of Camelot, and I had commanded you to guard my precious wife, to keep her safe and happy. And that's exactly what you did. I was never home and you were both unhappy, so you turned to each other and gave each other joy. In truth, there is nothing to forgive. However, Gwen begged my forgiveness and I gave it unreservedly. Now I do the same for you.

"Be at peace, Sir Lancelot. I forgive you."

* * *

"Arthur?"

He turned at the sound of his mother's voice, hoping that she wouldn't break down when she saw that he was packing his belongings. "Yes, Mom?"

"Oh, Arthur, look at you. My little boy is a grown man. A beautiful, strong man," Em said, her voice thick with emotion and her eyes welling with tears.

"Mom, please don't cry," he said quietly, reaching out to hold her against him. She seemed so small, or he was so large in comparison.

She wiped her tears away and valiantly pulled herself together. "I'm sorry. I know this is the way it's supposed to be, but it's hard to let go. Five years ago you were in my womb, barely conceived."

"I know. I remember." He stroked her hair and kissed her forehead. "I remember everything that's happened to me since I was a child in the fifth century, my life, my death, my rebirth in this century. It's been hard to comprehend." He made room for them to sit side by side on his bed and he took her hand in his large one.

"I haven't mentioned this to Dad, but it was so bizarre when he'd have those storytelling sessions, telling the people sitting next to me about my battles, my knights, my castle…my life. And I'm this old soul in a child's body, remembering everything and not able to say, '*I'm right here in front of you!*'"

Emily smiled, enjoying her own perspective of those memories. "Soon, you'll be able to say to the whole world: *I'm right here in front of you and I'll never leave you again.*"

They smiled at each other and held hands until Arthur finally stood up, pulling her into his arms again.

"I won't ever be far from you and Dad, I promise. But it's time for me to move on, to be with Gwen."

Emily smiled through her tears. "I know. It's meant to be this way."

He finished packing, which didn't take long, since he didn't need to pack all the clothes, coats and shoes that no longer fit him, or the toys of his brief childhood. She stood and watched him, wishing that he didn't have to go yet.

Arthur had an idea that might make her feel better. "Mom, why don't I help you and Dad at the shop on Friday? I know there's a large order being delivered and I'd be happy to work for a few hours."

"That would be great, Arthur, thank you."

As he nodded and turned away, she asked, "Aren't you going to say goodbye to your dad?"

"I already did when we talked earlier. I love you, Mom."

As he teleported back to Gwen's house, he felt bad about leaving his mother so abruptly, but he knew it was necessary.

* * *

Gwen was surprised to see Arthur materialize in the living room only a couple of hours later. "I thought you were going to spend the night at your parents' house?"

"I decided not to. It seemed kinder to have a clean break." He was facing away from her and she tugged him around.

Arthur had tears running down his cheeks. "I couldn't stay. I want to be with you, but I didn't want to leave them, either."

Gwen cupped his cheek. "Oh, Arthur. Life has been so hard for you, hasn't it? But, with any luck that will change now that we're back together again and ready to move forward."

CHAPTER 26
Moab, Tuesday, August 15, 2023, Evening

Still sexually stimulated by Arthur's experience earlier in the day, Seth gazed into his lover's eyes as he slowly penetrated her body. It was a tight fit, despite the fact that she had become accustomed to the size of him quite some time ago. He released a wee bit more of his scent, knowing it would help her relax and allow him to plunge even deeper. He began to move, slowly and sensuously. Chris smiled as she relished the feel of him inside her. He smiled back and kissed her, thinking about the differences between this incredible woman and others he'd known. For one thing, she loved him unconditionally. She had never said so, but her thoughts and emotions were an open book to him.

The Fae females he had joined with over the course of his immortal life had all been tall, slim, and anxious to have sex with him merely so they could flaunt having gained a prince's attention. It was all about prestige, and he hadn't cared as long as they satisfied him; he had never felt the urge to *mate* with any of them. The females of his race had an extraordinary flexibility in their spines, which always ensured the most satisfying positions. But they were cold and unemotional—true Fae—and he was never attracted to any one of them in particular. For a moment, he contemplated why he called the females "true Fae," as if he himself was not. But in truth, he was only half Fae, since his father was a god.

Without warning, his emotions spiked and it was clear to him that he did love Chris. He had never told her so because he assumed that he was unable to experience love. But this powerful surge of affection and protectiveness was unanticipated and it was a prelude to what came next.

His fangs lowered relentlessly, splitting his gums painfully. He'd been able to control them in the past, but this was different. They extended until they were completely exposed, and he thought that could only happen during sex with his soul mate.

Chris was his soul mate? But she was human, how could this happen? He started to panic when he realized that he was caught up in a ceremony as old as his race and that he no longer had control over his actions. As he bent closer to her and positioned his fangs against her throat, he finally understood. He was preparing her for the permanent mating with Fae royalty.

* * *

Chris was in Seth's thrall and sensed that he was going to possess her completely. Not just her body—after all, they had been lovers for five years—but all of her, body, mind and soul. She didn't know how she knew, and she didn't care. If this was her destiny, she intended to embrace it. He seemed to grow larger inside her, and her excitement grew with every thrust. Oh, God, it felt so good, and so right, that tears welled in her eyes. His body covering hers was heavy, even though he was very slender, and she felt deliciously pinned down, unable to move even if she'd wanted to. She could see his elegant wings spread out above them, as if they were going to take flight, their bodies melded into one.

For a moment, she thought she'd seen panic in his alien eyes as long sharp fangs descended from his mouth and he bit her neck. Initially she'd felt pain, but the sensation of him attached to her neck and inside her at the same time was so erotic that she shuddered rapturously, her climax obliterating conscious thought.

* * *

When Chris came, her inner muscles clenched around him so violently that Seth spontaneously climaxed as well, the intensity of his orgasm surpassing any other he'd ever experienced. And the rich, metallic taste of her blood gave him such mindless pleasure he almost passed out. However, in the midst of this combined ecstasy, he knew there was one more step he had to take to complete the ritual mating.

Akin to the rattlesnake here in the human realm, he had a gland attached to his fangs by a narrow duct, enabling him to inject a special serum into his partner at the peak of his orgasm. He did so, and Chris's transition began.

* * *

I had been lounging in bed next to my sleeping wife, contemplating Arthur's entry into the adult world, when my god senses registered an event that I hadn't foreseen: Seth had mated with Chris in an ancient Fae ritual that bound her to him forever. He had bitten her and introduced Fae DNA into her body, thus starting the process of making her his princess. And, although he wasn't aware he had done so, he had impregnated her.

* * *

Seth glanced over at his new mate, who was slumbering serenely. He'd helped her fall asleep so he'd have a chance to think about the ramifications of his actions. He winced as he touched the bloody fang marks on her neck and proceeded to heal them.

Sensing that Merlin was aware of his mating ritual, Seth sought him telepathically.

Och, Da, I'm a wee bit confused. I dinna ken how this happened.

You must have known what was going on when your fangs dropped. Or were you not aware you had them?

Oh, aye, I kent they were there, but I thought they were a wee evolutionary oversight. I never expected tae actually use them, let alone mate with a human. Although, since I bit her, she's turning Fae and soon willna be human anymore.

It's apparent this is your destiny, Seth, and hers. Do you love her?

Aye, I do. When I felt how much I loved her it could have triggered the mating. But that's the strangest part, Da—the Fae dinna mate for love. I'm no' sure any Fae have mated this way in thousands of years. We just have sex. I wasna sure I could truly feel love. That's one of the reasons I didna recognize the signs. And once ma fangs came all the way down, I wasna able tae stop the process as I have in the past. He sounded hesitant and even a bit fearful.

Seth, you have done what your nature has bidden you to do. I'm sure Chris understands that. She loves you—the real you—and she'll make an excellent mate for you; a true princess.

* * *

Surprisingly, considering my usual lack of perception of future events when it came to family members, I perceived that Seth and Chris's path led them to a destiny they could never have imagined. But I would keep that knowledge to myself for now since there were many stumbling blocks ahead of that momentous final step. I wasn't sure yet how Seth and Chris's future meshed with Arthur's anticipated proclamation of his return—and mine—but I had no doubt that it was all a part of my father's ambitious endgame.

CHAPTER 27
Moab, Wednesday, August 16, 2023, Morning

Chris Colburn gradually opened her eyes, still caught up in the peculiar dream she'd had, in which she'd been bitten by a vampire and became one of the **undead**.

She made a wry face. She seldom watched those movies. Why would she? She was surrounded by supernatural entities and magic every day. Hell, she lived with a Fae prince, worked for a god and his Elven wife, and her ex-husband was a powerful sorcerer, so why would she need to augment her daily quota of weirdness with Hollywood's largely inaccurate portrayal of supernatural phenomena?

She sensed that Seth was awake and staring at her. She turned her head on the pillow and looked at him, curious why he had such a worried look in his familiar yellow-green reptilian eyes. "What's wrong?"

"How're ye feeling?" he asked anxiously.

Chris thought about it for a moment. "I feel great. In fact, I feel incredible. Why?"

"Do ye remember when we made love last night?"

Of course she did, so why would he...

Chris clapped her hand to her neck "Oh, my God, you *bit* me! So that's why I dreamed about vampires!" She could still remember the sensation of needle-sharp fangs puncturing her skin, but she couldn't feel any kind of wound remaining.

"I healed it." He fondled the smooth skin of her neck, which made her shiver with desire and reach for him.

She panted, more aroused than she could ever remember being, and since she always desired him, that was saying something.

"I want you, Seth—now." And she pulled him on top of her, not stopping to speculate how she had the strength to do that.

But he knew, and he grinned, letting her discover her new reality as it unfolded.

He kissed her passionately and lightly traced the contours of her sleek body. He was heartily glad they slept naked. He had never adopted the human custom of wearing nightclothes and years ago had persuaded her to abandon her pajamas.

She caressed his smooth hairless chest, running her hands over his shoulders and onto the wing bones protruding from his upper back. She gently fingered a few of the feathers, causing him to shudder in ecstasy.

"I love your wings," she murmured, "and your ass." She emphasized her words by squeezing his muscular buttocks. Ready to be taken, she spread her legs until she could feel his hardness pressed against her, and pulled him inside her. She was so wet he entered her easily. And again, she didn't question how she had been able to manage that.

He flexed his hips and continued the penetration until he was buried deeply in her body.

She gasped at the sensation of intense pressure and cried out as pleasure raced through her.

He started to move, his thrusts taking her higher and higher until she screamed at the peak of her climax. He groaned at the gratification of his own release, and kissed her sweetly. "*Tha gaol agam ort, mo chridhe,*" Seth whispered.

Chris looked puzzled. "What did you say?"

"I love ye, ma heart."

"You…you love me?"

"Aye."

"Oh, Seth, I love you, too. I always have." She was ecstatic to finally be able to say it to him.

"I kent it, *mo muirninn*, ma darling."

"I'm so glad, but why are you telling me now, after all these years?"

"Because last night, when I bit ye, I made ye ma princess. We're mated forever."

"*What?*" She pushed him off of her and sat up abruptly.

"'Twas destined, Chris, and I couldna stop it," he said apologetically.

She felt dazed as memories of the previous evening appeared in her mind—he had held her in thrall while he bit her and injected *something* into her.

Seth saw the look in her eyes as she remembered everything, and he hoped that she could accept the inevitable, irreversible alterations that would make her Fae.

173

To his astonishment, she touched her belly, gazed into his alien eyes, and smiled brilliantly. "We're going to have a baby."

Seth inhaled sharply. "Are ye sure?"

"Absolutely. I can feel it." She grabbed his large elegant hand and placed it on her belly.

He closed his eyes and directed his senses inside her. And there it was. A microscopic collection of cells with the very beginnings of consciousness: A tiny new Fae being with a wee bit of human DNA.

He felt his eyes fill with tears, which hadn't happened since he had first come to Moab and connected with Merlin in 2018, as he realized he was going to be a father.

"Oh, Seth." Chris looped her arms around his neck and they clung together.

* * *

Later, as Chris was getting ready to take a shower, one of her ears ached and started to itch ferociously. She scratched it, thinking idly that she had been bitten by a mosquito. She froze, recalling again the earth-shaking events of the past twelve hours.

Oh, crap. Bitten, yes, but not by a mosquito. She dashed over to the mirror, tugged the hair away from her ears and felt her mouth drop open in shock. Her ears were pointed. And when she looked closer at her eyes, it was apparent that the pupils had changed to the typical Fae vertical pupil. Thank God they were still hazel, although they now had a faint yellowish cast to them.

As her upper back near her shoulder blades started to itch and throb, it occurred to her what else was going to happen and she blanched.

"Seth!" she screamed as nascent wings erupted and she experienced such excruciating pain that she started to black out.

He was there to catch her before she hit the tile floor.

Chris's eyes fluttered open a few minutes later and she cringed, anticipating more pain. Instead, she felt like she was floating in a warm bath, relaxed and pain-free. Seth was holding her, cradling her on his lap.

"Did ye think I'd allow ye tae suffer verra long, *mo chridhe?* I kent that yer wings would emerge at some point, but I didna ken exactly when it would happen. I'm sorry that ye had tae go through that." He kissed her and helped her up.

Chris stood with her back to the mirror and looked over her

shoulder at the reflection of wings protruding from her upper back. They didn't look like much yet. Rather like a newly hatched baby bird's wings, wet and unfinished. She wished she could tell what color they were going to be.

"Fae wings are typically black or gray. But since I turned ye, they'll nay doubt be similar to mine once they've dried—white feathers with black edges."

She met Seth's eyes in the mirror and felt a connection to him that she'd never experienced before, as though they were merging into one being. It was so all-consuming that she closed her eyes, afraid that she would lose herself in him.

"Aye, in ancient times Fae males were known tae force their mates tae merge their souls with them. I'd never do such a thing tae ye. 'Tis wrong."

Chris breathed a sigh of relief. "I'm happy you feel that way, because I'd hate to think that the price of being your mate was to lose my individuality."

His mate, she was his mate, and she was carrying his child! Her excitement grew as it dawned on her that it was real. She'd never dared to dream of it, or even to *think* of it, because she hadn't wanted to scare him away. But now she could ask for what she really wanted, which was to marry this man that she adored, in the human way, in front of her friends and family.

Seth's straight, white teeth gleamed as he smiled, hearing her thoughts loud and clear, as he had always done. "Will ye marry me, lass?"

CHAPTER 28
Moab, Friday, August 18, 2023, Early Morning

The entity occupying Jack Crandall's ageing body was getting impatient. He hadn't wanted to appear in human form since it required an immense expenditure of energy, but this body was deteriorating rapidly.

"Hellfire and damnation," the entity muttered darkly. For some inexplicable reason, he hesitated to take another mortal's body for his use—perhaps because he hadn't found anyone else in this town, or even in the state of Utah, who believed in the power of evil as unquestioningly as Jack Crandall had.

The alternative was to manifest as himself. It had been millennia since he had bothered materializing into the form he favored, but what the hell? Maybe Merlin wouldn't recognize him. After all, his brother had been keenly focused on his youngest son, Arthur, and not expecting Satan to show up in person. Besides, there had to be dozens of males in Moab with his exact height and coloring. He could change his features, and his eye and hair color, but he was satisfied with the appearance he had been given at the beginning of time; it was deliciously incongruous considering his dark personality. And the bottom line was that he had a few magical tricks Merlin wasn't aware of to keep the bastard guessing.

He decided to risk it. It was late, after midnight, and while he sensed no one in his immediate vicinity, the random human could still be seen walking along Mill Creek Parkway. He debated teleporting to a remote area of Grand County to dispose of good ole Jack, but he didn't care if or when the body was found. Screw it. He allowed the worn-out husk to fall to the ground as his energy left it.

Moments later, he coalesced into human form, curly blond hair gleaming in the bright moonlight and cold topaz-blue eyes brimming with hatred. He felt deliciously pagan as he stretched upward, naked beneath the dispassionate gaze of the distant stars in the night sky. Looking down, he studied his ample maleness, imagining the sexual encounters he could have now that he had vacated the older body he'd inhabited for so many years.

He conjured up the proper clothing to cover himself, and glanced disinterestedly at the pathetic carcass at his feet. He twisted his face into a sneer and disappeared.

* * *

Early for class, a teenage boy wandering along the banks of Mill Creek on his way to the high school discovered the grisly remains and hysterically reported his find to the principal, who immediately called the Moab City Police Department.

Shortly thereafter, Detective Colin Campbell gazed down at the stiff form at his feet and heaved a sigh. The body was that of a male approximately sixty-five to seventy years of age. There were no visible wounds and no obvious sign of foul play, so the man had possibly experienced a heart attack. He had apparently been walking along the creek when he dropped to the ground, unconscious, and died.

The corpse couldn't have been there long but it was already partially desiccated, and some critter had chewed on his face and neck shortly after death. Not a pretty sight, he had to admit.

The air was unusually dry, with the humidity no more than eight percent according to the weather report, and there was no wind, which helped explain why the student hadn't noticed the inevitable stench of death until he'd practically tripped over the body. Desiccation generally occurred after a period of exposure to extreme heat as well as dryness, thus Colin doubted that a few hours would be sufficient to cause such an effect.

Death had more than likely occurred about five or six hours ago, considering that rigor mortis had set in and not yet dissipated, and blowfly eggs were evident, but maggots had not yet hatched. Blowflies were attracted to a fresh corpse within minutes after death, so they would have been there at some point before the moisture in the body had been lost.

Colin ran through the probable sequence of events in his mind once more, and he came to the same conclusions. With the amount of foot traffic along this trail, there was no way the body had been there before midnight or someone would have seen it.

Something about the whole scenario felt off to Campbell, however, so it was lucky that the medical examiner's office would take all the facts into account during the autopsy and make the final determination as to cause and time of death. Colin would also request a toxicology screen to determine if there had been any drugs in the old man's system when he died. The lab would let him know the results.

Colin wondered what the holdup was. He had instructed his assistant to cordon off the area with yellow crime scene tape, but the young man still wasn't finished and was getting the wide plastic tape tangled in the brush and old tree limbs on the ground. There wasn't as much debris as there had been before the flood last year, but his assistant had managed to find it. They still needed to photograph the scene, bag any evidence they found, and look for clues.

The new guy irritated him, but the Chief insisted that he train someone, since there had been an unprecedented increase in crime lately and the team was short-staffed, as usual. The young man had recently come into the department as an intern, part of a college law enforcement training program. Colin had chosen him as the least objectionable of the candidates.

Colin sighed. Might as well help him with the crime scene tape and show him what to photograph. Damn it, he hoped the guy knew how to use a camera, because he wasn't looking forward to teaching his assistant basic photography on top of everything else. He started to call out but couldn't remember the man's name. He sure wished he had telepathy, although it was possible he did and hadn't learned to access it yet. It was worth a shot, so he closed his eyes and focused inside, where the magic vibrated quietly in his chest. He thought he could hear something...

A minute later, he shook his head—it wasn't coming to him by magical means, but he finally remembered what the guy's first name was.

"Hey, Owen, let me help you with that," Colin called out, standing up and walking with care to the perimeter of the area to be cordoned off.

The new assistant crime scene investigator jumped, startled that the boss remembered his name and was willing to help him. "Uh, sure," he said hesitantly. "Thanks."

"Officer Smith will keep the spectators away until we're done and the medical examiner gets here. It shouldn't take more than thirty minutes since they were in Green River when we called them. We're lucky—the Office of the Medical Examiner is in Taylorsville and it normally takes hours for them to get here."

"Why does it take so long?"

"They serve the entire state, not just Grand County."

After they finished placing the crime scene tape around the area, Colin returned his attention to the gruesome task at hand. He found a set of bare footprints—approximately men's size eleven—leading away from the body, but unfortunately, the kid who'd discovered the remains had disturbed them and Colin couldn't pick up the trail after that. He even used magic to enhance his senses and couldn't detect any trace of the perpetrator.

Owen worked alongside him, photographing the scene competently once he was told what to look for, and Colin had to admit he wasn't so bad after all.

A search of the victim's pockets yielded nothing—no wallet or any other form of identification.

"Shit," Campbell swore under his breath. Figuring out who the victim was could be problematic. Since most of the fingers were either missing or gnawed off at the first joint, he couldn't obtain fingerprints. He grimaced in disgust. There had been sightings of bears along the creek in this area in the past, but it was practically unheard of for them to eat human flesh. And if they did, it was unlikely they would have limited their meal to the fingers alone. He supposed they could use the rest of the fingers and the hand itself for identification purposes.

Colin needed to contact Merlin, since he had a strong hunch that dark magic was involved in this death. He wished he wasn't limited to calling him on the phone, or to dropping by the shop. His uncle had enhanced his innate skills and intuition about five years ago, and Colin also had his own magic to draw upon, which helped when he had to solve a crime, but it would be icing on the cake if he could initiate telepathic communication with Merlin.

Someday, if he was lucky, he might be able to do that. With an impatient sigh, Colin pulled his cell phone out of his pocket and called the station to confirm the medical examiner's estimated time of arrival. Colin would stop by the herb shop later; he suspected that Merlin would know the identity of the victim.

* * *

Unbeknownst to Campbell, the ghost of Derek's deceased partner, Ken Wilson, stood next to him, wishing he could communicate with the guy. He was confused why the detective, who apparently had some level of magical power, couldn't see or hear him. Ken remembered seeing the man, and hearing someone call him by name, at The Moab Herbalist, but he was fairly certain that Campbell hadn't possessed any magic then.

Despite the damage to the victim's face, Ken knew the identity of the dead man—he was Emily's father Jack Crandall. He had never met him, but he'd seen photos of Em's parents in her and Merlin's home. And at some point, Derek must have informed Ken that Satan had taken over Crandall's body.

Ken wished that he could tell the detective to be careful, that Satan was real and infinitely dangerous.

He pretended to chew on his incorporeal lip. How the hell had he gotten mixed up in this? He was terrified that the devil would come after him, although he was pretty sure God would protect him.

Ken shook his ghostly head in confusion. Why would he think that? Had Merlin told him so? He was a god, after all, so he could ask the Creator to keep Ken's spirit safe.

As he looked around at the area where he had walked when he was alive, it reminded him of his old friend Derek. It had been astounding to see him flying with his Fae brother, Seth. Oh, Ken had known when they'd been an item that Derek desperately wanted the ability to fly. But…*wings?*

Ken took one last look at Colin Campbell, had no choice but to presume he could hold his own, and wished himself to Derek's side. He ended up in the passenger seat of Derek's vehicle as his ex was heading up the hill above the visitor center at Arches National Park.

Derek saw Ken materialize out of the corner of his eye and barely kept control of the truck as it swerved.

"Whoa, ya startled me!"

Sorry. I'm trying to get more proficient at manifesting where I choose to appear. I didn't think to warn you ahead of time.

"Ken, where the hell have ya been? I figured ya moved on, went into the Light."

Huh. The last thing I remember was showing you where to find Jim Singleton out at Lion's Back after he'd been abducted, and following you back to the shop.

"That was five years ago, in the summer of 2018."

Ken was at a loss. Where could he have been for so long? Then it occurred to him that he existed outside of time; he was dead, after all.

He gave Derek a wry look. *I'm back and I need to tell you something. I just saw Detective Campbell crouched over Jack Crandall's dead body on Mill Creek near the high school.*

"What?!"

I'm surprised you didn't know about it.

"I'm not omniscient, Ken. That would be my grandfather—ya know, God?"

Ken missed Derek's sarcasm in his shock. *What? God is your grandfather? I thought Llyr was Merlin's father. Damn, obviously I've missed some things.* Ken pursed his non-existent lips and continued. *So…does that mean you're related to Satan?*

"Yeah, unfortunately. He's Dad's brother, which makes him my uncle."

That sucks.

"Yeah."

*I hate to tell you this, Derek, but I think your Uncle Satan…*Ken paused, frowning. *That sounds weird, so can you call him Uncle Lucifer? Or Uncle Sam? No, that won't work either, will it? Anyway, I think your uncle discarded Jack's body like a used suit. You might want to warn Merlin that Satan's running around town as a blond, blue-eyed human.*

Derek turned to his old partner with a look of disbelief that quickly became disgust. "Blond and blue-eyed? That evil son of a bitch? Wait, how do ya know that? Did ya actually see him assume human form?"

Ken looked puzzled. *Well, no, but I could see a faint after-image of his transition.* He realized that Derek wasn't paying any attention to the road ahead. *Hey, keep your eyes on the road. I don't want you to end up dead, too!*

Derek rolled his eyes as he turned around to face forward again. "Seriously? Immortal, remember?"

Yeah, I remember. But dying in agony wasn't pleasant, so I'd think you wouldn't want to experience that again, even if you'll come back to life.

They were silent as they both recalled their traumatic deaths after being abducted from the Devils Garden picnic area during Derek's and Em's joint birthday celebration in 2014. Ken remembered when Merlin had resurrected him, setting him on the irrevocable course leading to his second death at Morgana's hands, and current afterlife. *Such as it is,* he thought sourly. But at least he remembered everything again, including his love for Derek, thankfully. The time Ken had spent in Los Angeles had been dull and boring, and he'd always wondered why he'd moved away to begin with. Now he knew that he'd asked Merlin to send him away, and to make him forget his life in Moab.

At least he was a part of Derek's family again, even though he could no longer interact with the other people he'd previously known here.

"I'd better get back to town. Dad may need my help." Derek pulled into the parking lot at the upper end of Park Avenue and pulled out the other side, heading back towards the visitor center. He never noticed as Ken's ghost faded away.

I'll be there soon, Dad. Seth, meet me at The Moab Herbalist in twenty minutes.

Da, I presume ye heard that. I'll see ye shortly.

You presume correctly. I'm at the shop. See you both soon. Morry?

Yes, I hear you. I'll stop by on my way to work—see you in a few.

CHAPTER 29
Moab, Friday, August 18, 2023, Morning

I had been aware of the circumstances from the moment Colin found Jack Crandall's body, and I knew the detective would be checking in with me.

Emily, Arthur, and I were at the shop. We'd come in early to prepare for a large shipment of herbs, which was scheduled to be delivered in midmorning. I hadn't worked on a regular basis for several years, but lately we had been short-staffed and I had to step up and help.

Sarah had taken a temporary leave of absence when my grandson, Aidan, had been born. When she decided to stay home to raise her son there were still enough people tending the shop. But when Lumina left to attend college, Emily, Rae, and Chris had to cover all aspects of the business.

We decided that hiring someone unaware of our inimitable situation would be a grave mistake, so we made do, bringing Cathy Grant in occasionally when the work load called for an extra set of hands. Arthur had worked part time since he'd reached the age of eight, but I'd felt that it was essential for him to concentrate on the home study program I'd created for him, so he had been limited to working only a few hours a week.

I suspected Arthur had volunteered to help us with the shipment today because he felt guilty for moving out of our house so precipitously. His leave-taking didn't surprise me overmuch, since I was aware how desperately he'd wanted to reconnect with Guinevere.

Rae was attending an organic herbs symposium in Salt Lake City to enhance her knowledge and understanding of the craft, and Chris had taken several days off for personal reasons. As a result, it was just the three of us this day.

The scenario seemed to have been divinely inspired for Arthur and me to be present. I couldn't help but assume that my father had wanted us to be here when it was revealed that Sam was in town.

However, I wasn't sure it was smart to include Emily. She was already overwrought from Arthur's transition to adulthood and hasty departure from our home, and she evidently sensed through the powerful bond between us that something else was horribly wrong.

I hated to keep things from her because it always frustrated her so, but I was reluctant for her to discover that my brother, who had possessed Jack's body for more than six years, had finally discarded him. It was a devastating thing to subject her to on top of everything else.

I made the decision to get her out of the shop temporarily, hoping to give her a short respite from the emotional trauma, so I sent her to do errands. She complied reluctantly, frowning at me suspiciously, as she grabbed her purse and went out the back way.

I was surprised she hadn't complained that I was treating her like an employee, when she had been running the business for years. And more importantly, that she was my wife, not my servant.

As soon as I heard the door close, I took a breath and let it out slowly. I knew I would be in the doghouse when she returned.

"I wonder if we should have included her, Dad, since the man was her father," Arthur ventured.

"I know, but I wanted to spare her, at least temporarily."

"Is there anything I can do to help?"

I smiled sadly. "Nothing, I'm afraid, but thanks for offering."

"Are you sure, Dad? I'd be happy to tell her for you."

"No, it's my responsibility to do that."

"Do you think Satan has obtained a new body, or is he walking around in his original form?"

I shrugged. "Who knows? I can't see what he's doing or where he is. He's been able to stay off my radar so far, which is inconvenient, not to mention dangerous."

"It must be frustrating for you, not being able to see your family's current or future actions," Arthur said, tilting his head, his shoulder-length hair shining under the overhead lights.

"Extremely. But it's erratic. Sometimes I can, sometimes I can't." It seemed odd discussing these things with Arthur, although he must have been aware of my difficulties all along. His transition from young teen to mature adult a few days ago still had me bemused. I paused for a moment. "It has definitely been worse since my transformation. I asked Father about it years ago, but his answer was a mighty roll of thunder," I said. What I'd intended to be humorous ended up sounding sarcastic.

Arthur had opened his mouth to comment when Colin barged in.

The bell over the shop door chimed loudly and discordantly as he slammed the door behind him.

"Merlin! The body we found this morning is—"

"My father-in-law, I know. I could see the whole thing in your mind."

Colin blinked. "Oh, right, I forgot about that."

He saw the tall, strongly built young man standing next to me and his jaw dropped. Colin looked at me questioningly and I inclined my head.

"Yes, this is Arthur."

"Hello, Cousin," Arthur greeted him genially, in his mellow voice. His gaze was candid and friendly.

"Hello, Arthur. I saw you a few days ago and you were thirteen years old."

"As I'm sure my father told you, I was always meant to be full-grown in five years. It occurred somewhat sooner than we expected."

Colin noted Arthur's sandy-blond hair, his height and his regal demeanor, and it suddenly clicked exactly who was standing there before him.

"Oh, my God," he whispered as he sank to his knees and bowed low. "*King Arthur.* Your Majesty."

Arthur raised his eyebrows in a way that was reminiscent of my own habitual gesture and smiled crookedly. "It's been centuries since anyone called me that, and while I appreciate it, I'm no longer that king."

As Colin scrambled to his feet, he glanced over at me and muttered, "I don't think I'll ever get used to this."

At that moment, both Derek and Seth teleported into the shop and stood next to Arthur. Despite the tension in the room, I had to stop and admire each of my handsome sons.

Derek looked very little like me, although his eyes had my cat-like slant. He was the shortest of the three men at six feet, but what he lacked in height, he made up in sheer magnetism: he had become an extremely powerful sorcerer, in some ways exceeding Seth's abilities. His haircut was similar to Arthur's and the color was a shade or two darker, closer to light brown than blond.

Seth and Arthur were the same height, six feet three, and both of them resembled me closely. Seth's long, black hair was wavy, not straight, but the major difference between us was that he was Fae; grandson of the King of the Light Court Fae.

Arthur, while physically a mature adult, was still young and relatively inexperienced when it came to managing his magic, although he was rapidly acquiring an aptitude for it. After all, he had gained his basic skills when he was still a child. His stature was impressive—broad-shouldered and muscular—and his natural demeanor was as confident and regal as it had been in Camelot in his past life.

I was pleased with my offspring, and proud of them. But for a fraction of a second, I was unsure how they saw me. Instantly, I shook off that tiny remnant of self-doubt as being unworthy of a god. I received my answer anyway, in three short bursts of emotion from my sons. I practically staggered under the force of their love and regard for me. And surprisingly, I sensed a strong outpouring of sentiment from Colin as well. His feelings for me were far stronger than was warranted by our distant familial connection; they were akin to the feelings of a son, or a brother.

Rather flustered, I hurried to relegate all those exceedingly private revelations to a compartment in my mind to savor later, and returned my attention to the current unpleasant development.

Morry took that moment to burst through the door looking harried. "Sorry, I got here as fast as I could. I had to drop the kids off at my mother-in-law's."

"It's alright, Morry, we—"

I was interrupted as Ken's ghost coalesced next to Colin, looking as corporeal as the rest of us. This was the first I'd seen him in many years, and only I was aware he'd been with my father, who had allowed him to return to this plane to help him resolve some issues. Ken didn't remember he'd been in Heaven, or that he'd begged to come back here to this realm of human life.

Colin, I was trying to communicate with you when you were standing over Jack's body, but I couldn't get through.

"He can't hear you or see you, Ken," I reminded him.

Arthur saw a dark-skinned man about five nine in height, with curly black hair and light blue eyes, who seemed to be as corporeal as the rest of us. He glanced around at everyone else in confusion. "*I* can hear and see you, but you're...not alive. I don't understand. Who are you...and what are you, if you don't mind my asking?"

I'm the ghost of Ken Wilson, Derek's ex. Who are you?

"I'm Arthur Pendragon Ambrosius, Merlin and Emily's son, and—"

Wait a minute! You're King Arthur. That's how Merlin brought you back—your spirit at least—as his son. You must have been born only a few years ago, yet you're already an adult. How does that work? Is it Merlin's magic?

Arthur glared at him in extreme annoyance at the interruption and imperiously continued, "—what do you mean by 'ex'?"

Ken stared at the regal figure, dismayed at the rapid and startling reversal of Arthur's earlier affability.

Derek glanced at Ken briefly and answered for him, "Ex-lover."

Arthur's eyebrows shot up so high that they were hidden by the shaggy hair slanting across his forehead. He stared at Derek. "You're gay? But you're married to Sarah and have a child."

"It's a long story, little brother. And even though it's none of your business, I'm actually bisexual."

Arthur looked at Derek appraisingly and said with unexpected animosity, "By the way, I'm not little anymore. And you should remember that I'm considerably older than you are, and have an exalted status. Brother." He spit the word out as if it was poison.

Derek narrowed his eyes at Arthur's snide tone of voice and choice of words. He nodded curtly, knowing that he would have to address this subject sooner than later. *Exalted status, my ass*, he thought to himself. *And as far as age went, sure, Arthur had been born in AD 438 the first time around and I was born in AD 442. But this time? He's only been walkin' around in his current body for five years, so he's not older than I am. What the hell is wrong with him?*

I could hear Derek's mental commentary and knew that we would need to talk, but at the moment, we had more pressing matters to attend to. "All of this is beside the point! Let's get back to the main topic here. Colin," I snapped. "Tell us about finding Crandall." I already knew, but the others did not.

Stroking his long, dark moustache, Colin started to describe how Jack's body had been found.

I sat down in one of the comfortable chairs in the reading area, and listened and watched as my sons interacted with the detective, reading between the lines and asking intelligent, perceptive questions. Derek passed along Ken's observations of the crime scene to Colin, who pulled out a pocket-sized iPad and made notes.

I thought about Arthur's antagonistic response to Derek's innocent comment, and presumed that there was some hidden significance to it, but I didn't know what it was and couldn't concentrate. I felt myself becoming more and more disassociated from the interaction in front of me, as if I was watching a television show or a play. In the back of my mind, I recognized that this had happened before, but I couldn't remember when, and it didn't seem to matter as voices receded and I started to lose consciousness.

187

Merlin, you're fading, I heard a concerned voice whisper in my mind.

Ken's specter was with me in a circle of light, and then he, too, was gone. There was an all-encompassing Light, and nothing else mattered.

I couldn't be dead, but there was no doubt that I had reverted to a state of pure energy and returned to the realm of the gods. Could God have called me home? If so, why? This shouldn't be happening. I had assured Emily that I wouldn't leave her, so I prayed this wasn't permanent.

A Voice, familiar, powerful and supremely loving, spoke.

My son, you are correct, you should not be here. You have come very close to your goals, but you are nowhere near the final act of my divine play.

Father, I don't know why I'm here. I didn't intentionally choose this, although it's gratifying to be in your Presence.

It is clear that your troublesome brother has engineered this detour for you, so allow me to send you back where you belong. However, before I do so, be aware that you will need to take drastic measures to overcome his influence. Do not hesitate to do what you need to do. He has always been a problem child, I must admit, and he is overdue for an attitude adjustment...

I drifted in an eternal state while God paused, thinking his infinite thoughts. I waited patiently for what might have been a fraction of a second or a hundred years for him to continue.

You are dear to me, my son, and I have always been proud of you. I will come to Moab and visit you and your family one of these days... Alright, back you go!

I was abruptly conscious of being surrounded by familiar faces, all staring at me with concern. I was still sitting in the reading area, the center of attention. Since the shop was devoid of customers, I presumed that it was still closed and the front door locked to prevent outsiders from stumbling into an unexplainable situation. How long I had been away?

"Dad, you were just...gone. Body and all," Derek said.

"Are you okay?" Arthur asked just as Colin said, "Merlin?" and Seth said, "Da?"

I was still slightly dazed by my trip to the god realm. "My brother somehow sent me home."

"Ya mean Satan?" Derek asked.

"Yes, who else?"

Colin peered at me in confusion. "Home, what do you mean home?"

"The realm of the gods. Or you may call it the Other World, or Heaven."

"*What?*"

"Yes, and Father has informed me that he is coming to Moab for a visit."

"Fath…? You mean *God?*" Colin's voice rose several octaves. "God *himself* is coming to visit? Oh, crap," he whispered. His brow wrinkled in confusion. "But how could he do that?"

"We come to this realm in human form, so that is what my father will do. And I know for a fact that he has been to Moab several times in the past few years, manifesting as an old man, with green eyes like mine. He even came into the shop as a customer, although at the time I didn't recognize him. That was before I remembered the real truth regarding my origins.

"But back to the details of my unforeseen journey. Satan apparently manipulated me into reverting to my original state of pure energy and returning home. He could therefore manipulate any of us, including kidnapping Arthur, or any of your children. This is absolutely unacceptable and drastic measures must be taken. We need to locate him without delay and—"

"Kill the bloody bastard?" Seth snarled, interrupting me.

"Killing Sam would only be temporary. He is immortal, after all. But actually, that might be best as he'd be forced home, in the form of energy if his body is destroyed, and it would be awhile before he could regenerate."

"You can't be serious!" Emily exclaimed as she carried numerous packages in through the back room. "You're all standing here, including two men sworn to uphold the law, contemplating cold-blooded murder?" She bristled with outrage.

We were all taken aback as we stared at her and at each other. She was reacting as if Satan was an ordinary human. It was apparent she didn't remember a discussion we had years ago in which she and Derek had offered to help me destroy Beli. Was she truly unaware of who we were talking about?

"Yes, we're serious," six of us said in unison.

Em's eyes widened in shock, giving each one of us a withering glare to convey her vast disappointment in our conduct.

"Mom, there are developments you're not yet aware of that have prompted us to make this onerous decision." Arthur inserted smoothly, using the diplomacy he'd learned as the King of Camelot to try and diffuse the difficult conversation.

189

"Oh, and what developments are those? Enlighten me, please." She put her packages on the counter and put her hands on her hips in a disdainful manner.

"Well, uh..." Arthur turned to me for help.

Instead of answering her question, I decided to distract Emily with the information I had previous withheld, since for some reason she wasn't grasping the reality of the situation. I stood up and walked swiftly to her, pulling her into my arms.

"My dear, I'm afraid there's bad news," I said gently.

Emily jerked back and looked around frantically, noting who was present and who wasn't. "Is it my mom? Or Lumina? Or, God forbid, one of the children?" Em was especially attached to our youngest grandchild and our two great-grandchildren.

I cupped her face between my palms, looked into her frightened eyes, and said calmly, "No, Em, your mom is fine, as are Lumina and the kids. It's your dad. I regret to tell you this, but he's dead. Colin found his body this morning over by the high school. I'm so sorry, my love."

She stared at me uncomprehendingly. Her eyes rolled back in her head, and she fainted in my arms.

Without delay, I transported her to the small apartment above the shop and placed her on the old afghan covering the mattress. We used this space infrequently and it was stuffy and overly warm. I created a fresh, cool breeze that lowered the room temperature and caressed Em's face. Her eyes fluttered open and she looked around in confusion.

"What are we doing up here?" She stared up at the ceiling and the walls. "We really need to paint this room." Her gaze came back to me and she frowned uncomprehendingly. "What's going on?

I sat down next to her on the bed and stroked her hair. "You collapsed when I informed you of your father's death. I figured you'd want a few moments of privacy."

She closed her eyes and exhaled quietly. A tear trickled down her cheek and she flicked it away impatiently. "I've suspected for years that Satan had possessed Dad, and that his soul must be long gone. But I didn't want to believe it." She sat up and turned to lay her head on my shoulder.

I put my arms around her and held her quietly. I was reluctant to address this particular subject. "Em, I'm concerned about the way you reacted when we were discussing options for dealing with my brother. He's not human and can't be treated as if he is. And he can't be killed permanently anyway—he's too powerful for that. So we need to destroy his human form to get him out of this realm, as I did with Beli years ago. You didn't object to my actions then, in fact, you were so angry with him that you wanted to help me."

"Honestly, I don't know why I reacted that way today." She pulled away from me and got to her feet, pacing back and forth in agitation. "It's as if something is blocked in my mind, or covered up—it's hard to describe it. Remember something similar happened before, when I returned to Moab after the accident in Mesa Verde National Park?"

"I do indeed." When our relationship was in its early stages, Emily had been working for the National Park Service and had been transferred temporarily to Mesa Verde after a ranger there had been injured in a vehicular accident. Then, prior to her anticipated return to Moab, she had been involved in an analogous accident, resulting in head trauma and amnesia. She hadn't remembered me, or our relationship, even after she returned home, and it turned out that a supernatural entity had used black magic to block her memory and trap her soul.

I reviewed Arthur's unusual response to Derek's comment and what had happened with Emily, comparing those occurrences with the evil intent inherent in what had been done to her years ago. I came up with a startling hypothesis and I didn't like it one bit. Considering I was at full god status, the fact that I had been unaware of Satan infiltrating my family while Emily was pregnant left me horrified—and utterly furious with my father for allowing it to happen, no matter what his overall plan entailed. In addition, I wasn't impressed with the way Portunus had performed his "guard duty" since he hadn't even noticed anything wrong.

As I brought my fury under control and my common sense reestablished itself, I knew that ideally I needed to discuss my conclusion with certain members of my family. But it would be difficult to do so without including Arthur, and he, even unwittingly, was part of the problem. Even though I was tempted to do so, confronting my father wasn't necessary, since he had given me carte blanche to contend with my brother.

Apparently, Sam had established a connection with several members of my family that none of us were aware of, which acted as some sort of psychic probe or sensor. I needed to plan my actions so as not to alert him that I was aware of his involvement. I doubted such a thing could actually transmit our conversations, or we would have had feedback of some sort long before this. I could easily root out and destroy a simple spell, but this was an act of dark sorcery, akin to the evil that had been embedded in Morry's DNA. Removing that evil from him had taken all of our combined magic, and I anticipated this might take a comparable effort.

I decided it would be best to keep this information to myself for the time being. The damage had been done years ago and one more day wouldn't make any difference.

* * *

Emily watched her husband as he focused inside, attempting to make sense of recent events and to decide how best to deal with all the changes that had beset them. He was always so hard on himself, thinking he should have better control over their circumstances. Her heart ached for him. Merlin was not omniscient, and yet he berated himself for things over which he had no control.

She closed her eyes and gave a mental sigh. She would need to plan some kind of service for her dad, and arrange the burial. She couldn't imagine her mom would want to do it, since Rae had been divorced from Jack Crandall for years. Prior to that, she had suffered years of mental and verbal abuse until she had left him and come to live with them in Moab.

Maybe it was for the best that Satan finally let him go. Her dad's soul had been consumed many years ago and now it was time to lay his mortal remains to rest.

She understood that having a service would be very awkward, since they were all aware of who had been in control of his body for years. No, funerals and burials were for the living and none of them needed the reminder.

She would discuss it with her mother, but Emily felt the best way to handle it would be for Merlin to cremate what was left of Jack Crandall and release his ashes to the wind.

CHAPTER 30
Moab, Saturday, August 19, 2023, Between 2:00
AM and Dawn

Derek had difficulty getting the morning's events out of his head. He glanced at the clock on the bedside table—yesterday morning really, since it was past midnight.

The first thing that had upset him was discovering that Satan had cast aside Jack Crandall's body and was at large, causing an unknown amount of chaos in town. Second, Arthur's hostile response to being called "little brother," an endearment Derek had used in the past, and the imperious reference to his "exalted status," had annoyed Derek. In addition, Merlin's unexpected journey to the god realm—not to mention his announcement that God planned to visit in the near future —was alarming and would have been more than enough for one day.

But Emily's atypical reaction to their plans to do away with Satan was the last straw. Something was seriously wrong and Derek wondered why Merlin hadn't figured it out. Or he had and for some reason couldn't share it with him yet.

So it wasn't surprising that sleep had eluded him. In fact, Derek had been tossing and turning for hours. Sarah finally asked him to relocate to the guest room because he was keeping her awake, which didn't make him happy either.

He reluctantly abandoned their comfortable king-size bed, grabbed a lightweight blanket from the closet and left the bedroom, detouring for a moment to check on his son.

Aidan was sleeping soundly, as usual, so Derek backed out of the child's room and closed the door quietly. God, he loved that little boy. It was such a pleasure to be involved in his son's life as he grew up, to experience all the details he'd missed with Morry. He was actually glad his four-year-old had exhibited only a limited number of magical traits at this point—there was still plenty of time for him to explore his heritage and develop his abilities. Derek hadn't seen any evidence of

Aodh's presence since the god had communicated with them telepathically at the boy's birth. And that was fine with him.

Derek stood in the dark hallway and debated whether he should lie down and try to sleep. He decided he was too wound up and that he'd fly for a while. He walked into the living room and tossed the now superfluous blanket on the sofa, conjuring up clothing. He mulled it over for a moment and decided he didn't need shoes; after all, he would be flying, not taking a hike. It was pretty late, but he hoped Seth was still awake—he wanted to discuss what had happened at the shop.

I'm awake, Derek. And I have something tae tell ye, as weel. Where would ye like tae meet, Landscape Arch?

Oh, hell, no. Anywhere but there—too many memories, mostly bad. Why don't I teleport to your place and we can decide?

Aye, that works for me. Chris sleeps verra deeply, sae we'll no' wake her.

Derek materialized in their front room as Seth walked in, his entire being glowing. "Whoa, ya look happy, did ya just have sex?"

Seth laughed out loud. "Earlier, aye, but there's another reason for ma happiness. Let's go, lad, and I'll tell ye all aboot it." He teleported outside and shot into the sky, pristine white wings pumping rhythmically as he aimed for the stars.

Derek followed him and quickly unfurled his own wings, flapping them briskly to hold himself in one place while he scanned the area with his senses to make sure they hadn't been observed. According to guidelines Merlin had established regarding use of magic around mortals, they should have teleported up to the Rim and taken off from there, since even at this hour there were still a few tourists wandering around. But Seth seemed oblivious to everything except whatever had elevated his mood. Fortunately, it was nearly three in the morning and no one had seen them. It didn't hurt that the waxing crescent moon yielded only a trivial amount of illumination. Relieved, Derek hurried to catch up.

As the two brothers flew side by side, chatting aimlessly, the susurrus of air through their feathers was a constant background to their conversation. They talked about the weather, and shared the feeling of exhilaration that surged through them while soaring above the land. Finally, Seth couldn't wait any longer and blurted out his news.

"Chris and I are getting marrit, in the human way, verra soon. Are ye okay with that, Brother?" He glanced at the other man, his Fae eyes able to read Derek's expression in the dim light.

Derek was quiet for a moment before answering. "I guess it

shouldn't surprise me, since ya'll have been livin' together for years, but it never occurred to me that a Fae prince would want to marry a human."

They had arrived at Delicate Arch and settled on top of the iconic red rock formation before Seth answered. With a vaguely worried look on his face, he paused, and said, "I, uh, turned her."

Derek stiffened. "Ya did *what*?"

"I turned her, made her Fae."

"I don't understand. How in hell did ya do that? And why?"

"I bit her and injected a special venom from ma glands during an ancient Fae ritual tae claim her as ma mate."

"So, ya *bit* her, like a vampire?" Derek asked with a snicker, sure that his brother had to be joking.

Seth hesitated for a few moments, hoping what he was about to do wouldn't shock Derek. He opened his mouth and allowed his long sharp fangs to drop down, simultaneously releasing a natural bioluminescent substance in his saliva that made them glow in the dark.

Derek's amusement disappeared and he gaped in astonishment. "Fuck, ya *are* a vampire!"

Seth retracted his fangs, since it was difficult to talk around them. "No' as yer tales describe, although in ancient times we did drink blood. The legends began centuries ago when one of ma kind was seen with his fangs exposed, just as someone must've seen a Fae flying and thought he saw an angel. Och, who kens with humans?"

Derek sat staring across the dark landscape of the park, silently processing Seth's announcement. The gritty surface of the sandstone stuck to the seat of his jeans as he shifted position. He wasn't sure how he felt about Chris becoming Fae and mating with his brother. Did she ask to be changed or did Seth get caught up in their lovemaking, triggering a Fae mating ritual that had been hidden in his subconscious? Chris was Derek's ex-wife and his friend and he still felt somewhat responsible for her. Becoming Fae would completely alter her life and how she viewed the world. Did this mean she'd leave him behind forever? Abruptly, his perspective shifted, and it dawned on him that this was how she felt when he revealed *his* new reality—that he wasn't totally human, he was a sorcerer and an immortal demigod. As difficult as it was, he needed to let go and trust her to choose her own path.

He turned back to Seth, who had been quietly waiting for his brother come to terms with his revelation. "Has she completed the transition? Is she like you? I mean, the ears, the eyes, the wings? Is she immortal?"

Seth looked up at the glittering stars as if staring into eternity. "Aye, she's one of the Fae now, and ma princess. We'll be traveling tae Scotland soon and go afore the High Council of Elders, for they'll have sensed her transition from mortal human tae immortal Fae. Such a thing hasna happened for thousands o' years.

"I love her, and she's pregnant with ma child."

Derek felt a surge of compassion and understanding. He knew how it felt when he had discovered that his own wife was carrying his child. It changed everything.

"I wish you and Chris all the best, Seth. And congratulations on your baby."

"Thanks, *mo bràthair*," Seth said softly, more relieved than he wanted to admit that Derek accepted the situation. "Tell me what's bothering ye the noo. Is it what happened at the shop yesterday?"

"Yeah, the whole thing reeked of Satan. And I guess I was hurt that Arthur was such an asshole to me. When I met him in Camelot, I idolized him, pledged my loyalty to him. When he came back as Dad's son, our brother, I figured he'd grow up to be the same man he was in the fifth century. He's not."

"'Tis true, he's physically a different person. But his soul, what made him a decent man, should be the same as it was in his past life. I didna ken him in those days; I was young and I met him only once. But I kent his reputation." Seth clapped Derek's shoulder. "I'll no' say ye shouldna let it bother ye, but I think ye need tae talk tae Da afore ye give up on Arthur. Nay doubt Satan's got a hand in this, and Da willna sit idle and let him have his way."

"You're right. I'll get together with Dad and we'll figure somethin' out, we always do. Thanks, Seth," Derek said gratefully. He stretched and looked around, noticing that the sky was growing light in the east. "We'd better get back before our women wake up and wonder where the hell we are."

"Ye're right, 'tis getting on tae dawn. Let's go."

Both men got to their feet and leaped off of Delicate Arch, winging their way back toward the lights of Moab and their respective homes.

CHAPTER 31
Moab, Saturday, August 19, 2023, Morning

Seth rematerialized in their bedroom and stood at the head of the bed, watching his mate sleep as the room gradually lightened with the dawn. His mate. For a brief moment, he couldn't believe it and extended his senses out to her, into her, to reassure himself. When her scent, that of a mated female Fae, caressed his nostrils he instantly hardened.

He willed his clothing gone and slipped sinuously onto the bed next to her, pulling her toward him.

She blinked sleepily. "Hmm, what time is it?"

"Time tae make love, *mo leannan.*"

They were on their sides facing each other, their wings folded up snug to their backs. Seth raised Chris's leg, resting it on his hip, and slid inside her. She inhaled with a moan and pushing against him, welcomed him into her body.

Since he had made her like him, she'd been easy to arouse and wanted sex as frequently as he did. It was embarrassing for her. She only had to think about him to be wet and ready for him.

Seth knew this and it made him want her all the more. He surged into her unrestrainedly and they both climaxed. They clung together afterwards, with him still buried inside her, and nuzzled each other's necks.

"God, I love you so much. Do you know I used to have fantasies about it? That some miracle would happen and you'd love me enough to stay with me forever?" Chris whispered.

He did know. "Weel, ye got yer wish, aye?" he said tenderly. He pulled back a little so he could touch her belly, sensing the tiny being growing inside her.

"She'll be beautiful like her mother, with golden hair and hazel eyes," he murmured.

"You can tell the baby is a girl?"

"Oh, aye, 'tis a little girl growing inside ye."

Chris started to cry and Seth kissed her tears away. Still inside her, he moved, stroking her, calming her, until they both started breathing hard again. He thrust rhythmically, fast and deep. When they came, it was a sweet, warm rush and they finally relaxed, falling asleep still connected, their breath intermingling.

* * *

Later that morning, after they had showered and were back in the bedroom getting dressed, Chris decided she needed to ask about something that had been worrying her. She was staring at herself in the mirror, critically examining all the changes in her outward aspect.

"Seth, honey, I need to go back to work soon. How in the world do I keep people from seeing all these changes in my appearance?"

"Weel, ye create a glamour this way..." His Fae attributes disappeared and he looked human. He winked at her.

She made a face at him. "Seriously? I've seen you with that glamour dozens of times. What I want to know is *how* you do it."

Seth tilted his head in that inhuman way that always gave her goosebumps and said patiently, "I use magic, *mo chridh*, and ye'll be doing it yersel' when ye want tae hide yer eyes and wings. Look inside and ye'll find it. I wouldna worry overmuch aboot yer ears. Yer hair'll cover them." He ran his slender fingers through her long hair and draped it as he had described.

Over the years Chris and Seth had been together, she had let her hair grow until it was down to her waist. In the past, she'd always kept it fairly short, shoulder length, but once Seth had come into her life and he'd expressed a preference for long hair, she'd done no more than trim it occasionally.

She took a deep breath, let it out slowly, and focused her attention inside for the first time since he had turned her. What she saw amazed her: Light, color, sound...magic. Her very essence was composed of magic. So how was she to find which "button" to push to create a glamour?

Seth laughed. "Chris, there's no' a button. Remember what ye looked like as a human woman and focus on that memory. The magic will manifest itself. Open yer eyes, lass, and see yersel' in the mirror as ye wish tae be seen."

She opened her eyes and stared at the image she'd seen all her life: Chris Colburn, human.

She reached up over her shoulder and touched her new wings, but she couldn't see them. She turned to Seth and grinned widely.

He grinned back. "Ye see, we Fae—our species of Fae, that is—are typically no' shapeshifters, even though we can physically change our shapes if we must. But we are masters of illusion.

"Ye need tae give Em a call and tell her ye're ready tae get back tae work. She, Da, and Derek ken what ye are, and that we're mated, but no one else does. So, it's up tae ye tae announce it—if ye wish tae do sae." He raised his eyebrows questioningly and stroked a strand of her silky hair behind one pointed ear.

"Oh, I definitely want to announce it to everyone. I'm so proud you chose me and I'm pregnant with your child." She gazed at him with such smoldering hot love that he almost lost it.

He pressed up against her and whispered, "Ye'd better make the call or we'll end up back in bed, *mo chridhe*."

Chris saw—and felt—the evidence of his desire and nearly tackled him to the floor, wanting to take that delicious erection into her body again.

She closed her eyes and took a shaky breath. "Oh, God, I want you so badly I can't stand it."

"Aye, I ken it, but we canna spend all day making love."

"How can I want you so much when we've had sex at least a dozen times in the past twenty-four hours?"

He chuckled. "We're newly mated and you're with child. And Fae are naturally sexual, so there ye are. Ye can see how difficult it was for me tae hold back ma lust when ye were human, lass."

Chris stared at him until finally she had to walk away. She grabbed her phone off the bedside table and scurried into the kitchen to make the call to The Moab Herbalist.

She kept having to distract herself from thinking of Seth's body covering hers and—

"The Moab Herbalist, Emily speaking."

She took a deep breath and let it out. "Hi, Em, it's Chris. I wanted you to know I'm ready to come back to work."

"Are you absolutely sure?" Em sounded doubtful.

"Oh, yes, I feel fabulous."

"Chris, you weren't sick—you literally changed species, human to Fae."

"Em, believe me, I'm aware of that," she said dryly as she scratched her pointed right ear and felt the weight of her wings on her upper back.

"Okay, if you're sure."

"I am. I can even use magic to create a glamour, so people won't see what I look like."

"That's fantastic, Chris, and essential, since we can't have you showing up to work with Fae eyes and wings. Oh, and don't worry about your ears—just cover 'em up with your hair like Lumina and I do."

"That's what Seth told me."

"By the way, we're having a family gathering at Swanny Park tomorrow afternoon, and you and Seth are invited, naturally. I'm surprised he didn't tell you."

Chris cleared her throat. "We've been a little, shall we say, preoccupied the past few days."

"Ahh, of course you have. Anyway, the shop is closed tomorrow, so come to work on Monday morning at nine, okay?"

"Great, Em, thanks. I'll plan on it. And we'll see you tomorrow at the park."

"Yes, see you tomorrow…Daughter," Em replied softly.

CHAPTER 32
Moab, Sunday, August 20, 2023

Sam zipped up his fly and stepped over to the washbowl. Human bodies were a real pain in the ass, even temporary ones. As he washed his hands and dried them with a paper towel, he caught a glimpse of himself in the mirror. A tall, blond stranger, an Adonis, with classically aristocratic features and piercing topaz-blue eyes stared back at him. For a moment, he preened. He certainly was a handsome devil. He scowled. Why the hell *had* he decided to manifest his own human appearance? It took a great deal of energy to maintain this form—it would have been much easier to possess some other evil-minded lowlife after Jack's body died.

Jack Crandall hadn't been the only game in town when he'd possessed him, but he'd been the easiest to take over. And as a bonus, it had fucked with Emily's and her mother's minds, big-time. He'd enjoyed that immensely.

Sam grinned cruelly. Jack had been so full of hate it had poisoned his being, so he'd been the perfect host. Too bad possessing him had eventually eaten him up on the inside. Oh, well, the old bastard had been useful for many years. Except for sex, and that hadn't been a priority anyway.

He started to exit the men's room at the Moab Information Center and a young guy sidestepped him hurriedly, giving him a fearful look as they passed each other in the doorway. Sam knew he exuded a powerful aura of darkness that some mortals were more sensitive to than others were. He'd have to put a damper on it, though, or his brother and family would begin to sense a disturbance in town, and that was the last thing he wanted to happen. Yet.

He laughed out loud as he recalled the ease with which he'd interfered with Merlin's delectable wife and unborn child years ago, with none of them the wiser.

Soon, he would reap what he had sown.

They were weak, all of them. Even when Myrddin Emrys had transitioned, and several of his brothers had shown up for the big event, none of them had sensed his awareness of it.

Stupid. How could they be that careless?

As he strode aggressively along the crowded downtown sidewalk, considering what kind of mayhem to instigate next, he scarcely noticed people hastily getting out of his way, as if the aura surrounding him screamed, "Don't touch me!"

That afternoon, Sam teleported over to Swanny Park, drawn against his will to the gathering of Merlin's clan. Incorporeal, he watched as his brother's progeny and their mates socialized while their children enjoyed the playground. Their revoltingly sweet behavior towards each other made him want to puke.

What he really desired was to make them as miserable as he was. After all, what in hell was there to be so all-fired enthusiastic about? His relatives had females to bed on a regular basis, but he wouldn't want to be permanently attached to any of his sexual partners. Use, abuse and discard was his motto, and in his opinion, the only option.

* * *

I noticed Derek's agitation. He glanced at Seth, who seemed as uncomfortable as he was, protectively keeping Chris close to his side.

Somethin's wrong. Do ya'll feel it? Derek broadcast to me, Morry, and his brothers telepathically. His Southern drawl was thick today, which happened when he was under stress.

I waited to speak until they had all responded. I already knew the source of the problem and I wanted to see if they'd figured it out.

There's someone close by that has a verra dark aura, tae be sure. Seth cut his eyes at Arthur, who nodded surreptitiously.

"I'm positive that there's someone here in the park with us using a powerful spell to disguise himself. It's Satan, I'd wager."

"I agree—it has to be him. There's a feeling of both familiarity and overwhelming evil here, and it's not one of us, that's for sure. So who else could it be?" Morry ventured.

"You're all correct, it's Sam. Without our knowledge, he's been in the area for years, watching us." I knew now that he had done something to affect Emily and Arthur while she was pregnant. I had been so wrapped up in my transition, and in the wonder of knowing the child Em carried was truly Arthur, that I had naively presumed nothing could touch them. I was wrong. Somehow, at some point, my devastatingly evil brother had infected them both, but Arthur was the main target. It had started manifesting recently as distrust, resulting in a growing disrespect and disregard for what I stood for and aspired to. I experienced again the rage I had felt a few days ago, directing a great deal of it at myself. Emily knew how I felt, but I hadn't discussed the issue with anyone else yet. Arthur had already started distancing himself from the family and particularly from me. The others might not have noticed it yet since it was subtle—but I could sense it, and it wounded me to my very soul.

I felt strongly that my father should have informed me of Sam's presence from the very beginning, but ultimately, it was my fault that Sam had gotten past my defenses. I had been complacent, and worse than that, negligent. And I was afraid my family would pay the price.

Everybody go home without delay! The urgency of my thought galvanized us all into action and we grabbed our families and disappeared simultaneously.

* * *

Shit! Myrddin Emrys finally figured it out, at least in part, Sam thought, disgusted. The other day, after he'd forced his brother to leave this realm and return to Heaven, he'd congratulated himself on getting rid of one fly in the ointment, at least for now. Then their father had interfered and sent Merlin back, along with instructions that would be most detrimental to Sam if Merlin caught him.

He returned to his sparsely furnished apartment to brood. Hours later, he decided he needed a change of scenery, and the best bet was to check out the bars. Not for the alcohol, since he couldn't get drunk, but for sexual gratification. His human body, despite being a temporary construct, was experiencing the urge to mate—in the vernacular of this time and place, he was horny, and figured he could find a willing female in a place where humans gathered.

He walked into Moody's Tavern and slid onto an empty stool between two women who appeared to be looking for sexual partners, as they each reacted to his presence with a prodigious release of pheromones. He breathed in and felt his cock harden. It was auspicious that he'd worn loose pants and not those skin-tight denim jeans so popular in America. Becoming aroused now was premature, as he wanted to have a few drinks first, but it was gratifying to know that his physical form responded appropriately to human females.

He had finished his second beer when the woman on his left, pretty but not as young as he preferred, leaned over and touched his arm.

"Hey, baby, what's your name?" she asked in a low, sultry voice, her red-tinted lips unnaturally pouty.

He examined her for a moment, as if she was a bug under a microscope, mentally shrugged and responded gruffly, "Call me Sam."

"Well, Sam, I'm ready to call it a night. How about a drink at my place?"

Why not, he thought. He knew she only wanted him for sex, and after a thousand years of celibacy, he was more than ready for a good, sweaty fuck.

He escorted her home, which ended up being close by, a couple of blocks from Main Street, and scowled when he saw the dump she lived in. He tended to be fastidious, so he was disgusted by her less than sanitary living arrangements. But since he was simply there to use her body, he forced himself to ignore the filth and disorder. Sam followed behind her as she sashayed into the kitchen to pour shots of cheap bourbon into glasses of dubious cleanliness. He curled his lip in distaste, but drank it anyway. He certainly couldn't catch any diseases in this realm. She winked at him as she sipped her drink slowly, relishing every drop.

He reached the end of his patience. He put the glass down and ripped her blouse open, reaching with both hands to roughly fondle her breasts through her lacy bra.

"What the hell?" she cried, and slapped his face, hard.

As fast as a snake striking, he grabbed her hand and twisted it savagely. "I wouldn't do that if I were you," he said in a deep, gravelly voice.

She giggled, assuming his tough guy act was just that—an act. She purred, "You're in charge, Sam. Let's go in my bedroom and get naked. I might like it rough." She growled melodramatically and giggled.

He gave her a look that should have warned her she was messing with the wrong guy. The amount of alcohol she'd consumed had impaired her judgment, fatally.

Sam shoved her into the bedroom, noting the dirty sheets on the unmade bed. He decided he didn't care, as he hadn't planned to sleep in it. And the sheets would be much, much dirtier when he was finished with her.

He was considerably taller and heavier than she was, so it would be easy to intimidate her. Holding her wrists, he willed their clothing gone. She was so drunk she didn't even notice. Magnificently naked, he threw her down on the bed, pinning her beneath him. His cock rested in the valley between her legs and his muscular chest was cushioned against her plump breasts. The feel of her warm, soft flesh excited him, and being a selfish bastard, he didn't bother with foreplay. For one thing, he had no desire to kiss her—her breath was sour and stale—but he did want to fuck her, hard.

As if she sensed his less than gentlemanly intentions, she struggled and whimpered, which merely aroused him further and his cock throbbed in anticipation. He poked a finger into her and discovered that she was wet enough, so he pushed forcefully inside her. She squealed in protest at his brutality, which prompted him to pump even harder.

He'd forgotten how satisfying it was to bury his cock in a woman's tight heat, holding her down as he dominated her. He was tired of her whining, so he covered her mouth with his large cruel hand and rammed into her violently until he climaxed. He relaxed fully, causing her to struggle in protest of the considerable weight bearing down on her. He grinned evilly as she grew increasingly frantic to take a breath, gouging him with her long sharp fingernails, until finally she quit moving.

Sam got up in a leisurely fashion, unconcerned that he had killed her. He magically healed the bleeding furrows on his face and neck, conjured clean garments and new footwear and left the soiled items where they lay. He wasn't concerned about leaving fingerprints or DNA —he didn't have either. As he disappeared, his maniacal laughter filled the room.

CHAPTER 33
Moab, Monday, August 21, 2023

Colin was called out to the crime scene around four o'clock in the morning.

He'd been sleeping soundly, having a sweet dream of making love to an attractive blond woman who happened to resemble Cathy Grant, when the shrill ringtone he'd chosen for emergency calls rudely awakened him. He spoke briefly with the Chief, and dragged his carcass out of bed. He showered hurriedly, dressed in his usual business casual clothing, and slugged down an energy drink before leaving the house.

Fortunately, it wasn't far to the scene and he always carried a field kit in his vehicle containing everything he needed for an investigation: gloves, booties, Luminol, report forms, yellow crime scene tape, measuring devices, and a professional-grade camera.

In the past, he had worked crime scenes unofficially, but over the years, he had become so proficient that he was now the primary crime scene investigator in addition to his regular job. He didn't mind it, but he wished he was a better photographer. Colin admitted to himself that he should have Owen accompany him on after-hours emergency calls. The man had proven himself to be invaluable since he'd come on board —had it only been three days ago?—and Colin wasn't sure why he was keeping him at arm's length. No, that wasn't true. He knew exactly why —he didn't want Owen to see him using magic, which he had been doing increasingly often of late.

He focused once again on the scene. The victim's roommate had come home around three thirty and noticed that her friend's light was still on. She'd called out softly and opened the bedroom door, discovering the body. The roommate had screamed hysterically until a neighbor had called dispatch, who had notified the Chief of Police. Having his own night sleep rudely interrupted, Chief Baker hadn't had any qualms about ruining someone else's, so he assigned the case to Campbell.

The victim had apparently engaged in what at first appeared to be consensual sex with an unknown male. The bedclothes were disturbed, as if the victim had struggled with her sexual partner, but the body had no noticeable wounds, and there was no sign of a murder weapon. Initially, Colin figured it had been rough sex, but was persuaded otherwise when he noted the bloody skin under her fingernails. She had apparently tried to fight off her attacker, but perhaps he had been much larger than she was and he had suffocated her. Had he done so intentionally? If so, it was murder. If not, why had he left the scene? The odd thing was that there was a pile of men's clothing, as well as a pair of shoes, on the floor. Had he walked out of her apartment naked and barefoot? Didn't seem likely, but Colin would have an officer go door to door and talk to the neighbors as soon as it was feasible to do so, which was standard procedure anyway.

He bagged her hands to preserve the trace evidence, and thought, *Screw standard procedure.* He had used his magic in conjunction with his intuition before at crime scenes and these circumstances definitely warranted it, so he closed his eyes and extended his senses out into the room. He quickly discovered a residue of magical energy. It was apparent that the guy had conjured clean clothing—and shoes—and teleported away from the scene of the crime.

Colin shook his head in frustration. It was clear the man had known there would be no recognizable DNA on the clothing—thus there wouldn't be a problem leaving it behind. He wasn't human, consequently the skin cells collected from under the victim's fingernails wouldn't contain anything remotely recognizable.

Campbell paused for a moment as he realized his own DNA might not be recognizably human anymore either. He shook off a feeling of uneasiness and got back on track. When he felt the undeniable sense of evil left behind by the perpetrator he came to an inescapable conclusion, one that he could never include in his report.

He closed his eyes and sighed. Colin knew, without a shadow of a doubt, who had committed this rape and murder.

Crap. He'd still have to follow procedure, even though he knew it wouldn't accomplish anything. He sent a thought out to Merlin. Even though he couldn't initiate telepathic communication with him, Merlin would hear him anyway.

He was leaving the victim's apartment when he heard a familiar voice in his head.

Thanks for contacting me. It helps that you keep me apprised of Sam's activities since I can't sense him myself.

The jolt of pleasure he felt at Merlin's praise had him grinning like a fool. *You're most welcome, Uncle. Happy to help,* he responded silently, as if it was the most natural thing in the world to be conversing with someone in his head. Over the course of time, it was becoming just that.

* * *

I was leaning on the counter in my kitchen, drinking a cup of coffee, when I felt Colin's pleasure and feeling of belonging wash over me, and I marveled at the way the man had become an integral part of my life and family. It had been over four years since Lumina had mated with Josh—and two years since they'd married thus merging our two families —but there was a persistent sense of connection between Colin and me that was more than being in-laws. I loved the man and I knew without a shadow of a doubt that he felt that way about me. He couldn't be my brother or my son, and yet the feeling persisted that he was.

And there was that uncanny resemblance between Colin and Beli. I still had never gotten an answer from my father in regards to Colin's origins, and Beli seemed no more interested in Colin than as a distant relative, but I was convinced he was Beli's son.

I needed to focus on things that were more important, and yet it stuck in my mind, as irritating as a sliver in my finger that had broken off below the surface of the skin.

Llyr, Brother, I need help with something.

Hey, Bro, how've you been? Long time no see. What can I do you for?

I can't seem to get over the fact that Colin means more to me than an extremely distant relation.

I'm not supposed to say, but let me remind you that you felt much the same way about Derek, and he turned out to be your son—not that I'm saying Colin's your son, mind you, nooo—but, you know, keep an open mind. Heh, heh. And don't tell Father that I told you or I'll be in a world of hurt.

I chuckled and shook my head. My brother was a character, always had been, even when he'd been playing the part of my father when I didn't remember who I was. I thought, *What if he's serious?*

But how could Colin be my son? I'd never had sex with anyone besides Nimue in my youth, Seth's mother in the Fae realm in the fifth century, and Em in the current time. Or had I and didn't remember it? And if he was my son, it meant my daughter had mated with her own nephew, and that was unthinkable. Besides, she would have sensed it when she and Josh Saw each other.

I poured myself another cup of coffee and decided I needed to See Colin again. Somehow, I had missed something the first time around.

* * *

Cathy Grant had had a hard day at work. All she wanted was to have a nice, quiet, solitary drink and go home to a hot shower and her soft bed.

She accomplished part of that goal when the bartender at Moody's set a strawberry daiquiri in front of her and she'd taken her first delightful swallow of icy, fruity decadence. She savored the flavor on her tongue, feeling some of the tension release from her overworked arm and shoulder muscles. She rubbed a particularly sore spot on her right bicep. If she'd known how physically demanding her job at the T-shirt and gift shop would be, she would never have taken it. She'd been there for over a year and it hadn't gotten any easier. And folding innumerable sweatshirts day after day wasn't exactly rocket science, so her brain was getting sluggish.

Cathy had occasionally filled in at The Moab Herbalist when needed and enjoyed the work. Emily had been after her for years to come to work full time, since hiring someone who was aware of the magical nature of the family was preferable to hiring someone entirely clueless. She nodded to herself. She would accept Em's offer.

At that point in her thought process, a big man slid onto the stool next to her and she caught a whiff of familiar cologne. "I'd be glad to massage those sore muscles for you, if you'd let me, Cathy."

She groaned silently. Damn it, she wished he would stop bothering her!

"I don't think so, Colin," she said flatly.

He sighed and turned to order a drink from the bartender, who had been loitering nearby. Colin's muscular shoulders, encased in a light blue button-down long-sleeved shirt, slumped dejectedly.

Cathy's irritation left her as quickly as it had arisen as she noticed his weary sadness, and she felt ashamed of herself. She hated hurting his feelings. He was a nice man and she still cared about him—a great deal, if she was being honest. She forced herself to modulate her tone of voice.

"I appreciate your offer, Colin, but you can't keep holding on like this. We went out for a while and it didn't work for me—and you know why."

She reflected on the night of Merlin and Emily's dinner party when she had first returned to Moab, which was over four years ago. She and Colin had met, been attracted to each other and gone out on a date soon after that. At first, it seemed to be a match made in heaven—she rolled her eyes at the obvious pun—something they had both wanted. They seemed to be compatible, even though they had little in common except being a part of Merlin's group, and the sex was outstanding. Cathy admitted to herself, however, that it could have felt that way to her simply because it had been so long since she'd had a lover.

She glanced at him out of the corner of her eye and remembered why she'd been so attracted to him in the first place. Colin was tall, dark, and eye-catchingly handsome in a rough sort of way, with that long, drooping moustache of his making him look slightly sinister. His nose was aquiline and his cheekbones were high, his jaw firm. He had been in his early forties when they met, so he had to be at least forty-seven, but he looked thirty-two or thirty-three, at the most. Magically enhanced by Merlin years ago, he'd claimed. It must be true, because the man hadn't aged a day in four years. But she had. She decided not to dwell on that and continued her mental list of his assets versus his deficiencies.

Undeniably intelligent and hard-working, he had always taken his responsibilities as a detective with the Moab City Police Department very seriously. When he hadn't been working, he'd been helping Merlin out, which didn't leave much time for their relationship. And, she remembered, Colin hadn't yet been divorced from his wife when they started seeing each other, so that could have been part of the problem, as well.

At the moment, Colin was staring moodily into his drink, restlessly tapping on the counter in front of him, tiny blue sparks crackling from his fingertips with every tap.

She scowled and pursed her lips. Jeez, what was he thinking? This was another reason she'd stopped seeing him—he was often careless when using his magic in public, which always struck her as peculiar since he was so meticulous about other things.

Of course, it was miraculous and wonderful that he had magic, although he had confessed that when he discovered he didn't have telepathy and couldn't teleport or fly, he'd been depressed for weeks.

Damn it, she wished he would leave her alone to drink her daiquiri in peace.

He kept tapping and the blue sparks kept getting bigger. What if someone noticed what he was doing?

In fact, the bartender was turning around again and would witness Colin's magic at any moment. She leaned towards him and hissed, "Stop that! Someone will see you!"

He jerked his head toward her in surprise and she gestured at the sparks he was still generating.

"Oh, shit," he intoned quietly and made a fist, burying his still sparking fingertips into his palms.

"Ow!"

"What did you expect?" she muttered, utterly disgusted with him. He'd had the use of his magic for four years, for God's sake. You'd think he would have mastered it by now.

Cathy could tell when he finally got the sparks under control. It was obvious that between his lapse in judgment and her reprimand, he was embarrassed as hell. He tipped his glass and finished off his Scotch, and said without meeting her eye, "I still love you, Cathy, and I hope someday we can get back together. I miss you."

He got up, tossed forty dollars on the counter, more than enough to pay for both their drinks and a generous tip, and stalked out of the bar. She felt as if she was left in the wake of a hurricane.

She took a long, deep breath and tried to relax. She finished her drink and debated having another. As if he'd heard her thoughts, the bartender set another daiquiri in front of her and told her it was from the guy at the end of the bar.

She turned her head and glanced in that direction. A man in his early thirties, with long blond curls bright as newly minted gold coins, dipped his head in an old-fashioned gesture of acknowledgement. He was extremely attractive and Cathy's inner woman perked up in response.

Good God, what a physical contrast between the two men. Whereas Colin was dark and looked like a pirate, this guy was light and looked like an angel, so beautiful that it almost hurt her eyes. He was wearing a lightweight, loose white shirt with blousy sleeves that enhanced the image.

It was a shame the knowing smirk on the man's face spoiled the effect.

And what the hell was she doing checking out a total stranger—one that seemed to be an arrogant asshole, at that.

She was so tired, and disgusted with men in general, that all she wanted was to go home, so she dredged up a scant amount of courtesy and said, "No, thank you, I've had enough."

Cathy slipped down off of the high stool, grabbed her purse and walked rapidly towards the exit, feeling the blond's eyes focused intently on her as she passed by him.

It seemed to take an eternity, as if she was wading through molasses.

As soon as she was finally outside and the heavy door had closed behind her, she felt a surge of relief that seemed out of proportion to her experience. She tried to shake it off and focused on reaching her car, which was parked around the corner across from the City Diner. She ran the last few feet, feeling as if someone was chasing her. After she'd hastily unlocked the door and slid into the driver's seat, she relocked it at once. She rested her forehead on the steering wheel for a moment and breathed a sigh of relief. God, she needed to go home. Luckily, she lived in the low-income apartment complex on Kane Creek Boulevard, near Chris and Seth, so it didn't take long to get there.

As soon as she closed the front door of her apartment behind her, she set the deadbolt and immediately felt safer. While she showered and got ready for bed, she examined the sense of agitation she still felt regarding the encounter she'd had in the bar with that hunky blond man. Oddly enough, it was the opposite of the attraction and excitement she'd experienced when he'd initially looked at her. But she remembered his displeasure when she'd turned him down, and the heavy, threatening feeling weighing on her until she'd left the building.

She could have transferred the negative emotions she'd felt about Colin onto the encounter with the blond man, but that didn't seem accurate.

Phooey, she thought, *I'm done trying to figure it out*. As she walked barefoot into the kitchen to get a drink of water, she recalled a night when she and Colin had been together and he'd impressed her with his modesty. He didn't have an egotistical bone in his body, whereas the man at the bar tonight, beautiful as an angel or not, came off as a narcissist, and she hoped she would never cross paths with him again. She didn't need that kind of man in her life. Maybe she didn't need any man in her life. God, she was confused.

Cathy finally decided she'd imagined the whole thing and trudged off to bed. She'd consider giving the blond another chance if she ever saw him again.

* * *

Colin couldn't sleep. There was something he was missing, something vital. Out of the blue, memories of what had happened in the bar a few hours ago flashed through his mind. Cathy had been sitting on the stool to his left when the bartender had brought him his drink. After the man had turned away, he'd absentmindedly started tapping his fingers on the bar and emitting sparks of blue fire when Cathy had called him on it. He'd clenched his fist to extinguish the sparks until he'd felt the resulting intense burn on his palm. Then, he'd caught a glimpse of someone sitting at the end of the bar, watching him, someone who radiated evil…

Jesus H. Christ! He leaped out of bed and into his chinos, his fear for Cathy's safety motivating him to reach inside himself for a magical ability he wasn't supposed to possess, and finding it anyway. He teleported by sheer force of will into her bedroom.

Unaccustomed to teleporting, he was off-balance when he materialized and fell onto Cathy's bed, landing on her sleeping form.

She shrieked and fought like a wild animal as she felt a large man on top of her, thinking someone had broken in to rape her. She raked her fingernails across his face and he roared in shock and pain and pushed away from her, finally clambering off the bed.

Cathy flailed, her hand searching for the drawer in the bedside table. She pulled it open, found her pepper spray and pointed it at the intruder, catching him full in the face with the potent liquid.

He screamed and backed away. "Fuck! It's me, Cathy, stop!"

She leaped up, fumbling for the light switch. She discovered Colin standing next to her bed, his bare chest heaving, his face scratched and bloody and his eyes streaming.

"Colin, what are you doing here? How the hell did you get in?"

He mumbled a spell to rid his eyes of the burning sensation. "Whew, that's better," he muttered. He blinked rapidly and was able to focus on her in concern. "I remembered the guy in the bar and I teleported here to make sure you're okay."

"The guy in the bar? You mean the gorgeous blond man?" She looked bewildered. "Why wouldn't I be okay?"

"Cathy, that was *Sam!*" he bellowed.

"Sam who?"

"Samael, Merlin's brother." She still looked blank. "Oh, for Christ's sake. Satan, that was *Satan!*"

Every bit of color drained from her face and she collapsed limply onto the bed. "Oh. Oh, my God."

Colin sat beside her and pulled her against his big warm body. She turned and wrapped her arms around him, burying her face in the crease of his neck.

"I was so afraid for you, I couldn't think straight. I'm sorry I startled you."

She stiffened and stared wide-eyed at him. "Wait a minute—you said you *teleported* here. How? You don't have that ability."

"I have no idea. I was sure he'd come after you, so I dug deep inside myself and ...did it." He paused thoughtfully for a moment, a grin gradually replacing the somber look on his face. "I did it—I actually teleported!

"That's amazing. I'm happy for you." She saw that the scratches on his face were still bleeding, and she reached up tentatively. "Colin, I'm so sorry. Here you came to protect me and I attacked you."

"It's okay, you thought I was attacking *you* and..." His words trailed off as their eyes met and they both silently acknowledged that he was bare from the waist up and she was wearing only a thin, short, sleeveless nightgown that revealed more than it covered.

She cleared her throat nervously. She was acutely aware that his chest was bulging with muscle, and that the silky black hair around his nipples grew in a "V" down over his abs and teasingly disappeared into the waistband of his pants. "I, ah, better treat those scratches, before they get infected. Let's go into the bathroom, uh, you know, where the antiseptic and the bandages are."

"Okay, thanks." He wasn't sure it was a smart idea to move at this point as he had a noticeable ridge in his pants, and he didn't want to ruin this new rapport they had. But he got up and followed her anyway, sitting on the toilet lid while she stood close to him, tenderly washing and treating the gouges on his face.

Cathy was well aware Colin was intensely aroused, and she herself was having difficulty controlling her reaction to his nearness; her heart was beating double time, she was breathing hard, and she ached with desire. They hadn't had sex in years, but it was apparent they were still strongly attracted to each other.

As she finished the first aid, their eyes met and held. They each looked down at the other's lips and gradually leaned forward until they made contact, softly at first and then with hungry passion.

Colin pulled her onto his lap and her body pressed against his prominent bulge.

They both moaned and their tongues mated in a familiar dance as their hands roamed over bodies that hadn't been touched in a long, long time.

Colin suddenly stood up with Cathy in his arms and strode into the bedroom where he put her gently down on the bed and tore his pants off. He'd gone commando earlier, in too much of a hurry to bother with underwear when he thought she was in danger, and his erection, freed from the constraint of the taught fabric, reflected the strength of his need.

Cathy's eyes widened and she pulled her gown off and tossed it aside. She held her arms out in invitation and murmured, "Oh, Colin, come here, honey."

He wasted no time in going to her and holding her against him, caressing her slender naked body. Her firm breasts weren't large, but they were perfect in his estimation, and he covered one after the other with his hot mouth, running his tongue over and around each nipple until she shivered and moaned.

Cathy was amazed that she'd given in to him after all, but it felt natural to be in his arms again. His body was fit and athletic and as he pleasured her, she had to admit that he was the most skilled lover she'd ever had.

When he stretched out against her and used his mouth down below, his moustache tickling provocatively, she convulsed in a climax that drove all coherent thought from her mind.

Before her internal shock waves had subsided, she in turn took him into her mouth and caressed him with her tongue until he was ready to explode.

"God, Cathy, I have to be inside you!"

He turned around and covered her, and she guided him into her body. As he slowly filled her, she wondered how she'd ever be able to take all of him; it had been awhile since she'd had sex and he was quite large. But her body gradually opened to him, and as they began to move rhythmically together, the pressure built until she thought she would die from the pleasure of it. She ran her hands up his back, stroking his muscular body on top of her.

"I'm close, Cathy honey, come with me, now," he crooned, as he began moving faster, until he finally thrust deep and came, taking her with him over the edge of that magnificent precipice.

Basking in the soft, sweet afterglow, limbs intertwined, they gradually opened their eyes and smiled at each other.

"I love you, Cathy."

"I know, Colin." She was so tired of denying her feelings that she finally blurted out, "I love you, too."

He grinned, his white teeth a sharp contrast with his swarthy skin. "Then say you'll move in with me. What the hell, *marry* me!"

She was stunned. Was she ready for such a drastic step? Unexpectedly, a peaceful sensation washed over her, and she knew this is what she'd wanted all along. She grinned back. "Okay."

He was so surprised at her answer he couldn't speak, joy suffusing his craggy, masculine features. He cradled her face with his big hands and kissed her thoroughly, which led to them making love again, sealing the promise they had made to each other.

* * *

Finally, I thought to myself as I sensed the stars aligning at last for Colin and his lover. It had taken, what, four years? I was reconciled to being a matchmaker and a voyeur.

I chuckled. Cathy Grant was going to become Cathy Campbell. Yet another double "C."

Father, this is getting ridiculous.

I'm just having a bit of fun, Myrddin Emrys, God replied.

I sighed. *I need to ask you something. Is Colin actually Beli's son? They look exactly alike. And Colin's teleporting…*

My father's laughter echoed and reverberated through the valley and eventually became a low rumble of thunder in the night sky.

I shook my head. One day I hoped my father would give me an honest answer when I asked him something.

216

CHAPTER 34
Moab, Tuesday, August 22, 2023

Cathy practically floated into The Moab Herbalist around five that afternoon, she was so happy.

"Colin and I are getting married!" she sang out, doing a graceful pirouette in the middle of the shop floor. She held up her hand, exhibiting the diamond engagement ring they'd picked out that morning. In addition, they had decided to take the rest of the day off to start moving her things into his house. They'd been busy doing exactly that until half an hour ago, when, tired and sweaty, they figured they were done for the day.

Emily grinned and continued wiping the counter with an herbal disinfectant. Merlin had filled her in on the joyful news at breakfast this morning. She exchanged a satisfied look with her mother, who gave her a wink.

Chris squealed and ran around the counter, grabbing her sister in a bear hug, which effectively squeezed every bit of air out of Cathy's lungs. "That's awesome! Me, too!"

Cathy gasped for breath and Chris released her. "Oh, sorry, I don't know my own strength since I became Fae. Want to see my wings?" Since there were no customers in the shop at the moment, she dropped the glamour she'd been maintaining and let all her new Fae attributes show.

Cathy knew her sister had undergone a major change, but she hadn't imagined anything as drastic as this. Delicate white wings edged with black, pointed ears, reptilian eyes—and rounded abdomen.

"You're *pregnant*?"

"Sorry I didn't tell you about that. I wanted to surprise you, but I didn't realize she would grow so rapidly. We're going to need to get married pretty soon."

"She? You already know it's a girl?"

"Seth could tell as soon as she was conceived, isn't that incredible? Her name is Sorcha, which means light or radiance in Gaelic."

"That's a beautiful name, Chris," Cathy said, as a feeling of trepidation rippled through her. What if *she* was pregnant—they hadn't used any protection last night! Crap, this was all going too fast.

"Cathy, is something the matter?" Em asked, noticing the startled expression on her face.

"I, uh, might be pregnant myself, although I hope not. I'm not sure I'm ready to have a child."

Emily looked distracted as she received a telepathic message. "Merlin says you're not pregnant."

"How did...oh, never mind. I keep forgetting what Merlin can do." She paused to take a slow, cleansing breath. "I'm glad I don't have to think about that yet. Please tell him thanks."

"You just did. He says you're welcome." Em smiled crookedly. "Congratulations, Cathy, on your engagement. Merlin and I are very happy for you and Colin."

"Thanks, Em. It's kind of hard to believe it's truly happening."

"Have you two set a date yet?"

"No, we haven't." Cathy glanced at her sister, who had her human glamour back in place, and had an idea. "Hey, Sis, we could have a double wedding ceremony."

Chris looked thoughtful. "You, know, that might work. I'll talk to Seth tonight and get his opinion. And you'll need to mention it to Colin. I don't want a religious ceremony though."

Em and Cathy exchanged an amused glance and Rae chuckled.

Chris caught on right away and lightly slapped her forehead. "Oh, my gosh, what am I thinking? God's going to be my grandfather-in-law and yet I don't want a religious ceremony. That *is* funny."

The little bell over the door tinkled as someone entered.

"Oh, hello, Ann, how are you?" Em asked with a friendly smile as Lainie Colburn's mom strode decisively into the shop.

"I'm fine, thanks. How are all of you ladies doing today?" Ann Ogilvie was a tall, slim, attractive woman in her midsixties who loved to wear loose, flowing garments in bright, primary colors. Today's outfit of a short-sleeved blouse with matching long skirt had red and purple streaks on a dark blue background, which complemented her complexion and her short, curly gray hair. Large dangly red earrings completed her ensemble. While she was too young to have been a "flower child" in the 1960s, she still called herself an old hippie. She was a proficient witch, but had never admitted it to anyone, including her family, until her daughter Lainie had confessed to having shapeshifting abilities after she met Morry.

"We were discussing the possibility of a double wedding ceremony for Chris and Cathy, who have both become engaged recently," Em said.

"Oh, how thrilling! Formal, in a church, or informal, in the park, like Derek and Sarah's wedding?"

"I'd kind of like a church wedding, but my sister isn't a churchgoer, so informal would be best." Cathy looked at Chris, who nodded in agreement. "Colin was raised Catholic, but I'm pretty sure he hasn't practiced since he pledged himself to Merlin."

"And Seth is Fae, so I can't picture him in a church even if his grandfather *is* God," Chris said, glad that Ann was aware of all the magical and celestial details of the family.

"Do you have anyone to conduct the ceremony yet?" Ann glanced back and forth between the sisters. "The reason I'm asking is that I'd be happy to offer my services. Many years ago, I applied online with the Universal Life Church, so I'm legally ordained as a Licensed Wedding Officiant."

"Really? I didn't know the U.L.C. still existed. That would be great, Ann, thanks! Is that okay with you, Sis?" Chris asked.

"Absolutely, and the sooner the better." Cathy was so excited she could hardly wait to talk to Colin. "How about this Sunday? Our men can conjure up the appropriate garments, and everything else can be done pretty quickly with everybody pitching in. And I think the weather is supposed to be nice."

"Merlin says that sounds great and to go ahead with your plans. He'll take care of obtaining your licenses," Em said warmly. "But, do you have enough time to notify your parents or other family members so they can be here on Sunday?"

Chris and Cathy looked at each other solemnly. "Uh, we don't have any close family left. Our parents, well, that's kind of a long story," Cathy said, with a catch in her voice.

"No need to mince words, Cath. Our mother is dead and our father is in prison," Chris stated bluntly. She didn't think there was any point in spelling out exactly why their father was incarcerated.

Em looked chagrined. "Oh, God, I'm sorry. I didn't mean to bring up painful memories." *Merlin, were you aware of this?*

Yes, but Chris asked me years ago to keep it to myself. Obviously she's ready to talk about it.

"It's alright, Em, you didn't know. Cathy, does Colin have any family besides his kids?"

She started to answer, but realized she had no idea. They'd never discussed their parents, which, now that she thought of it, was sort of odd. "I guess I'll need to ask him tonight."

"So it's all settled, hmm?" Ann glanced at the brides-to-be, striving to get past the awkwardness. "Lovely, it's a date. I'd better get the herbs I came in for and head home. Emily, do you have any conize plant?"

Em took her cue, grateful to get back to business. "Do you mean fleabane or spikenard?"

"That's correct."

"Isn't that for inducing abortions?" She hoped Ann didn't want it for such a thing. The woman was way too old to need it for herself, but she might know someone who did.

Ann laughed, interpreting Em's expression correctly. "It was used for that purpose in medieval times, but I simply need it for killing fleas— hence the name fleabane. We don't have many of those pesky insects here in Moab, but what we do have are all on my cat."

Em grinned. "I have some in the back room. I'll get it for you."

"Thanks, Em," Ann said warmly. "Oh, and I need some peonia root if you have it. A friend of mine has sciatica."

"Certainly," Em said, and went to gather the requested herbs.

While they waited for her to return, the twins discussed the details of their hastily planned wedding and coordinated with Ann on a time that would work for everyone.

* * *

Seth came up behind Chris as she was fixing dinner, slipped his arms under her wings and around her waist, and gazed over her shoulder at the chicken she was frying. "Weel, ye've decided on this coming weekend tae get marrit, have ye?" He'd read her thoughts after she'd arrived home from work.

She turned her head and kissed his cheek. "I hope that's okay with you? To have a double wedding and everything?"

"Aye, 'tis fine. And Colin? How does he feel aboot it?"

"I don't know yet, but I'm sure Cathy will text me. By the way, I assume you don't have anyone in the Fae realm you wanted to invite to the wedding?"

"Nay, *mo màthair* couldna care less aboot me. I dinna even ken where she is."

"Are you okay with that?" Chris asked. If her own mother was still alive, she would want her to be present even if their relationship wasn't on the best terms.

"Aye lass, dinna fash yersel'. I havena seen her in three hundred years, sae I dinna need her tae be at our wedding."

* * *

Colin was getting frustrated trying to find his electric frying pan so he could cook dinner. He and Cathy had spent many hours moving her possessions into his house and the place was a mess. When they'd decided to call it quits for the day, she'd immediately taken off to show everyone at The Moab Herbalist her engagement ring, leaving him to figure out how to accommodate all her stuff.

He was ecstatic that she'd agreed to marry him, but the reality of combining their households on such short notice was daunting.

It was fortuitous that Merlin had altered his metabolism, because he was in his late forties and would otherwise be running on empty by now. As it was, he desperately wanted a beer, so he gave up on fixing dinner, popped the top on a brew, and took a seat at the kitchen table. He'd order take-out once his fiancée got home.

His fiancée. He was still getting used to the fact that she'd agreed to marry him. He hadn't expected much when he'd seen her go into the bar the previous night and made the last-minute decision to follow her. But as he thought back to everything that had transpired, he recognized that it was fate, or destiny, which led him to teleport into her bedroom and make love with her. He could envision the satisfied look on Merlin's face as he and Cathy made the decision to merge their lives. His uncle had told him years ago that the two of them were destined to be together, but when she'd broken up with him, he'd been crushed and assumed Merlin was wrong. Now, Colin realized he'd never given up hope.

At that moment, he heard the front door open and close and a voice call out, "Hey, Colin, I'm home." It was the sweetest thing he'd ever heard.

"I'm in the kitchen, Cath."

He saw her appear in the doorway, a big smile on her face, and happiness slammed through him, dissipating all the fatigue and frustration he'd felt earlier. He held his arms out in invitation and she rushed to his side, at which point he pulled her into his lap and buried his face in her sweet-smelling hair. "God, I love you, Cathy."

When he finally straightened and let his gaze linger on each one of her lovely features, she framed his face with her soft hands, kissing his mouth slowly, methodically. "And I love you. Want to get married this weekend?"

"Sure, I—wait, what? *This weekend?*" Colin wasn't sure he'd heard her correctly.

Cathy leaped up and started dancing around the kitchen. "Yes, on Sunday, this coming Sunday! I'm so excited! I wonder what I should wear…"

Colin regarded her with a certain amount of skepticism. He didn't know her as well as he thought he did. "Uh, how can we do it so soon? What about all the arrangements—a venue, finding a minister to marry us, wedding clothes, invitations, food—all that stuff?"

She danced up to him and grabbed his hands. When he only sat there with a peculiar look on his face, she knew something was wrong. "Colin, honey, are you okay?"

"Yeah, I guess. I, uh…" He swallowed nervously and blurted out, "Everything's going so fast, my mind can't keep up. After all, a few days ago you were avoiding me and now we're living together and scheduled to get married in five days."

"I'm sorry I didn't discuss it with you first, but Chris and I got carried away planning a double wedding and—"

"Double wedding? You mean, you and me and Chris and Seth?" Colin frowned, not sure that he wanted to share his wedding day with anyone else.

"Of course, Chris and Seth. Who else do you know in the group that's getting married? Besides Gwen and Arthur, and they haven't decided on a date yet."

"But Seth's a Fae prince and Chris is human. How is that going to work?"

"Oh, my gosh, I didn't realize nobody told you!" She still had Colin's big hands in hers and she squeezed them apologetically. "He turned Chris, made her Fae. She's got wings and everything. Oh, and she's pregnant."

Colin was momentarily speechless. Then he managed to say, "I wasn't aware Seth had the power to do that. I don't mean about getting her pregnant—it's pretty obvious how he did that—I mean that he had the power to change her *species*. That's mindboggling."

"Yes, it is." She stretched to tuck a stray lock of his glossy black hair back behind one ear. "So, are you okay with getting married Sunday?"

"Yeah, but don't you need a wedding dress? Won't you have to go to a bridal shop in Salt Lake City or Grand Junction?"

Cathy grinned and shook her head.

"No? Why not?"

"You have the ability to conjure things, don't you?"

"Yeah, some...hold on, you want me to conjure your *wedding dress*? I don't know, Cathy."

"Hang on a second." She pulled her phone out of a back pocket, opened up the Google app and searched for wedding dresses online. There were dozens, all different styles and fabrics, but she knew what she wanted. She quickly found the one she desired and showed him the gown, both front and back views. "Okay, close your eyes and visualize it, create it. You're familiar with the contours of my body, so I know you can do it, Colin!"

Initially, he was worried he'd mess it up and she would be disappointed in him, but it occurred to him that she'd definitely be disappointed if he didn't make an honest effort. He closed his eyes, calmed his mind, and focused intently inside, immersing himself in that well of power at the core of his being. He tingled as the Light seemed to fill every cell in his body. Had it always been so bright?

He pictured every detail of the dress in his mind's eye and how exquisite his fiancée would look in it—and made it real.

He heard a feminine squeal of delight and opened his eyes. Cathy was holding up a long, white, sleeveless satin gown, with a fitted bodice adorned with seed pearls.

He was dumbfounded. "*I* did that?"

"Who else?" Cathy gazed at him with such loving admiration that it took his breath away.

"Merlin could have done it."

No, Colin, you did it. Well done.

Thanks. I can't believe it.

* * *

Honestly, neither could I. It was an astonishing feat for someone with supposedly limited power. And he was using telepathy as easily as the rest of us—and wasn't even aware he was doing it.

Merlin, why are you so surprised? He must be directly related to you, somehow, more than a distant connection through Beli.

I looked up, startled. I had been so caught up in the mystery that

223

was Colin Campbell I hadn't realized I'd expressed myself on our private wavelength.

Emily shook her head in exasperation. "You need to try and stay focused when we're together. These days I feel like you're always somewhere else besides with me. I'm trying to be understanding, but it's awfully annoying!"

We were standing on the pedestrian bridge that arched over Mill Creek east of Main Street, not far from where Percival had threatened us on a dark evening back in 2013. Unbeknownst to me, Llyr had brought the knight forward in time from Camelot and dumped him unprepared in present day Moab. In his distress, Sir Percival hadn't recognized me and tried to rob us at knifepoint. He hadn't succeeded.

Similar to that day ten years ago, the creek flow had been reduced to a mere trickle by the diversion of water upstream for use by the Irrigation District. Em and I had been discussing the possibility of magically creating a way to keep the creek from drying up when I'd been distracted by Colin's inadvertent communication.

I dragged my thoughts back to the present and turned to look at my wife apologetically. I had been more and more distracted lately and it was affecting my marriage. I wished I could figure out how to be in more than one place at the same time.

"You're a god, Merlin, thinking like a human. Stop worrying about it. And you know I'll never stop loving you, no matter what you do or don't do. "

I smiled and pulled her into my arms, holding her tightly against me. I was aware of her full breasts and the warmth of her shapely body and became instantly aroused.

"I've said this before, but I don't know what I'd do without you, Em."

"Guess I'm indispensable, huh?" She batted her eyes at me flirtatiously.

"Indeed you are," I murmured, kissing her seductively, needing to caress her bare skin.

"Come on, magic man, let's go home," she said, pulling out of my grasp. "You need to conjure something suitable for us to wear to the wedding on Sunday. I've been practicing conjuring lately and I can probably handle the accessories. And we'll see what happens next, shall we?" She gave me a sexy look and a quick inconspicuous caress in a sensitive spot and I willingly took us home.

* * *

"Oh, I nearly forgot. Are you going to invite your family to the wedding?" Cathy asked as they finished getting the kitchen cupboards organized. After dinner, they had decided to make some kind of order out of the chaos.

"Josh will be here with Lumina, but my daughter Rose is out of town with my ex-wife. I have a distant cousin back east, but we haven't been in touch for decades. I don't even know if he's still alive," Colin answered, shoving the crockpot into an upper cabinet.

"Wait, let's put that down with the pans—I won't be able to reach it up there." After the crockpot was stored neatly alongside the pots and pans, she continued, "But, Colin, what about your parents? I've known you for years and you've never mentioned them." Cathy glanced over her shoulder as she rinsed out the rag they had been using to wipe the shelves.

He was quiet and introspective for a few minutes before he reluctantly started talking. "My mom died in the summer of 2017, a year before I got involved with Merlin's family. She and my stepdad, who I never got along with, were in a head-on collision in Omaha, Nebraska, while they were on vacation. They were both killed. I never knew my biological father and my mom never talked about him. They'd had a one-night stand and she got pregnant. She didn't even know what his last name was, so she gave me hers, which was Campbell." He leaned back against the counter with his arms crossed over his chest, looking somber.

Cathy patted his cheek. "I'm so sorry, honey."

He shrugged and looked into her eyes. "It is what it is, and at this point it doesn't matter anymore. You're my family."

CHAPTER 35
Moab, Sunday, August 27, 2023, Afternoon

Chris stood in front of the mirror mesmerized by her reflection. She didn't recognize herself. Seth had conjured a wedding gown that challenged the imagination. She wished she could show it off to all of her friends and neighbors, and the clients at the herb shop. But that couldn't happen since Seth had put a glamour on it so no one but the family could see it. Others would see a white blur. The alien fabric shimmered, all colors swirling together until they became one opalescent glow. And the texture was indescribable: as smooth as the finest silk and as light as air against her skin. The gown hugged her body, outlining her breasts and the slight curve of her pregnancy. It swept, rippling, to the floor, moving as if a light breeze meandered through the room. The v-neckline complemented her petite figure, and the fitted sleeves flared elegantly from her wrists to her fingertips.

It was magnificent. Her shoes were comfortable flat slippers of the same material. A lacy headdress in an unusual shade of gray-green framed her pointed ears and made her hazel eyes with the Fae vertical pupil look as yellow-green as Seth's. Her hair cascaded down her back to her waist in a silken waterfall of pure gold. Her delicate wings were fully open and extended from one side of the bedroom to the other, making her look and feel like a fairy princess.

"Ye look and feel like one because ye *are* one, *mo chridhe.* Ye're ma Faery princess," Seth murmured.

Her face glowing with love, Chris turned around and gazed at her tall, slender husband-to-be. He was wearing a suit of sorts, made out of the same rich Fae fabric, which molded flawlessly to the shape of his body and around his wings, with no zippers, no buttons, no fastenings at all. His slippers were identical to hers but noticeably larger to accommodate his long slender feet. His headdress was a masculine version of hers, emphasizing his own inhuman appearance.

He was gorgeous, with his long hair waving down his back like black satin. He looked every inch a prince and she hoped that she would do him proud.

"All we need are our crowns." He snapped his fingers and gold bands inscribed with ancient runes settled over the headdresses they wore.

"Do you really wear a crown? I've never seen one on you, Seth."

"Och, no' here in Moab. No one in town besides the family kens what I am. With ma glamour, I appear tae be Merlin's brother. But at home, for special occasions in the Fae realm, aye, I would wear a crown. I'm the grandson of the king, after all."

* * *

"Colin, are you ready yet, honey?" Cathy called from the master bathroom as she pinned on the delicate headpiece of seed pearls, her wavy blonde hair brushing the tops of her shoulders. Her makeup was nearly done and all she had left to do was put on the strappy, white, high-heeled sandals that made her three inches taller. She was still fairly short compared to Colin's six-foot-one, but at least with her new shoes on she came up to his chin.

As she finished applying her mascara, she reflected on what had happened the other night. After he had conjured her dress, Colin had managed to come up with the shoes and the headpiece before he had to take a break and re-energize.

He'd been quiet as they ate the large pepperoni pizza and green salad they'd ordered, and Cathy had wondered if he would be too exhausted to manifest his own wedding attire.

"No, I'll be fine, just give me a few minutes to relax after we finish eating," he mumbled.

She'd paused with a forkful of salad halfway to her mouth. "I thought you weren't telepathic."

"I'm not."

"Yes, you are. You responded to my thoughts. I never said anything out loud."

Colin's eyes had widened in stunned silence.

She grinned as she remembered the look on his face. She suspected Colin had been an active participant in many telepathic conversations with his uncle, all the while believing Merlin was providing the connection on both ends.

She put on her lipstick, spritzed herself with a light floral fragrance, then stepped into her sandals and went in search of her husband-to-be.

He was sitting on their bed examining the shoes he had conjured for himself last night.

"Hey, babe, what's the holdup? Don't they fit?" Cathy ventured.

He held them out to her, shaking in silent mirth.

She laughed. "No foot holes!" The shoes had tongues and laces but each one was a solid piece of black leather, with no way to put it on.

He took them back from her and held them on his lap while he focused his will and his power. As she watched, the shoe leather moved and reformed itself as if it was alive, until the shoes were wearable.

He grinned at her as he slipped them on and the laces tied themselves.

"Okay, let me look at you."

Colin stood up, threw his shoulders back and tightened his abs.

He looked incredible. The tuxedo he had chosen was as black as his hair and exquisitely tailored, and his ruffled white shirt was a stark contrast to his olive skin tone. The black satin cummerbund accentuated his trim waist. His hair was clean and lustrous and long enough to reach his shoulders. He had trimmed his moustache so that it wasn't as sinister-looking as usual, but she actually liked the hairy reminder of his unique self. She thought he looked like a god...

She laughed at herself. Naturally, he did—he resembled Beli.

Colin chuckled. "I wouldn't go that far, even if some of my other powers did finally show up."

Cathy smiled. "Beli has to be your father. I wonder why he won't admit it."

He looked panic-stricken, and she cried, "What's wrong?"

"I remembered something—I'm not supposed to see you in your wedding dress until just before we get married!"

"Whew, you had me worried for a moment. Since you created my dress, and I tried it on in front of you, I don't think that old superstition applies." She took his hand and looked up at him with love shining in her eyes. "Come on handsome, let's go get married."

* * *

I had arrived at Swanny Park an hour early—the wedding was scheduled for two o'clock—remaining in my incorporeal state to observe the crowd. Chaos would surely ensue if my tall, dark-haired self —with or without wings—appeared out of thin air in the midst of all the tourists taking advantage of the exceptionally beautiful late August weather. The air was crystal clear and there was a light breeze dancing through the trees, sporadically swooping down to playfully lift peoples' hair. The sky was a clear blue, so pure a color it was like my father had only moments ago painted it with his celestial brush. The grass had been cut recently and I inhaled the fresh, pungent scent with pleasure.

People sat at the picnic tables placed around the perimeter of the park eating lunch, or they were out on the lawn throwing balls for their children. A few individuals were lounging lazily in the shade. Some were organizing the camping gear in their vans or letting their dogs out to stretch their legs. A multitude of voices ebbed and flowed as people conversed with one another.

I was truly sorry to interrupt their Sunday in the park, but no humans could be allowed to witness the impending nuptials. Both Seth and Chris would be dressed as befitted Fae royalty, in distinctly alien garb, their wings and pointed ears displayed unapologetically. Colin and Cathy would be no less resplendent in their traditional wedding attire.

I regained my corporeal form behind a particularly large camper van, and casually walked over to the cluster of pine trees under which the ceremony would take place. In a friendly manner, I spoke to the people sitting in the shade and leaning comfortably against the scattered boulders.

"I'm sure all of you would be more than happy to vacate the park for a private wedding ceremony this afternoon, wouldn't you?" I asked pleasantly, the brilliance of my god Light pulsing unnoticed by the mortal crowd. Years ago, I had created an enchantment out at Delicate Arch that caused all the visitors to leave the vicinity in order to keep them safe from an energy vortex beneath the arch itself.

Now, I had no need to create a spell, I merely exuded the power that "persuaded" people to depart. They never realized it wasn't their own idea.

By one thirty most of the park was cleared out. The few stragglers in the westerly corner finally left and I created a magical barrier around the entire area. I merely glance at the points that delineated the border I desired and the barrier sprang into being, invisible and impenetrable to sight, sound and physical entry except by my family members and guests. I did the same thing with the parking area along Park Drive.

Satisfied with my work, I took a cleansing breath, stretched my wings out and back, and sauntered back toward the picnic tables closest to the pine trees. A tall woman stood there waiting for me whom I hadn't seen since the two Colburn families' joint wedding reception at the end of August, 2018. At this very location, as a matter of fact.

Ann Ogilvie looked radiant today wearing a long blue dress the color of her sparkling eyes. She was close to Rae's age and I wondered why they had never become friends. When I had a chance, I would encourage them to cultivate a relationship that would enrich both their lives.

As I approached her, I could see a strong though exaggerated image of myself in her mind. I appeared to her to be at least ten feet tall, glowing like a torch, my wings gargantuan. She seemed to be favorably impressed with the clothing I had chosen to wear for the wedding: a long-sleeved, tailored dress shirt in a warm smoky gray color and slacks in a darker gray with crisp creases, which gave me a suitably well-dressed look. My long black hair gleamed and the silver circlet I wore constantly these days reflected the sunlight like a mirror. Black belt and dress shoes completed her picture of me. It was high time to leave off dressing as casually as I had in the past and wear formal—or at least business casual—clothing more often. After all, I would soon be, along with Arthur, of course, the focus of attention when we revealed ourselves to the world, and it was vital that I look the part. I had briefly considered wearing a robe again, as I had in the fifth century, but swiftly determined that wouldn't do. I needed to be more modern.

I gave Ann a welcoming smile. Her eyes widened and her mouth opened with a gasp. I chided her kindly, "You know precisely who and what I am; there's no need to look so shocked." I held my hand out to her.

She stared at my outstretched hand for a moment, slowly relaxing. "Easy for you to say," she said with a laugh as she reluctantly surrendered her hand to me. "I've heard about your wings, and your Light, but I've never seen them. They're extraordinary. The powers I have are a drop in the bucket compared to yours."

"There's nothing wrong with your powers, you just don't utilize them to their full extent. I'd be happy to work with you. Think about it and I'll hear you. We can meet wherever you wish."

"You'd do that for me?"

"Of course. You're my grandson's mother-in-law, and you're my descendent, so I'd be happy to help you."

She looked uncomfortable when I mentioned our familial connection and nervously pulled her hand from mine. "I still don't understand how we can possibly be related?"

It was apparent to me—her nose was a feminine version of mine, and she had gotten her height from me as well. I replied with a grin, "One of these days Morry, Lainie, you and I need to investigate this most perplexing relationship we have and—"

I was distracted from our conversation as the bridal couples arrived. Colin helped Cathy out of their car, and Seth and Chris appeared next to them, having transported over from their apartment. One could sit in a car with wings on one's back, but it was uncomfortable and inconvenient. Yet another reason I was glad mine could be tucked away in that other dimension when not in use.

Shoving my reflections aside, I realized I'd better get busy. "Let's discuss it later, Ann. I need to take care of something before everyone else gets here."

I quickly turned to face the tables nearest the pine trees and raised my arms, power flowing freely to do my bidding. First, I removed all traces of dirt and trash, and any stray cobwebs that might be hanging from the shelter overhead. Second, I conjured fine, white Irish linen tablecloths on the picnic tables, with floral centerpieces reflecting the brides' colors in red roses, white carnations, and red and white "broken color" tulips. The plates, glasses, and silverware were arranged at the end of one table, with the white-frosted red velvet wedding cake and the Dom Pérignon champagne in silver ice buckets at the other end. The other table was set up with a lunch buffet, including various salads, rolls, and trays of meats and cheeses.

I perused my handiwork, added condiments, and asked Em if we needed anything else.

I don't think so, it looks wonderful—oh, wait, you forgot the fruit salad and the serving spoons. And you might want to drape some flowers around the edge of the tables.

I can do that. By the way, are you and Rae ready? I can bring you here as well.

Sure, we're ready to go.

Fruit salad in a pink Depression Glass bowl that had belonged to Em's paternal grandmother appeared and I placed it near the cake. With a flick of my wrist, I magically slid a serving spoon or fork smoothly into each dish that required one. Next, I affixed garlands of red bougainvilleas to the tables.

Finally, I raised my arms again and threw my head back, silver circlet glinting in the sun and long hair flying free in the breeze, and Em and Rae appeared in front of me. I was finished. And I had an audience. Derek and Morry and their families had arrived and acknowledged my theatrical touch in appreciative silence.

"What's everybody staring at?" Lumina asked as she and Josh teleported in from Logan.

"Nothing much. I used a trivial amount of magic to set up the food tables, that's all." I sent my wings back to that other dimension and turned to my daughter with a smile, showing her telepathically what I'd done.

"Trivial?" she scoffed. "That was a pretty flamboyant production, Dad, especially bringing Mom and Grammy Rae in at the end."

I grinned. "I was being overly dramatic, but I enjoyed myself thoroughly." She grinned back at me and we came together, hugging each other tightly.

"I've missed you, Daughter," I murmured, kissing her cheek. She was now slightly taller than her mother at five ten, and unlikely to reach the six foot mark I'd originally predicted. "I'm glad the three of you could make it."

"Is it that noticeable?"

"No, you've only been pregnant for a few days. Does Josh know?"

"Yes, I told him as soon as it happened."

I closed my eyes for a moment as my father sent me a message. "Her name is Cadence Campbell." I shook my head in exasperation. "Seriously?"

Lumina shrugged. "I know. But Josh and I kind of like it, so it's alright. Huh, Josh?"

He had been talking to his dad and turned around. "What was that, honey?"

"I was telling Dad we're okay with the baby's name being Cadence."

"Yeah, it's great."

This was the child I had foreseen when they first mated, and I knew my precocious granddaughter Cadence would in some way have a positive effect on Arthur's future reign. It was odd that, when I least expected it, my prescience would reveal itself.

"You'd better tell your mom and Grammy Rae about the baby before they find out from someone else."

"If I know Mom she's already sensed it, but I'll go and tell them anyway. I love you, Dad."

"I love you, too, Lumina."

At that moment, Ann walked up to us and smiled. "Hello, Lumina, it's nice to see you. We should get started, Merlin, it's two o'clock."

I noticed that Llyr and Beli hadn't arrived yet, and neither had Arthur and Gwen and the knights. "We're not quite ready yet, Ann, we're still missing a few people."

Arthur, where are you two?

Sorry, Dad, we're running late, but the knights should be there any minute.

Get a move on, there are two couples here who are anxious to get married.

I get it, Dad. We'll be there soon.

* * *

"I told you we should have gotten up earlier," Gwen complained as she finished applying her makeup and critiqued her overall appearance as best she could in the small mirror. She was wearing a simple, sleeveless sheath dress with a round neck in a shade of purple that complemented her brown curls. She wore small gold studs in her ears and low-heeled sandals that matched her dress. She knew she looked fine, but it annoyed her that she didn't have a full-length mirror. "One bathroom for the both of us is really inconvenient!"

"Why are you so grumpy?" Arthur came up behind her and put his hands on her trim waist, admiring her in the mirror. Gwen typically didn't wear a lot of makeup because in many of her past lives—including her most recent one—she had been a man, so when she did make the effort, she looked stunning.

She gazed at his reflection in the mirror and for a fraction of a second, she saw him as he'd been in the fifth century, his nose slightly aquiline rather than straight and his brown eyes focused on her with love. However, his ancient aspect was promptly dispelled by the sight of his modern clothing, creamy beige dress shirt with dark brown slacks, which went well with Arthur's sandy-blond hair.

"Why haven't we gotten married yet?" she blurted out, realizing this was the cause of her bad mood.

Arthur looked surprised. And amused. "Guinevere, my darling, we've only been back together for twelve days. Hell, I've only been an *adult* for twelve days!"

Gwen grimaced. "You're right. I'm sorry. Knowing that Chris and Seth and Cathy and Colin put their wedding plans together in less than a week, I start to wonder why we couldn't have done that."

"I suppose we could have." He turned her around and cupped her face in his large hands, kissing her seductively. He murmured in her ear, "Call me old-fashioned, but I want a big, formal wedding like we had in Camelot."

Gwen shivered as visions of the past flowed through her mind. Her long, white, silk gown, the juniper branches and autumn leaves interwoven with colored ribbons decorating the Great Hall, and Merlin in his best robe. All the knights standing tall and proud with their red and gold cloaks each adorned with a red dragon, and Arthur in his royal robe with the ermine collar and the gold crown on his head proclaiming him the King of Camelot.

She blinked and was back in their cramped bathroom in the small two-bedroom house in Moab, Utah, sixteen hundred years later.

As she looked up at his face, she noted again how different it was from his first life, but still somehow it was the same as it had always been.

"I love you, Arthur. We'll get married when the time is right."

"Yes, we will. Now, we need to get to the wedding before Dad comes to get us."

* * *

I was a bit aggravated that Arthur and Gwen hadn't yet arrived. It was disrespectful to the bridal couples to be late to their wedding, and I trusted that they would show up soon.

I sensed that my brothers were here, incorporeal, standing guard. *Thank you, Llyr, Beli. When did you arrive?*

You're welcome, Myrddin Emrys, Llyr responded. *We arrived a few minutes ago, in time to see you showing off, which I have to confess was most entertaining, Bro.*

Ignoring Llyr's needling, Beli added, *We'll still be able to see both couples during the ceremony and this way, we'll keep everyone safe if Sam tries anything.*

I appreciate it.

It's the least we can do for my twi—, uh, I mean, for my great-grandson.

Ah, finally, there it was. *Beli, why haven't you told him? He doesn't understand why he has magical powers, and he's remarkably adept without any training whatsoever. He thinks you're his father. How could he not—it's you he sees when he looks in the mirror.*

Naturally he sees me when he looks in the mirror—he is *me, or rather, my identical twin. I would have told you, and him, but I didn't know the truth myself until recently. Why do you think I stayed away? I didn't know what to tell him.*

This was most intriguing. Colin Campbell was my brother, which meant my daughter had married her first cousin. In ancient times, it was standard practice for cousins to marry, mainly in royal families, to assure continuation of the same family line. But in modern times, such a practice was discouraged. Science had determined that the human gene pool was not improved by marrying one's close relations. However, Lumina and Josh weren't normal and mostly not human, so it shouldn't make any difference. And since it was apparently part of my father's long-term plan, I decided not to worry about it overmuch.

That Colin was my sibling explained the depth of my feelings for him and his for me, but how had I not guessed the truth? How, when I Saw him years ago, was our true relationship not clear to me?

I remembered that the same thing had happened with Derek when he and I had initially Seen each other, and it turned out that Llyr had manipulated the situation at my father's behest.

Father, I need to talk to you right away.

Later, Myrddin Emrys. Trust me.

I heaved a sigh and opened my eyes. I sensed Ann looking at me, worried that things weren't going to plan. But at that moment the knights' Hummer pulled up and the men poured hurriedly out of the vehicle, looking suave and well-groomed. Arthur and Gwen teleported in, appropriately turned out for the occasion, and added their gifts to the others on the extra table Em had set up for that purpose.

Relieved I wouldn't have to chase after my overdue son and his fiancée, I directed Ann to go ahead with the ceremony. She got the couples situated in front of her under the pine trees, and called to everyone else to gather around them. It was time for the wedding to begin.

* * *

The attack started as a vague feeling of unease and quickly escalated. I spoke telepathically to Beli and Llyr, who confirmed that Sam was stealthily attempting to infiltrate the energy barrier we put in place over the section of the park we were occupying. As powerful as he was, he shouldn't be able to penetrate a shield or barrier created by his brother gods. But that didn't prevent him from trying. I was grateful for the others' assistance. Without it, the entire event could have been a debacle —I was at an extreme disadvantage when dealing with my devilish brother and wouldn't have been able to provide effective assistance.

Merlin, it appears the assault is gaining in strength, Llyr warned me.

I'll contact Portunus to help you. I presumed he would be useful. After all, my father had placed him here in Moab to support me should I need it and this indisputably qualified.

Portunus, we need your assistance at once.

Be there in a second.

I felt his presence as he joined our brothers and reinforced the energy shield over the park, and I hoped that three gods would be enough to prevent Sam from ruining the ceremony and endangering everyone there.

Dad, what's goin' on? Do ya need my help?

Sam is trying his best to force his way through the energy shield Llyr and Beli erected. Sam would still have to get through the barrier I put in place earlier as well, so we should be okay. Thanks, Derek.

I understand why ya don't want to disrupt the ceremony, but the bottom line is to make sure everybody's safe.

I'm aware of that.

At that point, Llyr let me know Sam had given up on his attack temporarily. I instructed them all to keep vigilant until I gave them leave to go.

* * *

"...you may kiss your brides. Ladies and gentleman, may I present to you, Their Royal Highnesses, Prince Seth and Princess Chris, and Mr. and Mrs. Colin Campbell!"

Rice and confetti filled the air as the wedding guests enthusiastically fulfilled the customary response and the two brides tossed their bouquets over their shoulders.

Laughter ensued when the bouquets were caught by Rae and Ann, who both emphatically denied having lovers, let alone plans to remarry.

Finally, after a great deal of toasting, socializing and well-wishing, everyone adjourned to the food table and filled their plates. I hadn't eaten all day and my stomach was growling.

I was sitting on the grass working on a shockingly large plate of food, waiting for Em, who was visiting with Lumina and Josh, when Colin sat down next to me and quietly waited for me to finish eating.

"Aren't you going to get something to eat?" I asked, scooping up potato salad.

"Later. I'm not hungry." He sat watching me consume my last bite of food and said casually, "I thought Beli and Llyr had planned to be here."

I wiped my mouth and turned to him. "I know, Colin. They both asked me to extend their apologies. They've been guarding us while we're here in the park, which was fortuitous since Sam decided to attack us."

He whistled through his teeth. "I sensed something earlier but assumed it was nerves. I had no idea what was going on."

"I didn't either until right before the ceremony began."

Colin was silent for few moments, not wanting to dwell on Sam's evil on this blissful day. Instead, he focused on his new wife and admired his wedding ring. But he couldn't help bringing up a topic that had been bothering him a lot. "I'd hoped, since we look alike, that Beli was my father and would stand with me when I got married. But he isn't, is he?"

I decided it was past time to tell him the truth. "No, he's not. But would it help to know that, although he couldn't stand with you, your *brother* was able to witness your nuptials?"

He whipped his head up and stared at me. "*What?*"

I grinned. "Beli told me you're really his twin brother."

"Holy Mother of God! But…that means *you're* my brother, too."

"Yes."

"And that means…" His eyes widened as he understood why he had powers.

"Yes, Colin, you're a god."

"Oh, shit, and—"

"And God is *your* father as well."

He was stunned. "I don't understand," he whispered.

"Neither do I, Colin, neither do I."

We fell silent as we gazed into each other's eyes, brother to brother.

"Merlin, I—"

"There's my husband!" Cathy called out happily, as she skipped barefoot through the grass carrying her heeled sandals in one hand and the hem of her gown in the other.

Colin broke off our gaze and scrambled to his feet, taking her in his arms to give her a resounding kiss. "Here I am." He beamed with love and pride.

She framed his rugged face with her small, soft hands and smiled up at him lovingly. "You're positively glowing, Colin, like you won the lottery."

"That's because I did. I married my soul mate *and* I found out I'm a god."

"Oh, that's so sweet—what? You're what?" She stared at him, glanced questioningly at me, and then stared at him again.

"It's true…Sister-in-law," I couldn't resist saying as I got to my feet.

Her mouth dropped open in utter shock, but she recovered swiftly and tugged excitedly on Colin's hand. "Remember, I told you this morning, that you looked like a god, like Beli. My God, you're twins, aren't you? Oh, that's so awesome! I have to tell Chris!" She whirled and ran exuberantly in her sister's direction.

I laughed as I watched her gesticulating wildly and pointing toward us. "I guess the secret's out, isn't it?" I turned to Colin, who was watching me with tears streaming down his face. I pulled him into my arms and hugged him. "It's alright, Brother."

"Merlin, I…I love you, man. I never had a brother, and now I have you and Beli and Llyr and—uh oh, wait a minute, crap, that means Sam's my brother." He stiffened in alarm and I tightened my arms around him reassuringly, then released him.

"Sadly, yes. But let's talk about that later."

"Yeah, that would be best." He gave me a startled look as it occurred to him who else he was related to.

Yes, JC is your brother, also…

He easily shifted to telepathy without realizing it. *Jesus Christ on a crutch! Oh, shit, I guess I shouldn't say that any more, should I?*

Probably not. He's used to it from the human population, but he would prefer his brothers be more circumspect in their language.

"That answers my other question. I'm not human, am I?"

"I'm not aware of the details of your creation yet. You might have been born to a human mother as I was, but I'm definitely not human and it's doubtful that you are. Tell you the truth, I'm baffled by the whole thing, because I don't remember you prior to the day you broke into my shop."

"Huh. It's a mystery, and *I* sure as hell haven't a clue. I don't remember anything before I was born. But you do, don't you?"

"I remember everything since I was created. But it took more than a thousand years for my memories to completely return."

Colin was quiet for a few minutes trying to process the unimaginable, but I was aware when he started thinking about flying.

He looked at me hopefully. "Do you think I have wings?"

I returned his gaze, intending to initiate the Seeing for a number of reasons, and it was like trying to bore through a solid wall. I frowned, increasingly puzzled by the enigma of Colin's existence. I'd been able to See him before, so why not now?

He asked anxiously, "What's wrong?"

"I can't See you and I can't sense your powers at all, which is illogical since I'm the one who triggered them. Or maybe I didn't since you had them all along. You *should* have wings."

Colin swallowed heavily. *Because I'm a freakin' angel,* he thought.

I tried again to See him and pursed my lips in frustration when it didn't work. "You'll have to look inside yourself, Colin; if you have them, you'll know it and be able to manifest them."

"Here goes," he said quietly, closing his eyes to help him focus. I could see the change come over him as he accessed the power and the Light. The otherworldly glow on Colin's face spread to his entire body as he attained his full god stature.

By this time, everyone had noticed what was happening and watched in fascination as Colin changed. It was obvious when he found the information he sought—wings appeared on his back. They were a unique color, the same as his olive skin tone, which was one of the few things that set him apart from his twin, who had black wings.

Colin stretched and rolled his shoulders, getting used to the added weight. When he opened his eyes, it was apparent that he had recognized and accepted his god nature.

Derek shouted, "You go, Colin!" As if it was a signal, everyone started talking and laughing excitedly, admiring his wings.

Beli appeared next to me, and he and I looked at each other in bewilderment.

I don't understand this at all. I literally don't remember Colin. How could he be our brother and we never knew him? What's his god name? I have no idea, do you?

Beli shrugged his muscular shoulders. *No clue. I knew he wasn't my son, but I didn't think I was his ancestor either, even though that was the most likely scenario. I did impregnate my human lover in Inverness—you remember Molly—but my last descendent from her died centuries ago and none of them had magic. Llyr let the information slip about Colin, though how he knew and we didn't is a mystery to me. Our father has to have done this.*

Yes, and he isn't saying anything but "Trust me." I have to let it go for now and go talk to Seth and Chris. They're teleporting to Scotland for their honeymoon this afternoon.

I'll congratulate them in a few minutes. I need to talk to Colin first.

Alright. Thanks for being here, Beli.

You're welcome, Myrddin Emrys. By the way, Llyr and Portunus are still watching over all of you while I'm socializing. He grinned and gripped my shoulder briefly before turning away.

* * *

"Colin," a deep, accented voice called out.

He sensed who it was and swiveled around, watching the god who was the mirror image of himself stride toward him.

He could hardly contain his delight. This man, this being, was his brother. Knowing Merlin was his brother filled him with joy. Knowing Beli was his identical twin gave him a feeling of completion.

Beli came up beside him, grinned, and threw an arm around him, drawing him into a manly embrace. "Well, Brother, I don't know how it happened, but you're one of us. I'm glad."

"Me, too. It seems unreal, though." His new wife took that moment to join them. He felt so much larger than she was that he allowed his body to revert to its human size and sent his wings back to wherever they came from. "Beli, this is my wife, Cathy. Honey, this is my brother, the god Beli."

Cathy gazed up into Beli's familiar face and smiled widely. "Nice to meet you. I feel as if I already know you."

"Don't be fooled by appearances, Sister-in-law. Colin and I may look the same, but our personalities are very different," Beli warned her.

"It's nice to meet you, though," he added hastily, realizing that he might have sounded harsh. His eyes flickered as he received a message in his mind. "Sorry I have to leave so soon—I've been called home. Again, congratulations to you both. I'll keep in touch, and this time I mean it." And he disappeared.

The two of them stared at the spot where Beli had stood seconds ago.

"If he's the Welsh god of death, what are you?" Cathy gazed searchingly into Colin's eyes.

"God knows. Literally."

* * *

I scanned the crowd for my Fae son and his new wife, and saw them standing with Derek and Sarah, who were listening with fascination as Seth described the Fae world beneath Tomnahurich Hill in Inverness. I knew there was an actual doorway at the base of the hill that led to another dimension, another realm, because I had walked through it myself when I'd been hurled into the past and lost my memory.

I forced myself to focus. I had been so caught up in Colin's transformation that I had sorely neglected the other half of this double ceremony. As I approached Seth and Chris, I was struck anew by their alien features. I had become so accustomed to my son's casual, day-to-day look, I'd almost forgotten—until I saw him dressed in his wedding attire and his crown—that he was Fae royalty. Seth stood tall and regal with his bride stationed proudly by his side, and my previous suspicions made sense. The Council of Elders had apparently planned it all out before I had appeared in the Fae Realm in AD 415, which implied that God had orchestrated this chain of events meticulously. I would bed the King's daughter, impregnating her, and our son would be a superior breed of Fae with the blood of the gods running through his veins, appropriate to be the next King of the Light Court Fae.

I watched Chris in her new form and acknowledged that she was the ideal partner for my son. She had accepted her transition from human to Fae with serenity and grace and truly looked the part of his future queen. Furthermore, and most importantly, she loved him deeply.

I wondered if Seth was, in fact, aware of his approaching destiny. There were many other males in line for the throne who he doubtless assumed had more claim than he did, being sons of the current monarch. After all, he was only the king's grandson, not a direct heir.

Seth glanced up at me and I knew he saw something telling in my eyes. His eyebrows lifted inquisitively. "Da, why are ye staring at me that way? And why are ye shutting me out o' yer thoughts?"

I wanted to tell him the truth, but it was neither the time to reveal such information, nor was it my place to do so. He and Chris would be appearing before the High Council within the week, supposedly in response to his action of turning a mortal woman into an immortal Fae, and I would be willing to bet they would inform him of the truth at that time.

"You both look so regal it makes me proud, and I'm a little over-come with the events of the day. Congratulations to you both."

"Thanks, Da." I could tell by Seth's tone of voice that he was aware I was deflecting.

I turned to Chris and took her hands in mine, kissing her softly on the cheek. "Welcome to the family, Daughter." I smiled as it occurred to me that she had been my daughter-in-law for many years as Derek's wife, long before I'd come to Moab.

She blushed and gave me a brief, embarrassed peck on the cheek in return. "I can't believe you're my father-in-law, Merlin, let alone that I'm a Fae princess." She gazed adoringly into her new husband's eyes.

She swiveled to look over at Cathy, standing starry-eyed next to her own husband, who had discovered he was a god. "My sister and I have just had all our dreams come true, and then some."

CHAPTER 36
Inverness, Scotland, Sunday, August 27, Late Night - Monday, August 28, Late Night, 2023

"Oh, Seth, what a cute cottage, I love it!" Chris whirled around, wishing she could see it all at once.

Still in their wedding clothes, Seth had transported them to Ballifeary Road in Inverness, directly to his front door. He hadn't bothered to make them invisible because he knew it would be late when they arrived and thus they wouldn't be putting on a show for the neighbors. Although it was dark, there was enough starlight that they were able to see clearly since Fae eyes adapted well to low light.

Seth had made a production of unlocking the door with the old-fashioned key and presenting it to his bride before he carried her across the threshold. Once he set her down, he'd shut the door, willed the lights on, and magically brought their luggage directly from Moab to his living room.

Chris commenced exploring her new home. "I never knew that you have such fabulous taste in antiques."

Seth smiled but kept silent as she checked out one room after another.

Chris bounced out of the master bedroom grinning excitedly. "The shower in the master bath is custom-built to accommodate wings. I can't wait to try it."

She glanced into the kitchen and approved of the clean, modern appliances. She had done most of the cooking in Moab, but Seth apparently had some culinary proficiency himself or he wouldn't have bothered to buy top-of-the-line stove and refrigerator. She decided to encourage him to do his share of the cooking henceforth, prince or no prince.

She realized the cottage was larger than it had seemed when they first walked in the door, and it started to sink in how many improvements Seth must have made over the years.

"If we were to purchase this house today, what do you think it would it cost?"

"Aboot £275 000, I'd wager. Why?"

"Oh, just curious. What is that, around $400,000?"

"Aye, more or less." He looked at her askance.

"When did you buy it and what did you pay for it?"

"Och, yer a nosy wee thing, aren't ye?"

"You knew that and married me anyway," she said, saucily.

"Aye, I did, *mo chridhe*," he murmured, pulling her into his arms to remind her how much he wanted her.

Chris moaned as she felt her body respond to his nearness. "Humor me and answer the question, okay?" she asked, breathlessly. Belatedly she added, "Please."

He chuckled. "I bought it a few months after 'twas built, significantly smaller than it is now, I might add, and furnished it, for aboot £1000."

She gaped at him. "When was that?"

"'Twas the year1820."

"That's over two hundred years ago," she said faintly. "No wonder you have great antiques."

He smirked. "What's yer point, lass?"

"I keep forgetting you're so old, even though you look my age."

"Except for the time I've been in Moab, I've lived in Inverness, or in the Fae realm beneath Tomnahurich Hill—the humans here call it Fairy Hill, by the way—all ma life. I've been alive for over 1600 years, Chris. Ye ken that, right?"

"Yes, but it seems so unreal to me." She wandered around the living room examining the things he had collected over the years—weapons, tartans, musical instruments, everything exceptionally old, and some items stained with what appeared to be dried blood.

He heard it when she thought, *It seems unreal until I see things like this.* His wife was a perceptive woman.

She pointed out a round, flat, well-used instrument hanging on the wall. "What is that?"

"'Tis a bodhran, a drum used fer centuries by Scots afore a battle tae frighten the enemy. In Ireland, it's said the bodhran was used tae summon the Fae on full-moon nights, so it's a wee bit ironic I played it masel'."

Chris grinned. "Were you ever tempted to drop your glamour while you were playing the, uh, bowrawn?"

"Nay, lass," Seth said with a brief shadow of a smile. Admittedly, he

243

had wanted to show the humans that even a Fae being could be dedicated to a cause. But it would have been extremely distracting, and possibly deadly, to reveal his inhuman aspect in the midst of a battle.

She continued to gaze at the other items displayed. "And what is that?" She pointed at the instrument hanging next to the drum. "Bagpipes?"

"Aye," Seth said. "Yon bagpipes make bloodcurdling sounds that instill fear in the enemy even more effectively than the drum. I played them both when I went tae war, many centuries ago. I played the bodhran at the Battle of Prestonpans in 1745 and the bagpipes at the Battle of Culloden in 1746."

She watched the expressions on his face change as he relived moments in his life that were events she'd read about in history books.

"But why would you get involved in conflicts that had nothing to do with your own race?"

"Ye see, I'm Fae, but I'm also a Scottish Highlander, through and through." He pulled himself out of the reflective state he'd allowed himself to lapse into, and said with a wry smile. "And 'tis verra useful that I'm immortal, since I was killed in both battles and wouldna be here with ye today if I hadna been."

Chris's eyes filled with tears. "You died? Oh, Seth, I can't bear the thought that you would ever cease to exist."

"Dinna fash, *mo muirninn*, it wasna permanent, as ye can see." He held her face in his slender hands and smoothed her tears away with his thumbs. "I dinna intend to die on ye, ever. We'll live forever, together, with our children, and our children's children and their children."

She pressed her mouth softly to his and gazed tenderly into his yellow-green eyes. He had scooped her up and was preparing to take her into the bedroom when she squirmed. "Uh, Seth, I, uh..."

"Ah, ye'll be needin' a toilet, I expect. 'Tis down the hallway, second door on the left."

"Yes, I remember glancing in there a few minutes ago. Be right back," she murmured and hurried away.

As the door closed, Seth's happy, alert expression sagged. He didn't want Chris to know yet what had been on his mind ever since they arrived. In fact, their inevitable visit to the High Council had been constantly in his thoughts for much longer than that.

His journey to Utah five years earlier had been mandated by that same High Council for him to spy on Merlin. As it turned out, he hadn't been in Moab very long before his father had discovered his duplicity. After he'd informed the Council he would no longer betray his father, Seth had heard nothing from them until Oengus showed up unannounced in Moab in 2019, joining the family for their holiday celebration. The Elf had told Seth he had "passed the test," whatever that meant, and Oengus seemed pleased by the way everyone treated Arthur, which had been one of the reasons Oengus had given for his unexpected visit.

Seth probably should have come back home to Inverness at some point, but hadn't felt the need—or the desire—to meet with the High Council or to visit with his Fae relatives, in particular the other princes. He was aware that in the future, one of them would have to take over as King, but he presumed he was at the bottom of the list, as the least qualified for the position.

However, the fact that he had spontaneously mated with a human, which was unheard of, and had turned her, which hadn't been done in millennia, made him suspect the Elders were preparing him to be King, with a ready-made Queen. He was fairly certain his da knew about this and that's why he'd been blocking his thoughts after the wedding. Seth hadn't shared any of this information with Chris in case it turned out he was wrong.

Gods, Seth hoped he *was* wrong because he didn't want to be involved in Fae politics, nor did he want to be King. He'd rather go back to Moab and help Arthur, Merlin, and Colin establish New Camelot. But he was the only son of the only daughter of the present monarch, and if he was chosen, he would have to accept.

Whit's fur ye'll no' go past ye, Seth thought resignedly. He snorted when he realized he'd lapsed into the Scots for "what will be, will be."

As he heard the toilet flush and the water running in the sink as his wife washed her hands, he took a deep breath and put a pleasant expression on his face.

The door opened and Chris burst out into the hallway. "Oh, I'm so excited to be here! You promised to take me flying, husband."

He had discouraged her from using her wings while they were still in Moab, promising her that once they arrived in Scotland, she could fly with him.

"Weel, I wanted tae make love, but we should take advantage of the night and go flying right awa'."

"Wonderful! I'll hold your hand at first, okay? And once I learn a little about—" Chris chattered on, describing how she pictured her flying lesson to play out. When she wound down, she said, "Let's change our clothes first and go do it!"

Seth felt his mood lighten as his new wife's giddy happiness washed over him. "I have a better idea." He spontaneously replaced their wedding clothes with black one-piece skinsuits and transported them to the top of Tomnahurich Hill. In an open area of what had been for hundreds of years an extensive cemetery, they launched themselves hand in hand up into the star-strewn night sky.

A clear night in Scotland was rare and Seth suggested that they make the most of it, so they started by soaring over the Caledonian Canal to Loch Ness, and on to Urquhart Castle, the ancient walls ghostly in the dim light. Built on the site of medieval fortifications, the castle perched on a cliff at the edge of the lake, as it had been since the thirteenth century.

"We're flying over the old Grant Clan lands on the west side of the loch the noo."

Chris had told him she'd wanted to come to Scotland ever since she'd discovered that her ancestors were Highlanders. She looked down, amazed that her Grant ancestors had lived there, for hundreds of years, until the Clearances after the Battle of Culloden had sent them fleeing to Ireland and ultimately on to America.

They finally circled around and headed out to the islands of the Orkney Archipelago off the north coast.

"I read about the Neolithic sites and seal colonies. I hope it's not too dark to see them."

"*Mo chridhe*, we can always fly out there during the day if we stay invisible. This night is merely a wee introduction tae the Highlands for ye. Besides, our eyes are made tae see efficiently with verra little light."

Chris squeezed his hand and smiled gratefully at him. "Thank you, Seth." Her love washed over him and he turned to look at her, his heart in his eyes and his body yearning for hers.

After a brief overview of the Orkneys, Chris was tired—as Seth knew she would be, as new to flying as she was—and they headed home, anxious to celebrate their wedding night.

After luxuriating in the large walk-in shower constructed of smooth, clear, glass blocks that prevented snagging their wings, they dried each other with lots of kissing and stroking. They went to bed but didn't sleep right away, wrapped up as they were in their enjoyment of each other's bodies.

The next morning they awoke in his king-size bed and immediately started making love again, their Fae nature dictating that they would partake in several hours of sexual pleasure before they could even contemplate leaving the house.

"Is it okay to lie on my back? Will it hurt my wings? I want you to be on top," Chris gasped as Seth thrust enthusiastically into her as they lay on their sides.

"Aye, ye need tae spread them out flat and they'll be fine," he explained while they repositioned themselves.

Chris looked up into his face and grinned as he entered her slowly, going deep. "God that feels amazing. You hit the right spot this way and—ooh, yes!"

Seth smirked at her, and proceeded to take them both to a most satisfactory conclusion.

They had finished a hearty breakfast of crisp bacon, scrambled eggs, and hot buttered porridge with cream and honey that they had prepared together, and were indulging in a second cup of coffee, when Seth stiffened. A look of incredulity crossed his face as he received an unwelcome telepathic message.

"What's going on?" Chris asked, concerned that something was wrong.

"Oengus has instructed me tae appear afore the High Council right awa'."

"Oh, I thought I'd be going with you," she said, perturbed at the thought of being left alone on the first full day of their honeymoon.

"As did I, *mo chridhe*, but apparently the High Council had a different idea. I'll be home afore ye can miss me overmuch, lass." He kissed her sweetly and disappeared.

* * *

As Seth materialized in the council chambers, he was dismayed to discover he was facing the entire High Council of Elders. The most likely reason for it was to remind him of his royal status. As the Elders stood and bowed deferentially, Seth wished he had anticipated this occurrence and clothed himself more formally than in T-shirt and jeans.

Oengus, whom he had neither seen nor conversed with since the Elf's visit to Moab at Christmas in 2019, remained standing as the rest of the council returned to their seats. The Elder looked not a day older than he had in 2019, and Seth speculated that he was at least 3,000 years old. It took many centuries to attain a position on the High Council, and many more to become the leader of that illustrious group.

"Yer Royal Highness, thank ye for responding sae quickly."

"It seems I dinna have a choice, as it wasna a request, but a demand for ma presence."

"Apologies, Yer Highness, but the message was, and is, rather urgent."

Seth's brow furrowed in confusion. "Oh, aye? If ye dinna mind, perhaps ye'd best explain exactly what the message is."

Oengus stood quietly for a moment, as if contemplating the correct wording for his response. "The King has 'requested' yer presence, along with yer mate's, at a banquet this night in the Hall of Gems. The other royal offspring of the King have been invited as weel. Ye're expected tae be there." He eyed Seth's casual attire critically. "Surely ye'll dress appropriately, Yer Highness." It was more a statement than a question.

Seth's eyebrows rose up practically to his hairline. The King wanted him to attend an event in the Hall of Gems? He was afraid his grandfather was going to select his successor, and for the lowliest member of the family to be included didn't bode well at all.

Interview concluded, he transported himself home, but before he completely materialized, he hovered incorporeally at ceiling level to observe his wife while she thought she was alone. It wasn't fair of him to do so, but he did it anyway.

Chris was in the kitchen making brownies, singing to herself as she worked, meticulously keeping her wings back and out of the way. He'd only been gone a short while, but she had already cleared up the breakfast dishes and had a batch of brownies in the oven. He loved brownies. He loved her and their unborn child. And he didn't know how to tell her that her life could change yet again before the day was done.

He rematerialized in the doorway and as she saw him, her eyes lit up and she rushed to his open arms.

"You're home!"

"Aye, I'm back, and I'm ready for brownies." Seth decided he'd wait to tell her the news.

After Chris had finished baking and both of them had eaten their fill of the rich chocolatey treats, they donned lightweight jackets and walked the scant quarter mile from their cottage to the river. The day was bright and breezy and they both had to tie their long hair back in tails.

The peat-brown water of the River Ness was incongruously clear, reminding her of the color of strong tea. The river flowed relentlessly northeast toward the Beauly Firth, and seemed terribly deep and dangerous to Chris until she glanced up, laughing as she noticed a fisherman standing in the middle of the river, chest waders wet to midthigh.

"'Tis no' verra deep here, as ye can see, but the current can be strong and the water's cold. I dinna recommend taking a swim," Seth said wryly.

Chris rolled her eyes at him; he was aware of her aversion to cold water.

They continued to stroll along the river's westerly bank until they came to a large footbridge suspended over the tumbling water.

"Let's cross here," Seth suggested with an innocently forthright look.

Chris glanced at him suspiciously. "Okay." She gazed at the old bridge that seemed to sway and buckle as a noisy group of young people tramped enthusiastically toward them, purposely stepping in unison. "Are you sure it's safe?"

"Aye. I helped a man named Manners design and build the thing back in 1880 and 1881."

Chris made a face. "I can't picture you doing civil engineering work."

"I've done many things in ma life—some things I'm proud of, some no' sae much." He seemed lost in thought until he shook off the siren call of old memories. He turned to her with a smile. "Come wi' me, *muirninn*."

She gripped his slender hand tightly as they started to walk over the bridge. By the time they reached the middle of the central span, she felt queasy from the motion of the bridge platform.

Seth gave a hearty laugh. "We in Inverness call it the 'bouncy bridge.' It tends to startle the tourists."

"I can see why," she muttered as they stepped off on the other side.

As they made their way toward the downtown area, the plaintive sounds of a bagpipe began, and they noticed a tall man in full Highland regalia playing the pipes near the ivy-covered entrance to a stately old hotel.

She turned to ask Seth about it and caught him trying to disguise the troubled look on his face. "What's wrong, my love?"

He pointed out a bench facing the river. "Let's sit for a wee bit. There's something I must tell ye."

Chris stared at her new husband, her Fae eyes seeing through the glamour to his true form. In the back of her mind, she knew no one else could see the striking evidence of his—and her—inhuman attributes, but it still made her nervous to be out in public with wings on their backs.

She was concerned that Seth looked so unhappy for someone who had recently gotten married. She wondered if the interview with the Elders hadn't gone the way he'd expected. "You know I love you."

"I love ye as weel, and our wee one growing in yer belly. That isna the problem, ye ken. The Elders had some news that perturbed me and it wasna aboot turning ye Fae." He closed his eyes and took a deep breath.

"We've been invited to attend the King this night at a banquet in the Fae Realm beneath Tomnahurich Hill."

Chris opened her mouth as if to comment and closed it again without saying a word. The shock of his announcement left her speechless.

"I think he plans tae announce his successor."

She finally found her words. "Oh, is that all? You've told me before there are many others ahead of you and it's not likely that you'll be chosen."

When he didn't answer she started to get worried. He noticed her concern and took her in his arms. "Aye, ye're right. I'm worrying for naught, most assuredly. Let's go home. We can make love afore we have tae get ready tae go." He glanced around surreptitiously, confirmed that there was no one watching them, and transported them back to the cottage on Ballifeary Road.

After an eminently satisfying sexual encounter, he created clothing for them in a style similar to what they'd worn to their wedding, but in royal purple. As they stood next to each other in the master bathroom finishing up their ablutions, Chris turned to pull his head down, kissing him reassuringly. "Seth, if the impossible happens and you *are* chosen to be the next King of the Light Court Fae, I'll be thrilled to be your Queen."

He brushed an errant strand of long, blond hair behind her pointed ear. "I ken it, and I thank ye, *mo chridhe*. Ye're a bonny wee lass and I'm glad tae have ye in ma life."

Chris beamed at him. "Let's go if you're ready, my handsome prince. It's not every day an ordinary mortal, er, ex-mortal, gets to have dinner with a king."

Seth was charmed by his wife's reaction and felt a tug of excitement. It had been centuries since he'd attended an event such as this and he wondered if his family had softened in their attitude toward him. Long ago, their rejection had caused him to seek acceptance and companionship in the human world, and he had made a point of staying away from the Fae realm.

Seth kissed his wife again and remembered one more thing. Their crowns appeared on their heads. "Now we're ready tae go."

* * *

She held Seth's hand and watched the now-familiar surroundings of their cottage fade out as they transported to the Fae world. They rematerialized in the entrance to the Hall, where bright light was interspersed with dark shadows, making it difficult for Chris to discern her surroundings. When Seth realized her problem, he showed her how to adjust her eyes, but assured her that the Hall proper would not have such a stark contrast; the sparkling crystals and gemstones on the walls and ceiling gave off a soft, reflective glow.

They followed an oddly shaped being—a different species who was evidently a servant—into the Hall of Gems. They were seated on comfortable cushions at a low table that had been placed on a dais, high enough above the floor to allow their wings to hang down comfortably. Chris looked around and saw that everyone had been seated in like fashion, whether or not they had wings. At one end of the spacious room was a throne and table on a much higher platform. "Where's the King? Why isn't he here yet?" Chris whispered.

"I dinna ken, but he'll want to enter last. It does appear that all ma uncles are present."

"Only a few of them have wings—why is that?"

"They're throwbacks to a time when all Fae royalty had wings. These days, 'tis only Unseelie—Dark Court Fae—royalty who are born with them every time. Except for masel', of course; I have wings because Merlin does."

As she glanced around, she caught a tall woman of ageless beauty eyeing her contemptuously, and wondered who it could be, since she knew Seth had no Fae siblings.

When Chris mentioned it to him, he turned surreptitiously toward the woman and quickly looked away with a grim expression on his face. "I was hoping she wouldna be here, since she isna in line for the throne. 'Tis ma mum."

"That's your mother? She looks so young."

"She's older than she looks, *mo chridhe*."

"Shouldn't you introduce us since I'm her daughter-in-law?"

"The Fae dinna acknowledge such things, Chris."

"Do you think she'll accept that you married—mated with—someone that used to be human?"

"In truth, it willna please her, lass." He chuckled briefly, and looked thoughtful for a few moments before continuing. "I suppose I can introduce ye, but it'll no' be a pleasant experience. She willna be kind tae ye. She's true Fae and has ne'er understood ma involvement with humanity. The fact that ye're no longer human willna matter tae her."

Seth leaned over and kissed her cheek. "'Twas destined that I turn ye and mate wi' ye, sae she has nay choice, ye ken. She must accept ye whether she likes it or no'."

As it turned out, there was no opportunity for Chris to meet her mother-in-law. The lesser Fae servants entered the hall with steaming platters of food, some of which looked familiar to Chris, some exotic and strange, and they both stopped thinking about his mother and focused on the abundant, delectable repast.

It may have been her altered physiology or the distinctiveness of the experience or both, but Chris relished every bite of the meal. The first course of soup had odd bits of surprising crunchiness, which was disconcerting until she realized it was similar to the cream of celery soup her mother had made when she was a child. The next course was vegetables—at least she assumed they were vegetables—which had a pleasantly mild flavor and a texture like squash. The dish was served smothered in savory spices and some kind of clear buttery oil that reminded her of ghee. The meat was tender and bursting with flavor, served with fresh crusty breads with which to sop up the juice. She presumed the meat was lamb or veal, but she couldn't be sure. She turned to Seth to ask him, but found him lost in thought, so she decided to enjoy it, whatever it was. When the dessert course was served, she eyed it with delight since she loved sweets, and managed to consume a substantial amount of something that reminded her of crème brûlée, all creamy custard and caramelized sugar.

Finally, the remains of the elaborate meal were cleared away and warm, damp linen hand towels were offered. They wiped their hands and Chris surreptitiously wiped her mouth as well, then swiftly reapplied her lipstick, which she'd brought in the tiny pocket Seth had made in her gown.

The King had still not appeared and she watched her husband grow more and more agitated. She conjectured that Seth's grandfather had dined apart from his guests, and knew she was correct when two servants came in and removed the table from in front of the throne. She almost wished the old monarch had changed his mind about announcing his successor so they could go home.

At that moment, atonal musical notes announced the King. His long, wavy, dark hair was threaded with silver and held back with a thick band of gold encrusted with glittering gemstones. His face was lined, showing his great age, and Chris guessed wildly that he could be at least 10,000 years old. After all, Seth considered himself to be a fairly young Fae, and he was 1608 years old this year. The King's luxurious robe flowed around his tall slender body, constantly in motion as if it were alive, caressing the old Fae. She wondered why the King looked old if Fae beings were immortal, but perhaps he chose to appear that way.

She took Seth's hand and she could hear his thoughts in her mind. *I'd forgotten how impressive he is, powerful and wise. How could anyone else possibly fill his shoes? And yet, all ma uncles desire tae take his place, each one convinced he's the better choice.*

Seth turned to look at Chris and smiled. *Any of them are more qualified tae be King, sae 'tis doubtful I'll be chosen.*

Oh, okay. She could feel him relax, content to watch the scene play out before them. She was so focused on the King that she never considered it curious that she had heard and replied to Seth's thoughts.

* * *

Seth transported them home late that night, still numb with shock. He had been certain it would never happen. He was the youngest and least experienced of any of his family members, and yet his grandfather had singled him out, praising his integrity, his common sense and his intelligence, complimenting his choice of mate, ultimately announcing that he was the chosen successor.

Once the King had departed, most of Seth's uncles and his mother couldn't decide whether they should curry favor with him or shun him, and for that reason they merely ignored him. However, a few of his uncles gave him such threatening looks that he knew he would need to watch his back. He was grateful to have abilities he'd inherited from Merlin that they knew nothing about, not to mention the fact that he was a demigod. It occurred to Seth that these were the real reasons the King had chosen him.

"When do you have to take over as King?" Chris asked shyly, more than a little intimidated by the proceedings.

"I'll meet wi' the High Council in the near future tae discuss it, but it mayna be for several years yet. Time passes differently in the Fae realm." He pulled Chris into his arms, holding her close. "I'm verra sorry tae have gotten ye into this…"

"I told you I would be honored to be your queen if you were chosen, and I am. It'll be alright." Chris held him tight and kissed his soft lips. "But I hope we can go back to Moab beforehand."

"Weel, I think that can be arranged."

* * *

I blinked, instantly back in Moab. My perception of the proceedings in the Fae realm had been so vivid that it was a shock to see the walls of my office around me.

So, I was correct. The King had chosen Seth, out of all the candidates available, to take his place when the time came. I knew my son wasn't altogether happy about it, but I was exceptionally proud of him. And it was one more increment in the timeline of the ultimate destiny we all shared.

CHAPTER 37
Inverness, Scotland, August 29, 2023, Early Morning

"Oh, this is so much fun," Chris gushed as she soared over Loch Ness, catching an air current that lifted her higher.

"Dinna forget tae control yer rate of ascent, *mo chridhe*," Seth called, glad that the news they'd received earlier hadn't put a damper on her enjoyment of their honeymoon. They should have changed out of their formal clothing before flying, but he'd felt so—what was the word he'd heard in the late 1800s?—discombobulated, that they'd flown off promptly after the banquet and subsequent succession announcements, which hadn't ended until after midnight.

"Seth, who is that?" The apprehension in her voice coincided with his sensing the presence of another Fae in the vicinity, who appeared to be as shocked as they were to discover he wasn't alone in the night sky.

Seth flew unerringly toward the intruder and hovered threateningly in front of the young male with black wings, ready to protect his mate. The unknown Fae seemed taken aback by Seth's greater size and aggressive behavior, and said nothing.

Seth demanded, "Who are ye? I thought I kent all male Fae in Inverness, but I've never seen ye afore. Speak up!" As the other male cringed, he realized he was making matters worse with his menacing tone, and added, "I willna hurt ye, lad."

The young Fae said in a timid voice, "Uh, my name's Randy Hartwell. Who are you? Do you live around here?" He seemed to be struggling to control his wings, as Chris had done when she first tried to fly.

"I'm Seth MacAdam, and this is ma wife, Chris. We live in Inverness. Ye're no' from here are ye?"

"No. I, uh..." He seemed unable to continue, apparently still feeling anxious about meeting other Fae.

Seth waited for a few seconds, and when the man remained silent, he extended his senses, searching for any intent to harm them. He sensed no danger from him, in truth, the young man needed help. He glanced at Chris and she nodded, having sensed his intentions. "Randy, I have questions for ye, but dawn will be here shortly, and 'twould be better if the humans dinna see us, ye ken?" he asked calmly. "We can go back tae my house tae talk, aye?" He didn't wait for a response, merely made a small hand gesture and the three of them stood in the middle of their living room.

Chris looked rattled. "How did you do that, Seth?"

He shrugged. "I dinna ken, I just…did it. I think ma grandfather is already starting to transfer his powers tae me."

* * *

Randy was in awe of the older male's magical abilities and continued to glance back and forth between the two elegantly attired Fae. And became aware of something significant he'd missed in the dark despite his augmented vision: they were both wearing gold crowns.

He gave in to the urge to kneel down to this distinctly royal couple.

As soon as he did so, Seth motioned to him to get up. "I'm no' the King yet, ye ken."

Randy's eyes practically popped out of his head. The Fae King?

"Call me Seth, aye?"

He choked on his reply and managed to nod as Seth narrowed his eyes and subjected him to a close scrutiny.

"Ye're American?"

"Yeah, I came to Scotland trying to find my roots. Guess I found 'em," Randy told him with a hysterical giggle.

"I need tae hear yer story afore I can be certain, but I think ye may be ma uncle's son by a human woman. Ye look like him, and besides that, ye both have black wings. And if that's true, ye and I are cousins, as the humans figure it."

"Huh? You th-think we're related?" Randy stammered, reluctant to believe such a thing.

Seth said, "Aye," and was going to explain what that could mean when Chris interrupted. "You look familiar, Randy. Where did you say you're from?"

"I, I didn't say, but I'll bet you've never heard of it. It's a tourist town in southeast Utah."

The Fae couple exchanged a glance.

"I'm from Utah, myself. In fact, both Seth and I have family in Moab," Chris announced with a grin.

Randy jerked in shock. "What? Are you kidding me? That's where *I* live!"

And then it hit him. "You both have family there? But you're Fae!"

Do you mind if I tell him, honey?

Ye might as weel. I'm fairly certain he's family.

"Seth was born in the Fae realm in the fifth century; his mother is Fae. His father and brothers—who aren't Fae—live in Moab. I was born human in the United States, and my ex-husband—who is Seth's half-brother—lives in Moab." Chris took a breath, aware that she had been chattering away like a magpie, but she needed to tell him the rest. "When I mated with Seth, he turned me Fae." Chris gazed at Seth with such a look of adoration that Randy's breath caught.

Seth returned her look with one of his own and said in a loving voice, "We just got marrit."

Randy was so impressed that he hardly knew what to say. It was obvious that they would both understand his state of affairs if he could work up the nerve to tell them.

As he focused once more on Chris, he realized why she looked so familiar to him. "I recognize you. You work at that store on Main Street, The Moab Herbalist, right? But when you waited on me last, you were human, not Fae."

"Oh, I use a glamour to hide my Fae features when I'm working. Sounds like you've been in the store more than once."

"Yeah, I've been going there for years. I was there just before I left for Scotland—when I still thought I was human." Randy's voice was rough with emotion. "I haven't figured out yet how to get used to my transformation. I didn't even know I was a Faery."

* * *

Seth was starting to feel sorry for the lad. *He's no' a danger to us,* mo chridhe. *He's young and confused—and I think he's hungry. Have we any brownies left?*

Yes, I made extra because I know you crave them. Chris beamed at her husband as she responded silently.

"Randy, why don't I get us something to eat and drink and then you can tell us your story, okay?" Chris jumped up and went out to the kitchen. "I hope you like brownies. And would you like coffee or hot chocolate?"

Seth smiled at her enthusiasm and his eyes followed her with such a possessive look that Randy stared at them both, a grin gradually spreading across his face. At that moment, they seemed like any other newly married couple. "I like chocolate in any form, thanks!"

A few minutes later, Chris came back with a tray of refreshments, and they all helped themselves. Mug in hand, she snuggled up against her husband, who put his arm around her affectionately, and they waited for their guest to begin.

He took a long swallow of his hot chocolate and a bite of brownie and began to tell his story. "I've always wanted to visit Scotland, so when I lost my job, I decided it was excellent timing. I made reservations and left as soon as I could. It was a long flight from Salt Lake City to Inverness, and I spent every minute I wasn't sleeping studying my copy of Lonely Planet Scotland. I didn't want to waste time once I got here. I planned to hike up to the top of Tomnahurich Hill first, since I'd read about it once and thought it sounded, you know, magical.

"It was early morning when the plane landed. I caught a bus into town and found a hostel a few blocks from the bus station. You must know the one I mean—the Black Isle Hostel? It's painted yellow."

"Aye, I ken it," Seth said and gestured for him to continue.

"Luckily, they let me check in right away, so I left my stuff there and I started walking. Crossing the river at Bridge Street, I went south along Ness Walk until I arrived at Ballifeary Lane. Then I took a left on Ballifeary Road and walked through a nice neighborhood of old cottages and bed-and-breakfasts—"

"That's where ye are the noo," Seth interjected.

"Oh, ah, sure, yeah. Anyway, when I got to Glen Urquhart Road, I saw the gate on the other side, at the entrance to Tomnahurich Cemetery, and I dashed across the street, dodging traffic. The gate was open, so I went through and up the old cemetery road that winds around the back of the hill. Halfway up the slope I caught sight of the Caledonian Canal through the trees and snapped a few photos with my phone. Man, it's beautiful! I was pretty happy it wasn't raining, but it was obvious it had been, since everything was soaking wet.

"I continued up the slope and finally reached the top of the hill, which wasn't as natural as I'd hoped. There were large open spaces with lots of old grave markers scattered around, some of them from the 1600s. For some reason, I'd assumed the area would be thickly wooded. And you know what happens when we assume things, right?" he asked jokingly.

"Right," Chris said with a smile, cutting her eyes at Seth, who chuckled and kissed the top of her head. "Ye'd never do anything like that, would ye, *mo muirninn*?" he teased her.

Distracted by their show of affection, Randy cleared his throat. "Anyway, I wandered around for a few minutes, but something happened that didn't make sense. I was suddenly surrounded by a thick grove of conifers that hadn't been there a moment before. I was so excited I forgot to get my bearings before heading into the woods, and never thought how peculiar it was for all those trees to have appeared spontaneously like that."

He took a quick sip of chocolate and said in a hushed voice, "It was…awesome. There were so many shades of green, and the light that came through the branches overhead was a brilliant white, like a laser. It was quiet and felt, well, *ancient*.

"I wandered around for a while, hungry and thirsty, and it occurred to me I hadn't thought to bring food or water with me. I was upset with myself, but decided to use my head. I drank water that had been caught in some of the leaves when it rained. A beam of sunlight shone on a large bush covered with purple berries. I ate one and it tasted so good that I picked and ate them all."

Randy made a face. "You're probably thinking I must be the most ignorant guy who ever lived. I knew Tomnahurich was also called 'Fairy Hill,' and that there were tales of folks who'd entered the hill itself to entertain the Fae, only to find when they eventually were allowed to leave that hundreds of years had passed. But I hadn't gone into the hill, so I didn't think I'd have trouble leaving."

Seth agreed. "Ye took a chance, but ye'd have tae enter the Fae realm itself under the hill—which would be nigh impossible tae do since the entrance is concealed by a glamour—and ye didna. Go on wi' yer tale, lad."

Randy took a long breath. "When the light dimmed I knew I should leave, but I had no idea which way to go. I got scared. I ran down a path that seemed to go in the right direction, ran out into the open, and ended up near the headstones I'd seen earlier. It was dark, so I must've been in that forest all day. I was so relieved I almost cried. I made it back to the hostel in record time. It was a few hours ago—" he glanced at the antique clock on the wall, "—uh, seven hours now, that everything changed.

"I was so tired I went to bed without eating. I woke up a few hours later with my ears and eyes aching and my upper back between my shoulder blades itching. I crawled out of bed and stumbled down the hallway to the communal bathroom, scratching my upper back as I went. The itching stopped, so I used the toilet and had turned to go back to my room when I experienced an excruciating pain and a sudden weight on my back. I looked in the mirror—and got the shock of my life.

"I'd sprouted wings. And if that wasn't enough, my ears were long and pointed, and the pupils of my eyes had vertical slits like a damn snake's! Oh, uh, like yours." Randy looked sheepish, hoping he hadn't insulted his hosts.

Seth shrugged his shoulders. "'Tis true, lad. We have the pupils of a predator."

"I was so wigged out, I wanted to be back in my own room before anyone saw me. And I was."

Randy stretched his shoulders and rearranged his wings, the weight of which he still hadn't gotten used to. "I could see clearly in my dark bedroom, and I felt around the wing bones that had come out of my upper back. There was blood everywhere. I was grateful the other bunks in my room weren't occupied. I don't know what I would have done if someone had seen me.

"The funny thing was, I knew I'd become Fae, and that I'd used magic. I never once questioned it."

"Why was that?" Chris asked.

"Because I'm a fan of fantasy and science fiction, and I'm familiar with Irish and Scottish folklore. 'Course, I used to assume it wasn't *real*."

He leaned toward them to emphasize his words. "I thought I'd figured out what must have happened to me—I'd wandered into the Fae realm somehow, ate and drank there, and it had changed me. But that didn't make sense. People never changed to Fae from human—they always returned to the human realm eventually, years or centuries later. I hadn't had any problem at all returning to the same time period, some hours later than I'd left." Randy stopped to drink some of his chocolate, now cold, and to munch halfheartedly on a brownie.

By now, Randy was running out of steam and Seth was losing patience. He and Chris hadn't had any sleep last night and it was breakfast time. His wife could hardly keep her eyes open. He shifted in his seat, wishing Randy would finish up, but the young man still droned on.

"So I decided to be logical about it. I'd come to Scotland because I wanted to find out who I was. I knew I'd been abandoned as a newborn, wrapped in a tartan, so my birth parents were probably Scottish. I was adopted by an ordinary human couple and raised in a middle class home, but I'd always wondered about my birth parents.

"Then I came here to Inverness and entered part of the Fae realm somehow. I might have been under some kind of spell all along, and being in Faery caused me to revert to my actual appearance. I suspect that's what actually happened.

He let loose a quick bark of laughter. "My God, I have magic, and I can *fly*." He took a deep breath and let it out slowly. "I'm flipping out, but in some ways, I feel better than I've ever felt in my life." He glanced over at Seth, who barely managed to contain a yawn. "Am I a changeling? If so, how did I end up in Utah?"

"I think ye might be, but finish yer story first, aye, and hurry it up," Seth responded gruffly.

Randy nodded, weary as well, but so self-absorbed he didn't notice how exhausted Seth and Chris were. "So, uh, as I'm staring at myself in the mirror, I realize that I have to create a glamour to hide what I look like, 'cause I can't walk around Inverness in my true form. But first, I gave in to an irresistible urge to fly. I transported myself to a secluded spot on the river—you know that area like a park on the east side of the river south of the bouncy bridge?"

Seth gritted his teeth and inclined his head slightly, thinking he was going to strangle the lad any minute.

Honey, he's scared to death of you. Lighten up! Chris glared at him. She'd apparently roused when she'd sensed how frustrated he was. She'd been so easy-going since she became Fae that her reaction surprised him. He made an effort to rearrange his features into a more pleasant expression, but inside he was still fuming.

"Anyway, I launched myself into the sky. I went up until I could see the entire valley, Loch Ness, and south to Fort William, even though it was dark. It felt bizarre to have wings and I had some trouble controlling them at first. I was hovering over Loch Ness when I saw you two flying toward me, and I didn't know whether to be excited or terrified. And now, here I am, and I'm, uh, really nervous again…" His voice tapered off apprehensively.

When Randy finally stopped talking, Seth at first felt an overwhelming relief. But the ordeal wouldn't be over until he decided how to handle this new relative of his. If, indeed, he was a relative. Randy seemed to need a mentor, but Seth's first preference was to wish him *"Beannachd Leat"* and send him on his way. He had enough on his plate without taking on a ward. And he had just gotten married. Chris wanted his undivided attention and he needed hers. But this was not a decision he should make without discussing it with Chris. However, by the look on her face and her transparent thoughts, she was so infatuated with Randy that she was ready to adopt him, despite the fact that he was a grown man, not a child.

One way or another, it was imperative for Seth to confirm whether Randy truly was related to him, and not some interloper trying to get close to him. After all, it was a wee bit suspicious for such a thing to happen immediately after he had become the King's successor.

What if his uncle—Randy's biological father—planned a coup by insinuating his son into Seth's life? And there was a remote possibility that Merlin's brother Sam was orchestrating this meeting for some nefarious purpose.

As Seth was about to suggest that Randy go back to the hostel and get some sleep, and come back later in the day, Chris turned and spoke to him telepathically.

I think you should See him before he leaves, to make sure he's who you think he is.

He was relieved she'd sensed his intentions. *Aye, I'll do that,* mo chridhe.

Seth noticed that Randy was getting restless, as if he was curious why the two of them were silently staring at each other.

Seth stood up and motioned to Randy. "Come here tae me, lad. I need tae find out a wee bit more aboot ye and this is the best way tae do sae. And I can find out aboot your being a changeling at the same time."

Randy wasn't at all sure he wanted to get that close to the next King of the Fae, so he dragged his heels, but ultimately he wasn't able to resist the male's mesmerizing gaze.

Impatient, Seth yanked him closer and adjusted his grip on the young man's forearms. He wasn't experienced with Seeing into some-one's soul, but he should be able to do so—he was Merlin's son, after all. He struggled to direct the process so that he would See Randy's life and allegiances, but the young male would experience only an edited version of Seth's life.

Both of them were bombarded by a kaleidoscope of color and sound until Seth gradually fine-tuned what they were Seeing. After a tumultuous few minutes of discovery, the two of them opened their eyes and stared at each other.

Seth took a long breath and let it out slowly. "Weel, I ne'er would have guessed *that*...Cousin."

* * *

I stopped filling potion bottles and frowned. Em poked her head in the door between the back room and the front of the shop and gave me a startled glance. "What's wrong?"

"My connection with Seth has been erratic since they discovered he's going to be the next king. I've been getting the impression they've met someone, but I can't perceive the details. Our bond has... dissolved." I turned to gaze into Em's beautiful hazel eyes and hoped I didn't look as lost as I felt. "He and I have been in constant contact since they arrived in Scotland, but I can't get through. I can't feel him at all."

"Oh, my God, do you think he's *dead*? But he's immortal so that can't be it."

"I think he's started to assume the old king's powers and they're blocking our connection."

Em put her hand on my arm. "Assuming the old king's powers doesn't sound like a bad thing."

"It is if they're creating a barrier between us."

"What about Chris? Can you contact her?"

I sought my daughter-in-law's unique life 'signature' with my god senses. "She's there, and I don't sense anything wrong, although I can't seem to connect to her telepathically. She may have started to take on the mantle of the Fae queen."

My wife and I locked gazes. "Looks like we have no choice but to wait until they return."

CHAPTER 38
Northern Ireland, Early September, 2023

The newlyweds gazed at the magnificent view of the Giant's Causeway, with the vast, turbulent expanse of the North Channel and the distant coast of Scotland hazy in the background. Unfortunately, the impressive geological formation was overrun by tourists in brightly colored jackets clambering over it like ants on an anthill.

Colin remembered reading in the guidebook that there were 40,000 basalt columns formed by an ancient volcanic fissure eruption at the edge of the pounding surf.

Each one appeared to have a person sitting on it.

"I'd like to take some photos, but there are too many tourists in the way," Cathy complained.

Colin looked thoughtful. "I think I can fix that." He closed his eyes and projected a subliminal message that everyone should hurry back to the buses without delay or be left behind.

Cathy giggled. "Whatever you did, it worked."

He opened his eyes and chuckled. People were gathering up their errant children and streaming up the hill to the visitor center parking lot, eventually leaving the formation unoccupied except for Colin and Cathy.

"Good work, god man." Cathy turned and looked up at him proudly.

"Thanks." He leaned down to kiss her. "But you shouldn't call me that. Em calls Merlin 'god man.'"

"I'll think of something appropriate before we get home, I promise. You know, it's difficult to comprehend that you're one of them."

"Yeah, I know. It's crazy."

What he really wanted to do was leap up into the air, his wings pumping strongly, and soar high over this country of his mother's ancestors. He managed to curb his desire, with difficulty. He could do it later.

They were on a day-long bus tour that included many popular tourist destinations in Northern Ireland: Carrickfergus Castle, Carrick-a-rede Ropebridge that spanned a hundred-foot gap above raging ocean waves, 400-year-old Bushmills Distillery, and the Giant's Causeway, and while it was gratifying to see the countryside without having to drive, flying over it would have been infinitely more satisfying.

"Go ahead and take your photos, Cathy, and we'll walk back to the bus when you're finished. I'll make sure the driver doesn't leave without us."

"Okay." She used her phone, preferring it to her camera, since she'd discovered she liked the quality of the shots better. "I think when we get back to the apartment I'm going to take a shower and a nap before dinner. Care to join me?" Cathy murmured, batting her eyelashes seductively at her ruggedly handsome husband.

Colin looked down at his petite wife and practically purred. "Sure. I'd be happy to wash your back, or any other part of you, for that matter, and a 'nap' sounds good, too." He knew that they wouldn't do much sleeping, if any. They'd been enthusiastically making love whenever they had a chance since the night he'd teleported into her room.

Since the wedding, he'd been riding such a high it was unreal. Between the constant lovemaking and the knowledge that he was a god, he was so happy he could scarcely handle it—in shock at the unbelievable turn of events, but deliriously happy.

With a wide smile, he held Cathy's hand while they walked back to the visitor center. He located their bus driver with his mind and ensured he would wait for them while they bought a few postcards. Afterwards, they found their bus, climbed aboard and took their seats.

When they had first arrived in Belfast and settled into the two-bedroom apartment they'd rented on Salisbury Court, he had taken Cathy flying around the area. He'd shielded them from view with an invisibility spell, although the fact that it rained most of the time might have rendered his spell a bit of overkill. The power that he'd had before the wedding was nothing compared to the glowing well of Light and energy he now had access to, even if it was a drop in the bucket compared to Merlin's.

And Colin was positively thrilled with the knowledge that he was Merlin's and Beli's brother. He didn't know Llyr very well, but he had eternity to get acquainted. JC was another story—he still couldn't fathom how he could be related to *him*. And Satan? He didn't want to contend with that bastard at all. Being an angel was exciting, unnerving, but the fact that God was his father made him distinctly uneasy.

It was odd to realize that the heritage he had always accepted as his, at least on his mother's side, was such an inconsequential part of who he was. It was a mystery. How was it that a god was born to a human mother? He needed to discuss it in depth with Merlin when they got home.

In the interim, exploring Northern Ireland with Cathy was delightful. Neither of them had ever been there, so they had no agendas to pursue other than searching for his "roots." His mother's ancestors had been born in the city of Antrim, on the north shore of Lough Neagh, so they had spent the better part of a week exploring there, hoping to find some evidence of distant cousins who might still be in the area. Colin's mother had done some research on her family tree, but he and Cathy hadn't been able to find any of the people whose names she'd uncovered, despite the fact that the area was crawling with Campbells.

Colin wasn't worried. How significant could it be to have roots in the human world if he wasn't human?

All that mattered was that he was having an incredible time and thoroughly enjoying the area and the people, whether he found any relatives or not.

He did wonder what they would look like if he found them. Possibly like his mother, who had been a brunette with blue eyes and fair skin. It was obvious that his swarthy skin tone hadn't come from his Scotch-Irish forebears.

While he had been lost in thought, the bus had pulled up in front of the Tourist Information Center in downtown Belfast, and everyone was disembarking.

Cathy glanced at him as she stood up and grabbed her jacket and her purse. "Were you taking a nap or thinking?"

"I was trying to figure out how I could have been born to a human mother. Merlin was, but I don't know the details."

"Uh, maybe you shouldn't bring that up until we're alone," Cathy said under her breath.

Colin cringed as he realized people were giving him weird looks. "Yeah, you're right. Not exactly a topic to discuss in public."

They stepped out onto the sidewalk and started back to the apartment. It was an easy fifteen-minute walk and they decided they both wanted the exercise after sitting in a tour bus most of the day. Colin and Cathy were debating what to have for dinner when she let out a strangled noise.

"Cath, what's wrong, honey?"

266

"I, I think I saw him…over there." Her hand shook as she pointed to a spot at the side of the Belfast City Hall and Government building.

"Saw who?

"Now who's being dense? Satan, that's who!"

"Shh, keep your voice down, people are staring at us. And if you did see Sam, you don't want to alert him."

"Colin, what if he's here because we're here?"

"True. Crap. Hold on." He swiftly initiated a combination invisibility and forgetting spell that would affect the people near them and teleported the two of them back to the apartment. They'd planned to stop at the Tesco Express around the corner on Dublin Road to get some groceries, but shopping would have to wait.

Rematerializing in the cozy kitchen of their home-away-from-home, Colin realized Cathy's skin was ice cold, so he glanced at the thermostat to turn up the heat. He held her tightly against him until she warmed up.

"I'll keep you safe, I promise," he murmured. He felt extremely protective of his new mate.

She pulled away from him and started pacing back and forth agitatedly. "I wish you had your gun. You could shoot his ass."

He wanted to chuckle at her reaction but figured it wouldn't go over well. "I'm sure the Police Service of Northern Ireland would take a dim view of a cop from America carrying a weapon while he was on vacation in their country. Besides, I don't need one since I transformed; the magic is more than enough. And, let's face it. Shooting Sam wouldn't accomplish anything in the long run anyway. He's a god."

She dropped into a chair at the kitchen table. "I know, but I don't like feeling so helpless and vulnerable."

Colin hesitated, pondering if he should say anything to her, but finally decided he should tell her the truth. "Uh, if I understand correctly how this whole thing works, since you're married to me and I'm immortal—"

"You're *immortal?*" Cathy interrupted, aghast.

"Well, yeah, I'm a god, so I'm immortal. Like Merlin. Like Beli. Didn't I mention that?" Colin glanced back over his shoulder while he set up the coffeemaker and got clean mugs out of the cupboard.

"No, you didn't." She blinked. "Holy crap."

"No kidding. I feel like I must be dreaming. How can it be real, you know? Hey, watch this, it's pretty cool." He walked into the center of the living room and closed his eyes. A nimbus of golden Light flared around him as his wings appeared and he rose a few inches off the floor.

His wore a long white robe instead of the khaki pants and long-sleeved denim shirt he'd had on before, and his feet were bare.

Cathy leaped out of her chair, gazing raptly up at her husband. He had always looked like a pirate with his long black moustache and swarthy skin, but at this moment he actually looked like an angel.

His eyes flew open. "Oh, yeah, so I didn't finish what I was going to say, that since you're married to me and I'm immortal, so are you."

She gawked at him.

He appeared in front of her with a sexy look on his face, totally naked, no robe, no wings, just a big, muscular man with an erection that left no doubt in her mind what his intentions were. "Let's take a shower."

Cathy didn't answer for a moment she was so overwhelmed. Then her body responded to what he was offering. She smiled enticingly, hurried to strip her clothes off, and headed for the bathroom with her trim hips swaying.

As she leaned over to turn the water on, Colin came up behind her without a word, and pressed against her. She leaned back against him and sighed, happier than she'd ever been in her life. She couldn't grasp the concept of being immortal, so her solution was to consign that disclosure to the back of her mind.

Under the drenching spray of the wide showerhead, they stroked soapy, slick hands over each other's bodies, kissing feverishly as they embraced their rising lust. Colin's wet, dark hair hung long and straight down to his shoulders and he looked so fabulous that Cathy could hardly grasp that he was nearly fifty years old. She stared at him, hard, and had a startling thought. *Oh, my God, he looks like Je—*

Colin raised the corner of his mouth in a crooked grin. "He's my brother."

Her jaw dropped.

"Don't forget, it's a secret."

She swallowed with some difficulty and whispered, "I promise I'll never say a word."

"I know you won't, honey. Besides, who would believe you?" Colin smiled and looked deeply into his wife's eyes for a few seconds, long enough to feel the pull of their love connection but not long enough to initiate the Seeing. Despite the fact that he was becoming comfortable with his magic and his god powers, he wasn't anywhere near ready to try something like that. And he certainly didn't want to admit to his fear that, god or no god, once Cathy saw his tarnished soul, she might not love him anymore.

* * *

Several hours later, Cathy stirred and carefully extricated herself from her husband's arms. As she padded out to the kitchen to get a glass of water, her stomach growled and she remembered that they hadn't had dinner. She opened the refrigerator door looking for something to eat, but her thoughts whirled madly and she ended up staring blankly into the cold space. She was married to a god, an immortal god, and if he was correct, she was immortal as well. How could that be? She'd think she was dreaming if she hadn't seen the evidence of his transformation with her own eyes. And felt the difference when they made love. The first time he had slid inside her on their wedding night, the sensation was so shocking she came immediately. God, she must have orgasmed continuously for ten minutes It was pure luck their house had double-paned windows, was well-insulated, and had lots of tall hedges around the perimeter of the yard. Otherwise, the neighbors would have heard some loud moaning and repetitions of "Yes, yes!"

No wonder her friends and relatives who were married to gods or demigods always had smug, satisfied looks on their faces.

She closed the refrigerator door and took sip of water. She hoped that Chris's honeymoon was going well with her Fae prince.

Cathy laughed. How could it be anything other than spectacular?

CHAPTER 39
Moab, Thursday, August 31, 2023

After the debacle at Swanny Park the previous Sunday, Sam was still fuming. If that interfering Roman son of a bitch, Portunus, hadn't shown up, he would have had a chance to finish off everyone in one fell swoop. Despite the presence of three of his brothers, no, make that four, counting Colin—and wasn't that a pain in the ass to discover Beli had a twin, whatever the fuck his god name was—Sam knew he was powerful enough to have accomplished his goal.

And the presence of his self-righteous nephew, Seth MacAdam, had reminded him of all the work he'd put into infiltrating that damned Fae Elder High Council to plant the seeds of distrust and fear of Merlin. For nothing, as it turned out.

Sam had known he wouldn't be able to stop the insertion of King Arthur's soul into Emily's womb, but he could make them think his brother would ultimately put the newly reincarnated Arthur in grave danger. He'd never anticipated Merlin would discover Seth's treachery so quickly, or that Seth would have the strength to break free of the compulsion to disrupt Merlin's family life and instead, to become an integral part of it. And to find out Seth had been the chosen replacement for the old Light Court Fae King all along, and that the Elders had used Seth's perfidy as a test, was the final straw. His anger erupted like Mount Saint Helens had years ago.

Time for retribution. Dressed all in black as befitted his nature, Sam stood in the center of the huge cavern beneath Balanced Rock, the corners overhead lost in deep shadow. The light he exuded—his own god light—was red, the color of hellfire, bathing the expanse of the lower cavern in a demonic glow. He noted the large, flat, raised rock surface where Nimue, inhabiting her daughter Adrestia's body, had restrained his unconscious nephew Derek. She had used him to lure Merlin to his doom, but Nimue had grossly underestimated Merlin's power and had paid the price. Adrestia's body, containing Nimue's essence, lay unnaturally still in a supernatural sleep in an alcove off the end of the vast room, still awaiting her fate at Merlin's hands.

Sam had decided that since Nimue had proven herself to be weak and stupid, she no longer had any real value to him. After all, Morgana and her minions were still in his thrall, anxious to do his bidding, and he had no patience for dealing with the complicated enchantment that had been placed upon Adrestia-Nimue. He had no particular grudge against the girl, but would experience a great deal of satisfaction from killing Merlin's daughter in order to cause him grief. The fact that she was Sam's own niece meant nothing to him.

Sam called up a shining black sword and contemplated slicing her up into bloody chunks, but he determined that one specific blow would produce the most long-lasting effect.

He lifted the preternaturally sharp blade high and brought it straight down, cleanly bisecting her neck. Blood sprayed everywhere, soaking him. The severed head remained in place for a few seconds then fell to the side. He sensed two souls departing hastily, one to Heaven and one to Hell.

Sam grinned wickedly. He looked forward to torturing that one for eternity.

Sensing his brother was on his way to this chamber of horrors, he made himself scarce, but reserved a portion of awareness for witnessing —and savoring—Merlin's shock and grief.

* * *

Sam must have deliberately allowed me to sense him at the exact moment the blade entered Adrestia's neck, so I would have no way to prevent him from executing her. If it had been anyone except Sam, I could have been there instantly and prevented it, but he affected me in ways no one else did and he took advantage of my weakness.

I fell to my knees in front of the rock bier upon which the grisly remains of my eldest daughter lay. Knowing it was futile, I sent out every last sense I had anyway, hoping that some spark of her life energy and soul remained, but I felt nothing. She was gone—forever.

I was absolutely devastated. I had arrived too late to prevent Sam from killing Adrestia in his endeavor to destroy Nimue. Not that I cared one whit for the stone-cold bitch who had been my nemesis for century upon century, despite that she was my brother Beli's daughter. The fact

271

that I had impregnated my own niece was not something I liked to think about; I hadn't been aware I was related to her when she had seduced me back in the fifth century. But I had loved my daughter Adrestia even though she and I had never seen eye-to-eye.

I had known that Adrestia's soul was submerged beneath her mother's essence and had tried for years to come up with a way to rid Adrestia's body of its parasitic burden, but I had never succeeded. I was supposed to have met with Beli to jointly resolve the situation, and neither of us had felt any urgency to do so. Now it was too late.

Raw emotion swept over me like a tidal wave, drowning me in rage, sorrow, and guilt, and my lament filled the vast cavern beneath the geological structure that would be known in the future as Balanced Rock. Nimue's lair for an unknown period, this cavern existed thousands of years in the past, and I'd only discovered the full extent of it in 2014 when she had abducted Derek. Her ploy to lure me to my destruction had been an abysmal failure for her. She had no idea that I'd changed a great deal since her attack on me and mine at Matheson Wetlands Preserve the previous year.

The bitter taste of failure gagged me. I was a powerful god, and yet I hadn't been able to stop this horrific event from occurring. What did that tell me about my real effectiveness? How could I support Arthur, or save all of humankind, if I couldn't save my own daughter?

I didn't realize how intensely I blamed myself until I felt an ethereal touch upon my shoulder, and heard a faint, sweet voice in my mind.

Father, it is not your fault. I'm at peace. Grandfather has forgiven me and guided my soul back home. I'm with him now.

Adrestia, I'm so sorry I couldn't save you.

Please do not grieve, Father. It was never my destiny to be a part of your life, in the olden days or in modern times. I played the part God assigned to me and it is finished.

I felt what might have been a kiss on my tear-washed cheek and then my daughter's presence was gone.

* * *

Emily had been shaken when her husband abruptly stiffened in horror and disappeared from the table as they sat down to lunch. He hadn't shared with her what had happened to distress him so badly, but she'd sensed—from what little he had allowed her to feel—that it had nothing to do with their closest friends or immediate family members. While it was a considerable relief to know that, she was concerned that

Merlin hadn't felt it necessary to let her know through their bond what was wrong.

She thought about it until he returned, and decided she would have to be patient. He'd had so much on his plate lately she didn't want to add to his burden by being the demanding wife. He'd let her know what was going on soon enough. She hoped.

CHAPTER 40
Moab, Monday, September 25, 2023, Early
Afternoon to Late Evening

I stood in the living room staring out the window, lost in thought. I was still reeling from my daughter's death more than three weeks ago, unable to get back to even a semblance of normal. I hadn't told Em about Adrestia, but had incorporated that devastating experience into the rest of my many issues that needed to be resolved.

I was mired in apathy and a sadness that I couldn't shake. I had been distant with my wife and withdrawn from our everyday activities. I felt like I was wearing a dark, heavy, hooded cloak that I couldn't take off.

"Merlin, we need to talk."

I slowly turned and saw Emily standing near me, waiting for me to acknowledge her. I was surprised to see her, thinking she was at work, until I remembered that she had taken the day off.

"What is it, Em?" I was weary to the bone with the weight of the world's problems on my shoulders and I could hear it in my voice.

"I don't know what's gotten into you lately to make you depressed —you haven't shared any information with me so I have no idea what's wrong—but I can see that it's affecting you profoundly. I've tried to be patient, hoping you'd confide in me, but you haven't done so. Frankly, I'm at my wit's end.

"So, here's what I think is going on, and please, correct me if I'm wrong. You're worried that you've failed somehow, that you're not good enough. For centuries you've yearned to be human and have hidden from yourself the fact that you never were or could be a human being. And humans make mistakes. The reality has always been that you're a sorcerer, a god, an angel, a being who—supposedly—shouldn't make mistakes. So there seems to be an unacceptable contradiction in your mind.

"Merlin, the bottom line is, you're the finest *man* that has ever existed, and you're the only one who can't see it. You're kind and loving and concerned about everyone else's welfare. That's what really counts in this world. You're a shining example of what humanity should strive for."

Emily's statement was so powerful that it jolted me out of my misery. Her frankness stirred my awareness, and her love and appreciation soaked into me like the parched earth absorbs the rain. The Light shone once again in my heart, illuminating the dark place that I had somehow created for myself.

I wrapped my arms around the compassionate, intelligent woman I'd married and held her close, breathing in the intoxicating scent of her skin.

I kissed her tenderly. "I'm sorry I've shut you out, Em. As usual, you've saved me, helped me to refocus on what's significant and what I need to do."

"That's what I'm here for, and I'm glad, since I can't stand to see you so damned unhappy."

"The main reason I've been melancholy is that Adrestia is gone. Sam kil…" My breath caught as searing pain washed over me again. I fought to get past the lump in my throat and continued, "…killed her. He decapitated her. She'll never be able to come back."

"Oh, my God, I'm so sorry." Her eyes filled with tears as she touched my face tenderly. "I've wondered what had happened for weeks. Why didn't you tell me sooner?"

"I couldn't. I buried it inside with everything else I've been dealing with. But it's time to resolve those issues once and for all." Reconnecting with the Light inside me had finally burned away the indecision.

Em smiled through her tears. "Alright, god man. Go for it."

* * *

In my office, a cup of strong black coffee in hand, I recalled the conversation Derek and I'd had years ago, when he'd suggested my problem was that I wasn't all together, that I might need to merge with my clones in all times and dimensions to truly be whole again.

I had been procrastinating for far too long. I'd been focused on raising Arthur, which had been crucial, but I could have dedicated some time to figuring out what to do regarding my other selves. Could I have been afraid to examine the situation and its ramifications?

Afraid. That wasn't like me at all. And yet, hadn't I reacted in much the same way when I met another version of myself? I had been driving up the La Sal Loop Road, ostensibly searching for portals through which I could finally reconnect with Arthur in Avalon, when I had spotted one that looked promising.

However, the portal I stepped through not only failed to reunite me with Arthur, but it brought me face to face with another version of *me*. After a brief conversation with the other Merlin, I had fled that encounter in abject fear, racing home to my wife, who had comforted me fiercely and assured me of her unwavering loyalty and support. Of course, at that time I hadn't been aware of certain aspects of my celestial nature, but that shouldn't have mattered.

There had to be something I wasn't seeing—or facing.

I was a god. I was completely connected to the vast energy of the universe and to my father, the Creator of said universe. How could there be something lacking in me?

I conjectured that the problem was the hypothetical difference, a schism or separation, between my two personas: the sorcerer, Merlin, and the god, Myrddin Emrys. But every time I started to examine this vital issue, which could be the basis of all the troubles I had been experiencing lately in the human realm—other than the obvious interference by my devilish brother—I was either distracted or I conveniently forgot about it.

I gritted my teeth and decided to take action. I remembered that I had a whiteboard I'd purchased and never used. I hauled it out of the closet and hung it on the wall near my desk, then rummaged through one of the desk drawers for the markers and proceeded to make a list. It seemed ironic that I would choose to employ a method similar to Colin's investigative techniques when solving a murder, but it was appropriate, after all. A heinous act—a murder—*had* been committed.

I wrote, *Step One: Recognize and Acknowledge the Problem,* and then grimly checked it off. I had done that. And I wouldn't forget that my fear seemed to be the major problem.

Next I wrote, *Step Two: Analyze and Face My Fear.* I stepped back, stared at what I had written. Why in the world would I be afraid? It didn't make sense. I tried to open myself up to it, to face it head on, and immediately realized that it was an obstacle of pure emotion—one of those human emotions I treasured—inside of me. It had always been there but I'd never perceived before that it was preventing me from accomplishing my goals.

I seemed to be getting to the root of my issues. Emotions, including fear, were inhibiting my ability to reconnect to all other aspects or clones of myself, and worse than that, they were blocking my ability to see the necessity of doing so. With that simple discovery came a burst of clarity: Once I had scaled that seemingly insurmountable wall, bypassed or breeched that obstruction, and had identified and reunited with all my other selves, I could become the unique "super-being" that God intended me to be. And it dawned on me that I'd had glimpses of this truth all along and had forgotten, which was a very *human* response to life-changing realizations. But even while understanding this intellectually, I still needed to act on it.

So I wrote, *Step Three: Do It!*

I grinned wryly. How did the old saying go? *Easier said than done.*

I could begin by opening myself up to all those other selves and inviting—I paused, considered what was at stake, and realized that *inviting* wasn't going to cut it and changed my wording—*summoning* them to return to me, to come home. What a daunting prospect it was, knowing there could be as many clones of me as there were worlds, timelines, and dimensions. I assumed my other selves would know how to merge with me, but what if they didn't? Or even worse, what if they didn't want to merge with me? And if that happened, would I even be aware of it?

How would I force someone to give up his own existence, as he saw it, even though *I* knew his life was but a shadow or faint reflection of mine?

All I could do was try. Not knowing what to expect, I closed my eyes, pictured blasting a large hole through that wall of emotion, and through that imaginary aperture I sent out an urgent message to all aspects of myself—a call-to-arms, as it were—to return to me.

At once I was filled with dozens, then hundreds, of my clones returning, merging with me, my spirit swelling as each one became reintegrated; the memories of their separate existences adding to my considerable store of information. Time passed unheeded as more and more of my alternate selves became reabsorbed, until at one point, the flow slowed and stopped. Something wasn't right—

—I was standing in my own spacious quarters in Pembroke Castle. Arrow slits in the outside wall allowed a few weak beams of sunlight to cut through the otherwise gloomy space and gave a limited view of the Pembroke River below. The room was chilly and damp, even though the coals in the brazier were glowing hotly and colorful woven tapestries covered the walls of cold, gray stone.

It was early January in the year 1486, the sky mostly overcast and promising snow before nightfall. It had been over four months since my master Henry Tudor had defeated King Richard III in battle at Bosworth

CARYL SAY

Field. He was currently in London preparing for his marriage to Elizabeth of York and he had left me to manage things in his absence. I took my responsibilities seriously, yet I yearned to witness the nuptials scheduled to take place on Sunday next. It would be a significant event, effectively uniting the House of Lancaster and the House of York, bringing an auspicious end to the decades-long strife.

I had been advisor and companion to Henry Tudor for many years, having previously served his father Edward. 'Twas I who had encouraged Henry to claim direct descent from King Arthur, since he was determined to be seen as the embodiment of a virtuous hero. Descended from the English King Edward I on his mother's side, Henry would be a powerful force able to unite Britain as Arthur had striven to do.

Referring to Arthur stirred memories of my previous life, and I remembered awakening in the Crystal Cave in the year 1469. It was the tumultuous period the English called the War of the Roses, in which the warring factions of the Plantagenet family and the influential barons supporting them laid waste to the countryside in one vicious battle after another.

Having experienced firsthand the majority of Arthur's battles in the fifth century, I had neither stomach nor tolerance for the carnage, the wasted lives that came with the power struggles existing in a kingdom such as this, and—

I wrenched my own consciousness free of my clone's memories and realized I was in his body in Pembroke Castle, which was located some thirty miles—little more than a hard day's ride on dry roads—from my old hometown of Maridunum in the southwest part of Wales.

This Merlin had readily acknowledged the summons to merge with me, and therefore he should have relinquished his own reality as the others had done. So what was *I* doing *here*?

I, the original Merlin, had never been awake during the fifteenth century, nor had I ever advised the Tudors. Yes, Henry Tudor had become the King of England and had married Elizabeth, the daughter of Edward IV. He had claimed descent from King Arthur, and even named his first son Arthur. Yet history as I knew it had never mentioned that King Henry VII had a sorcerer by the name of Merlin at his side.

Sadly, Arthur Pendragon had produced no legitimate descendants, so Henry Tudor's claim was patently false. Arthur had sired many "natural" children, as illegitimate offspring were called in those days, but none survived to an age to procreate. Even Arthur's son with his sister Morgana had died before he had sired any children who survived to child-bearing age.

278

And Arthur Tudor, the eldest son of Henry VII, had died childless at the age of fifteen.

There was no doubt in my mind that I would have to leave this alternate reality posthaste and return to my own, somehow taking this other Merlin's consciousness in tow and reconciling the incongruity. But I was finding it difficult to extricate myself from the body of my alter ego.

Finally, I concentrated on all my connections in the twenty-first century: my wife, my children, and their children and grandchildren, not to mention all the other individuals who had allied with me and whom I loved. Using those connections as an anchor, I pulled my mind back to 2023, hoping my ploy would work and both of us would end up in Moab.

* * *

I gradually opened my eyes, taking in the artwork on the walls of my office, the whiteboard with its list, my oak desk and chair. My counterpart was standing beside me giving me a concerned look.

"Are you alright?" he asked solemnly. "I hope you know what you are doing, as I most certainly do not."

This didn't bode well. "You do agree to merge with me?"

"Of course, Merlin, you are the source. I am but a reflection of you, after all. Once I received your call, I recognized the truth and let go of all else so you could take over."

"So it was obvious to you to do so."

"Yes." His familiar face looked bewildered.

There had to be something I had overlooked or hadn't done correctly, which was odd since at least a thousand of my clones had come back to me so far, without any problems whatsoever.

The truth came to me. How simple. I smiled as the Light inside me embraced the Light that was now evident around the other Merlin.

"I knew you would figure it out," he said as his Light and mine became one. He seemed to dissolve into a mist as his molecules merged with mine, causing a sensation that defied description.

I came to standing with my arms out to the sides as if welcoming a long lost relative. In a way, I suppose I was—he was a hard-won part of me.

"Oh!" A shocked exclamation and a movement in the doorway had me turning to face my wife. She had apparently witnessed the other Merlin's essence joining with mine.

I felt the weight of my concerns lighten even more and I grinned widely at her, happier than I'd been in ages. I'd finally started to put myself back together.

We stepped toward each other, meeting in the middle of the room. We held each other tightly, and then I kissed her with carefree abandon.

"Mmm, what was that for?" she murmured after she had recovered from my unanticipated assault on her senses. "Not that I'm complaining, you understand."

"Since I was gone so long, I had to make up for lost time."

Emily looked at me askance. "You walked in here less than twenty minutes ago, Merlin."

"Oh? I was in 1486 for what seemed like hours. In actuality, my mind was there but my body was still here in the office."

"I thought you had never been awake in 1486."

"I hadn't been. But in that alternate reality, my clone was. He answered my summons to join with me, and somehow I ended up with him there, in his body, and had to forcibly bring his essence back here."

"I did see a shadowy form disappear into your body. It was like seeing a double image of you, out of focus, and having the two images become one."

"That's exactly what happened, Em." I kissed her again and held her against me as I made a few more notations on the whiteboard. "With the exception of the Merlin from 1486 reuniting with me one on one, I've reintegrated a multitude of my alternate selves who accepted my initial summons, but there is one in particular who refused to do so."

"Really? That's unexpected. Which Merlin refused you, and how could that happen?" Em asked.

"It's the Merlin from the alternate Moab, the one with whom I've interacted before and whose existence upset me so much. I've tried to enter his mind and he's powerful enough—or desperate enough—to prevent me from doing so. I'll need to go there physically, through the portal in the La Sals, to confront him face to face, to look him in the eye when I tell him it's imperative for him to merge with me."

"I'm going with you."

I was taken aback. "I don't think that's a good idea, Em."

She was adamant. "Merlin, when you came home to me that day, years ago, you were shaking like a leaf, you were so frightened. I admit I was surprised, since I didn't think you were afraid of anything. So I'm going with you, to support you. What could possibly happen? You could always make us invisible."

I still had my doubts and she saw them on my face. "Oh, for Pete's sake, you're an immortal god and the other Merlin is a part of you. And besides, your father has dominion over that reality, also. So, let's go."

I grinned crookedly. It had been a long time since she had asserted herself like this.

"Okay, you win, Em. Remember, the other Moab is exceedingly different from ours. Magic is commonplace, used openly, but is considered a necessary evil. Practitioners are free to use magic—no one has been burned at the stake for at least a century in the alternate Utah—but they are regulated closely and there is substantial mistrust of the magical community by the human population."

"I understand." She looked down at her casual attire, which was like mine, jeans and T-shirt. "Are we dressed appropriately?"

"Yes, we'll do." I put my arm around her. "Ready?"

She nodded and we vanished from my office, reappearing at once on that brushy hillside in the La Sal Mountains where I had found the portal years ago. The late afternoon light shone harshly on the dry vegetation.

"Is that it?" She pointed to a spot twenty feet off to the left and up the hill a ways.

"Yes, right there."

I parted the brush so we'd have a relatively clear path, and as we approached the wavering distortion in the air, I opened the portal, allowing a hazy light to shine out into our reality.

She gave me her hand and we stepped through. The terrain looked like I remembered it, in other words, exactly like the section of hillside we'd just left—chest-high brush all the way up to the ridge. There had been a major fire in 2021, but the brush had grown back as thick as ever.

"Hmm, so far I'm not impressed." She grimaced and I chuckled.

"It's not the countryside that's different here, Em. Anyway, your suggestion earlier about being invisible in the town was a sensible one, and necessary, at least at first. I'm going to take us to The Moab Herbalist, where we'll check both the store and the upstairs apartment. If that doesn't pan out, we'll search for his home. If he never found his own Emily, he wouldn't be living in your old mobile home, and it's highly unlikely he would be in the house on Doc Allen, unless he's sharing it with other single men." I thought about alternatives he might have chosen—or been forced to choose—as an abode, but quickly rejected them as not practical for this Moab's Merlin.

We were still standing in the brush when Em spoke.

"Uh, why are we still here?"

I shook myself. "Sorry, I was lost in thought for a moment." I made us invisible and then we were standing on the sidewalk outside The Moab Herbalist. No work had been done on the storefront. It was badly in need of repainting and the windows hadn't been washed in years. The sign hung crookedly and the paint was peeling so badly it was difficult to make out the lettering. We looked at each other in dismay. If the store had been taking in even a fraction of what it did in our world, Merlin should have been able to maintain the store's exterior appearance.

I glanced around, noting that many stores on this block had been boarded up, including the bank across the street, and there were nowhere near as many people out and about as there should have been at this time of day. Traffic was sparse, and most of the vehicles were old.

"This reminds me of the future Moab we traveled to where magical creatures had invaded the town," Em said.

"But that wasn't real, it was a vision of the future Llyr had created to help me understand my powers. This is an alternate version of our reality."

I took another look at the crooked sign and winced. "Let's go inside. With any luck at all, he'll be there."

The inside was as shabby as the outside. The old vinyl flooring was cracked and dingy, and the walls had never been re-painted. It was clear that this Merlin had never created a reading corner, never stocked fantasy or science fiction books, never held storytelling sessions in which he could unobtrusively share his magical past. A glance at his unadorned front counter confirmed that he made and sold basic charms, potions and herbal tonics. There were no fragrant soaps or lotions or gift baskets to encourage customers to add to their initial product choices, no bright posters or artistically lettered signs or price tags.

We stood in the corner and watched a few customers come slinking in, evidently uncomfortable visiting a practitioner of magic. We glanced at each other, imagining the sadness and loneliness this Merlin must experience on a daily basis. And I wondered why, if he was so miserable, he wouldn't want to come home to me.

Then he came out of the back room. He was dressed in clothing that, while it was patched and worn, appeared to be clean. His long hair had been combed and was neatly tied back. But the most impressive change was his dazzling smile, which lit up the room like the sun coming out from behind a cloud.

It was obvious what must have happened. He'd finally found his

Emily, or his Derek, and he was happy. I had told him to keep searching and he had. And now I was insisting he leave the person and the happiness it had taken him so long to find.

Em turned and caught my eye. *Oh, my God, he met someone who loves him!*

Yes. What should I do? I could force him to leave but I can't bear the thought of taking him away from his loved one, I replied silently.

"What are you doing here, Merlin?" A familiar voice with a strong Welsh accent inquired. "And this must be your Emily. She's lovely."

I had been so focused on Em I hadn't noticed the customers leave, or that I had allowed us to become visible again.

I turned my head and gazed at my other self. He stared back at me, looking as startled as I felt. On closer inspection, it was apparent that he had aged a great deal in the ten years since I'd seen him last. He appeared to be in his early fifties in human years, and his ebony hair was liberally threaded with gray. Could this Merlin have lost his immortality and had started ageing again?

"You look the same as the day we met! How can that be?" He looked shocked.

"Merlin, I'm immortal, a god, and you're my alternate self, thence you should be the same. How can you have aged?"

"Me, a god? Hardly." He laughed faintly. "As soon as I came to this God-forsaken town, I started ageing again. It could have had something to do with the fact that Satan took up residence here around the time I opened my shop. Moab has become like hell on earth. The reason I refused to obey your summons is that I can't leave now. I finally found my own Emily after all these lonely years and she has a son I've adopted. His name is Morry, and I love him as if he were mine. Em had married Derek Colburn, the other person you told me to find, but he and his partner Ken Wilson had burned to death in a freak wildfire out in the park several years ago."

I closed my eyes. I, who never suffered from illness, felt nauseous. My brother had caused such suffering, in so many places, times, and dimensions it boggled the mind.

Em was still standing at my side, tears coursing down her face.

I had to make a decision and return us to our own Moab.

"Merlin, I have no choice, I must gather all my clones and become the complete being I was meant to be, before I can accomplish the task for which I have always been destined. Arthur has been reborn, and he and I will save the world, but not until I am reunited with all aspects of myself. However, for now, I will leave you in peace, to enjoy the life and the love you've always dreamed of."

"Arthur is back? It is truly a miracle." For a moment, his narrow face gave away that he longed to see his king again, then the look faded. "Thank you for telling me, and for giving me some time with my wife and son. Who knows, time in this Moab may move faster than it does in yours and when you finally summon me again, I'll be dead and gone. I can't say I'm sorry I'm no longer immortal—it was always a heavy burden to bear."

We gazed silently into each other's eyes until he abruptly turned and walked away. He didn't look back as he slipped into the back room and pulled the door shut.

I clasped my wife's hand tightly and we returned to the portal, where we swiftly walked through it, leaving that desolate Moab behind.

* * *

Still blinking away tears, Emily stood next to her husband on the hillside in her own reality, and allowed the magnificent view of ridge after ridge of red rock, shadowed blue with evening, to soothe her soul. She turned to look at Merlin and realized tears were also trickling down his cheeks. The encounter with the ageing Merlin in the alternate Moab had been one of the most distressing things she'd ever experienced.

"What are you going to do, god man? You can't take him away from his family."

"No, it would be too cruel." He wiped the tears away. "I'll continue gathering in all the other parts of myself that are still out there. I'll leave him until last, and if he's correct, and time is passing at an accelerated rate in his reality, he may be dead by the time I summon him again. Somehow, I never anticipated such an occurrence. The thought of an aspect of myself ceasing to exist is inconceivable."

"And unbearably sad."

"Yes." They stood hand in hand as darkness fell, and one by one, the distant stars blazed brilliantly in the night sky.

Emily stirred and stretched up to kiss his cheek. "I'm getting cold and hungry. Let's go home, my love."

* * *

We were both quiet during dinner that night. I was feeling uneasy, as if I was missing something vital. Then I realized my error. My father had created my alternate selves to take over some of the responsibilities of my god self on this earth and I had been calling them all back to me! How could I have been so obtuse? But perhaps it wasn't too late. After all, there were still an untold number of my other selves that hadn't yet answered my summons. Deep in thought, I heard my wife start to speak and dragged my attention back to the present.

"Merlin, that's a great idea! The rest of your clones can keep track of certain areas of responsibility for you, kind of like the way computers can be programmed to run different tasks simultaneously and store lots of information so it can be retrieved later."

I laughed. "We're back on the same wavelength, Em. It should work. Since I can't undo the summons, I can send out an addendum to let the rest of them know what I want them to do."

We made short work of the kitchen cleanup and decided to retire early. Although I didn't need to sleep, I wanted to feel her body next to mine in bed. I had spent a great many nights away from her recently, working in my office, and our relationship had suffered for it.

"Would you like to…shower together, my love?" Em murmured.

I hugged her close and kissed her cheek as we headed for our bedroom. "That's a brilliant idea."

"Why do you think I suggested it, big guy?" she smirked.

I didn't bother pretending we were anything but magical beings. As we entered the bathroom, our clothes disappeared, the water was flowing from the showerhead at the perfect temperature and our large fluffy towels were ready on the rack. In a moment, we were in the shower, and I was holding my wife tightly against my body, my arousal making it clear to her that I wanted her badly. She reached down to stroke me and I moaned, taking her mouth voraciously.

In my urgent need, I lifted her up, held her against the wall of the shower enclosure and surged deep inside her, causing an explosion of erotic sensation for us both. As the warm water beat down on our straining bodies, we quickly brought each other to climax. It wasn't romantic, but it was what we both wanted and needed. Sex had always been imperative to me in this guise of humanity that I maintained. Some things weren't available in the spirit world of the god realm. Physical intimacy was one of the more important ones. The love bond with a mate was another.

As we stood facing each other, water cascading over us, we gazed into each other's eyes and recognized how privileged we were to have found one another, no matter how it had happened. And as immortal beings who were husband and wife, we had the opportunity to cherish our existence and everyone in it with us, forevermore.

We dried off and brushed our teeth, and I smoothed lotion over my wife's curvaceous body. We got into bed and I held Emily until she lost the battle to keep her eyes open, and slept.

I watched over her, seeing her dreams, and I had an idea.

CHAPTER 41
Moab, Tuesday, September 26, 2023, Early Morning

Emily smiled as she danced with her handsome husband on the most exquisite beach she had ever seen. The fine-textured white sand was pleasantly soft and silky beneath her bare feet and there was a gentle, warm breeze caressing her body, which was clad in a long, white, gauzy négligée. Merlin was dressed in thin, white pajama pants, his chest bare and glowing in the bright moonlight. His long, glossy black hair flowed over his shoulders and his eyes glittered the color of emeralds. The clear night sky above her was filled with millions of stars, and graceful night birds glided above an ink-dark sea, placid waves continuously meeting the sand and retreating in a never-ending rhythm. She could hear a song on the breeze, old yet familiar, which brought tears to her eyes though she couldn't quite make out the lyrics.

Merlin had flown them to this secluded spot, holding her safely in his arms, over a tropical land filled with sweet-scented night-flowering vegetation, rivers and streams flowing lazily along and eventually merging with the endless sea. They had reclined together on a patch of soft grass at the edge of the beach and made slow, delicious love, his body glowing with the Light from which he had been created and his glorious wings spread wide above them.

Afterwards, they danced. The music swelled around them and she recognized the song as Merlin began singing to her in his angelic baritone.

"'Like the river flows, surely to the sea, darling so it goes, some things are meant to be…Take my hand, take my whole life too, for I can't help falling in love with you.'"

He kissed her passionately, held her against his chest and leaping up, he soared skyward toward the moon as he sang again, "'…for I can't help falling in love with you.'"

* * *

Em awoke slowly, stretching luxuriously, the lovely, sumptuous dream and the refrains of the old Elvis Presley song still resonating in her mind.

She sighed, wishing Merlin still slept beside her. *It can't be helped; gods don't need to sleep*, she thought resolutely, and sat up on the edge of the bed, automatically reaching for her slippers with her bare feet.

In place of her fleece-lined slippers, she felt something gritty and looked down.

Her eyes widened in disbelief as she saw grains of pure white sand on the carpet and noticed the gauzy white négligée draped over the arm of her rocking chair. It was the same garment she'd had on in her dream.

"Merlin?"

He appeared in front of her, wearing the pajama pants from her dream.

Em pointed at the sand and the négligée and gave him a questioning look.

He smiled and began to sing softly, "'...darling so it goes, some things are meant to be...'" He reached for her hand, and pulling her to her feet, he continued, "'Take my hand, take my whole life, too, for I can't help falling in love with you.'"

As he finished the last strains of the romantic song, he framed her face with his elegant hands and kissed her sweetly.

Emily burst into tears.

* * *

"It was real, wasn't it?" she asked as she hurriedly dressed in her favorite gray leggings and a long-sleeved pink T-shirt. They had made love for the past hour and she was late for work.

"Yes, darling Em, it was. I did whisk you away to a South Sea island. I remembered how much you loved that old Elvis Presley movie from 1961, *Blue Hawaii*, and the song he sang in it."

"It was one of the most romantic, wonderful things you've ever done for me, Merlin. Thank you, my love." She put her arms around him and kissed him, breathing in his intoxicating scent that always reminded her of how extraordinary he was.

"You are most welcome," he said solemnly. "I love you, Em."

They were both remembering what had happened the day before in the bleak world of that alternate Moab. "And I love you, Merlin. I'm so grateful we have each other."

She wished she could stay home with him, but she needed to open the shop soon since she was going to be on her own today.

"I'll come in and help you later on if I'm able to, alright?"

"Okay, god man, see you then," she said, and blew him a kiss as she ran out the door.

CHAPTER 42
Moab, Tuesday, September 26, 2023,
Midafternoon to Early Evening

Emily was tired and it was only two in the afternoon. Even though Merlin's romantic South Seas gift had lifted her spirits immeasurably, yesterday's adventure in the alternate Moab had been traumatic. She knew she should be able to go inside her own being and connect to the limitless energy that fueled the universe, but somehow she couldn't quite remember how to do it.

She'd had no choice but to cover the shop by herself. Her mother was spending a week with her Fae grandfather, Oengus, who had shown up on a whim a few days ago, and she couldn't begrudge her that. Chris and Seth were still in Scotland getting over the shock of him being chosen as the Fae King's successor. She understood their desire to take as much time together as they could as an ordinary couple, but hoped they planned to come back to Moab before Seth ascended to the throne. Em assumed that Chris would be resigning, but she didn't know for sure. Colin and Cathy had returned from Northern Ireland but she had requested a few days to recuperate before coming back to work.

Em urgently needed to find someone to help her in the shop, but hesitated to hire a person she didn't know, particularly one without magic. She wished she could count on her husband to pitch in on a regular basis, but he was focusing even more stringently upon finding and reconnecting with as many of his clones as was possible and she hesitated to ask him. She could ask Arthur to fill in once in a while, but asking the former King of Camelot to work as a retail clerk seemed wrong.

So she bit the bullet and worked by herself. She used magic often, but she couldn't let anyone see her and there always seemed to be a nonstop flow of customers.

Lumina could help her a few days a week. It would be a simple matter for her daughter to teleport from Logan. She could encourage her to move back here before the baby was born.

The thought of a new grandbaby made Em feel better, as did looking forward to going home and taking a hot shower before dinner. And knowing it was Merlin's turn to cook put a grin on her face.

Em looked up as the tiny bell over the shop door tinkled its usual high-pitched melody and an elderly Latino man in a worn, ill-fitting jacket entered. He had a slim build, stood approximately five feet seven and seemed oddly familiar, although she couldn't remember exactly when she had seen him in the shop before. But familiar or not, she always tried to be polite and welcoming to every customer, so she fixed a bright smile on her face and nodded in greeting. He gave her a nod in return and headed toward the book shelves.

Over the next hour or so customers filtered in, chose merchandise and made their purchases. Em was busy, but she tried to keep an eye on the old gentleman. Fortunately, she didn't have to go into the back room for any bulk herbs. He sauntered around the shop in a slow but sprightly manner, peering at the various potions, herbs and soothing lotions. On his third circuit around the room, he started whistling a haunting melody that, while she didn't recognize it, sent chills up Em's spine.

She saw unexpected movement out of the corner of her eye; she was certain someone as old as he appeared to be couldn't move that fast. She turned to face him and did a startled double take. The old Latino man was gone and a middle-aged Asian woman had taken his place. She was wearing a flowered dress from the 1940s and had the hairstyle to match.

Emily stared. She knew the individual hadn't been Asian—or female —when he entered the shop, and she'd never seen an Asian woman regardless of age come in or the Latino man go out. What the hell?

The phone rang and as she answered, she kept her eyes on the door to make sure the person didn't abscond while her attention was elsewhere. As Em finished up the conversation, she realized she was nervous, for some reason. She glanced around expecting to see the woman and instead noticed a man gazing directly at her, his eyes like chips of obsidian in a wrinkled face as dark as strong, black coffee.

This is getting weird, she thought, and reaching out with her magic, she sensed…nothing. It was as if there was no one there. She could see the man standing in the reading area, but now he was Caucasian, his eyes bright and ageless despite his stooped posture and numerous age spots sprinkled liberally across his face and hands. He was over-dressed for Moab in a long-sleeved white shirt, conservative gray suit and maroon and gray striped tie. She realized that she had seen this man in the shop in the past; she had even helped him with his purchases.

The store was quiet so she decided to speak to him.

"May I help you find something, sir?" Em asked, pitching her voice a little high and a bit loudly, assuming he was hard-of-hearing.

"I imagine you can, my dear. But there is no need to shout, my hearing is quite good, actually," he said in a cultured British accent.

Emily flushed in embarrassment. "I'm sorry, I just assumed..."

"And that is the root of many problems, is it not? People make assumptions and don't think before they speak," he said kindly. "Well, not to worry, my dear."

He straightened, walked fluidly up to the counter, and stood relaxed in front of her, most indicators of his apparent old age gone. He was over six feet, possibly as tall as Merlin, with shoulder-length black hair streaked with gray, and laugh lines radiating from the corners of his eyes.

She looked startled at this even more abrupt change in the man's appearance and demeanor. And then he spoke again.

"I came to see you, Emily."

She gasped. "You did?"

"I'm your father-in-law."

Feeling as if she might faint at any moment, Em belatedly noticed the familiar green eyes and the undeniable resemblance to her husband. "Oh, God..."

The man grinned mischievously, revealing perfect white teeth. "Yes?"

* * *

Em was dumbfounded.

"Perhaps you would consider closing the shop for the remainder of the afternoon, so we won't be disturbed." His voice was a beautifully modulated baritone like his son's and should have made her feel at ease. It didn't.

She forced herself to respond without her teeth chattering or her voice shaking.

"I can do that," she said hoarsely and walked mechanically over to the door, locked it, and flipped the sign in the window. She forgot that she now used magic for such mundane and repetitive tasks.

"Would you...like some tea?" she asked him uncertainly, her lips numb.

God said, "That would be lovely, Emily, thank you," and waited patiently while she fetched hot water, mugs, and a small basket of assorted tea bags from the back room.

"Shall we sit down?" he asked, and when Em didn't respond, he took the tray from her and set it on the coffee table. "Sit down, my dear, and be at ease."

Looking into his ancient green eyes, she perched on the edge of the chair cushion. She understood that he wished her no harm, but relaxing in the presence of God was not an option for her.

They sat facing each other in the reading area, sipping mugs of British Blend black tea.

"I can't believe it," Em said, finally.

God smiled benevolently. "You know, Daughter, I've been here before. I've even purchased things. I'm surprised you didn't recognize me when I entered the shop today."

"All I saw was an elderly man, or, uh, several elderly men and a middle-aged woman, in need of my help, and, and—" she stuttered, her stiff posture indicating that she was about to bolt like a frightened horse.

"I'm sorry, my dear, I didn't intend to put you on the defensive." He patted her hand and tilted his head inquisitively. "I'm positive my son mentioned I was coming for a visit."

The hot tea had relaxed her to some degree and loosened her vocal cords. "Oh, he did, but that was some time ago, and he said it might be years before you came."

"Ah, I see. Your mind decided my visit was in the future so it was acceptable to forget about it. Understandable. But I'm here now, Emily, and I'm going to allow you to entertain me."

Her eyes widened and her face paled.

God smiled sweetly and patted her hand again.

Anxiously, Em glanced at the clock on the wall above the counter. "It's getting late and I usually leave at six o'clock. Would you like to join us for dinner? Uh, I mean, that is, if you eat. Dinner. Or whatever." She covered her eyes in mortification.

God took pity on her at that point and went to her, pulling her into a fatherly hug. He kissed her cheek affectionately and gave her a reassuring pat on the back. "My dear Emily, you are my favorite son's wife in this human realm and you are a part of the humanity I created, so in essence you're my daughter any way you look at it. I love you. And in contrast with the human male whose sperm contributed to the creation of your body, I created your soul, and I can assure you I will always be with you."

Emily gradually relaxed and was able to bask in the joy of being held by the Creator of the universe. She put her arms around him and exhaled happily. "Thank you...Father."

"Let's go home—to your house, not Heaven—" he hastened to clarify his wording when Emily looked alarmed, "—and I can help you fix dinner."

She sat up, blinked, and stared into her father-in-law's twinkling eyes, a laugh bubbling up inside of her at the thought of God helping her in the kitchen.

"Okay, I'll take you up on that," she said, forgetting that Merlin was supposed to be cooking.

The two of them materialized in Em's living room, and she was grateful she had cleaned the house recently.

"Merlin must be in his office. He's been having a hard time since Adrestia died. Now he's connecting with his other selves, bringing them all back together in his being, and—"

"Father?" Merlin stopped and stared as he entered the living room. "What are you doing here?"

"Is that any way to greet me, Myrddin Emrys?" God's Voice reverberated through the house and, Em suspected, out to the city limits. "Come here, Son." And he held out his arms as if Merlin was a small child.

Merlin stepped forward eagerly and Emily inhaled sharply at the sight of her husband and his true father embracing each other. She had witnessed Llyr and Merlin hugging each other quite often, when everyone thought Llyr was Merlin's father, but their coming together was nothing like this. These two flowed together like two swiftly moving streams intersecting, merging into one body and dissolving into pure Light.

* * *

My father and I returned to our human forms and grinned at each other. I couldn't remember when we'd ever met and interacted like this before in the human realm. Of course, he had been here when I didn't remember who *I* was, and didn't realize who *he* was. I was thrilled and grateful he had come to me when I needed him most.

"I have so many questions to ask you, Father."

"My dear Merlin, why do you assume I'm going to answer them?" God grinned in amusement.

My face fell. "But...I thought that was why you're here."

"My goodness, you've become self-centered, Son. There are others here on this plane that I came to see as well."

I clamped my mouth shut. How could I have forgotten? His human appearance notwithstanding, this was the being that had literally created the cosmos and everything in it. I was his son, yes, even his favorite, but it was rare to get an intelligible answer out of him. I had experienced his machinations and his capriciousness innumerable times over the eons since he created me.

"You're correct, Father, as usual," I said, bowing my head reverentially. There was no point in pursuing my questions. If he decided to answer me, I'd know about it. I glanced at Emily and saw her shaking with suppressed laughter. I raised my eyebrows at her.

"Shall we make dinner, children? I'm looking forward to eating tonight. I haven't consumed food in, oh, let me see, several millennia, at least."

"We were planning on having tacos tonight, if it's alright with you," I said tentatively.

"Splendid, I've never had tacos before." God rubbed his hands together in anticipation. "By the way, you need to invite Arthur and Guinevere. It's high time I met King Arthur and his queen."

"Certainly, Father, I'll take care of it."

Arthur, you and Gwen are invited to have dinner with us tonight. There's someone visiting who would like to meet you.

We were planning to have a quiet evening at home, Dad. Can we do it another day?

I noted an undercurrent of impatience in his thoughts that I didn't care for and replied implacably, *No, I'm afraid not. My father is here, Arthur, and he has requested your presence and Gwen's specifically. So be here by seven fifteen.*

What? God is having dinner with you? Alright, we'll be there shortly.

* * *

Gwen, who had gotten the salad fixings out of the refrigerator and started to rinse the lettuce, noticed Arthur standing silently in the middle of the room.

"What's the matter? You have a really weird look on your face," she said, drying her hands on a kitchen towel.

"Dad contacted me telepathically. He wants us to come for dinner tonight."

She glanced at the food on the counter. "Did you ask him if we could have a rain check?"

Arthur looked at her blankly.

"Sorry, it means a postponement."

"Oh, right. Yes, I did, and he said that wasn't an option, that his guest requested our presence."

Gwen hastily put the food away. "Who is this 'guest'?"

Arthur took a deep breath and let it out. "My grandfather."

"I thought Emily's father was dead."

"He is."

"Oh…God," she said faintly, as it occurred to her who Merlin's father was.

"Exactly."

"Should I change my clothes?" she asked, fretfully smoothing the fabric of the trim black slacks and white blouse she'd worn to work.

"No, you look fine. Should I? Do I look okay?"

Gwen examined him critically and winced. "You should put something on besides jeans. Merlin's a bad influence on you when it comes to clothing."

Arthur closed his eyes. Instantly, navy blue linen slacks and a long-sleeved pale blue dress shirt replaced the jeans and cotton T-shirt he'd been wearing. Bernard tassel loafers took the place of athletic shoes.

"Ooh, you look *delicious*, er, I mean, handsome, very handsome." She put her hands on his shoulders and stood on tiptoe to brush her lips against his. It took every bit of willpower she had not to ravish him right there in the kitchen.

Arthur groaned as her erotic thoughts aroused him. "Sweetheart, we don't have time for that, but by all means, keep it in mind for later." He gently held her away from him while he struggled to control his physical reaction to her nearness—and her thoughts.

"Sorry, I can't help it, you're such a gorgeous man that I can't keep my hands off you," she teased, then glanced at the clock. "Uh, oh, when are we supposed to be there?"

"Now." He retained his grip on her arms and teleported them promptly to his father's house. As soon as they materialized in the living room, he let go and they turned toward the kitchen. Merlin and an older man who looked very much like him were making salsa and heating corn tortillas and refried beans.

God was making tacos.

Arthur felt an irresistible urge to laugh. This was his grandfather?

He turned to Gwen, who was staring at the scene in the kitchen and they shared an amused look.

* * *

I sensed Arthur's and Gwen's arrival and their reaction to seeing my father helping me with the meal. I glanced at God as he glanced at me and winked. Naturally, he knew. He knew everything, continually, and enjoyed every second of it.

"Come on in you two. What would you like to drink?" I wiped my hands on a dish towel and got a bottle of Lagavulin out of the cupboard.

"A shot of that would do nicely, Dad, thanks."

"Beer for me, please. I could never drink something that smells like burnt cat piss," Gwen said, her noise crinkled up in disgust.

My father started laughing, which was so contagious that we were all still chuckling as Em came out of the bedroom to see what the commotion was. She was wearing the leggings and long-sleeved T-shirt she'd worn to work but had her comfortable slippers on.

"It's nice to hear laughter in this house no matter what the reason is." She greeted Arthur and Gwen with hugs and kisses and helped herself to a beer.

We were getting ready to put the food on the table when God turned to me. "You know, Merlin, there is enough here to feed two more. I think we also need to invite Colin and Cathy, don't you?"

I hesitated for a fraction of a second. "Absolutely." *Colin, you and Cathy are invited to dinner tonight. Father is here.*

* * *

Uh, sure, Merlin, we'll be there in a few minutes. Colin stood still, trying to comprehend that God had decided to have dinner in Moab, Utah. He didn't know how to react. Even though he'd spent his honeymoon confident and happy in the knowledge of what he really was, he hadn't considered what it would be like to come face to face with his father.

He finally drew a long, deep breath and tried to summon a bit of equanimity.

"Colin, was that Merlin?"

He looked down at his wife of four weeks. "Yeah, he invited us to come over tonight because God is having dinner with them and he wants us to be there."

297

Cathy froze in place, shock registering in her eyes. The lyrics to Joan Osborne's song, "One of Us," started playing in her head. *What if God was one of us? Just a slob like one of us? Just a stranger on the bus, tryin' to make his way home...Like a holy rollin' stone...back up to heaven all alone...*

Colin's facial expression reflected outrage, horror, and amusement one after the other. "Please don't tell me you're going to have that song in your mind when we get there."

She blushed, having forgotten that he could read her thoughts. But she rallied, "He's probably got a great sense of humor. And he's omniscient, so he already knows. Besides, he *is* one of us, in a way."

He closed his eyes and groaned. "I suppose so, but the thought of meeting him is kind of freaking me out. I was Catholic before I met Merlin, and even though I haven't gone to church in years, part of me is saying it's sacrilegious to think about God that way."

He ran his fingers through his hair and started pacing back and forth. "I'm a friggin' cop, Cathy, and I've done some terrible things in my life. How do I face *God*, even if he is my—" he paused in trepidation "—father."

Colin, you two need to get over here ASAP. Dinner is on the table and we're all waiting for you.

* * *

I was standing in the living room when Cathy and Colin finally appeared, looking flustered.

"Sorry we're late," he said uncomfortably.

"It's alright, you're here now. Come in and say hello to our father." I motioned for them to precede me into the dining room, where God had risen from his seat at the head of the table.

In a panic, Colin glanced at me before gazing apprehensively at our father, who smiled at him in welcome and understanding.

"Hello, Colin, it's lovely to see you, my son."

"Oh, uh..."

God ignored Colin's less than succinct greeting and turned to Cathy. "And this must be your charming wife. How are you, my dear?" His British accent made his words sound a bit formal, but his slanted green eyes were filled with loving warmth.

Cathy could barely speak she was so dazzled. "I, I'm fine, thank you...sir."

God smiled at her, then turned back to Colin and waited for him to speak.

"I…Father? Is that really you?"

God smiled. "Who else? I have come to reassure you that all is as it should be. You and Myrddin Emrys have found each other again, and you can begin the real work I sent you both here to do."

I swiveled around and stared at him in astonishment. Real work? Colin was crucial to the work Arthur and I were destined to accomplish? I had known Colin would be an asset to Arthur, and he was destined to be a part of New Camelot, but I'd had no idea his presence was essential to *my* efforts.

God changed his features to look like an older version of Colin and Beli and turned to face me. "Son, you should know better than to make assumptions or to second-guess me."

I managed to choke out, "You're right. I apologize."

He tilted his head slightly in acknowledgement of my capitulation. "Well, let's eat, shall we?"

It took a few moments to get everyone seated and beverages distributed. Considering who was attending our meal, it wasn't surprising the food had maintained its optimum temperature while we waited for my brother and his wife to arrive and greetings to be exchanged.

Father seemed to enjoy the meal and consumed an impressive number of tacos, loaded with cheese, onions, lettuce, refried beans and ground beef, and topped with sour cream and our homemade salsa. When he had swallowed the last bite and wiped his mouth with great care, he leaned over to speak to Cathy, and said as though continuing a previous conversation, "And you know, I've always enjoyed that song. It was I who suggested to her, in a dream, that she should sing it."

Cathy's breath caught as she realized that God was referring to Joan Osborne's song, still running in a loop through her mind. "I was only ten when it came out, but it's always been one of my favorites."

"Ah, we have something in common, don't we, Daughter?"

"I guess we do…Father." She grinned, feeling at once happy, lighthearted, and peaceful in making a small but meaningful connection with him.

When we were all finished and had pushed back from the dinner table, I suggested adjourning to the living room for a digestif. After everyone had been served Courvoisier, I motioned to Colin to come and talk with me. "This might be your best shot to ask Father your questions."

"Are you sure? I'm feeling nervous about this."

"Colin, when you were a churchgoer, did you feel as if you were communicating with God?"

"Yeah."

I looked over at our father, who was sipping his cognac and chatting animatedly with Arthur and Gwen. "He's the one you communicated with, the one who listened to your heartfelt prayers. He knows you better than anyone else does because he created you. Go and talk to him —he's waiting for you."

* * *

At that moment, God glanced over at Colin with a look calculated to dispel all of his mental reservations, a look of such love and acceptance that Colin started walking toward him without hesitation.

"Let's talk privately, shall we, my son?" God said, back to his British accent and resembling Merlin and Llyr again.

Colin had scarcely nodded in agreement when he looked around and realized they were standing on the Rim in Merlin's favorite spot.

"Father, why can't I remember you or Merlin or Beli from before I was born in this body? I can feel my real self, so I know what I am, but I don't understand it." Colin couldn't keep the uncertainty and distress from his voice as he questioned the one being who knew the truth.

God reached out and stroked Colin's hair, offering comfort and paternal affection.

"You'll remember when it's time, my son. It's necessary, for now, for you to be ignorant of your celestial past. I can tell you—however difficult it may be to accept—that you begged me for this opportunity." He beamed. "Know that I love you, Colin."

"I'm glad, Father." He paused for a moment and came up with one last question. "Is Colin even my real name?"

"As real as any other, but not your original name, no."

Before Colin could blink twice, they were standing in the living room again, and God had turned toward Merlin.

* * *

I shall leave soon, but first I must tell you something, Son. Be aware that Samael's presence in Moab is not a recent occurrence. To the detriment of your family, he has been here off and on for many years, spying on you and worse. I should have warned you, but I presumed that you would discover his presence and banish him. I admit, I have always expected more from you than from any of your siblings, since you are my firstborn.

By the way, how is Portunus doing at his post? Another unfortunate choice of mine; not necessarily the most effective one I could have made.

I responded cautiously, *Yes, Father, I'm aware that you have had Portunus "guarding" us, and no, he hasn't been able to stop Sam from infiltrating my family. The results of that fiasco have yet to become known, and they won't be desirable. As I'm sure you know.*

I'm certain you will prevail, Myrddin Emrys, now that Colin is more or less aware of his true self. He doesn't remember the details of his origins, but that will come in time.

I don't remember him at all, and neither does Beli, his own twin.

That is inconvenient, isn't it? Oh, and by the way, it was an interesting evening. I thoroughly enjoyed myself.

And on that unsatisfactory note, without saying goodbye to anyone, he departed. I don't know why I expected anything else. It put me in mind of a quote generally attributed to Saint Theresa of Avila: "Well, if this is how you treat Your friends, no wonder You have so few of them." We were family, not just friends, but the sentiment still applied.

I had hoped, even expected, that Arthur would come to me with questions, observations, or even basic conversation once God had taken his leave, but he and Gwen teleported home without saying more than 'Good night.' It didn't escape my notice that neither one of them thanked us for dinner. Em and I had raised Arthur better than that, and I knew Gwen was normally polite, so I was unhappy at their rudeness. This might be one more subtle yet sinister indication of Sam's influence.

"I'd hoped Arthur and Gwen would stay and chat. After they made such a point of reminiscing about their first wedding during dinner, I thought for sure they'd want to discuss this one," Em said, disappointed and hurt.

"I know, and I'm rather upset with both of them."

Em looked around at our kitchen, leftover food, dirty dishes, and pots and pans covering the table, stove, and counters. She sighed dejectedly and I took my cue. "No worries, I'll do it." As I intentionally ran my gaze from the dining room and through the kitchen, dishes were cleared and washed, food was put away, pots and pans were scrubbed, counters and stove were wiped down.

"You're certainly efficient at that, god man. I knew I kept you around for a reason," she quipped.

I gave her a wry grin and she held my face while softly pressing her lips to mine. "Thank you, Merlin. I could have used magic myself to clear things up, but I appreciate your thoughtfulness."

I returned her kiss tenderly. "You're welcome, my love."

"I think I'm going to take a bath and read a book, okay?"

"Sounds like a plan, Em. Personally, I'm going to do some thinking." I watched her appreciatively as she sashayed down the hallway and into our bedroom.

Turning to stare out of our living room window into the night, I thought about everything Arthur and Gwen had discussed. Em hadn't realized that they were hinting at somehow duplicating their first wedding, and I knew I would have to find or create a specific venue for them, and soon. It was imperative that Arthur focus on our mission, but it seemed he wasn't going to do that until the two of them were married again.

My father had made it clear that I must deal with Sam's evil activities posthaste. I wasn't going to forget it was a priority—I was sick to death of my brother's hold on us—but Arthur's wedding had to be arranged and accomplished without delay.

CHAPTER 43
Moab, Tuesday, September 26, 2023, Evening

I was gazing out the window, lost in thought, when I heard the back door open and close and realized Colin was still here.

"I took Cathy home a few minutes ago. I was in the back yard getting some fresh air and thinking about everything that happened earlier," he explained.

Without warning, pure happiness filled my being. I had a brother who lived here in town, and wouldn't constantly be leaving me to return to the god realm. And the knowledge that he was a close friend warmed me to the core. Derek had been my friend long before we knew we were father and son, but there was something about the feeling of comradeship I had with Colin that I'd never experienced before.

He saw something in my expression and quickly walked over to me, pulling me into an affectionate hug. I held him tightly, inhaling the richness of his cologne and his own, distinctive male scent. He was Beli's twin, but in so many ways he was entirely different. I loved Beli, but not the way I loved Colin.

"Christ, Merlin. If we keep this up, people will think we're lovers," he said kissing me playfully on the cheek.

I laughed out loud as Colin released his grip on me. We both knew we weren't so inclined. Since we were brothers, we could hug each other any time we wanted, regardless of what anyone might think.

He winked at me, and made himself at home by pouring each of us a glass of Lagavulin. "*Slàinte mhath.*"

"*Lloniannau,*" I replied as I tapped my glass against his.

Colin's eyebrows pulled together in a puzzled frown. "What language is *that*? Chinese?"

"It's Welsh," I said with a grin. I had seldom spoken my native tongue since I moved to Utah, and it seemed strange to use it again.

"Could have fooled me, Brother." Colin took a long sip of his Lag and gave me a lopsided smile. "I was so in awe of you when we first met."

"And…now you're not?" I raised one eyebrow.

"Not the way I was, but I sure as hell respect you even more, now that I understand the colossal responsibility you've got on your shoulders. And with that being said, I, uh, have something to confess."

I felt his guilt wash over me as he cringed.

"You know Cathy and I returned from our honeymoon a week ago."

"Yes." I wondered where this was leading.

"I went directly back to work because the department caught a case. I didn't want Owen to go out alone if Sam might be involved, and I—"

"Colin, cut to the chase, will you?"

"Well, I was using a touch of magic like I have been at crime scenes for years. I made the mistake of getting caught up in it, and Owen must have seen my aura, because he commented that I was surrounded by a bright light. Oh, and I forgot to mention I was levitating twelve inches off the ground. And, uh, my wings kind of…popped out." He hunched his shoulders. "Shit, how much trouble am I in?"

I was at a complete loss for words. Years ago, Cathy had confided in me that Colin wasn't disciplined with his magic. I was concerned at the time, but thought he would have gained experience and restraint over the years. And now that he was aware he was a god, I figured he must have acquired some self-control.

Bollocks. I should have confirmed his ability rather than assuming he knew what he was doing. "Did anyone else see you besides Owen?"

"No, there was no one else around."

"Thank God for small favors," I muttered. "What did Owen say when you inadvertently revealed things he shouldn't have seen?"

"He said, and I quote, 'OMG! That's sick!'"

I looked at him blankly. "What does that mean?"

"I think it's teen slang from a couple of years ago meaning, 'Oh, my God! That's awesome!' Owen isn't a teenager, but he's still fairly young."

I never understood why people couldn't manage to use straightforward speech. But then again, teens were a different breed and making up slang expressions apparently helped them to feel unique. I didn't remember Lumina ever saying things like that, but she'd never spent any amount of time with other young people as she matured.

Colin glanced at me nervously. "And he said, 'I suspected all along that you were using magic.'"

I scratched my head, considering what type of damage control I should do. Something occurred to me. "Owen's been working with you over a month, correct?"

"Yeah, he started the same day we found Jack Crandall's body."

"Could he be an unwitting tool for our brother?"

Colin froze with the glass part way to his lips. "Oh, fuck me a runnin'. That never occurred to me. Can you tell? Without Seeing him, I mean?"

"If he wasn't your assistant, I could. But as it is, we're back to that same issue I've had for years, of not being able to sense the details about people connected to my family members."

Colin looked pensive as he shook his head. "I can't picture Owen as a pawn of Satan."

As I started to protest that literally anyone could come under Satan's influence, he interjected, "Wait, I have an idea." He pulled his iPhone out of his pocket, touched the icon at the bottom of the screen and selected a number. He waited impatiently for the call to go through. "Come on, answer…Oh, hey, Owen, it's Detective Campbell. Sorry to call you so late. What? No, it's not about a case. Meet me at—" he rattled off my street address "—in the next few minutes. We need to discuss something vital. Yeah. Okay, thanks." He ended the call.

"What good will it do for me to meet him? I'm still not going to be able to tell if Sam's infected him," I said.

"I think you can, with my help. Are you willing to try it?"

I was taken aback, since I'd never even considered such a thing. But it made sense, particularly when I recalled that my father had said Colin was an integral part of the work I needed to accomplish.

We were replenishing our drinks when there was a knock at the door. I opened it, and a man in his early twenties looked at me expectantly.

"Hi, is Detective Campbell here? I'm Owen, his assistant."

"Yes, come on in, Owen, I'm M—" I caught myself and merely said, "I'm Detective Campbell's brother."

Owen stepped into the living room, saw Colin, and looked doubt-fully between the two of us, comparing our appearances.

Anticipating his comment, Colin glanced at me with a smirk. "Different mothers."

I returned his look impatiently. It was the truth, more or less, but had nothing to do with our pressing need to See Owen.

I offered the man a drink and went into the kitchen to get him the beer he'd requested. I hoped having a drink together would help to alleviate the awkwardness between the three of us.

Even as Owen tipped up the bottle and drank, he was intently focused on Colin, who finally said, "I wanted to talk to you about what you saw the other day."

Oddly enough, Owen appeared to be relieved. "Is that all? Hey, it's all copacetic. I won't tell anyone I saw your wings, or that you were working magic."

Colin gaped at him. "How come you're not shocked out of your mind at what you saw? Do you have magic yourself? Are you Fae, or a shapeshifter?"

Before Owen could answer, I perceived enough about him that I could tell he was a normal human being. He had a brilliant, insightful mind and a wild imagination, and had possibly encountered magical or celestial beings in the past.

Owen shrugged. "I spend my free time immersed in fantasy and gaming. In my world, anything is believable."

He smiled at me as if he'd finally recognized me. "You own The Moab Herbalist, right? Where all the knights hang out and some of the clerks are Elves?"

Colin and I stared at each other in astonishment.

"Jesus H. Christ!" Colin exclaimed. He muttered a quick apology toward the ceiling.

I took a deep breath and decided to introduce myself. We'd gone way beyond keeping our secret and it was apparent that Owen needed to know.

"Alright, Owen, I guess I should introduce myself properly. I'm Merlin Ambrosius, the Sorcerer of Camelot."

With perfect aplomb, Owen said, "Yes, sir, I know."

I blinked at him, and turned to Colin. "Alright, let's do this."

After briefly telling Owen what to expect, Colin and I grasped each other's wrists, then Owen's, and Saw him. Having Colin boost my perception was like putting a higher wattage light bulb above the bathroom sink—every detail of Owen's existence appeared with absolute clarity in the mirror of my mind.

Minutes later, all three of us emerged from Owen's journey of self-discovery. I was relieved that there was not one iota of evil or dark influence in the man's being, nor was there any trace of traditional magic, which confirmed my preliminary assessment. He did however, have the ability to sense and accept the existence of the supernatural. I had never encountered any other human being with such a gift and speculated that my father had planted him in our midst.

Sure seems that way doesn't it? Colin responded to my thoughts.

Yes, and I appreciate his assistance.

Unaware of our silent conversation, Owen exclaimed, "That was incredible, thank you so much!" His face was alight with excitement.

"Okay, kid, I guess you're going to have my back at work. Are you up for it?" Colin asked in a mock-stern voice.

"Oh, yes, sir, totally!"

Colin cut his eyes at me and back to Owen. "I'm sure you realize you can't let anyone know about us."

Owen looked at both of us earnestly. "I understand and I won't let you down."

"Excellent. I'll see you at work tomorrow."

Owen said, "Yes, sir," and started out the door.

"By the way, what's your last name again?" Colin called after him.

"Douglas, sir. It's Douglas."

* * *

As the door clicked shut behind him, Owen stood unmoving on the steps, more overwhelmed than he wanted to admit at what had transpired. Not only did his boss have magic—and wings, how amazing was that?—but he was Merlin's brother. And they had showed him his past lives, linking him with his ancient Scottish roots. When he'd gotten the call from Detective Campbell, he'd wondered if he was getting fired. Although, he would have expected his boss to tell him something like that at work.

He couldn't wait to talk to his roommate about what had happened. He'd technically given his word that he wouldn't tell anyone, but he figured he had a free pass with Randy. The roommates had suspected the truth about the owner of The Moab Herbalist years ago, ever since the two of them had attended those storytelling sessions when they were teenagers.

It was like he and Randy were involved in a superior, real-life video game.

And Owen hoped the news he had to share would persuade Randy to open up to him. Since the guy got back from Scotland a couple of weeks ago, he'd been hiding something. Owen couldn't imagine what had happened during a simple vacation to cause Randy to spend so much time locked in the bathroom or to take long walks day and night.

Could he have found out something disturbing about his biological parents? Randy had been obsessed with finding his true origins ever since his folks had finally admitted to adopting him as a newborn, and the adoption agency had had some evidence that one or both of his biological parents had been Scottish. Owen couldn't imagine what type of information a newborn baby could possess. He was no expert, but the fact that baby Randy had been wrapped in a tartan seemed to be rather flimsy evidence, circumstantial at best.

When Owen got home, it was late and his friend still wasn't there. He decided to wait up for him, because he would be disappointed if he couldn't share right away what had happened to him earlier in the evening. Undoubtedly Randy would reciprocate with the reason for his irregular behavior.

He decided to sit on the porch, in the dark, even though it was a little cool for comfort. He ended up falling asleep on the bench next to the front door, and didn't wake up until he heard a strange whooshing sound in the air above the lawn.

When he saw what had made that sound he thought he was dreaming.

It was Randy, with dark wings sprouting out of his shoulders, touching down like some outlandish creature out of a fairy tale.

Owen stumbled down the porch steps until he was face to face with his roommate. "My God! What happened to you? Why didn't you tell me?"

"I didn't know if I should. It's been a lot for me to deal with as it is."

"Are you, uh…" Owen's question stuck in his throat.

Randy gave a quick grin. "Fae? Yeah, I am."

"Let's go in so I can see you better."

"If you need light, I can help with that." Randy held out his hand, where a glow of radiance lit up his features.

Owen stared slack-jawed at the ball of light and examined his friend's face. "Whoa, your eyes kind of look like a snake's, and your ears are pointed. Damn. You obviously have magic. Can you can create a glamour to hide your new form?"

"Sure," Randy said, and called up the glamour he'd first created in Inverness.

"Way cool. Literally." Owen shivered and suggested they go inside. "I have something to tell you, too. You want coffee?"

"Yeah, it's cold out here. I'm hoping at some point to be able to regulate my body temperature, but I haven't figured out how to do that yet."

As they trooped into the house, Randy had to bend over and tuck his wings down to keep from snagging them on the door sill. He went into the kitchen and turned a chair around, sitting in it backward, and let go of his glamour. "One of the problems with having wings, is they're always getting in the way. You may have noticed that I haven't been driving around town."

Owen looked at him over his shoulder as he started the coffee brewing. "Yeah, I wondered what was going on."

"I don't know where to put the damned things. Try getting into the driver's seat with 'em!"

"You know, I never took stuff like that into account."

"Neither did I until I had wings hanging off my shoulders, practically dragging the ground." He pinched his shoulder blades together, which lifted his wings a few inches off the floor. He glanced down at the lower feathers and grimaced. They were dirty again and some were out of alignment. "Now I get why birds are always preening."

Owen handed his roommate a big mug of strong coffee, liberally laced with cream and sugar, the way he liked it. They'd been friends for so long they knew each other's preferences for almost everything.

"It looks like you found your roots in Inverness," Owen said with a laugh. He took a careful sip of his hot, black coffee as he eyed Randy's new appendages.

"Yeah, smartass, you might say that." Randy went on to describe what had happened when he'd been drawn into that small segment of the Fae realm atop Tomnahurich Hill, and when he'd transformed that night. He scratched one pointed ear. "Chris told me her ears itched when she first transformed, too."

Owen looked puzzled. "Who's Chris? You met another Fae?"

"Two of 'em, Chris and Seth, and they've been helping me adapt. You'll never guess who they are."

Owen's mind made a creative leap, considering the magical information he'd already received this evening. "I'll bet they're from Moab and they're somehow connected to the people at The Moab Herbalist."

Randy's alien eyes very nearly popped out of his head. "How the heck did you come to that conclusion?"

"Remember I told you there was something uncanny about my boss, Detective Campbell?"

"You said he acts abnormally at times and you thought he was using magic."

Owen described what had happened when Campbell had used magic at the crime scene, levitated, and sprouted wings.

"What? You mean he's *Fae*?"

"That's the thing. He's not. He's Michael Reese's half brother. You know, the guy that owns the herb shop? The guy that we always thought was really Merlin? We were right! He admitted it earlier tonight when Campbell asked me to meet him at a house over on Doc Allen Drive; Merlin's house, it turned out."

"Merlin and his brother live in Moab? How cool is that? And, Owen, there's more. The Fae I met are royal. Seth is the next King of the Fae, and Chris is his wife, so she'll be Queen. She works at The Moab Herbalist. And it turns out Seth is my cousin. My biological father—Seth's uncle—is a prince, so that makes me royal, too."

Owen gawked. "Seriously?"

"Yeah, I'm a changeling, according to Seth. And get this: Seth told me his father lives here in Moab. What do you want to bet Merlin—"

"—is Seth's father," Owen finished.

They grinned hugely at each other and high-fived enthusiastically.

CHAPTER 44
Moab, Wednesday, September 27, 2023, 1:00 AM
to Late Morning

It was late, the house dim and quiet, and still I sat at the kitchen table mulling over my father's visit. It had been an exceptional evening, which should have left me with a sense of accomplishment, and yet I felt restless and on edge. It was as if some particularly thorny bit of information was trying to work its way into my conscious mind.

Colin had departed shortly after his human assistant, dematerializing as if he had been teleporting all his life, and I had gone into the bedroom to kiss my wife goodnight. Uncharacteristically, neither one of was in the mood to make love, so I had tucked her in and gone back out to make myself some coffee.

Mug in hand, I left the kitchen and walked into my office, sat down at my desk, and started concentrating on our current dilemma. I sipped at the dark, hot, unsweetened liquid I favored while considering the next steps that my evil brother might take, and determining which strategy would be sufficient to stop him. I was beginning to fear the depths to which Sam's demonic influence had been subverting my life's work, and what form that influence would take once it reached the tipping point. I pictured the scene like the eruption of Vesuvius, the molten lava of his hatred erupting once the pressure became too great, and the resulting pyroclastic flow of corruption destroying everything around me.

This truly was a war we were waging, not merely a family squabble or an inconsequential disagreement between brothers. So why hadn't my father sent one of the gods of war to assist us instead of Portunus, who was, in my admittedly biased opinion, completely ineffectual?

With a jolt, that missing bit of information, the essential piece of the puzzle, fell into place, and the elusive truth finally became clear to me. I knew who Colin was and why I'd been motivated to bring him into the family to begin with.

As usual, my father was way ahead of me.

311

My brother was Týr, the Norse god of war, law, and justice. How could I have forgotten that? My original assumption was flawed. Colin didn't have to be a Welsh god just because his twin was.

Týr and I had always had a strong emotional connection. Millennia ago, he and I had been the closest of all of our brothers.

Merlin, it does not surprise me that you have recollected Colin's true identity. I knew you would do so. But I would prefer you do not mention it to him at present. He must discover it for himself.

I was not surprised to hear my father's Voice in my mind and I responded in like manner. *As you wish, Father.* There was no percentage in asking him to explain his reasoning.

Now that I had recalled who Colin really was, it freed my mind to concentrate on other things. I spent untold hours contemplating how best to organize both defensive and offensive responses to the catastrophic event Sam's actions would trigger. And I thought about all the people that comprised my extended family, and how they might be affected by this terrible event, should I be unable to stop it from occurring.

I had a realization that stopped me cold. Back when the pandemic had first hit, and before a vaccine had been developed, I had ensured that everyone in our close-knit group who needed protection had received immunity, including Gwen and the knights.

And of course, once Gwen became Arthur's wife, I would make her immortal and she would be permanently immune to disease.

The knights, however, had no such thing to shield them for the long term. I could still protect them from disease, but they were growing older as humans always do, and I had done nothing to prevent that.

I had been inexcusably remiss. Those gallant men had continued ageing over all the years they had been in my service, and I had blindly expected them to go on serving me and Arthur in the future. I thought back to the last meeting we'd had, and reviewed it in my mind, paying special attention to the physical appearance of these men who had always been there for me.

Sir Lancelot, in his current incarnation as Ryan Jones, had been in his midthirties when we first reconnected here in Moab in 2013. Now, ten years later, his hair had changed from blond to pale silver, and there were many more wrinkles on his rugged face. He was still in excellent physical condition due to his rigorous daily workouts, but he wouldn't be able to continue that regimen forever.

Sir Gawain, also known as Gary Gardner, had gray hairs streaking his long dark brown hair. He was the same age as Ryan but didn't look as careworn; his wrinkles appeared more like laugh lines. He was in excellent shape, but not as dedicated as his roommate was to maintaining it.

Percival's original body had aged, but he had been younger than the others when Llyr had transported him from fifth-century Camelot to twenty-first century Moab. At thirty-five, he was still relatively young, and he was dedicated to bodybuilding and watching his diet, so I had no concerns for him on that score.

Sir Leon, also in his original body, had been in this century for five years, but he had served Uther Pendragon prior to Arthur's reign and had to be in his late forties. His curly hair was steel gray and the lines on his face were cut deep, partially due to the unhappiness he had experienced when he'd initially arrived here. For the first few years he had been in Moab, he had neglected his health, and it was only recently that he'd begun to participate in the nutrition and physical training sessions Ryan held regularly, so he was not in the best of condition.

I had been quick to grant extra years and enhanced health to Colin after I had caught him breaking into my shop, knowing he would be useful to me. That was long before I had known who and what he was, and that he hadn't needed my assistance at all. Colin had been in his early forties and looked it, and had reacted to my gift by becoming younger and fitter. I frowned in confusion. Why would he have aged to begin with since he was a god, even though he hadn't been aware of his true nature? I imagined as with many other aspects of this scenario that my father was responsible, so I just had to be grateful and let it go. And since Colin was immortal I didn't have to worry about his welfare ever again.

However, I had shamefully neglected my knights, Arthur's knights, those dedicated souls who had renounced normal lives in devotion to our cause, and it was time to rectify my negligence.

But would a quasi-immortality be something they would want? Should I give them the choice or go ahead and change them? Of course, if they refused my gift, eventually they would no longer be able to continue in service to my son and me.

I decided I would tell them, but make them understand that they would need to accept the gift as I had originally given it to Colin: enhanced health and a longer lifespan. I couldn't justify granting any of them complete immortality, as such was not their destiny, but a long life and sustained good health would give them more years than any mortal man would normally have.

I glanced at the clock on the wall. The knights would be in bed, but

I felt an urgent need to accomplish this task and vowed to do so first thing in the morning.

* * *

I was somewhat distracted as I joined Emily for breakfast, and she noticed.

"What's on your mind, god man?"

"I'm sorry, Em, I'm out of sorts this morning."

"Really? Why?" she asked as she handed me a toasted bagel and a container of cream cheese.

I took the bagel and spread a thick layer of cheese before answering. "I'm going to confer a partial state of immortality on the knights today and I'm concerned how they'll react. Do we have any strawberry jam?"

Emily's calm acceptance of my statement—to which I had appended a banal domestic inquiry—was typical of my wife. She had put up with me and my issues of one sort and another for more than ten years and I considered myself a lucky man to have her.

She handed me a new jar of jam she'd levitated from the pantry without reminding me I could have done the same thing myself or conjured one.

When had I become so lazy?

"You're not lazy, Merlin, you merely have more important things to think about than to keep track of the contents of our pantry. Mom and I will continue to take care of the household while you keep the world safe from your evil sibling. Okay?"

"I don't deserve you, Em, I really don't."

"Yes, you do!" she shouted unexpectedly. "Stop being so hard on yourself!" For a moment, she looked ashamed for raising her voice. "Sorry."

I got up and walked around to her side of the table, pulled her up and into my arms and held her close to my heart. "Do you feel that?"

"Your heart beating?" she whispered. "Yes."

"It beats for you, Em, always has. And always will."

* * *

Later that morning, I hovered in my incorporeal state above the knights' front yard until I perceived that no one would observe me rematerializing. Fortunately, it was a dark, gloomy day threatening rain, there were no pedestrians in the vicinity, and there was a lull in the traffic on 400 East, the wide street that supposedly had been the main thoroughfare in Moab early in the twentieth century.

As I started to knock on the door, Gary pulled it open.

"Come on in, Merlin. You don't have to knock, my lord. Why didn't you teleport into the living room, as usual?" Gary obviously didn't realize I could appear anywhere spontaneously, without teleporting.

"I'm trying to reform my ways and be more polite, since I hadn't called ahead."

The rest of the knights had gathered around us, having heard Gary's response to my arrival.

"Oh, screw that," Percival said bluntly, all trace of his old world accent gone, and his original vocabulary replaced by current idiom. "We're here for you and Arthur, Lord Merlin, and for no other reason. Besides, you own the house, so you can show up whenever you damn well please."

His outburst was so out of character that complete silence reigned until Gary piped up, "Why don't you tell us how you really feel, Percival?"

That broke the ice and we all laughed until our sides ached. Finally, I said, "We all needed that. We've been under a lot of stress and uncertainty lately, and some of that has been my fault. I haven't done enough for you."

Several men voiced protests.

"No, I truly haven't. I intend to remedy that starting with something I've been meaning to do for a while now." I gazed slowly and intently from one loyal face to the next and used my god powers to bestow upon each man that which they would need to continue in my service, and Arthur's. The power and the Light flowed so effortlessly through me that it took no more than a few seconds, passing over and through the men before me.

"I feel different," Leon said.

"Me, too," Gary said. "And you look younger. So do you, Ryan."

"Merlin, what did you do?" Ryan asked quietly, gazing at his arms and hands, the skin of which had been scarred from many altercations over the years and was now as unblemished as it had been in his early twenties.

They all took turns staring with disbelief at their reflections in both bathroom mirrors, until they gathered in front of me in the living room again. I could see in their eyes that they'd forgotten for a moment that I was a god.

"You have all been serving me for years and I want you to be able to do so for many more decades. Therefore, I have given you the gift of enhanced health and of a partial immortality. In other words, you will feel and appear as if you are around thirty years old, living healthy lives free of disease and the infirmities of old age, for hundreds of years."

There was dead silence until Ryan had the courage to ask what they had all been thinking, "What's the catch?"

"Isn't it obvious? Arthur and I are immortal, hence you will be serving us for the rest of your lives." I didn't intend to sound as lofty and untouchable as I had, from the looks on their faces. But it was the truth. "You can decline the gift I've given you, but be aware that continuing in service will no longer be possible. Or you can accept and be a part of a glorious future."

I waited while the four of them cogitated on my ultimatum and finally each of them stated, "I accept," and knelt at my feet, one after the other.

In the past, when faced with overwhelming gestures of fealty that bordered on worship, I had denied its appropriateness or felt undeserving of such gestures.

Today I recognized it, in all humility, as my due. I was what I was and there was no point in denying the truth of it. And in that humble acceptance, I was one step closer to being what God wanted me to be.

CHAPTER 45
Moab, Friday, September 29, 2023, Early Evening

Several days after my epiphany regarding Colin's god name and after doing my duty to the knights, I contacted Derek telepathically and suggested we spend some time together. I missed my son; we had not had any quality time together in months. With all the transformations, child-rearing, weddings, honeymoons, confrontations and tragedies happening this year, not to mention a visit from my father and Lumina's pregnancy and probable return to Moab, we had all been justifiably preoccupied.

Derek and I had discussed getting a few beers at Moody's, so he dropped in after dinner, figuring we'd go together. I wanted to show him what I called "stepping over the threshold." I had been spontaneously transporting myself without consciously teleporting for a decade and I'd decided to have fun with it, like walking through a doorway from one reality into another.

As soon as I mentioned it, though, he jumped in and asked me about a specific phenomenon others had noticed when he teleported.

"Everyone's been seein' these glitterin' colored particles as I vanish and when I rematerialize. It started years ago, but I hadn't noticed until Lumina pointed it out to me. Isn't it that way for everybody?"

I took a measured breath, putting aside the irritation I'd felt when he interrupted me, and I chuckled at his bemusement. "You're creating your own special effects, Derek. Do you remember telling me that you liked the way the transporter beam in Star Trek glittered as it broke down peoples' bodies into their component molecules? Well, subconsciously you decided to do it."

His brows furrowed and he gazed at me skeptically. "Are ya sure? You'd think I'd know if I was doin' it deliberately."

"I'm sure," I said dryly. "And this is exactly the reason you need to be careful. You have considerably more power than most demigods, and creating magic subconsciously at your level of power could have unintended—and possibly harmful—consequences."

"I'll be more careful in the future, Dad. By the way, Lumina's been doin' it for years."

"She's mimicking you, Derek, because she likes the effect. In her case, she's doing it deliberately. And she's a goddess, and thus has more inherent control over her powers."

All of a sudden, I felt as if the whole purpose of his chat about glittering particles had been to distract me. Perhaps he hadn't meant to do it, but I'd been so suspicious of Sam's interference with my family lately that I kept seeing negative influences where there were none.

I decided to put that edgy feeling aside and demonstrate, as opposed to talk about, the subject I'd tried to introduce when he had come over tonight.

He looked puzzled when I mentioned it.

"Why don't we drive down to Moody's in the truck? It's like, two minutes away."

"But this is instantaneous, Derek, like stepping into the past, very much like you did while searching for me when I was lost in time." I put my hand on his back, guiding him forward, and we walked over my front door threshold—directly into Moody's Tavern. It would appear to the patrons as if we had come through the entrance from outside the building.

"How long did ya say you've been doin' that?" he asked me quietly as we relaxed in one of the high-backed booths with bottles of Heineken and a couple packages of pretzels.

I shifted to telepathy to make sure we weren't overheard. *I don't know, at least since 2013, but over the years I'd forgotten, especially when I started flying. Colin, of all people, noticed in 2019 that I was doing it and called me on it. His god self was trying to manifest even then. And by the way, I remembered his god name. He's Týr, the Norse god of war.*

Derek eyebrows shot up. *Damn, I never would've guessed that.*

Keep it to yourself, alright? Don't even mention it to Sarah or Morry. Eventually, Colin will remember, and that's the way God wants it.

Ya got it, Dad.

Anyway, back to our discussion. You know, it may seem like teleportation is immediate, but it's not. It requires certain steps to be taken. One has to focus on a destination—and it's best to have been there or at least know what it looks like—and consciously allow your body to dissolve into billions of tiny particles. Next, by will alone, send those particles to that destination, and will those particles to restructure themselves back into your unique self.

Seriously? That's how we do it? It's so natural, so automatic, I don't even think about it anymore.

And Derek, you're choosing *to allow the minute particles of yourself to be seen as you leave for your destination and again when you arrive and rematerialize.*

Can mortals see me? He sounded worried.

Yes, so I hope you haven't been teleporting in front of people. I gave him a solemn look, but I was teasing him. I couldn't imagine him being so irresponsible.

He tossed a few pretzels in his mouth and started munching on them as he rolled his eyes. *Oh, for Pete's sake, Dad, of course not!*

I winked at him and took a long swallow of the cold brew. He shook his head and gave me a crooked grin. I decided to bring up the topic I truly wanted to discuss with him. *I have an idea for Arthur and Gwen's wedding and I'd like your help.*

He raised his eyebrows. *Oh, yeah? He mentioned to me that he wanted a formal weddin', kinda like the one they had in Camelot. But neither of them wants a church weddin', so I don't know where they're gonna find a venue that looks like the Great Hall of a fifth-century castle, do you?*

As a matter of fact, I do. And I began to outline the steps I would take in order to accomplish the impossible.

"You're gonna do *what?*" In his astonishment, Derek forgot and exclaimed out loud.

Recreate Camelot.

CHAPTER 46
Somerset County, England, September 30, 2023

As I deliberately trudged up the steep, winding, interminable steps, enjoying the exercise, I pondered the dogged persistence of human beings to hold onto ideas that intrigued them. Case in point, man's continuing fascination with all things pertaining to Camelot, King Arthur, and me, despite the more than 1500 years since he and I had first walked the earth together.

When I eventually attained the flat summit of Glastonbury Tor, I reveled in the view. At first glance, it seemed the landscape hadn't changed in hundreds of years. The lake that had surrounded the cone-shaped hill had been gone since before my visit in 1191, and by the time I was there in 1700, the ancient forests had disappeared as well. Interestingly enough, I could still feel a faint vibration of magical energy emanating from deep beneath the Tor.

Once, the Tor had been called the Isle of Glass, and after that Avalon, when a major portal to the Other World had existed on its slopes. The Fae realm had been accessed through that portal time out of mind, but the portal had disappeared—or been deliberately closed—at least 1200 years ago. And as far as I knew, most if not all of the Elven Fae had retreated to the portion of the Fae realm accessible through the doorway at the base of Tomnahurich Hill in Inverness, Scotland, and Avalon as it had been in the fifth century existed only in the memories of those of us who had lived then.

As I strolled around, noting the view from every direction, a large brass plaque mounted on a concrete base drew my attention. The lettering on the disc pointed to landmarks in the valley below and even included the nearby hills. I was particularly drawn to the lettering which indicated various points of significance relating to the Arthurian legend. The people standing near me were expounding upon the subject in loud and pompous voices with various European accents, debating with each other which locations might have been Camelot. I had a strong urge, quickly stifled, to direct their attention to where the real Camelot had actually stood.

In modern times, the Iron Age hillfort known as Cadbury Castle was thought to be Camelot, and as I gazed in that direction, I could understand how it had been mistaken for Arthur's castle. But I knew better. Camelot had been on a high point of land south of the Cadbury Castle location, surrounded by rolling hills forested with towering oaks and sycamores, interspersed with alder and ash. Those magnificent trees had been cut down centuries ago, replaced by pastures, houses, barns, and paved roads. It was still a sparsely populated area compared to a city like Glastonbury or Bath, but not as remote as it had been in the fifth century.

As I stood there, unaffected by the cold wind that whipped my long hair behind me, I felt the gaze of several people on me and realized I'd been talking to myself in the old language.

I turned and smiled, broadening my accent as I said, "You can almost feel the past come alive here, and see King Arthur and his knights riding out of Camelot." From the shocked look on their faces, they seemed to believe it. I was dressed in denim jeans, with a long leather coat hugging my broad shoulders, but I swore it felt like a robe swirling around my ankles as I walked away.

As I headed back down the steep steps planning my next move, I heard one man ask, "Did he look familiar to you?"

I heard his companion snort and say sarcastically, "Hey, maybe it was Merlin."

I laughed out loud, tempted to turn around and confirm their hypothesis. I didn't give in to the urge.

I would be doing that soon enough, on a much grander scale.

When I was out of sight of another group of tourists swarming up the stairs toward the summit, I stepped through the gap in the boundary fence and instantaneously appeared on the site of Camelot. I stood where the proud castle had once been and closed my eyes, envisioning it as it was when Arthur was King.

I sensed the boy before I heard him call out to me from across the field. "Hey, mister, what're you doing?"

I answered unreservedly, "I'm remembering Camelot."

He stared at me intently, taking in my long black hair, my height and my dark leather duster that billowed in the wind. "You're Merlin, aren't you?"

I don't know what possessed me to do it, but I answered, "Yes."

"Oh, that's brilliant. It's about time, isn't it?" he said, and giving me a wave, he rode off on his bicycle.

I stared after him and thought how odd it was that a human child could be so in tune with a realm and a reality so far removed from his own.

I returned my thoughts to my purpose here today.

In the fifth century, the wedding of Arthur and Guinevere had taken place in the Great Hall of Camelot, and I intended for their twenty-first century wedding to be held there as well. The main problem was that the castle no longer existed except in my memory. However, I sensed multiple ancient foundations beneath the ground. The original stones from Camelot's walls were closest to the surface, the next layer down building materials from Roman times, and below that the remains of an Iron Age hillfort.

I walked around the site and made note of every detail I would have to attend to in order to accomplish this seemingly impossible task I had taken on to please my son and his fiancée. Energy emanating from the earth itself beckoned, offering itself to me should I require it for such a colossal undertaking. I accepted the gift with pleasure.

Satisfied with my plans for resurrecting Camelot, I paused to appreciate the sunshine warming my shoulders, the crisp feel of the autumn air, and the scent of burning leaves. The seasons were changing once again in this material realm, the wheel of time turning inexorably to the death of another year—and the birth of a new era.

Ready to depart, I took a step out of England and appeared in my home in Moab, Utah. I definitely wasn't teleporting. I could call it flashing, but Em told me that sounded like I was the comic book character, The Flash. Or, worse yet, that I was naked beneath my long coat and going around revealing my private bits in an unacceptable manner. I grinned. I needed to put some fun back in my life—but not that way.

"Well, did you get all the information you needed?" my wife asked from the kitchen as she sensed my return.

"I certainly did, and I'm confident that I can do it." My coat disappeared from my body and appeared in the coat rack near the door.

As I joined her, Emily handed me a large mug of steaming hot coffee and picked up her own. "It sounds risky, god man. What'll happen if someone sees it there, as real as it was all those centuries ago? If a gigantic castle with a dragon banner flying above it spontaneously appeared, the locals would know without a doubt what it was, and who created it! When I was in England, I noticed that everyone still believes in King Arthur and Merlin and they're waiting for both of you to return. I imagine they would be beside themselves with joy and anxious to spread the news. It could cause a *multitude* of problems with the timing of your plans for announcing yours and Arthur's return."

I stared at her, coffee halfway to my lips, caught off guard by her outburst. "I'll make sure no one can see it except our people. Trust me, Em." I put the coffee mug down on the counter, cupped her face with my palms and looked into her worried eyes. "Why is this bothering you so much?"

"I feel like it's tempting fate, or inviting your horrible brother to interfere." She leaned into my hand and kissed it. Turning to grab her own mug, she took a healthy swallow of the cooling brew and said in a conciliatory tone, "Don't get me wrong, I think it's an awesome idea. Do you think Arthur and Gwen suspect anything?"

I shrugged. "They know I have a plan, but I don't think it would occur to either one of them that I'd do something so outrageous."

"It is outrageous, but I don't doubt that you can pull it off. Were you planning to get Derek to help you?"

"I was, but I think he's got his hands full at home with Aidan and helping out with his grandkids. And he doesn't want to neglect Sarah. Same thing with Morry and his family."

"Then get Colin to help you. Cathy won't mind, and I think he'll get a kick out of it, don't you? After all, Arthur is his nephew."

"True." Em was aware of my realization about Colin, and that I was still getting used to the idea that he was actually Týr. It made sense, when I considered how easily he had initially handled his magic, with no training and no hesitation whatsoever. I wish I was permitted to tell him his god name, but I didn't dare ignore my father's "request" to keep his identity a secret.

Bollocks, I had to focus. Continuing to ponder Colin's transformation and question Father's machinations wouldn't get Camelot built.

Colin, would you like to help me set up the venue for Arthur and Gwen's wedding?

His answer came promptly. *Sure. I'm not working this week, so it's ideal timing.*

Then come on over.

He appeared in front of me in jeans and a long-sleeved, maroon T-shirt with a gold Celtic knot on the front and the word "Belfast" under it. He'd obviously gotten the shirt while he was on his honeymoon in Northern Ireland. I'd never seen him looking so casual.

"You might want to conjure up a jacket. It's a bit cold and windy where we're going."

He looked at me thoughtfully, and a brown leather bomber jacket appeared on his upper body. It suited him.

"Follow me, Brother," I said as I headed out the front door and disappeared.

"Merlin, wait, where are you going?" Colin asked, as he followed in my wake and ended up on the site of ancient Camelot with me.

"Where are we?" Colin looked around at the relatively open and unremarkable English countryside from where we stood in the middle of a wide, level, slightly raised mound covered with blackthorn.

"You mean you can't see it?"

"See what?" He peered at me as if I'd lost my mind, and perhaps I had. I could see Camelot in my mind's eye as it had been centuries ago. And it was massive. This project was going to require a great deal of effort and energy. But I had an infinite source from which to draw more if needed. Every so often even I forgot what I was.

Colin rolled his eyes. "Oh, come on, man. You never forget what you are, you just like to pretend you have. Makes you feel more human or something."

I laughed out loud and gripped his muscular shoulder in acknowledgement. "I love you, Brother. Em never lets me get away with anything and neither do you."

"I love you, too, Merlin, and I suspect that's why our father originally sent me here: to keep you on the straight and narrow, focused on what's essential." He chuckled, his rugged, swarthy face alight with intelligence and humor, and I felt my typically somber demeanor lighten considerably.

"And I'm grateful for it, Colin." I paused as I gazed into his dark eyes that were like Beli's. "Alright, back to business. This is where Uther Pendragon originally built Camelot."

"Wait a minute. I thought you and Arthur built it."

"So the legend would have it, but no, Uther built the original castle upon the foundations of an old Roman fortress. Later, Arthur and I redesigned and fortified it until it became the Camelot you're thinking of."

"Now you've ruined the whole thing for me," he complained facetiously.

"Regardless of your vast disappointment, we need to get going so we can re-create Camelot for the wedding."

"*That's* your plan? Christ, you never do anything halfway, do you?"

"Not for something this momentous."

"Well, what would you like me to do?"

I described the various tasks that would have to be completed prior to the wedding day, which Arthur and Gwen had finally agreed upon as October fifteenth. I'd refused to tell them my plans, but had assured them I would take care of everything. When the time came, I would personally transport the guests to the venue and handle all of the details. Until the day of the ceremony, the location and those details were a secret.

"I'd be happy to do miscellaneous chores for you, but won't you need a hand with the actual creation spell, or whatever?" Colin gazed at me questioningly, apparently concerned that I had overestimated my abilities. I hadn't, but I realized that it would be easier and quicker—and a better experience for both of us—if we did it together.

I smiled. "You're right. We can do this now if you're ready."

"Okay, but you'll need to clue me in on the procedure so I don't screw it up," he said a trifle apprehensively.

"Stand next to me with your arms out and your fingers touching mine, and link with my thoughts. I'll guide you."

As he followed my directions, we turned to face the stretch of ground where the rubble of Camelot's past was buried.

I shared my vision of its resurrection with him and we merged, the glow of our energy increasing until our bodies vanished into a huge sphere of Light, which spread out until it encompassed the original dimensions of castle and courtyard. It continued to expand upwards until it reached the maximum height of Camelot's highest tower. At that point, the earth rumbled and a sharp cracking sound exploded across the valley.

All was quiet again except for the sound of the wind through the tall grass. We returned to our human forms and opened our eyes.

Colin looked up…and up…and his jaw dropped. "Oh, my God," he whispered.

CHAPTER 47
Moab, Sunday, October 1, 2023

"Chris, I'm glad to see you! When did you and Seth get back?" Emily exclaimed as her daughter-in-law walked through the front door of The Moab Herbalist, a glamour obscuring her Fae features.

"We got home late last night. I was going to call you but decided to come in this morning instead," Chris said as she stepped aside and motioned to a slender young man to follow her in. "Em, this is my new friend, Randy Hartwell. You might remember him—he's been in the shop before."

Em came around the counter and shook Randy's hand. "Hi, it's nice to meet you." She turned to the other woman with a puzzled look. "You said you got back last night, so when did you two meet?"

"In Inverness. But he's from Moab."

Em's eyebrows shot up in surprise. She took a closer look at Randy. "Oh, I recognize you. You came into the shop years ago, when we first started doing the storytelling sessions."

"Yeah, my buddy and I came in pretty regularly while we were teenagers, and I've been in for herbs and potions off and on for years." He glanced uncertainly at Chris, who gestured at him to continue. "Um, Chris suggested I, that is, I'm looking for a job, and I was hoping you might need someone to work, you know, here in the shop?" He fidgeted, wiping his hands on his jeans as if they were damp with nervous perspiration.

Emily was thunderstruck. Why would Chris think it was appropriate for someone she just met to work in a shop run by magical immortals?

Sensing Em's concern and bewilderment, Chris laughed. "It's okay, Em." She confirmed there was no one else in the shop and used magic to lock the door and close the blinds. That done, she dropped her glamour.

"What are you doing?" Em cried, cutting her eyes at Randy.

"Don't worry," he said apologetically. "I already know about Chris and Seth."

Em looked skeptical. "You do?"

He dropped his own glamour.

She exclaimed, "My God, you're Fae!"

Randy and Chris grinned at each other.

"I reacted that way, too, when Seth and I were hovering over Loch Ness and Randy flew up to us. Amazingly enough, he's Seth's cousin— and he's my distant cousin, too, on his birth mother's side."

"Are you kidding me?" Em couldn't take her eyes off him. He didn't look at all like Seth. He had medium brown hair, a snub nose with scattered freckles, black wings, and beautiful yellow-gold reptilian eyes. And he was shorter than Seth, around five feet eleven. *Merlin, did you know about him?*

No, I didn't. Remember, I lost contact with Seth shortly after they left their house the night they must have made contact with Randy.

* * *

I was eager to meet this young man, so I instantaneously transported to the shop. Since he was Fae and related to both Seth and Chris, there was no reason to hide my powers.

Randy stared at me intently. "Oh, my God, you really are Merlin. Owen and I thought so, ten years ago when you started speaking Old British at one of your storytelling sessions, but we had no way to prove it. And you must be Seth's father; he looks like you."

Caught up in his fascination with me, Randy hadn't stammered once. And he was surprisingly bold, considering his initial meeting with Seth and Chris, the story of which I gleaned from Chris's open mind. And after meeting Owen and Seeing him, and sensing his lifelong friendship with Randy, it confirmed that the two had figured out who I was a decade ago. I remember thinking that I would have to keep an eye on them. They were so serious about their gaming and their sword and sorcery role-playing, I knew if anyone could discern my true identity, it would be them. But as with many of my best intentions, I hadn't followed through and kept track of them. Apparently, my father had, though, and patiently brought them to my attention again, in a particularly outrageous fashion.

"You're correct, I am Merlin, and Seth MacAdam is my son." I called forth my wings and spread them wide in a show of dominance.

* * *

Randy quailed and got down on his knees, bowing his head. He didn't remember any of the old legends stating that Merlin had wings. And the bright circle of light around him that looked like a nimbus put him into a whole different category of being. Randy figured getting humble would at least show respect.

When he heard Em say, "Should we invite him to the wedding, Merlin? He's Seth's cousin, after all," Randy was utterly confused and shocked and threw his head up to ogle the three people standing above him.

Chris bent down and grabbed his hand. "It's okay, Randy, you can get up." He clambered awkwardly to his feet, his wings throwing him off balance. Merlin was both taller and heavier than he was—more muscular—his wingspan was greater, and his aura of power was intimidating, to say the least. Randy felt uncoordinated and insignificant next to him.

"Yes, he's part of the family. What do you say, young man? Would you like to attend the second wedding of Arthur and Guinevere?"

"Arthur?" Randy looked baffled for a split second and then his eyes crinkled in delight. "*King Arthur and Queen Guinevere? Are you serious?* Arthur's *back?* Damn straight I'll come! Can I bring my roommate Owen?"

As Randy waited for the man—or sorcerer, or god, or whatever the hell he was—to respond, Merlin suddenly grinned, making his stern face appear boyish and carefree. "Arthur is indeed back. But I expect you to keep that to yourself. And you may bring Owen." He abruptly disappeared.

Emily and Chris exchanged glances.

"Has he always been so...dramatic?" Chris asked.

"Oh, yes. In fact, he used to be worse. He's toned it down some in the last few years." Em glanced at the newest member of her family. The poor guy looked snowed under by recent happenings.

"Well, Randy, I happen to have a job opening, so welcome to the crew of The Moab Herbalist. Chris, can you work today? I realize you'll have to go back to Scotland eventually, but I can certainly use you until then. Yes? Both of you hide your Fae attributes and let's get to work. There's a lot to be done before Arthur and Gwen's wedding."

CHAPTER 48
The Wedding, Sunday, October 15, 2023

"God, I'm so nervous. What in the world is Merlin planning that he couldn't tell us ahead of time?" Gwen muttered to herself as she pulled her long, white, silk gown over her head and tied the intricately embroidered girdle, allowing the long tail of what was essentially a belt to hang down the front. She'd wanted to replicate her wedding gown from her first wedding in the fifth century, but it proved to be difficult to attain an exact match using modern fabrics and available accessories. Arthur had attempted to conjure her gown from her verbal description and his own memory, but to his dismay and embarrassment, it wasn't quite right. She'd assured him it didn't matter, since what she had ended up with was beautiful anyway. After all, it was their love and their desire to reaffirm their commitment that mattered, not their clothing.

The gown had a wide "V" neck, plunging down almost to her breasts, and long sleeves that fanned out from the shoulder down to her wrists. The girdle was soft leather dyed red, with a pattern of wildflowers embroidered on the wide back, which definitely wasn't what she'd worn originally, but she'd loved it so much she'd bought it anyway. It cinched in the loose white gown at her waist, accentuating her womanly figure. She'd also found delicate red leather flats online—which surprised the hell out of her—but she didn't care where they came from since they fit exactly and matched the belt. She sent out a silent thank you to Arthur's grandfather, just in case it was his doing.

At five six, Gwen was short compared to Arthur's six three, and it would have helped if she'd been able to wear three-inch heels, but she hated them. Those negative feelings probably stemmed from living nearly four decades in a man's body—more, if you figured the other lifetimes she'd been male—or because heels were so damned uncomfortable. Either way, she refused to wear them. Fortunately, Arthur didn't care how tall she was, since she couldn't change her height in any case.

Gwen was glad to switch her runaway train of thought to a different track, and contemplate Arthur's success in conjuring duplicates of his own fifth-century wedding garments. He had worn his best robe of fine, soft, white wool, and his red velvet cloak with the gold dragon emblem and ermine collar, with his golden crown resting on his royal brow.

Gwen remembered everything about that day, especially how Arthur had entered the hall flanked by his knights, who had worn their best tunics and trousers and their own red cloaks—the more utilitarian wool, rather than velvet, of course—with the dragon emblems. As soon as Arthur had arrived at the dais at the front of the Hall and turned to watch her enter, she had begun her long, measured walk down the aisle toward her destiny. The Great Hall had been decked out in red and gold fall leaves, juniper branches loaded with purple berries, colorful ribbons—

"Gwen, do you need any help?" Em's voice effectively jarred her out of her reminiscing.

"Sure, come on in," Gwen called out. Emily opened the door to the small bedroom and entered, followed by Sarah, and then Lumina, who was wearing maternity clothes. "You might think of something I missed."

"You look stunning, Gwen!" Sarah exclaimed. "And you'll look even more so after I braid your hair and pin it up. I recently learned a new technique and I know it will be just the thing for your long curls."

"Great, thanks. I didn't how I was going to manage. Back in the fifth century, in Camelot, I had servants to help me dress and do my hair and occasionally I miss that. And my quarters were larger than this entire house." She happened to turn and catch the look on Sarah's face, and grinned. "Forgot who I was for a minute, didn't you? These days, it seems unreal to me, too, it was so long ago. I'm more likely to remember things that happened in my life as Jim Singleton. Being a man is a whole lot simpler than being a woman.

"Anyway, I appreciate your help." She turned to address Lumina who was standing behind Em. "Hey, Lumi, how are you, honey, besides preggers?"

"Doing fine, but I'll be relieved when Cadence arrives. Of course, that's four months away. I guess I'm impatient; being pregnant is uncomfortable."

"Oh, come on, you're a goddess! How hard can it be when you can literally manipulate everything going on around you, and, I presume, in your body."

Lumina looked embarrassed. "Sorry, I shouldn't be complaining.

Yes, I could manipulate the whole thing, including how my body functions. But I'm choosing to experience my pregnancy like a human woman does—except it'll only take six months gestation instead of nine." She glanced at Sarah, who was working assiduously on styling Gwen's hair. "And there's someone else in this room who is going to give birth right around my due date. Gosh, I wonder who that could be?"

Sarah looked up and grinned happily. "Yep, I'm pregnant again, due about a month later than Lumina so I'm not *quite* ready for maternity clothes. I had a few days of morning sickness but it's gone now. Derek says it's a girl, and she's a regular immortal, which is fine with me. We decided to call her Aisling, which is appropriate since I'm part Irish and her brother has the soul of an Irish god."

Gwen chuckled. "I won't hold it against either of you. But when I get pregnant, I'm going to hope it's relatively easy since I'm not the most patient person. I think I'll be joining the immortal ranks as soon as Arthur and I are married." She glanced at Em.

"That's how it works when a mortal marries a god, or an immortal like a Fae. Cathy became immortal as soon as she officially bonded with Colin, and Chris became immortal when she transitioned to Fae. I was granted immortality through my Fae ancestors—the Elves—as well as through my mate bond with Merlin." She tilted her head as a thought occurred to her. "You know, since Arthur is a demigod, Merlin will make you immortal as soon as you two are married."

"Okay, I was just curious." Gwen looked speculatively at Em and Lumina as Sarah finished her elaborate braid. "What's going on with the wedding venue? No one seems to know where it is and it's driving me crazy! I assume you two know all the details. Can you give me a hint?"

Mother and daughter grinned slyly at each other. "You'll find out soon enough."

Gwen exhaled noisily. "At least tell me if Arthur is going to be ready soon. I badly want to get this show on the road."

Before anyone could respond, Gwen's phone sounded off with the forceful beat and dark tones of Destiny of the Sword, from the 2017 movie, *King Arthur*. "Ah, there he is. He must have read my mind," Gwen said as she picked it up and thumbed 'accept.' "Hello, my darling, are you ready to get married again? Okay, we'll be there soon. Love you, Artie." And she disconnected the call.

Em and Lumina both intoned, "Artie?"

"The name Arthur is so old-fashioned I thought I'd jazz it up." Gwen grinned. "Relax. It's a joke. He laughs when I call him that."

* * *

As Em, Lumina, and Sarah helped Guinevere with her last-minute primping, Derek, Seth and Morry assisted Arthur at Derek's house—or hung out with the groom and gave him moral support, which was more likely—while I was busy riding herd on the guests as they arrived at my house.

I had once again enlarged the interior of the living room to accommodate all attendees. If I had counted correctly, there were twenty-five individuals I would transport en masse to the staging area in the field just outside of Camelot.

As I met the gaze of each one of the beloved members of my immediate and extended family, including the knights, I envisioned the expressions on their faces when they realized where they were. It would be hard to miss that they were standing outside a huge castle, and most people, other than the children, would understand the significance of it straightaway, especially Arthur and Gwen. And I expected at least a sense of satisfaction from Oengus, who had accompanied Rae, since this was a major step towards the culmination of his life's work.

When I caught Colin's gaze, he silently acknowledged that his initial skepticism had been unwarranted. We had done it. The combined power of two gods had easily accomplished the task.

Originally, I had planned to do the whole thing myself and leave the peripheral details to Colin. But I had thoroughly enjoyed our joint effort. Using my memories of the layout and dimensions of the castle, and the location of the Great Hall within, we had created a perfect facsimile of Camelot.

As the children started to fuss, I surfaced from my private reverie and noted that we were almost ready. Arthur was here and the women had just arrived with Gwen. I had previously directed Derek to inform the knights as to their roles in the ceremony as soon as we arrived, without revealing where the venue was located.

I made sure everyone was standing in the configuration I desired before I spoke. "I'm sure you are all curious about what I have planned, but it must be obvious that I will be transporting all of you to Arthur and Guinevere's wedding venue. That is the reason I have positioned you as I have, so don't move. I know it's difficult in view of the children's restlessness. But please trust me. All will be well, and I promise this adventure will be memorable. Many of you are concerned Satan will interfere as he has in the past, but we have a surprise for him this time, so no need to worry." I sent a wave of love and calmness out to settle over the crowd like a soft blanket, and I heard a quiet sigh of happiness and contentment emanate from adults and children alike.

Arthur and Gwen stepped up to stand hand in hand in front of me, and as I gathered my power, I felt the two of them experience a rush of excitement as I transported everyone to...

Camelot.

"Oh, by all the gods," Arthur breathed. "Dad, what did you *do?*" He gazed up at the familiar towers of gray stone and massive hewn timbers holding the partially thatched roof high above us. Bright pennants and flags bearing the iconic red dragon outlined in black flew from the different levels of the structure, moving lazily in the breeze. The castle was large and imposing, constructed only partially of the stone blocks described in the legends; many sections were built of wood, which was common in fifth-century Britain.

The sunlight seemed particularly bright and warm this day. Puffy white clouds in the flawless blue sky seemed to gambol like fat sheep in a grassy meadow.

Tears welled in Gwen's eyes as she beheld the home she'd never expected to see again. She kissed my cheek and whispered quietly, "Thank you, Merlin."

"You are most welcome, Guinevere, my queen," I said in the old language.

Arthur gripped my shoulder and pulled me against him, practically trembling with emotion. "I'm so grateful. How can I ever thank you?" For a moment, I thought his sincerity seemed forced, but I assured myself that I had to be imagining things.

"No thanks are needed, Arthur. I've said it before and I'll say it again: I would do anything for you. You're both my son and my king, and we're both immortal. We'll be together forever."

* * *

Cathy gazed up at the magnificent structure in awe, and whispered to her husband, "You helped Merlin create this?"

Colin grinned in satisfaction and pride. "Yeah, I did."

"How did you know what to do?"

He paused a moment. "It's hard to describe how it works when I utilize my powers. For something as massive as this, I had to follow Merlin's lead. I added my power to his while he did everything else. It feels amazing, like energy, Light, and love inside me, and when I'm in it, my being is set free. In fact, I think we became pure Light at one point."

She held Colin's hand and looked into his eyes, knowing that she would never be able to comprehend what it was like for him to be a god. She paused and looked around, her brows pulling into a slight frown. "Wait a minute. We left Moab around noon, which means it should be evening here in England, and dark. But it's not. And it's autumn, so why does it look and feel like late spring?" It was warm, there were flowers blooming on a nearby hill, and the trees boasted newly unfurled green leaves. Cathy noticed that others were questioning the inconsistency as well, nodding in agreement with her or simply gazing curiously at their surroundings.

Colin's face reflected the awe he felt as he described what his brother had done.

"We created Camelot in our own dimension, but then Merlin decided to move it to an alternate reality, which is the reason the time of day isn't what you expected it to be. I don't know if you're aware of this, but when we're not using our wings, they exist in a place only a hair's breadth away from the dimension we live in. I think the reality we're in is parallel to that place."

Cathy was speechless, as were others who had heard Colin's words.

* * *

Total silence reigned behind me and I turned. As one, every single adult present bowed to me, even my wife, my son the future Fae King, and my brother. I wasn't expecting to be honored in this manner and I felt a little embarrassed. After all, I had not done it for self-aggrandizement, but out of love for my son and soon-to-be daughter-in-law.

Colin smiled as he caught my eye. *Take what's offered, Merlin. We're all devoted to you and that devotion must be expressed—and accepted.*

I acknowledged his wisdom with a barely perceptible nod and bowed my head toward my devotees in grateful acceptance.

I cleared my throat and began to speak. "It is now time for Arthur and Gwen to renew the ancient vows they made so long ago. And to keep us safe from harm, *all* of my brothers and sisters from the god realm will be watching over us this day."

I heard many sighs of relief among the guests, who had been on edge at the possibility of Sam making an appearance and causing mayhem.

As Arthur, Gwen, and I led the way into the castle, and thence to the Great Hall, I felt a weight lift from my spirit as I sensed who was waiting on the dais to conduct the ceremony. I had hoped my father would show up, but I knew better than to make assumptions, so I'd been prepared to officiate if necessary.

Thank you, Father. I am most grateful you came.

How could I not? This is one of the milestones in your journey and Arthur's. And I'm happy that you allowed Colin to assist you. It takes great compassion, understanding, and teamwork to share an accomplishment such as this. I'm proud of you.

I should have known he'd been observing all along. I was relieved that he approved of what I'd done. I thought I had been veering from my true path while planning and finalizing this celebration, and all along, he had been guiding my steps.

I smiled. Of course he had.

As everyone filed into the Great Hall and stood in the predetermined spots as if directed there, light filled the space and all the original decorations appeared by prearranged magical design. It was spring outside because I'd made it so, but the leaves and garlands were in flaming autumn colors to satisfy a cherished memory.

* * *

Unseen horns sounded and King Arthur strode regally up the aisle to the dais and turned. He gazed at all the familiar faces. Only a few of these individuals had been present at his wedding in the fifth century, but somehow they fit perfectly into the current scene.

The woman he'd been in love with for centuries appeared in the entryway to the Great Hall, outlined by light. She gazed up at him with her heart in her eyes, and his thoughts became focused solely on her.

Horns sounded once more, and Queen Guinevere glided elegantly toward what was once again her destiny. As she approached the dais to join her past and future husband, the King of Camelot, the crown that had been buried with her when she died over 1500 years ago appeared magically on her head.

Arthur guided her up the final step, placing her squarely by his side where she'd always belonged. They gazed into each other's eyes and turned as one toward Arthur's grandfather, ready to reaffirm the loving bond that had linked them through time.

God smiled and began, "My dearly beloved, we are gathered here in my sight to bring these two lovers full circle, through life and death and life again, to join them once more in the bonds of holy matrimony…"

* * *

As Gwen stood hand in hand with Arthur before the Creator of the universe, listening to him recite the age-old service, she felt as if she would burst with happiness. However, underlying that giddiness was a sense of unreality. Memories of her life in Camelot, and of her many other lives over the centuries, both male and female, raced unchecked through her consciousness. But her most recent life as Jim Singleton was absolutely clear and steady in her mind, in particular the night when she had met Merlin again.

* * *

I experienced Gwen's memories—which were similar to my own—of a certain night back in 2014 when I had transported Derek, Morry, and Jim Singleton from Moody's Tavern to my home, intent upon discovering why Jim, Morry's supervisor at the newspaper, and I seemed to recognize each other...

I gazed silently at the man before me and knew I had to solve the mystery of his true identity. He was in his thirties and his soft, curly brown hair framed his animated features. He stared at me boldly with a faint smile and a knowing look that disturbed me. I held him immobile by my will, initiated the Seeing, and moved back in time through the fabric of his past lives until it had unraveled to the original thread of his beginning. And I discovered the one life, the one soul, that I had least expected to encounter again.

"Your Majesty," I uttered, as I bowed in acknowledgment of her status in the fifth century.

Jim's features morphed into a familiar feminine visage as the soul of Guinevere Pendragon peered out of those expressive brown eyes. "Lord Merlin. It is wonderful to see you again. You were my best friend after Arthur died and I would have done anything in the world for you."

As I refocused on the present, I had tears in my eyes. I could sense Gwen's emotions as she remembered that scene as well. We had treasured the experience of reconnecting after all those centuries, and now we had come back to the beginning again.

I listened to my father's mellifluous voice as he continued with the service, until the time came for Gwen and Arthur to exchange rings along with their vows. I could sense Arthur's hope that she would approve of the ring he had chosen for her. The original wedding ring that he had slipped on her finger so long ago had been lost, and surprisingly, I had been unable to find it. The gold ring had been wide and ornate, with ancient symbols of devotion etched on it. He hadn't wanted to duplicate that ring, figuring he needed a new style for a new century and a new lease on life.

I grinned to myself. Both Arthur and Guinevere had unknowingly chosen the same ring for each other: a simple 24 karat gold band with, appropriately, an eternity symbol engraved upon it.

As they each slipped the bands of purest gold on the other's fingers at God's prompting, I sensed the love flowing around me as relentlessly as a river flows toward its joining with the ocean. The magic of that moment filled every heart in the room with joy.

I held Em's hand in mine and we repeated our own vows to each other silently as God performed the miracle of making two hearts one.

* * *

I felt more relaxed than I had in a long time as I watched my loved ones enjoying themselves. I thought about all the effort and planning that had gone into this wedding celebration, and I realized that this facsimile of Camelot, which I had originally intended to dismantle once it had fulfilled its main purpose of wedding venue, would be just right for the European headquarters of the new State of Albion. I had re-created the castle in all of its glory, complete with bedchambers, kitchen, storerooms, dining hall, meeting rooms, infirmary, library, armoury, Great Hall, and Council Hall, wherein the Round Table held pride of place. I did add a few bathrooms for the convenience of the wedding guests, but everything else was authentically replicated. Outbuildings such as the stables and blacksmith shop were unnecessary in this day and age, but once we had declared our aim to create a new world order, we would need offices and all the modern accoutrements. I could create those when the time came.

And when it was appropriate, I would move New Camelot back to our dimension in order to be available to everyone. Until then, it would be safe and undisturbed in this unpopulated dimension.

I put aside my thoughts of both past and future, and joined everyone in a toast to the newlyweds. I had set up the reception here in the dining hall, having conjured furniture and all necessary and assorted tableware, utensils, and decorations. I had also brought in an abundance of food and drink and set it up buffet style, to which everyone applied themselves with hearty appetites.

On a whim, I conjured my old lap harp from The Crystal Cave, and proceeded to play and sing for the bride and groom and all the assembled guests.

In stunned silence, my audience listened to entertainment they had never foreseen: A god who was also a fifth-century bard singing and playing an ancient harp in a legendary castle as the King and Queen of Camelot looked on.

When I finished to rousing applause, I smiled and bowed to my appreciative audience.

I was immensely pleased and satisfied with what Colin and I had accomplished here.

As a soft hand touched my face, I turned.

"Good job, Merlin," my wife murmured.

CHAPTER 49
Moab, Sunday, November 5, 2023, Early Morning

E ver since he had attained his adult growth, Arthur had found it difficult to keep the reality of his present life separate from his memories of the past, and it often kept him awake at night. He would get out of bed and pace around the bedroom pondering if being reincarnated in this complicated time had been worth the hassle, and if he could manage to reconcile it all before it drove him insane.

Then he would gaze at his sleeping wife, his precious Guinevere, and he would thank the gods he had been reborn, the two of them reunited in this incredible century.

One such night, lying in bed wide-awake and lost in reminiscing, he decided to fly. The fact that he could do so never ceased to amaze him. He cautiously got out of bed, not wanting to disturb Gwen, conjured clothing, and teleported into his shadowed back yard.

The home they had recently purchased on Doc Allen Drive was only a few blocks from his parents' house. His property was slightly higher in elevation, so he could see the top of their vine-covered back wall from his own yard.

He hadn't been able to bear the thought of being very far away from them, although he wondered why he felt that way when he constantly doubted—and criticized—his father's objectives. He had been experiencing surges of increasingly intense anger, disgust, and betrayal ever since he had transitioned to adulthood and he didn't understand why. It might be his mind's way of protesting the existence of two sets of memories, and the necessity of keeping them in order constantly. Or did he blame his father for bringing him back to life?

It was confusing and distressing, and since he didn't want to let his emotions ruin his flight, he shut them down, at least for the time being.

Arthur stared up at the stars, their configurations so different from those he remembered in fifth-century Britain. For a moment, he became lost in the old memories again. But that was an exercise in futility and he deliberately shook off the transitory sense of homesickness that always accompanied his reminiscences.

He closed his eyes, sought the place inside his being where his magic resided, and called forth his wings. The sudden weight on his upper back near his shoulder blades—not to mention the sensation of having extra limbs—always startled him. And he still wasn't fully accustomed to the intensity of the magic flowing through his adult body. He could conjure clothing and household items, and teleporting and telepathy were easy for him. But whenever he felt like he'd reached an appropriate level of accomplishment, something would occur that made him realize he was still a novice. And it irritated the hell out of him.

He thought about his father's magic, and how blind he had been in his previous incarnation not to have recognized the truth: Merlin commanded power far beyond that of a mere magician. The fact that he was a god, and moreover, an angel of God, was hard to accept even now.

Arthur grimaced. He had spent an evening in September with both his father and his grandfather, the Creator of the universe, but even so, he'd had a difficult time comprehending the reality of his situation.

When Arthur had died that fateful day in the fifth century at the Battle of Camlann, his body and spirit had gone posthaste to Avalon, to be protected by the Elves until he was needed once more, resurrected to fight for justice.

He'd never anticipated that his resurrection would be like this. He had assumed he would get his original body and life back, the son of Uther Pendragon and a normal human being. Instead, he was the demigod son of Merlin, with a new body, magical powers, and the ability to fly.

Filled with a sudden, desperate need to be aloft, Arthur launched himself into the night sky, winging higher and higher until he attained a height beyond which he was out of his comfort zone. He caught a strong air current and soared out toward Arches National Park, one of his favorite destinations. He hoped he wouldn't run into Derek, as they had been at odds for months and Arthur didn't feel like dealing with his brother tonight. Simply thinking about it left a bad taste in his mouth.

As he was gliding over the imposing sandstone structure known as The Three Gossips, he was startled by a dark form with ghostly white wings off to his right that seemed to be on a collision course with him. He was relieved to recognize Seth. After all, who else could it be?

Hello, Brother, Arthur said telepathically.

Halò, Arthur, Seth responded.

He and Chris had returned a little over a month ago from their honeymoon in Scotland, having spent some of that time meeting with the Fae Elders. When he'd told his family that the old king had proclaimed Seth his successor, Arthur had been shocked, but Merlin seemed to take it in stride, as if he'd expected it.

Arthur planned on meeting with Seth once the main headquarters for New Camelot was established in America and Seth had become King of the Light Court Fae, so that they could coordinate efforts to bring about Albion in both the human and Fae realms.

What're ye doing here this night? Ye should be cuddled up wi' yer wife the noo, aye? Seth's Scottish burr was so thick Arthur could scarcely understand him.

Arthur glanced over at his half sibling, recognizing the lack of warmth when they spoke to each other, despite Seth's effort to make conversation. That reserve was even more evident since Seth's return from Scotland.

For the past three months, Arthur had noticed that both Seth and Derek seemed resentful and suspicious of his relationship with their father. It never occurred to him that he was the one experiencing those feelings.

He scowled. It was ridiculous and they'd both have to get over it. He was going to be King Arthur again soon enough and they had no choice but to accept it. In fact, Merlin needed to accept it, too. Arthur remembered when as a child he had knelt submissively at his father's feet. It had felt like the right thing to do, but now the memory infuriated him. He glanced over at Seth, who hadn't seemed to notice the angry look on his face. Arthur hastily replaced it with a polite half smile. The light was pretty dim but he knew Seth's eyesight was exceptional at night.

The brothers flew together in a tense silence until Seth finally addressed him again.

Weel, it's time I headed fer home, but I'm certain we'll see each other again soon.

I'm sure we will, Seth. Fly safe. He congratulated himself for learning to shield his inner thoughts as he added, to himself, *you smug bastard.*

Apparently none the wiser, the Fae prince gave him a solemn nod and banked sharply, flying swiftly back toward the bright glow in the sky over Moab.

Flying soothed Arthur when he was confused and upset (so much for controlling his emotions) so he decided to continue on a bit longer, wings spread wide as he caught an updraft of slightly warmer air. Dawn was approaching, the sky lightening in the east to streaks of soft gray and peach.

He was so caught up in his roiling thoughts he never noticed the car parked below him in the Fiery Furnace parking lot until he had almost flown past it. But he didn't worry about it since the car was dark and no one seemed to be around. And if someone did see him, it shouldn't be any concern of his. Humans tended to exaggerate, so who would believe them? He didn't even notice that he now considered himself apart from humanity.

* * *

Beth Douglas stepped out from under the shelter of a scraggly piñon pine next to the parking lot and lowered her phone, which she'd been using to record the action in the sky above her. The light was still fairly low but she was sure the device would pick it up.

She wasn't worried about being seen. Her jacket had a desert camouflage pattern which blended into the landscape seamlessly.

She felt vindicated in spying on the man—well, maybe not a man, but what the hell was he?—with blond hair and wings as he flew overhead. It was a public place, after all. And the one with black hair and white wings who had flown in the opposite direction had features that were so similar to the blond's they could be brothers. Probably were, and she didn't see how either of them could be human.

It dawned on her that she recognized the blond one. He was Gwen Singleton's husband. Beth remembered when tall and sexy—minus the wings—had strolled into the office back in August and surprised Gwen at her desk. They'd had a whirlwind courtship, moving in together without delay, and were married by mid-October. They'd acted as if they'd known and loved one another forever, but she didn't know how that could be. Gwen never talked about having had a relationship with anyone; she'd always been alone whenever Beth saw her around town.

She sensed a major story here, one that could blow the lid off of whatever colossal secret those guys were keeping so assiduously. As a reporter, she needed something to boost her standing at the newspaper, and this could make her career.

She'd see what happened when she released the video and photos she'd taken and had written an exposé. Or posted everything on Facebook, *and* on her blog.

* * *

Arthur had flown as far as the Devils Garden trailhead when he began to feel as if something was terribly wrong, even though he had no idea what it was. It galled him to admit it, but he needed to contact Merlin. He wouldn't be waking him up since his father never slept anymore. A dubious benefit in Arthur's opinion.

Sorry to bother you, Dad, but I need your advice. He gritted his teeth in frustration.

I'm always here for you, Son. What do you need? Arthur figured his dad knew everything already, but couldn't seem to break the habits of a lifetime, so he continued to use polite conversation rather than getting right to the point. Often, Merlin didn't seem like a god at all. But Arthur had limited experience with gods, so in all probability this was typical.

I'm not sure. I have a feeling something's amiss.

No sooner had he expressed that thought when Merlin was beside him, his enormous wings dwarfing Arthur's own. He shivered involuntarily, still a bit awestruck when confronted with his father's magnificence. And a whole lot more annoyed.

* * *

I extended a magical field of energy around the two of us as we hovered in midair over the trailhead, rendering us invisible to the mortal eye. It was too light for us to be flying out here in plain sight.

"Arthur, I'm surprised you didn't remember that hikers have been known to show up in the park as early as five o'clock in the morning, and it's now seven. And during a full moon, people hike to Delicate Arch in the middle of the night. So you shouldn't be flying around Moab—or any other inhabited area for that matter—without having a powerful invisibility spell in place. I taught you that sometime ago." I eyed him impatiently, sensing that Arthur's thoughts and emotions were in turmoil, although I couldn't perceive exactly what was wrong. Had he learned to block me?

"I never even considered it when I left home earlier," he said dismissively. "I was caught up in trying to reconcile my past with my present, as usual."

Arthur didn't seem at all concerned by his error. In fact, lately he had been displaying an increasingly blatant disregard for what I'd taught him, and an inexcusable lack of caution when it came to using his magic.

The duality of his existence might be causing his issues, as he had mentioned, and his memories of olden times could be interfering with his current perceptions. But that was highly unlikely since Arthur had spent centuries in Avalon anticipating his resurrection and what it meant.

It was imperative that he adapt his thinking and his behavior to this new age. He had been an adult for almost three months and should have become accustomed to applying adult reasoning to his everyday life, as he'd done in his previous one.

He had been paying more attention to his love life and his marriage than to his duty, for which I wouldn't normally blame him. But the ever-growing crises in the world that would lead up to our establishment of the new world order were coming to a head.

Satan's previous influence was yielding a profoundly negative effect on my son.

As his father, it was easy to make excuses for his behavior, but in view of his recent transgressions, I couldn't, and shouldn't, do that.

In the modern vernacular, Arthur had screwed up big time.

As we hovered a hundred feet above the ground, I allowed my god senses to fan out in all directions to confirm what damage had been done by Arthur's negligence. At least half a dozen individuals who had been drinking had seen him flying over Moab and would attribute their experience to inebriation, so I didn't bother with them. A few others had been driving into the park and had seen glimpses of Arthur's wings and assumed they'd seen a large bird. This was acceptable—barely. The human mind was able to deny hints of the supernatural, which was to our benefit.

My eyes narrowed when I sensed the major problem. I glanced at Arthur and snapped, "Come." I vanished, reappearing in the Fiery Furnace parking lot face to face with a woman I recognized as Morry's coworker, Beth Douglas. I lifted my hand, stopping time. In the past, I had used a spell, triggered by the Latin word *desino*, which prevented the subject from moving. However, devices and spells were no longer necessary to utilize my magic—I *was* the magic. It was ironic that I could accomplish literally anything, except to anticipate my family's thoughts and actions, which would continue to be a problem until I had reconnected with all my clones *and* defeated my brother and his elusive minions. I was tired of dealing with that, but it was difficult not thinking about it.

Arthur had followed me and stood at my side, staring at the young woman as she gazed at images of my two sons in midflight with a satisfied smirk on her face.

"I had hoped this wouldn't happen so soon."

"I don't understand why this woman is taking photos of us. Who is she?"

I was dismayed at his naiveté. In his life in the fifth century, Arthur had been brilliant, shrewd, and intuitive—he'd had to be in his position as both warrior and king. In this century, life didn't present the same kinds of challenges on a daily basis, so he hadn't had the opportunity to relearn those skills.

I reined in my temper and filled him in. "She's a reporter working with Gwen and Morry who has become obsessed with revealing our secrets. She and her friend Chloe used to attend my storytelling sessions when I first opened the shop, and somehow they figured out who I was. Years ago, prior to the Battle of Matheson Preserve, they saw me appear out of thin air on top of the Rim where they were hiking, and I erased the information from their minds. Or so I thought. Apparently, Beth retained at least a fragment of it. It seems fate has decreed that she will be a part of our lives in some way. So, instead of erasing her memory along with those incriminating images, I'll only erase the photos and videos."

Arthur looked wary. "But…"

"Destiny will prevail and everything will come together in the end. But right now it would be best if you headed home." I followed him closely as we left Arches National Park and I made sure he didn't take any detours, which irritated him to no end.

I didn't realize until later in the day that I had sounded as enigmatic and removed from human affairs as my father always did. If I completely lost touch with my "humanity," I would lose my reason for being at Arthur's side once he was King of Albion, and that wouldn't do at all.

However, I may not have a choice, since my human emotions blocked my intuition as well as my communication with the clones that hadn't yet merged with me.

I sighed. This day had started out on a sour note, and having to send Arthur home in disgrace hadn't helped any. He had been furious with me for treating him like an errant schoolboy.

I told him to quit acting like one.

* * *

Beth frowned and glanced around the parking lot, which a few seconds ago had been empty of cars other than hers. Now there were a whole slew of them, a dozen or more. She glanced at her phone, thinking she'd review the images she'd taken of the flying men.

They were gone, every single one of them. She searched frantically through every photo, every album, and every video she'd stored on the device and they weren't there.

In the midst of her distress, she had a flash of memory, a fleeting glimpse in her mind of a black-haired man with piercing green eyes and mammoth black wings swooping down in front of her, followed by Gwen's husband, and then...nothing. It was as if she'd been unconscious. Or time had stopped for her alone.

She generally had a mind like a steel trap—she never forgot anything—so she concentrated until she found the information she wanted.

Michael Reese. It was Michael Reese from The Moab Herbalist, or, as she suspected, *Merlin*. But where had the wings come from? What the hell was going on in that family? What *were* they? Did they all have those fucking wings? If so, what did they do with them when they weren't using them? God, she'd give several years of her life to get the real story on them; it could earn her a sizeable raise, for sure, maybe even a Pulitzer.

But they were gone and so were her photos and the video. She gritted her teeth and growled in frustration. She might as well go home.

Beth took off her jacket and climbed into her car, the interior of which had heated up as the sun rose higher. She tossed her jacket in the back, grabbed the water bottle she'd left on the seat, and drank thirstily. It was a damn good thing she always used metal water bottles as opposed to that plastic disposable crap, which released toxins into her drinking water when heated. She put the cap back on the bottle and reflected that, despite the heat here in the parking area, which was unusual for November, it would be cool within the fins and spires of the Fiery Furnace even on the hottest days of summer.

The name actually referred to the warm glow of the afternoon sunlight on the red rock, not the air temperature. Many years ago, she had spent a few seasons as an interpretive ranger, giving guided tours in the Fiery Furnace, and she'd had to memorize all the descriptive details for the tourists. She was glad she didn't have to do it anymore. News reporting was more her style.

She glanced at the time on her phone and realized she'd been standing there, oblivious, for an hour or more. No wonder she felt so dehydrated. She pushed her wispy brown bangs back off her forehead. Her face felt sunburned, even though it seemed rather late in the year for that.

Beth had started the car, opened the windows to get some air inside, and prepared to put the car in reverse, when she spied a slim dark stick lodged in a clump of blackbrush. She did a double take and got back out of the car.

She picked it up and excitement surged through her. It wasn't a stick, it was a feather, an iridescent black feather some thirty inches long. Sure, there were large ravens in the area—several of them were hanging around hoping for a handout—but this was no bird feather.

As she returned to the car with her prize she received a text from Chloe. She read the message and huffed out a breath.

WHERE R U? THOUGHT U WERE COMING 4 BRKFST??

Her best friend always used caps when she was pissed off. Beth texted back, *Sorry, got held up out in the park. Be there ASAP.*

She drove as fast as she dared up the winding entrance road to the stop sign, looked both ways, and turned left onto the main park road. As she continued past the turn-off to Delicate Arch and accelerated up the hill toward Balanced Rock, Beth asked herself if she had the courage to confront "Michael Reese" in his shop, and decided that might not be the wisest course of action.

But hey, she could talk to Morry, her coworker, and get his advice on how best to proceed, she thought to herself sarcastically. Although they had always maintained a cordial working relationship, she was hesitant to reveal her obsession with the owner of The Moab Herbalist since Morry was clearly related to him. She could ask Gwen, but she and her boss had never hit it off. She'd honestly tried to make friends with Gwen when the woman had replaced Jim after his death, but Gwen apparently wasn't interested.

The funny thing was, Gwen and Morry seemed to be close friends, having nearly the same relationship as Jim and Morry had had. That Gwen was Jim's sister could account for it, but it was still an odd coincidence.

Thinking about Jim made Beth feel depressed. His death had really thrown her. They hadn't been close, though she wouldn't have minded dating the man. She'd always had the desire to run her fingers through his brown curls. But she'd been reluctant to say anything, and he, to be honest, hadn't seemed to be overly attracted to her. He had treated her the same way Gwen did—with polite detachment.

Jim and Gwen might as well be the same person, which was logical since they'd been twins, but...

Her mind, which was adept at making odd connections, jumped to an implausible conclusion—that Jim and Gwen *were* the same person; that he'd been reborn as a female after he died.

Beth shook her head and laughed. How stupid could she be?

CHAPTER 50
Moab, Monday, November 6, 2023

After the conversation Merlin had with him the previous day regarding Arthur's exploits, Morry wondered if Beth would try to talk to him at work this morning. He had always gotten along with her, but they weren't friends by any means, so he wasn't sure if she'd want to confront him. Merlin had warned him about her quest to expose their family secrets, and wanted Morry to talk to her if she approached him. But what in the hell should he say to her?

He was aware that the shape of his eyes reflected a relationship with his grandfather. The question was, had she noticed? She must have if she thought that Michael Reese, owner of The Moab Herbalist, was actually Merlin. But how the hell could she have figured that out when Merlin had erased her memory?

"Daddy, can I have hot chocolate?"

Morry roused himself from his thoughts and looked at the kitchen clock before answering his daughter. "You'll have to wait 'til you get to Grandma's, Bonnie. We have to leave pretty soon or I'll be late for work. Are you ready to go? Where's your brother?" Ever since Lainie had decided to go back to work this past summer, he'd been in charge of dropping the twins off at her mother's house on his way to the office, since he started work later than she did.

"He's getting dressed," Bonnie said in her serious little voice.

"Tell him to hurry—we have to leave in five minutes. And put your coat on, it's pretty chilly outside." Damn it, he shouldn't have spent all that time lost in thought.

"Brady, Daddy says hurry up we have to leave!" she yelled at the top of her lungs.

"I could have done that myself, kiddo. Go in there and—oh, never mind."

Morry hurried into the kids' room, to find a roly poly brown wolf pup sleeping on the bed.

349

"Brady, what are you doing?" he shouted. Startled, the pup fell off the bed, turning into a naked four-year-old boy who started sobbing when he saw his father's furious expression.

"You know you're not supposed to shift in the morning when you have to go to Grandma's. I have to go to work!" He gritted his teeth in frustration as he picked up his son off the floor. This happened often, and he figured Brady was acting out because Lainie wasn't there.

He didn't have the patience for this. He didn't bother to dress his son the traditional way and instead conjured clothes, shoes, and coat with a thought.

Brady looked down at the clothes that had appeared on his body and scowled at him. "Mommy says not to use magic to get dressed!"

"Well, Mommy's not here and I'm running late. Tomorrow, dress yourself instead of shifting." He conjured his own jacket, and the two of them headed to the front door, where his daughter stood waiting for him. "Okay, you two, let's go."

He finally got them strapped into their car seats, jumped into the car, and fastened his own seatbelt. It was a pain in the ass to use mundane, non-magical ways of doing things outside the house, but they had to keep a low profile. Their neighbor, Mrs. O'Kelly, had proven to be nosy and he'd already had to make her forget several incidents that could have revealed sensitive information about the family.

Morry backed out of the driveway and headed toward his mother-in-law's house on Rosetree Lane. Lainie drove his Jeep Patriot to work and he had to drive Lainie's old Ford Escape—which was on its last legs —since it supposedly had more room. Personally, he didn't think so; it looked the same size to him. He figured she liked his vehicle better than her own. He couldn't blame her, so did he. They needed to eliminate one source of controversy in their lives and get a new vehicle, like a Suburban, or an Explorer. They should be able to afford it since they had two incomes again.

He looked at his children in the rearview mirror. He loved them dearly, but having two young kids to raise was way more work than he'd thought it would be, and he never had any time to himself. In fact, he and his wife rarely had any quality time alone anymore either.

He gritted his teeth, and tried to remember that he'd asked for this.

* * *

Morry pushed through the big glass office door and hurried over to his desk. He quickly logged onto his computer, noting as he did so that he was ten minutes late. Yesterday it was five minutes. He needed to get the morning routine under control so he could arrive at work punctually in the future. He didn't think they'd fire him, since Gwen was his supervisor, but he didn't want to take the chance.

"Kids giving you trouble?"

Morry glanced up as he heard Beth's amused voice. Jeez, he didn't want to have to cope with her yet. He took a long, slow breath to calm himself before he answered.

"Yeah, they miss having their mom there in the morning. Lainie stayed home with them until she went back to work recently."

"I'm sure you'll get it straightened out. Hey, I have a question for you if you've got a minute."

Shit, he'd hoped to have a few minutes to prepare. She sounded reasonable and friendly, but he wasn't fooled—he knew she was neither. He figured he'd better get it over with. "Uh, sure, I need a cup of coffee anyway, so why don't we talk in the break room."

He stood up and headed down the hall, with Beth following him. He saw Gwen give him a questioning look as he walked by her desk. He raised his eyebrows and hoped she'd interpret his expression as 'I'll tell you later.'

He poured himself a large mug of coffee, fortifying it with sugar and powdered creamer and took a big gulp as he turned to Beth expectantly.

"What do you know about Michael Reese, the guy at The Moab Herbalist?" Even though he'd expected her to question him, it was still a shock and he swallowed wrong, causing him to almost cough up a lung. He finally got his breathing under control.

"Uh, like what? How long he's owned the business? Stuff like that?"

She stared at him and smiled disingenuously.

He swallowed another, smaller mouthful of coffee. And did something he normally considered shameful—he read her thoughts without her permission.

The stupid ass thinks I don't know that Michael is Merlin. He thinks I don't see that his eyes are slanted like Merlin's. I bet he can fly, too.

Morry stared back at her until he had to look away, reluctant to initiate the Seeing between them.

Aw, look, he's embarrassed, or maybe even nervous. Poor guy. Her mental voice dripped with sarcasm.

"It seems you know the answer, Beth, so why bother to ask me?" He paused to take another sip of coffee before continuing. "Embarrassed? Nervous? Hardly. As a matter of fact, I *can* fly."

351

He put the coffee mug on the counter, and crossed his arms over his chest to await her response.

A look of surprise flickered across her face and was gone.

"You read my mind."

He bobbed his head impatiently.

"You're his son aren't you?"

"Grandson." Morry's expression turned hard. "Not that it's any of your business."

"So you have wings, huh?"

His eyes narrowed and his lips thinned. If he was in his wolf form his teeth would be bared and he'd be growling menacingly.

"No, I'm a shapeshifter. I can turn into a bird." He lost what little patience he had left. "You're too fucking nosy! You have no idea what damage you could do with the information you have, and—"

"You mean like tell the world all of you can fly? People have a right to know, after all. And that Merlin, the sorcerer, is living among us? Who's to say he's not plotting against regular folk? And who is the guy that looks like Merlin but has pointed ears and white wings? Obviously he's not human and could be a threat to society." Beth smirked, hoping to goad him into more revelations. Unbeknownst to him she wore a voice-activated recorder on a silver chain around her neck, in plain sight. It resembled a simple pendant, but was in reality a highly technical and expensive piece of investigative equipment she'd recently purchased.

Goading him was the right move to get him all riled up. It distracted him from being aware that his every word was being recorded.

"Gwen's husband is my uncle. And the guy with the white wings, who is Fae, is also my uncle. They both happen to be very powerful, but my father is even more powerful than they are, and my grandfather most of all. I wouldn't mess with any of them if I were you." Morry was so angry he could scarcely speak coherently, and he finally had to shut up so he didn't give away any more information than he already had.

He took a couple of deep breaths to regain at least a modicum of composure. "People are not entitled to know our personal business." *Not yet anyway*, he thought. He tried to find the most effective words to get through to her. "And you should know that our supervisor, your supervisor, is my aunt Gwen. Don't be fooled by the fact that she appears younger than I am. She's not. So be careful what you say and do around here. Oh, and by the way, Merlin *allowed* you to keep your memories even though he wiped your phone."

Beth still had a defiant, snarky look on her face and he wondered if he dared to try something he'd only thought about doing. What the hell, he should test it out on her. So he projected an image of his wolf—ears back and teeth bared—directly to her mind.

Beth screamed.

Morry smiled toothily, satisfied with his effect on her. He casually sauntered out of the break room, coffee mug in hand, and back to his desk.

Everyone looked worried and asked him if Beth was okay.

"Oh, yeah, she just saw a spider," he said, loud enough for her to hear him.

* * *

That supercilious bastard, Beth seethed silently. She had finally gotten herself under control enough to go back to her desk, worried she would have a dismissal letter waiting for her. It turned out she didn't and Gwen didn't even come over to talk to her. But she was determined to ruin Morry, ruin them all. So after she got her regular assignment finished, she surreptitiously plugged the recording device into a USB port on her computer and downloaded the information she'd collected earlier. She typed a narrative and posted it on her Facebook page and on her blog, revealing everything she knew about Merlin and Morry and every last one of those magic-wielding bastards. Finishing the last post with a flourish, she clicked enter, avidly anticipating the havoc her disclosures would wreak.

Everything she had posted disappeared.

She emitted a frustrated squeak and Morry said in a normal tone of voice, but loud enough to be heard throughout the office, "Gosh, Beth, did you see another spider?"

She glared daggers at him and he merely raised his upper lip in a sneer. He started typing and she saw his words come through to her on Microsoft Teams: DID YOU THINK YOU COULD GET AWAY WITH THAT? DO YOU WANT TO MEET THAT WOLF I SHOWED YOU? JUST KEEP IT UP; I'D BE HAPPY TO INTRODUCE YOU.

Beth noticed that Gwen was standing at Morry's desk, talking to him quietly. If the look on his face was any indication, she was ripping him a new one.

Since Gwen was facing away from her, Beth smirked at him again, hoping to piss him off even more. She laughed to herself and thought, *Serves him right. Asshole.*

"Beth, can I see you in the break room for a moment, please." What was worded as a request came across as a demand.

Oh, damn it. She glanced up at Gwen's furious expression and wondered if she'd hung herself. But she realized that, unless Gwen could read her mind, she wouldn't really know what Beth had been thinking. A wave of relief swept through her and she looked into Gwen's eyes with an insincere smile. "Sure, happy to oblige."

Beth got up and followed Gwen, giving in to the urge to look back at Morry smugly. But as she saw the look of satisfaction on his face, she faltered. Oh, God, was she going to be fired?

Morry watched as it dawned on Beth that she was in trouble. But he was worried Merlin's plan was going to backfire. The woman was totally unscrupulous, and revealing more information about their family seemed like an extremely bad idea. True, she had known, or at least suspected, way more than she should for many years, and had never, up to this point anyway, revealed her knowledge to anyone. But she would have if Morry hadn't removed her online posts a few minutes ago.

Beth decided she had nothing to lose, so when she entered the break room she leaned against the counter with a confident smile, positive that she could talk her way out of this mess and get back to work.

Gwen eyed her with distaste and got right to the heart of the matter. "So, my nephew tells me that you know all about us."

Beth's smile disappeared and she wondered if she was walking into a trap. "My goodness, what do you mean, Gwen?" she asked disingenuously.

"Don't play games with me. I've known you far longer than you think, Beth, and I know that while you're a competent writer, your ethics stink. Do you remember the article you wrote back in early 2014? The one alleging a misuse of funds by National Park Service personnel? The misuse that *you* created out of whole cloth?"

"How the hell do you know about that?" she asked hotly. "You weren't even here then! I never let that article go to print because your brother, Jim, gave me a break."

Gwen's lips turned up in a smile that held no amusement. "I wish that I'd fired you for it, Beth, as you deserved."

"*You* wished you'd fired me?" After a moment of confusion, Beth remembered the highly improbable scenario she'd imagined, that when Jim died, he'd somehow come back as a woman. She stared hard at Gwen, picturing her with shorter hair, no makeup, no boobs, and dressed like a man, with a package that made the front of his pants bulge slightly. "Oh, shit, you're Jim Singleton," she whispered.

Gwen nodded curtly. "I used to be Jim, but now I'm who my soul has always been: Guinevere, wife of King Arthur."

Beth's mouth gaped unflatteringly.

"Better close your mouth or you'll attract flies."

"The blond guy you married is *King Arthur?*"

"Yes. He was Arthur Pendragon when we both lived in Camelot in the fifth century. Then he died and was in Avalon—or the Other World you might call it—for many centuries. Since he's been reborn, he's Arthur Ambrosius, son of Merlin Ambrosius, better known in Moab as Michael Reese, owner of The Moab Herbalist. Which you were about to reveal to the world, with no more thought to the damage you'd cause than you had back in 2014 with that article."

Beth swallowed with difficulty, her mouth dry. She'd thought if she could ferret out the truth, she would feel a spiraling sense of accomplishment that would send her on her way to fame and fortune. Instead, now that she knew everything, she felt diminished, ashamed, as if she had kicked a puppy, or told a child there was no such thing as Santa Claus.

She rallied, pushed those thoughts ruthlessly aside, hardened her heart, and glared at Gwen defiantly.

"Merlin seems to think this fiasco can be salvaged, that allowing you to work for him will be enough to keep you from doing irreparable harm to our family." Gwen examined the expression on Beth's face gravely. "Personally, I think it's a horrible idea, but who am I to argue with Merlin? So, what's your decision? Are you for us or against us? Oh, and by the way, if you decide you're against us, Merlin will permanently wipe your memories—every single damn one of them. So I suggest you choose wisely."

Her face white as chalk, Beth still maintained her stance. "I need time to think it over."

Gwen sighed. "You have to be the most intractable person I've ever met, Ms. Douglas. And that includes all the pig-headed, chauvinistic men I dealt with when I was Queen of Camelot. Alright, you have less than twenty-four hours to think it over." She glanced at the clock on the wall. "Meanwhile, I want you to take the rest of the day off—without pay, I might add—to allow things here in the office to get back on track. Be here at nine sharp tomorrow morning with your answer."

* * *

Morry watched Beth walk stiffly to her desk, grab her coat and her purse, and storm furiously out the door. As soon as the whispers died down and everyone got back to work, he stood up and hurried into the break room. He knew what had transpired between the two women but was anxious to chat with Gwen about it.

His aunt was leaning against the counter, a brooding look on her face. "I don't think I've ever met a more disagreeable human being. How could I have condoned her behavior for so long?"

Morry was concerned that this confrontation had troubled her more than she expected. After all, she had been the office supervisor for at least ten years—the last five as Gwen Singleton—and had handled many altercations and disagreements successfully.

"Maybe you had a different outlook on life when you were Jim. After all, men's brains work differently than women's."

"That's unquestionably true, but honesty and integrity shouldn't depend on one's gender."

"No, they shouldn't."

The two of them stood for a few minutes in companionable silence.

"Do you think she's going to choose to work with Merlin, or to have her memories erased?"

"She's egotistical enough to think she can manipulate things to go her way no matter what she chooses," Gwen said wryly. "I guess we'll see what happens tomorrow morning, won't we?"

And a plan began to take shape in Morry's mind.

CHAPTER 51
Moab, Tuesday, November 7, 2023

Beth was sitting at her desk, diligently typing away, when a shadow fell across her keyboard. She looked up to find her coworker standing in front of her, scowling menacingly.

"What the hell do you want, Morry? Or is your name really Mordred, the man who killed King Arthur?" She was getting a kick out of taunting him, hoping he would cause a scene in the office.

"You need to leave my family alone," he growled low in his throat as he stalked around her desk until he was standing next to her chair, glowering at her.

"Ooh, I'm so scared. What're you going to do, turn into a wolf and eat me all up, right here in the office? I don't think so. I think you're a wussy little boy hanging onto your daddy's, your uncles', and your grandfather's shirttails." She noted with glee that his face was getting red, his silver-gray slanted eyes mere slits, and she could literally see the steam coming out of his ears.

Beth looked away nonchalantly, figuring it would piss him off if she ignored him. She heard an eerie sound, like joints popping and cracking, and her coworkers' screams pierced the air. She swung around and saw a gigantic wolf standing next to her, hackles raised and mouth open in a show of fang that had her shrieking in terror. As if from a great distance, she noted dispassionately that he was the most beautiful animal she had ever seen. The wolf was tall and muscular, considerably larger than normal. He had thick fur in the same multicolored hue as Morry's hair, and his eyes were the same silver-gray with flecks of green and brown.

As the monstrous creature growled at her, she trembled in fear, unable to move, and realized her bladder had let go. In the midst of the chaos, she thought she heard Patty say with satisfaction, "I *knew* it. I knew he was magical."

Then the beast lunged at her and tore out her throat.

* * *

Beth sat up in bed, screaming and crying, clutching her untouched neck. When she finally calmed down, she remembered what Morry had told her: she would see his visage again if she didn't behave herself.

He had been deadly serious, if the images in her mind were any indication, so it was fortuitous her hot new boyfriend hadn't spent the night. They were still getting to know each other and had only had sex twice. It would have made a very bad impression on him for her to wake up screaming.

She crawled out of bed, still shaking like a leaf, and headed into the bathroom to take a hot shower. She glanced at the fanciful bathtub clock on the wall next to the sink as she was drying herself and decided she had enough time for a few cups of coffee and some toast before she had to get dressed for work. She had a decision to make.

Breakfast over and feeling better for having the caffeine rushing through her system, she dressed more professionally than usual in dark blue slacks and matching jacket over a white, long-sleeved, tailored blouse, to bolster herself for the ordeal she was about to face. Just as she was slipping on her black low-heeled ankle boots, she thought she heard Morry's voice in her head.

My father and I are sorcerers and demigods, and my grandfather is a god. So you won't win this one, Beth, no matter how hard you try.

She shook her head impatiently. *Oh, bullshit, I'm imagining things,* she thought. How dare they treat her with such disrespect? She was going to make them pay.

* * *

I was appalled that my grandson had resorted to such tactics, and yet my god self admitted that they would be more effective than anything else in persuading the devious young woman to accept my offer. I thought I was being fairly generous, considering the depths of her perfidy—not that she was violating any previously pledged loyalty to me personally—but her plans reeked of disloyalty to her coworkers, her employer, and even to the human race.

She was only human, after all, and fallible, but that didn't excuse her unacceptable behavior. I knew Beth's future, and it wasn't going to be the way she'd planned it. Not at all.

* * *

Morry had gotten the kids up half an hour early, which they hadn't been happy about; neither had his mother-in-law when he'd dropped them off at eight thirty. It had been like pulling teeth to get them fed and dressed—in the regular way, without resorting to magic—so that he could leave on schedule, but at least he'd made it to work early, for once. He'd wanted to be present when Beth came in at nine. He had no idea how Merlin was going to handle the situation, because he was positive that Beth wasn't going to be cooperative in any way.

Nine o'clock came and went, and Gwen and Morry looked at each other cynically. Gwen made sure everyone else in the office had plenty of work to keep them busy, so when Beth did arrive—and Morry figured she would show up eventually—they could confront her in the break room without too much commotion.

She just pulled up in front of your office, Morry,

Okay, thanks, I'll let Gwen know. I presume you'll be here?

Yes. I'm here, incorporeal.

Great, thanks, Grandpa. Morry glanced at Gwen, shifting his eyes toward the door to indicate that Beth would be here momentarily.

She nodded, and they waited for the woman to walk through the office door.

Finally, Beth strutted in twenty minutes late, as if she hadn't a care in the world. She went over to her desk without looking at anyone, stowed her purse in a drawer, and made a big production of doffing her coat and hanging it up on the rack behind her.

Before she could sit down, Gwen and Morry stood up simultaneously and ushered her peremptorily towards the break room, their hands unobtrusively grasping her arms. She didn't say a word, but her lips were pressed tightly together in annoyance and a frown wrinkled her smooth forehead.

* * *

When they entered the room, Morry sensed my presence. Even Gwen apparently felt something, her eyes flickering back and forth.

They released Beth simultaneously, apparently hoping that she would behave in a civilized fashion.

She didn't, so it was fortunate I had anticipated her action. As she pulled a subcompact handgun out of her pocket and aimed it at Gwen, I slowed time. When Beth pulled the trigger and the bullet headed unerringly for my daughter-in-law, I snatched it out of its trajectory, silencing the noise of the explosion and levitating the gun out of Beth's hand.

I allowed time to flow normally again and became visible, wrath personified.

The look on her face when she saw me was almost worth all the problems she had caused.

Gwen smiled at me gratefully then turned to Beth. "Needless to say, you're fired."

"Bethany Douglas, you're under arrest for attempted murder," Lieutenant Colin Campbell stated as he stepped into the break room and pulled her hands behind her back, slapping handcuffs on her wrists. "You have the right to remain silent. Anything you say can be used against you in court. You have the right to an attorney…"

As Colin continued to recite the Miranda Warning to Beth, Morry, Gwen and I stood back and helped ourselves to coffee.

"You must have known she was going to do this, Dad."

I loved it when Gwen called me that. "Yes. Although she decided on this drastic action this morning, I sensed her subconscious intentions as I erased the photos from her phone on Saturday. I contacted Colin yesterday and told him to be waiting out front—concealed by an invisibility spell—when she came through the office door." I turned to my grandson, sensing that he was disturbed by the whole situation.

"Morry, I know you have doubts about my plans for Beth, more than ever since she pulled this stunt, but you have to understand that things are not always as they seem."

"Well, she *seems* pretty dangerous to me, and I can't figure out why in the hell you would want such a nasty, scheming bitch in our group!"

"I don't, but my father does, and I will accede to his wishes."

Before we could continue our conversation, Colin spoke. "Do you need to speak to her before I take her to jail, Merlin?"

"Just for a few minutes, Brother."

* * *

Beth had been hanging her head dejectedly until she heard the cop, a big, burly, dark man with a long, drooping moustache, address Merlin in a familiar manner, to which Merlin responded similarly. She jerked her head up and stared at Colin with narrowed eyes.

"You're Merlin's *brother*? Are you even a real cop?"

"Yes, ma'am." Colin obligingly pulled his jacket back to reveal the badge clipped to his belt.

"No way. I think he put you up to this."

"He let me know what you intended to do so I could be prepared to arrest you, but he didn't put me up to anything."

"It's entrapment!"

"Entrapment? Really? You fired a weapon, unprovoked, at an unarmed woman. At point blank range. In front of witnesses. Sure looked like attempted murder to me."

Morry shook his head. "You should stop talking, Beth. You keep digging your hole deeper. Didn't you hear Lieutenant Campbell read you your rights? Anything you say can be used against you. And it will be."

Beth glared at him poisonously.

"Alright, Colin, I'm going to talk to her for a few minutes, if you don't mind waiting until we get back," Merlin said.

Colin, being an agreeable sort, said, "Sure, take your time, man."

Beth looked back and forth between them and started panicking. "Wait a minute, what do you mean? Where are you taking me?"

Merlin smiled grimly and dropped her gun into the evidence bag Campbell was holding out. Then he folded his long fingers around Beth's arm and they vanished.

"I wonder if he's taking her up to the Rim?" Colin mused.

"I kind of wish he'd drop her off in the Hell realm and let the demons have at her," Morry stated, causing Gwen to glance at him sharply.

"Jesus, Morry, that's callous. What's gotten into you?"

"No good can come of having her around. She's treacherous," he countered unsympathetically.

Concerned something else was bothering him, Gwen told Colin she and Morry were going outside for some fresh air. She guided her nephew through the office and out the front door. Six inches shorter and much smaller than Morry, she hadn't any advantage over him, but he didn't resist.

"What's going on?" she demanded.

"She's going to hurt my kids." Morry's voice sounded strained and his usually calm facial expression was frantic with worry.

"What? Are you sure?"

* * *

Beth and I stood on the Rim, gazing down on the city of Moab below. I sensed the fear and the anger and the underlying misery surging through her, but I felt no pity or compassion.

I had dispensed with my wings and resumed my everyday garb of jeans and T-shirt, hoping that Beth would feel more comfortable with my human appearance and communicate with me. But I wasn't feeling human, and she may have sensed my disconnection. My imperious god self had taken over, coldly furious at her attack on my family.

She turned to me and her face tightened. "Why did you bring me up *here*, of all places?" It was apparent she was cold, as she shivered in the chilly November air a thousand feet above the valley floor, but I honestly didn't care.

I looked down at her and shrugged. "It's my go-to spot. I like to come up here to think, to ponder what to do next. It's the place you first saw me work magic, you and Chloe. I'm sure you remember, despite the fact that I tried to erase your memories of me here. It worked with your friend, but not with you. Why is that? Who are you?" The fact that I couldn't determine her true identity rankled.

Beth scoffed. "I'm a regular old human, sick and tired of being a second-rate reporter at a hick town newspaper. You have everything at your fingertips and don't even appreciate it. I have nothing."

I gritted my teeth as my temper broke through. "Do you think it's easy being a god, living in the human realm, dealing with mortals and their irrational behavior? Hearing and experiencing *everything* that happens on this planet and not being able to fix things?" I roared. I had no idea why I was revealing such a personal sore spot. My assignment and my behavior here in the human realm were none of her business. She was a problem I had to solve, an undisciplined, self-centered, greedy human, nothing more.

"Boo-hoo, poor Merlin," she sneered. Abruptly exhausted, she seemed to wilt. "Why do you care what happens to me?"

"Actually, I don't give a *damn* what happens to you." At that point, I should have realized something was wrong; I rarely used such words. However, I didn't notice and continued on in the same manner. "I'm sickened by people like you. But my father cares, God cares, and therefore I have to care. And with all the other people out there who truly need and deserve my help, it galls me to have to care what happens to *you*. All I want is to put Arthur back in power and eradicate the evil in this world."

My resentment and anger had grown to an intense degree and my control had slipped dangerously. She gaped at me incredulously.

"Your…father? God is your *father*?

I lifted the corner of my mouth in a semblance of a smile as I called forth my wings again and let the god Light shine through me, surrounding me with radiance like a nimbus.

"What do you think?"

Beth's eyes bulged and whatever words she had planned to say stuck in her throat.

* * *

Under his piercing stare, a long-buried memory stirred, a memory of another time and place in which Merlin had stared at her like this. She was Beth but she wasn't, she was taller, with golden hair, and she had a sister she envied, one that had the higher-level magic she coveted, the power and influence she needed….

Beth's eyes fluttered open and she realized she must have passed out. She was lying on the ground, face up, cold rock under her and washed out denim sky above her, her hands still in handcuffs uncomfortably underneath her. A familiar male face with long black hair restrained by a silver circlet peered at her with cool detachment.

"What a surprise to see you here, Morgause. I wondered if you'd been reincarnated," Merlin commented as he unceremoniously hauled her to her feet. "Beth's unreasonable anger and frustration finally make sense."

Beth blinked uncertainly as the new set of memories vied for a place in her mind. Once, long ago in a past life, she had been King Arthur's half sister. She glanced at Merlin and recognized the silver circlet he used to wear in Camelot, as Arthur's official sorcerer.

"I remember you from the past, but you're different now than you were then. More powerful. Less tolerant."

Merlin looked amused. "That's an understatement." Without further ado, he again clamped his large hand around her arm and returned them to the break room of the newspaper office.

* * *

Colin seemed surprised. "I thought you'd be gone longer. Gwen took Morry outside a few minutes ago for some air."

Feeling more like myself again now that I was with my brother, I drew him aside and filled him in telepathically on what I had discovered.

Aw, shit, really? She used to be Arthur's sister in the fifth century? Was she as evil as Morgana?

Nowhere near. I didn't like her, mind you, but she didn't have that dedication to evil for its own sake as Morgana had—and still does.

Do you still want me to take Beth in? I should, you know. Not only is she guilty of premeditated attempted murder, but she doesn't have a CFP— Concealed Firearms Permit—for that SIG Sauer P$_{365}$ she pulled out of her pocket. I checked while you were gone. Man, that piece is impressive. I'm considering getting one for Cathy.

My lips tightened in annoyance and he hurriedly continued.

Anyway, with those charges against her, Beth should stand trial. In which case she'll go to prison and it will be impossible to get her out of there without some major magical intervention. I suppose you could have Gwen drop the charges, but I don't recommend that. I can sense the evil in Beth. If she wasn't that bad in her previous life, she is now.

I know, Colin, and I happen to agree with you, but Father apparently wants to give her another chance. I thought about recent developments. *Go ahead and take her to jail. Let her stew a bit. I need a day or two to make other arrangements for her.*

I decided to try again and speak with Beth briefly before Colin took her away. When I walked over to her, she looked up at me. Defiant. Unrepentant.

I stood there a moment with my arms crossed and realized there was nothing to be gained by trying to have a conversation with her.

I shook my head and turned back to Colin. "You can take her away." And I left.

* * *

"Like I said, she's going to hurt the kids—at least that's the feeling I'm getting, along with a vision that's kind of vague."

"Morry, you need to trust your grandfather. I've known Merlin forever, and I'm sure he'd never let anything happen to his great-grand-children." Gwen looked up into Morry's worried face, and put the palm of her hand on his cheek.

He gave a tentative grin. "Thanks, Gwen, I guess I got all worked up for a few minutes. Being a father is more intense than I thought it would be."

"But it's rewarding, isn't it?"

"Yeah, sure."

Gwen had never been a mother, and the way things were going she was afraid she never would be. *No, she said* to herself, *no more negativity. I failed before, but not this time! It doesn't have to be today, but I will get pregnant and give Arthur an heir.* An old-world way of looking at things, she realized.

As she dragged herself out of her thoughts of Arthur, she caught how odd Morry's statement was. "You make it sound as though you've never been around kids before. Didn't you and Lainie have children together in other timelines and you both remember those lives together?"

"That's true, but I never had anything to do with the kids' care on a daily basis. In the past, it was the woman's job to take care of the house and the kids, and the man's job to work and support the family."

"Why don't you talk to your dad later tonight, if you're hesitant to discuss it with Merlin."

Morry looked relieved. "You're right. Great idea, thanks."

"Shall we get back to work?"

He agreed and opened the door just as Colin brought Beth out in handcuffs. They stepped aside and watched dispassionately as he protected her head while seating her in the back of the patrol car. Colin cut his eyes at Morry and gave him an ironic look. *I'd just as soon let her hit her head, but as a dutiful public servant I can't do that.*

I hope she gets what she deserves.

Yeah, me too, but in this case, it's going to be up to Merlin—and my father. Colin turned to Gwen and gave her a nod and a grin, waving at them both as he opened the driver's door.

Morry returned the wave, acknowledging how much he liked Colin. It was easy to accept that the man had turned out to be his great-uncle and one of the gods.

* * *

Sitting in the back seat of the police car, Beth narrowed her eyes as she watched the three of them interact. She wished she hadn't brought the gun into play so soon, but she'd been terribly distraught after the dream Morry had sent her and she hadn't been thinking straight. She stared at him, standing there looking and acting like an ordinary man, and pictured him turning into that huge, terrifying wolf. He wasn't human —by his own admission he was a sorcerer and shapeshifter—and she wondered if this was where the tales of werewolves had come from. She watched him communicating silently with the cop who looked kind of like a pirate. Merlin's brother. Shit, she hadn't seen that coming. The guy was slightly shorter than Merlin and looked nothing like him, but she guessed it didn't matter. She didn't look like her sibling, either.

If they were angels—which totally blew her mind, she had to admit —it would certainly explain why they had wings. She shifted her gaze to Gwen and contemplated what she'd said, that she'd been Guinevere Pendragon, King Arthur's queen, in the past. That intrigued her. If she herself had been Morgause, Arthur's half sister, it would explain why she felt such antipathy toward these people. But it was strange that she didn't remember Gwen from her old life. She closed her eyes and thought, *Crap. I should have taken Merlin up on his offer instead of resorting to violence.* If she played her cards right, she might convince him that she'd had a change of heart. In any case, she fervently hoped Morry would keep his alter ego away from her.

* * *

That evening, Morry and Derek were hanging out in Moody's Tavern enjoying a few priceless minutes together apart from their wives and kids. They'd done very little socializing one on one in the past four years and they needed the time with each other. Derek knew something major was bothering his son, but he waited patiently for him to start talking.

Morry looked at Derek across the table and took a long pull on his brew before setting the bottle down in front of him. His father had grown immeasurably more powerful in the past four years. It remained to be seen if he'd grown wiser. "I know this is going to sound awful, but there are times I wish I'd never asked for this."

"By 'this,' you mean bein' a parent?"

Morry nodded and scrubbed his face with his palms, trying to erase the signs of fatigue. "I love my wife and kids, but I never dreamed it would be so…"

"Difficult? Exhaustin'? Frustratin'? I get it, I'm a father, too." He wiggled his eyebrows as if to remind Morry whose son he was.

Morry chuckled. "At least you never had to deal with me as a kid."

"I would give anythin' to have raised ya."

"I know. Be that as it may, Aidan is easy compared to my two hellions."

At that moment, Derek felt the difference in their ages and the gap in their levels of magical proficiency. "Admittedly, your brother is calm, and his god nature tones down the part of him that's human. But remember, as sorcerers and demigods we have the ability to overcome the exhaustion and the frustration. It's easy to forget that." He cocked his head. "There's somethin' else eatin' at ya, isn't there?"

Morry stared at the empty bottle in his hands. "Yeah. Let me show you what happened today and it'll help you understand where I'm coming from." He projected a mental image of everything that had transpired lately at the newspaper, with Beth and her visions of earning a Pulitzer by exposing the family. And he revealed who she really was, showing Derek his vision of her harming his kids as a result of Merlin's insistence in adding her to their midst.

Derek looked solemn as Morry related his story and didn't let on that he was aware of what had happened. "Hey, I don't blame ya for feelin' that way." He paused thoughtfully and continued, "It's been too long since we Saw each other. We can do it here and now, and nobody'll know."

A wide smile transformed Morry's troubled countenance. *Sure, Dad, I'd like that.*

They gazed steadily into each other's eyes and merged. Morry experienced a welcome sense of relief as he was engulfed by his father's love and compassion. All of the concerns of his everyday, flesh-and-blood life dropped away as they went deeper into the realm of the spirit, into the Light that was the source of all things. They were two different souls and yet they were the same.

Finally, they reluctantly pulled back out of that state of oneness, into their separate bodies, their separate lives in the human realm. Morry felt as if he had been gone for an eternity, but according to the clock on the wall of the pub, just a few minutes had passed.

Derek opened his eyes and watched his son reorient himself to the physical world. He had long ago become accustomed to his reality as a demigod, the son of Myrddin Emrys. He wasn't perfect, not by a long shot, but he'd learned.

He smiled. *How're ya doin'?*

I feel fantastic, Dad, thanks. I feel like going home and hugging my kids and making love to my wife.

Derek smiled and looked forward to doing the same with his own wife and child.

* * *

It was late when I stood in the dark atop the Rim, staring down at the city I considered mine, and impassively reviewed my behavior from earlier in the day. Except for losing my temper with Beth—Morgause—

I had been as detached from my emotions as I had ever been. And it felt...wrong. It was the height of irony that I had been striving to set my emotions aside in order to achieve my goals, and yet when I succeeded in doing so, I didn't like myself at all. Even Emily had commented on my uncharacteristically cold behavior (she even reminded me that I'd done the same thing once before, which I hadn't remembered) and said she hoped I'd snap out of it.

I didn't know if I would be able to do so. I was completely stymied. I couldn't attain all of my goals unless I put my emotions aside, but if I did that, I couldn't be effective in supporting Arthur. More importantly, I couldn't feel love. And that was unacceptable. As was being doomed to repeat these lessons until I finally achieved clarity.

I closed my eyes as a chill wind blew my hair back and a metaphysical cold cut through my heart and soul.

* * *

Beth tossed and turned on the narrow bed in her cell. She'd been given one phone call, and she'd used it to call her best friend Chloe, who'd been horrified that Beth had been arrested. They promised to keep in touch, but Beth doubted she'd be able to do so.

She'd been thinking a lot in the interminable hours since she'd been incarcerated. How could any story—even one as mind-blowing as this, about King Arthur and Merlin, magic and angels—be worth committing murder? What had happened in her life to make her so bitter and jaded that she'd lost touch with her humanity?

She couldn't seem to figure out when or how she'd started down this path, and she couldn't fathom how quickly everything had gone to hell in a hand basket.

She stilled. What did that phrase mean, anyway? Beth searched her memory and finally recalled looking it up when she'd been writing an article on archaic sayings. The best explanation she'd been able to find was that a hand basket caught heads after they were chopped off by a guillotine during the French Revolution. The choppee went to straight to Hell with his head in a basket. Damned appropriate for her situation. She'd never considered the consequences of her actions and had ridden a wave of overweening fury and a burning desire for revenge. Now, even though her head wasn't literally in danger of being chopped off, her life as she'd known it was over. Merlin was going to wipe her memories and she'd be in jail and not even remember why. And it hurt to know she'd never see that sexy new guy of hers again. She was sure they were soul mates, he made her feel so good about herself. And that body of his… the sex was so incredible she couldn't believe her luck in finding him. Her eyes swam with tears of self-pity when she realized she might never have him inside her again.

But maybe she could still take Merlin up on his offer. Her heart felt lighter as she thought about it. And a memory surfaced from the distant past, of a certain sorcerer showing a young Morgause a simple spell, and her feeling of gratitude that he had been kind enough to help her with her first magical endeavor. Although he didn't seem like that sorcerer anymore—far from it—perhaps he would consider overlooking her actions earlier today and help her again.

A few more tears escaped, trickling down her cheek. The moisture dampened the pathetic excuse for a pillow and she punched it a couple of times to teach it a lesson.

She would definitely ask Lieutenant Campbell to contact Merlin for her in the morning, and she would sincerely begin to make amends. Then, she would give her boyfriend a call and they could hook up. She needed him badly and he would know just what to do to make her feel better.

I'll see you soon, babe, she thought.

CHAPTER 52
Moab, Wednesday, November 8, 2023

E m and I had just finished the breakfast dishes when Colin teleported into our kitchen with an apologetic look on his face. He was dressed for work looking professional and competent, as usual.

"Sorry to show up out of the blue."

Em put her hands on his shoulders and bussed his cheek. "It's okay, Colin. You know we love you. Now if you'll excuse me, I have to go to work." She paused and turned to face him. "By the way, Lieutenant, congratulations on your promotion. It took them long enough to reward you for all your hard work."

"Thanks, Em, I appreciate you saying that." He watched her as she gave me a quick kiss, grabbed her purse, and went out the door. "Man, she is a gem." He hurried to add, "Not that Cathy isn't."

"No need to explain yourself to me, you know that." I offered him a cup of coffee and he accepted with alacrity.

Colin took a healthy swallow. "This hits the spot, thanks. You know, it might sound like a cliché, but it's true—police department coffee sucks."

I chuckled briefly then got serious. I knew why he'd come. To put it succinctly, Beth couldn't handle even one night in jail and wanted to finagle a pact with me.

Colin easily perceived my thoughts and responded to them. "You know, I thought that at first, too, Merlin. But when she spoke to me this morning, she didn't complain, and she was polite and humble. I still don't trust her and have grave doubts about her, but I think she might actually be on the up and up. I realized it wouldn't be a smart idea to See her, but I did allow myself to be open to her surface thoughts and feelings, and I think she's honestly repentant." He paused, his forehead wrinkling into a frown. "I'm kind of concerned though. I encountered a blank spot in her emotional grid. It's as if something's been erased, or concealed, or something. Or it might be a glitch."

"I'll come and evaluate her. If she's completely ready to commit herself to me, I'll take care of manipulating the system to erase her presence from it. I've made arrangements for her to move in with the knights so they can keep tabs on her."

"Huh, I bet that didn't go over well."

"It didn't, but they have no choice. It's what I want, at least for now." I sighed. "I don't blame them. It's been males-only for years. But it's a big house and there happens to be an extra bedroom—"

"No there isn't." Colin interrupted as he looked at me askance. "There's four of them and four bedrooms and... Wait a minute, did you add a room?"

I gave him an innocent look. "Why, no, it just happened to show up out of thin air." I rolled my eyes. "Of course I did it, Colin, who else?"

"Okay, okay, I forgot. So sue me."

I grinned at my brother. I enjoyed giving him a hard time. "Anyway, it has an en suite bathroom so she doesn't have to share a toilet or shower with the guys. It turned out nicely, if I do say so myself."

"You already knew what she was going to do."

"Yes. My knowledge of the future worked for this, even though she's connected to me through Arthur—and to you through her brother."

"Her brother? What are you talking about?" He read my thoughts and his jaw dropped. "Beth is Owen's sister? Oh, shit, her last name is Douglas. I should have remembered that. It's Moab, after all, and everyone seems to be related or connected in some way."

I clapped my hands together briskly. "Now that we've hashed that out, let's go."

* * *

We materialized in Beth's small cell and scared the living daylights out of her. I have to admit it was gratifying. As she opened her mouth to scream, I used my powers to prevent her from doing so.

It took me a mere second to evaluate her feelings and intentions. "Are you ready to get out of here?"

She had her hand over her heart and was breathing heavily. "Oh, my God, you scared me. Couldn't you have come in the door like normal people?"

"Seriously? Do we look like normal people to you?" Colin sniffed, insulted.

"We don't have time for this," I said sharply. "Do you want to get out of here or not?"

"Yes, but I haven't even…"

"Haven't even what?"

"Begged and pleaded and convinced you I was sorry," she muttered and stared down at her feet glumly.

"*Are* you truly sorry?" I knew she was sincerely repentant, but I wanted her to say it out loud.

"Yes," she whispered.

I nodded brusquely and transported the three of us to the large house on 400 East where the knights had been living for years. They had originally rented it when I was lost in time, but when I returned I had purchased it as an investment.

The men had been forewarned of our arrival and were standing in the living room waiting, quiet and stern. As a rule, they reveled in their duty to me, but this assignment was not to their liking. That worked for me, because I wanted them off-balance and edgy. I wanted one or more of them to guard Beth at all times, despite the fact that I had erected substantial wards around the outside of the house, making it escape-proof. I'd made a round-the-clock guard mandatory outside the door to her private quarters when occupied. She needed to be constantly aware that I meant business.

When Beth saw the knights, and realized she had traded one type of incarceration for another, she was irate. "What the hell is this? I thought you were releasing me!"

I grabbed her arm and jerked the ungrateful little wretch around to face me. "Did you honestly think I would let you go free after what you did? I magically manipulated your information in the justice system so you won't go to prison, and I haven't erased your memories. So you will accept my guidance in all things and will work for me when I think you're ready. In the interim, you won't leave this house unattended—if you go out for a doctor's appointment, for example, you'll have one of my men with you. You'll have a certain amount of freedom within the house but you are *not free*." I glared at her. "Consider yourself extremely fortunate, Miss Douglas." It was a wonder she didn't freeze solid under my glacial stare.

"But what about my brother, and my friends? And my boyfriend?"

"What about them?"

"Can I text them? Or call them? What about emailing?"

"I don't see why not, but any phone or computer use will have to be monitored."

"But what if my boyfriend and I want to, uh…."

I raised one eyebrow. "What, have sex?"

She glowered at me belligerently. "Yes, or I want to have someone come over just to visit me."

"Visitation can be arranged, under supervision. In the case of intimate relations with your boyfriend, you can be in your private quarters with one of the men standing guard outside your door."

"Will I ever be able to go home?" she asked in desperation.

I pursed my lips. "It depends on you, Beth. If you don't change your ways—and believe me when I say I *will* know—you'll go back to jail with your memory wiped."

* * *

Colin and I stood on the knights' front porch with Ryan, whose expression was stony. I knew what he was going to say and I responded before he could do so.

"This is the way it has to be, Lancelot, and trust me, I don't like it any more than you do."

"I'm concerned about the men's morale, my lord," he replied stiffly.

"I realize that, but you'll all have to consider this a test of loyalty."

Ryan nodded reluctantly. "Now that Arthur is back, the men had assumed he would be working with us in person. That hasn't happened yet, and they're getting restless and irritable."

I stood facing him, grim and unyielding. "It can't be helped. We're not yet ready to announce our presence to the world. You'll all have to have patience, and continue to have faith in me—and in Arthur."

"I'll inform them of that," Ryan said. "By the way, I'm puzzled. If you've warded the house, how will the rest of us be able to leave?"

I stared at him in disbelief. "How can you even ask me that?"

"You made the ward specific to Beth alone?"

"Naturally. Lancelot, you know me better than that."

He paused for a moment. "I thought I did," he said sadly.

* * *

Colin had gone back to work and I had the house to myself. I paced the floor of my office until I was afraid I'd worn out the carpet again. Had I handled this affair with Beth incorrectly? Ryan's last comment bothered me—and hurt my feelings—and I was afraid the knights no longer trusted me. Was I losing sight of the big picture?

Merlin, stop it! You're playing into Sam's hands. This is exactly what he wants, for you to lose confidence in yourself. Em's voice rang out sharply in my mind.

I stopped in midstride and let her words clear the doubt from my mind. *Thanks, Em.* I shook my head. This had to stop.

B eth had been in the house with the four men since yesterday and she was sick of all the testosterone permeating the atmosphere. Admittedly, it had been an eye-opening twenty-four hours—after all, how often did one have the chance to hang out with the Knights of the Round Table? Percival was particularly intriguing; he was tall, handsome, and built like a brick house. If she didn't already have a boyfriend, she'd be interested in him. All the knights were attractive guys, although none of them were overly friendly. It was obvious they were devoted to Merlin and King Arthur (*Duh*, she thought, rolling her eyes), but it was equally obvious that they were disgruntled by the necessity of "babysitting" her.

Screw 'em, she thought. She wouldn't be in this place forever; she planned on getting out as soon as she could manage it.

She had persuaded Ryan—did she understand correctly, he was actually *Sir Lancelot?*—to let her call her boyfriend and invite him over for the evening, so she had something to look forward to. She'd sweet-talked Gary—Sir Gawain—into going out and buying emery boards and polish so she could do a quickie job on her nails. She intended to spend the rest of the day in her own quarters, getting ready for her date. Luckily, her bathroom had been stocked with soap, shampoo, conditioner, lotion and a woman's razor. Merlin's wife had done this, she was certain, as the products were all decent quality. There was also an adequate supply of tampons in the cupboard. She wasn't scheduled to start her period for a few days, but she was relieved they were there. Having to ask the men to buy those for her would be the absolute last straw.

* * *

Sarah called Lainie early in the day to confirm their plans for the evening. They had become close friends over the years and spent time together as often as they could arrange it, which had the added benefit of allowing the children to socialize frequently.

But this night was special, just the two couples going out for dinner. It was nice to look forward to an adults-only conversation. They had decided on the Hillside Grill, as they all had favorites on the menu. The restaurant had originally been an elaborate private home, built by a man who had made a fortune during the uranium boom of the 1950s. It was perched on the red rock slope north of town and commanded an outstanding view of the Colorado River and the entire Moab valley.

Sarah had been surprised when Arthur had spontaneously offered to watch the kids, and she felt guilty for accepting. After all, he and Gwen were still newlyweds. They had stayed for several weeks in the elegantly furnished room in New Camelot that Merlin had prepared for them, while they explored the countryside of that alternate reality. They had only recently returned to Moab, but according to Arthur, he and Gwen were willing to give up their evening to babysit. They planned to take the kids out for pizza, so it should be an enjoyable evening for everyone. Sarah had a brief thought that she should have confirmed the plans with Gwen, but if you couldn't trust King Arthur to tell the truth, who could you trust?

Derek arrived home from work in time to change clothes before Morry and Lainie picked them up. "Hey, Sarah, is this blue shirt okay?" He hadn't worn it recently and hoped it would do. They hadn't had a night out in months and he was looking forward to it.

"It looks fine, honey. Besides, you could always conjure something else up if you wanted to."

"That's true, what was I thinking?" He winked at her.

"Oh, by the way, Arthur should be here any minute to pick up Aidan."

"I'm relieved to have family watchin' the kids tonight. Arthur and Gwen will keep 'em safe." Derek felt a brief twinge of uncertainty but dismissed it as his mind playing tricks on him.

"Me, too." Sarah smiled as Derek caught her eye. "Hmm, we can even make love tonight."

He laughed. "Ya must've read my mind."

* * *

The tall blond man grinned wickedly to himself as he knocked on the door of the house on 400 East. He was looking forward to seeing Beth and to everything he'd scheduled for the evening.

The door swung inward and a hulking individual who reminded him of a soldier—one of Arthur's knights?—stared distrustfully at him. "Hi, what can I do for you?"

"Yeah, hey, I'm Beth's friend, ah, Lucas. She's staying here, apparently." He was careful not to allow even a hint of sarcasm to leak into his speech. He was all too aware of the reason she was in this house, against her will, but he wouldn't let this moron know that.

"Come on in. I'll take you to her." The man gave him a wary look and moved aside.

Sam stepped deliberately over the threshold, detecting the potent ward that, fortunately for him, didn't prevent him from entering, and followed the man through the living room and toward the back of the house.

The knight rapped lightly on the closed door at the end of a thickly carpeted hallway. "Beth, it's Percival. Your friend is here." The guard who had been standing there turned the key in the deadbolt and unlocked it.

The bedroom door flew open and Sam's brown-haired beauty was in his arms, warm and sweet-smelling.

"Oh, Lucas, I missed you so much," she whispered in his ear.

"I missed you, too," he responded, surprised that he meant it. He kissed her cheek, swung her into his arms, and strode confidently into her bedroom. The door shut, a bolt was thrown, and he could sense the presence of a guard standing outside.

The two kissed frantically while throwing off their clothing. Sam didn't hesitate to push her down on the bed and immediately climb on top of her, and she moaned at the feel of their naked bodies pressed together. Spreading her legs, she willingly took his considerable length inside her. She had been ready for him for hours. They both gasped at the intimate contact and started to move, the bed thumping rhythmically against the wall.

* * *

Leon gritted his teeth as he listened to the explicit sounds emanating from the room at his back. He hadn't had sex in years and this assignment was challenging his strength of will.

"You okay?" Ryan asked as he stepped into the hallway to check on the knight.

"Yeah, I'll do," he said hoarsely, in physical discomfort but not wanting to admit it.

"I wanted to let you know that Arthur's bringing the kids over to visit in a few minutes, and we've got that box of toys to keep them occupied while we play cards. If you've got the deadbolt locked, it won't be necessary for you to stand there all night listening to them having sex. Come on out and have a beer."

"Thank the gods. I need to get the hell away from them." He hesitated, confused. "But I thought... didn't Merlin say we had to keep a guard on her at all times?"

"He did, but what's the point? The lock is sturdy and there's no other way for them to get out. Besides, we're still in the house. Don't worry about it."

Leon thought it was odd that Lancelot, who had always been the most obedient of them all and thoroughly devoted to Merlin, would brush off the sorcerer's explicit orders so casually. But hey, Lancelot was in charge, so it must be okay.

As the men set up the card table and put the beer and snacks out on the counter, Arthur arrived with the twins in his arms and Aidan following along behind him. As soon as he set them on their feet, Bonnie and Brady ran to Gary, who scooped them up and kissed their cheeks. Aidan was more sedate, greeting Ryan and Percival with a hug and a handshake, which they thought was rare for a four-year-old, but Aidan had always been mature for his age. All three children said hello to Leon but withheld hugs and kisses. The older knight was standoffish with them as a rule and they didn't like him.

Greetings concluded, the kids began playing with their toys in the living room, and the five men each grabbed a beer and sat down to play poker.

* * *

Temporarily sated, Beth and Sam lay entwined, lazily stroking each other's bodies and pressing gentle kisses to lips swollen from passionate activity.

He hadn't planned on falling in love with her, and wondered if he was losing his touch. In the past, he'd never had sex with the same woman twice. And he killed them if he could get away with it. But this woman had apparently bewitched him—they had been exclusive for several weeks. This emotional crap could royally fuck up his real plans for the night. He stiffened and gritted his teeth in annoyance. No, he wouldn't let that happen. He could handle Beth and she'd willingly follow his lead. She had no choice in the matter.

"Lucas?" Beth whispered tentatively.

He turned his golden head on the pillow to gaze blankly into her expressive, dark blue eyes. He'd forgotten for a moment that he wasn't using his own name with her. "What?"

"I love you," Beth said sweetly, caressing his beautiful face.

His mouth went dry. No one had ever said that to him before. Except that wasn't entirely true, was it? His father had said it to him once, eons ago, but he hadn't believed it then, and he didn't dare believe it now. He was evil and evil wasn't lovable. He closed his eyes and bared his teeth in a grimace of pain.

"Lucas, honey, what's wrong?"

Hell, he was going to have to go into her mind and manipulate her thoughts—it was the best way to ensure her cooperation. Love screwed everything up.

With a miniscule pang of regret, he savagely yanked her up against him and forced her head around so she had no choice but to look deep into his eyes. She started to cry out in pain. He slapped a palm over her mouth as he initiated his version of the Seeing—so that it was all about him—and took control of her mind.

* * *

"I fold," Ryan said with a sigh, discarding his cards face down. Everyone else continued to play the hand, and no one commented on his action, which was uncharacteristic, to say the least. The usual jesting and good humor wasn't in evidence at all this night. He was especially concerned about Arthur, since the two of them were supposed to be friends again, and yet Arthur had been distant, brooding, and barely civil.

Ryan stretched and noticed it was pitch dark outside. They had a light on over the table and there was one lamp glowing in the living room where the kids were playing, but otherwise the house was dim and quiet. Too quiet, he recognized, vaguely curious why that bothered him. He was feeling out of kilter, and as he watched Arthur continue to play, he grew more and more anxious. It seemed bizarre to him that his king had chosen this specific night, the first night Beth was in the house, to bring the children to visit. Arthur was normally great with the little ones, attentive and loving, but this time he'd totally ignored them after they'd entered the house.

Ryan knew the two Colburn families had planned on going out to dinner together tonight and were leaving their children with Arthur and Gwen. So what had happened? Where was Gwen? Ryan frowned. This wasn't right. He had a sensation in his gut that something awful was about to happen and he should contact Merlin, but an unnatural lethargy engulfed him and he blacked out.

* * *

The lock fell apart, the door opened, and Sam walked out of the bedroom holding Beth's upper arm in a vise-like grip, forcing her to walk awkwardly beside him. Her eyes were glazed and she moved stiffly, as if she was in a trance. He shook her roughly. "Hey, wake up and do as I say, you hear me?"

Beth stiffened and a tear trickled down her cheek where a red palm mark stood out against her pale skin. He shook her again, more violently, and she said hoarsely, "I hear you."

"I want you to grab the redheaded kid and hold him tightly—don't you dare let him go! I'll take the twins. Then we're out of here."

"Okay." Oh, God, how could she have been so foolish. This man she thought she loved was a criminal. He was going to abduct these poor, innocent children, and she was helpless to do anything but obey him.

When they entered the living room, she saw the children glance up and see two adults converging on them in a threatening manner. The girl started whimpering and the brown-haired boy's lip quivered in fear. The redhead seemed to sense that something was off and she saw him look over at the card players for support. All the men except one appeared to be unconscious, their heads resting on the table in front of them. Before the boy could react, Beth snatched him up, and Lucas—or whatever his real name was—stuffed one screaming, struggling child under each arm, and turned to the familiar blond man at the table and commanded, "Come with me." The man stood up stiffly and he and Beth silently followed the evil bastard out the door.

* * *

Derek appeared in my office, panicked. "Dad, the kids have disappeared."

"*What?*" I surged to my feet.

"We got back from dinner and went to Arthur and Gwen's to pick up the kids. The house was dark and I couldn't sense where anyone had gone." Derek's voice shook with fright.

Clarity speared through me and I remembered Morry's vision that Beth was going to hurt the kids, and every pertinent occurrence for the past five years raced through my mind. The conclusion I came to chilled my blood.

I could think of only one place Arthur would take the kids. *Follow me, Derek.*

We materialized in the knights' residence and discovered them out cold at the card table. The front door was open and there was no sign of Arthur or the children, although there was ample evidence they'd all been there: Arthur's jacket was hanging on the back of a chair and the kid's jackets and toys were strewn around the living room.

Beth's bedroom door was open, the lock in pieces. It was evident from the smell of sex in the air that her boyfriend had been here, and that he had taken her and the kids and absconded, with Arthur following along. How could I have been so oblivious that I didn't realize Beth's boyfriend was none other than Satan himself? And how did he penetrate my ward? Yes, he was incredibly powerful, but there was no way he could have gotten through. And then I comprehended what had occurred. I'd created the ward to keep Beth, a human being, from escaping. I hadn't even entertained the possibility that a supernatural presence would enter the house and then shield her as they left the building.

I revived the knights and tasked them to utilize mundane investigative techniques, with Colin supervising and making use of his god powers, to track Arthur, Beth, and the missing children. I didn't try to fool myself into thinking *I* could track my evil brother at this point. The rest of us would explore all supernatural and celestial alternatives that might help us find our missing family members, Beth included. She was a pawn in this debacle, after all, and I felt obligated to rescue her along with the others.

* * *

After many hours of fruitless searching, we all gathered at Derek's house, both sets of parents beside themselves with fear and worry.

Derek, Seth, Morry and I had merged our minds in an attempt to discover Sam's and Arthur's whereabouts. When that effort failed, I tried to communicate with my father and had no success whatsoever. I contacted Ryan, instructing him and the knights—who had also been unsuccessful in their endeavors—to return to their residence and remain there on the off chance that the abductees might somehow escape and return.

Colin joined Portunus, along with the rest of my closest brothers from the god realm, and did everything possible to assist in the search, but even those efforts failed.

I was convinced that Sam had taken Arthur, Beth, and the kids somewhere in town, but the location was being hidden effectively from us all.

My wife had been helping diligently from the start. The first thing Em had done was to call Gwen's cell phone, and she didn't waste any time with social niceties.

"Gwen, it's Em. Arthur and the kids have been abducted. Where are you?"

I heard Gwen's reply as clearly as if she was standing in front of me.

"What? *Abducted*? How? When? Oh, God, I—"

Em cut in and urgently repeated her question. "*Gwen, where are you?* Arthur told Sarah you two would watch the kids while the parents went to dinner. Instead, he picked them up and took them directly to the knights' so he could play cards."

"I'm out having dinner and drinks at the new hotel downtown with a few friends. I had no idea that Arthur had arranged to babysit the kids, let alone that he'd planned to take them along when he went to play cards," Gwen said, plainly upset and close to tears.

Although I was concerned that she might have been compromised by Sam, I sensed she was genuinely shocked and distressed.

"I'm coming over. I want to help. Are you home or—"

"We're all at Derek's place. See you soon." Em ended the call and turned to me.

"Do you suppose Sam has influenced her?" she asked.

"No, I don't, but I'll try to See her when she arrives. And you can probably sense if anything is off with her."

I gave Em a quick hug and she pulled away to check in with her mother.

I was terribly worried about the children, but at the same time, I was appalled and saddened that Arthur had succumbed to Sam's apparent long-term manipulation. All the hints of infiltration by Sam since Arthur's birth, or even while he was still in the womb, became clear in my mind. I had known for years there was that possibility, but had assumed Sam's influence hadn't actually affected Arthur. Now I knew that it had been dormant inside him, very much like Nimue's black magic had been infused into Morry's DNA when he was conceived.

My clever, wicked brother had fooled us all. My father had known the seeds had been sown, had even warned me, but since I had seen no indication of evil in my son, I had assumed Sam hadn't succeeded. How arrogant I had been to make that assumption!

He'd meticulously set it up to manifest so gradually that none of us paid attention to the hints that something was wrong.

I wanted to rant and rave about the unfairness of it all, but I knew it would do no good whatsoever. And strangely enough, the feelings welling up in me overrode the anger and the fury and the desire to destroy my brother. Indeed, alongside those intense emotions was sorrow and pity. Sam was pathetic and desperately unhappy. I didn't welcome such feelings; in fact, I was exceedingly confused by them. I filed them away to examine later, once we had found and rescued everyone.

It was getting late, but going home to bed wasn't an acceptable option for any of us. We would all stand sentinel throughout the night, waiting for some communication, some bid for ransom or other demand. Finally, I followed my instincts and pulled out those unwelcome feelings about Sam and truly examined them.

You are starting to understand, my son. By morning, you will receive a sign.

What sign, Father? He didn't answer, which shouldn't have surprised me, but it did under these dire circumstances.

Em looked up from her seat beside Rae and Gwen, having sensed that God had contacted me. *Merlin, what did he say?*

We will receive a sign by morning. I have to assume it will be something positive. I hardly think he would allow Sam to hurt or kill Arthur or the kids—or Beth, since he was so anxious for me to bring her into the family.

Should we...say something? she asked me hesitantly.

I hated to see my family in pain, but my father hadn't in truth said that we would find or rescue anyone, so I hesitated to get their hopes up. *No, I hate to say it, but I don't think we should.*

She nodded grudgingly and a tear trickled down her cheek. She swiped it away and closed her eyes, resigned. Even though Arthur was an adult, in her mind he was still her little boy and in danger.

I felt helpless and ineffectual. I should be able to do more. But all I could do was wait impatiently for morning.

* * *

Beth was exhausted. She was also hungry and thirsty and needed to pee, but she knew *he* wouldn't allow her to address those basic needs. To make matters worse, she was cold since he hadn't let her dress as warmly as the season required. And she was miserably uncomfortable perching on a backless wooden stool for hours—who even had this kind of stool anymore, for God's sake? She knew it would be futile to ask him if she could lie down.

She followed her captor with her eyes as he paced frenetically around the living room. When he had first brought them here, she assumed this immaculate place with no personal belongings or mementoes was some kind of hotel suite or condo, the typical off-white walls and beige carpet lending credence to her assumption. However, as Lucas moved around in the rooms as if he was intimately acquainted with every square inch of them, she realized he lived here.

The children had been locked in a small room with no furniture in it that was probably meant to be an extra bedroom. They'd cried and screamed for hours—at least the twins had, the red-haired boy had been unnaturally calm and composed—but they had finally quieted down and presumably gone to sleep.

Her erstwhile boyfriend hadn't even let the poor kids use the toilet, so God knew what kind of mess they'd find in the morning. The bastard would make *her* clean it up.

How could she have been so gullible? The man she knew as Lucas was somehow connected with Merlin's family, and taking revenge for some real or imagined insult by abducting the children. It was clear that the twins, at least, had to be Morry's kids—the boy looked just like him. And the clincher was that both kids in Lucas's arms had changed into wolf pups and back to human, when they had reached their destination. Lucas had growled something under his breath that sounded like "fucking shapeshifters."

She glanced over at the man Lucas had brought with them. She'd realized as soon as they left the knights' house that it was Gwen's husband, Arthur—*King Arthur.* He seemed to be under some kind of spell and didn't seem regal now, merely a dazed and confused human being.

Wait, he couldn't be human. She'd watched him flying with his brother out at Arches National Park.

She closed her eyes, trying to concentrate. What the hell was going on? If Arthur wasn't human, how did Lucas take control of him? Was

Lucas a being like Merlin? Merlin was an angel. He had wings and a light glowing around him, and God was his father. Lucas could be Merlin's and Colin's brother and therefore, Arthur's uncle. If he was indeed part of their family, and an angel, yet he was evil and hated them all passionately, then...

Beth's eyes flew open in horror as she came to the logical conclusion: Lucas was *Lucifer*. Satan. She'd had sex with the devil.

Sam paused in his pacing, swung around, and narrowed his deceptively beautiful blue eyes at her. "You think you've got it all figured out, do you? You know nothing!" he shouted at her, venom in his voice.

She cringed and turned her eyes away, trying to make herself smaller. She started to weep silent tears and wished she could go home.

CHAPTER 54
Moab, Friday, November 10, 2023, Early Morning

Aidan had stayed quiet and bided his time throughout the long night. The other two had curled up in the corner, fussing and sniffling. They finally slept when they were worn out, and as usual had shifted to their wolf forms, curling up around each other. All three of them had been handled roughly and were bruised and battered, but Aidan knew instinctively that it would not be advantageous to complain and cry. He had always been an easy-going child, and he was aware that wasn't common for a boy his age. He knew it was his god self, Aodh, who provided the calm, unwavering support and understanding far beyond his physical years.

It was clear to him the woman who had carried him off had done so against her will. She was being controlled by the evil man who had grabbed Bonnie and Brady. Aidan's god self was aware of the man's identity—he was Samael, otherwise known as Satan. Aodh had known Sam in the god realm millennia ago, and had never been on the best of terms with him. Sam was fractious and unreasonable and had become more and more dangerous over the eons since all of the gods had been created.

Aidan grimaced. It was apparent he was the only one capable of rescuing them. He was fairly sure he would recognize when it was time to act. He was tired, but he knew he could depend on his god energy to keep going. He was tempted to contact his father telepathically, but since he had never done so in his short life and had never even shown any aptitude for using his powers, he figured it would be more effective to contact his grandfather. Or his god self would do so, since Aodh could communicate telepathically in such a way that Sam couldn't intercept it.

Aidan closed his eyes and pretended to sleep. Opening his mind to his god self, he became a conduit.

Myrddin Emrys.

* * *

Just before dawn, a voice spoke in my mind that I hadn't heard for years, but I knew instantly to whom the Irish accent belonged. *Aodh, are you and Bonnie and Brady alright?*

Tá, yes, but we might not be for long, I'm thinking. And I have no idea what state Arthur is in; I'm concerned about the extent to which Sam is directing him. However, I wouldn't advise trying to rescue us as Sam would be alerted immediately. The woman is under his thrall, and I'm that convinced she had no choice, despite the appearance that she collaborated in the abduction. His influence plainly overwhelmed her, it did. She'll be the instrument of our destruction, whether she wills it or not.

"Dad, who're ya communicatin' with? Is it the kids? Are they okay? What's goin' on?" The anguish I heard in Derek's voice was enough to tear my heart out.

"Yes, they're well. Wait a moment and I'll fill you in." *Aodh, are you positive that Beth doesn't wish you any harm?*

I'm as sure of it as I can be. She wasn't lying to you when she asked for your forgiveness and promised to serve you. Truly, she had no idea who her boyfriend was, and she didn't know Sam's evil was infecting her. Uh, oh, sorry, I must go.

I turned to Derek and sent a private message to him. *Aidan, that is, Aodh, says they're not harmed. Bonnie and Brady are upset and a little bruised, but alright. He—*

Aidan contacted you telepathically? But he's never used magic, so how could he—

Derek, calm down and use your head. You knew before he was born that your son is really the god Aodh. Aidan has always known who he is and chose not to use his magic and telepathy until now. I think he's going to try and get them out of there, but something happened and we were interrupted before he told me what he had in mind.

* * *

Aidan quickly scooted closer to his niece and nephew, who were back in human form, and lay still with his eyes shut as the woman came into the room to check on them. He could tell she suspected that he was awake and up to something. He doubted she would hurt them, but he was afraid she would tell Sam. And that could be deadly since Sam wouldn't hesitate—he'd kill all three of them and savor it, inciting an all-out war between the gods. He couldn't imagine what fate Sam had in store for Arthur. Whatever it was, it wouldn't be good.

As he lay quietly curled up with the other kids, he could think of but one option open to him.

As soon as Beth left the room and locked the door, he completely and irrevocably surrendered to his god powers. He moaned as indescribable energy rushed through his being and he permanently merged with his god self. His small body couldn't contain the vastness and it changed, altered, became *more*. He became an adult. The transition didn't hurt, but it wasn't pleasant either. He shrugged off his discomfort along with the ragged pieces of his child's shirt and pants and conjured simple adult-sized clothing and donned it. Before the children could wake up and cry out, he picked them up and tried to transport them all to safety instantaneously, as his god self had always done. It didn't work. He felt a flash of irritation until he recalled that he could use basic teleportation, and to do so, he'd have to properly visualize his destination—home, with his father and mother.

He tried again. He pictured his house across the street from his grandparents' place, the patio in the back yard with its spectacular view of the Rim. He pictured his bedroom with the Star Wars-themed bedspread and curtains, and his mom holding his clean pajamas, reminding him to take a bath. And he pictured his father, with his sandy-brown hair and warm brown eyes, glowing like the sun as he told the story of his trip to Camelot with Merlin in early 2014.

Aidan/Aodh and his precious cargo disappeared from the room in which they'd been imprisoned just as the door crashed open and a tremendous roar of male fury filled the air.

* * *

Sam had sensed a sudden build-up of magical energy from the room in which he'd been holding the children. He'd flung the door open and raced into the room just as a red-haired young man disappeared with Morry's twins in his arms. "Fuck!" he shrieked. He hadn't realized Derek's son was in reality his old adversary from the god realm, the Celtic god, Aodh.

* * *

It was 6:00 AM and Derek and Sarah huddled together, holding hands with Morry and Lainie on the couch, meditating in spite of their exhaustion. Emily, Lumina, Chris, Cathy, and Rae stood by ready to provide food and drink and loving support. I spoke quietly with my brothers, still attempting to discover the location of Satan's lair.

Without warning, a tall, slender red-haired man holding two small children appeared in front of me, staggering a few steps. He managed to hold onto the traumatized twins, who struggled in his arms and howled in fear.

Chaos ensued as the parents rushed to their children. Morry and Lainie took Bonnie and Brady into their arms, laughing and weeping, while Derek and Sarah paused in bewilderment when a grown man turned to them in place of the four-year-old boy they had waited for. "Sorry, it was my first time teleporting in this body and I lost my balance, I did," he explained in a deep, lilting voice.

Derek instantly understood what had happened and stared at Aidan in shock, but unchecked maternal emotions clouded Sarah's mind and caused her to react instinctively.

"Where is my son? What have you done with him?" she screamed.

As she pounded furiously on Aidan's muscular, T-shirt-covered chest with her fists, he gathered her against him, gazing calmly into his father's eyes over the top of Sarah's head.

Derek blinked back tears. Aidan was a grown man, and it would be the most difficult thing he'd ever done to accept that his little boy no longer existed.

* * *

Aidan heard his father's thoughts and knew Derek was stunned, but would eventually accept the new reality. He returned his attention to his mother, who finally collapsed against him, sobbing in exhaustion and confusion. Aidan put his hands on Sarah's shoulders and gently pushed her away from him so that he could look down into her sad, deep blue eyes.

"Mom, it's okay, I'm right here," he said reassuringly, stroking her hair.

Sarah stared uncertainly into the moss green eyes of a man who was at least as tall as Merlin. He was in his early twenties and strikingly beautiful. His skin was golden, with no sign of the freckles he'd had as a child, his straight nose and heart-shaped face mirroring her own. Hair the color of flame hung down his back to his waist. Sarah gasped. "Oh, God."

He grinned, his teeth perfectly white. "No, I'm afraid not. I'm

Aodh, but I'm also your son **Aidan**. Don't you remember when I spoke with Merlin, er, Grandpa, before I was born?"

"Of course, I remember…Aodh," she replied, warily pronouncing the Gaelic name. "But it may take me awhile to get used to." Sarah wiped away tears and whispered, "Son."

"It's okay, Mom, I'll still be around, I promise. I'll be living here with you for a while yet, although we'll have to get larger bedroom furniture, won't we?" He could conjure it easily enough, but it might help his mother if she had something to concentrate on other than his unbelievable change.

Sarah smiled hesitantly, making a valiant effort to keep her emotions in check. "I guess we will. You've definitely outgrown it."

"That I have. Sure and you don't have to call me Aodh, just Aidan."

Relieved, she said, "Okay, Aidan. That makes it easier for me to accept. I love you."

"I love you, too, Mom, that I do." He kissed her cheek, and dropped his arms as Sarah went to check on Bonnie and Brady.

He glanced up as Derek approached him tentatively, as if his father couldn't decide how to act or what to say. "It's me, Dad, not a stranger," Aidan said dryly.

"I know, but it would make me feel better if I could See ya. Do ya mind?"

Aidan smiled. "No, I don't mind."

Derek took a breath. "Here goes." He put his hand on his son's arm and Looked intently into Aidan's eyes. Their souls merged seamlessly.

The Light that flared around them was more intense than Derek had anticipated and he blinked.

Aidan winced. *It's sorry I am, Dad, I'll dial it back a notch. I restrained my god powers as my body developed, but now that my two selves are one, I'm at full power.*

Once more Derek became immersed in their connection, and he realized he didn't know his son as well as he thought he did. Naturally, Aidan had experienced the trials and tribulations of a child during the past four and a half years as he grew, but Aodh had always been there in the background, a part of Aidan, enjoying his human body.

Derek felt the deep love Aidan had for him and knew that his son's nature was as affectionate, compassionate, and understanding as he had anticipated. But Derek also experienced firsthand the benevolent yet fiery spirit of the ancient god, and it was so mind-boggling he found it difficult to accept. He concentrated on the fact that Aodh and Aidan were one inseparable being, and there was no going back.

Derek and Aidan gradually came back to normal consciousness, their eyes still locked on one another. As they stepped into each other's arms and held on tightly, Derek grinned. It would be difficult getting used to the fact that his son was two inches taller than he was.

* * *

I stood and watched as Derek, Sarah and Aidan—Aodh—came to terms with their new relationship, and Morry and Lainie took their leave with their exhausted, traumatized kids in tow. Morry gave me a wave as they went out the door and I waved back, understanding his desire to take his family home quickly.

Beli, Llyr, and Portunus stood patiently beside me, awaiting further instructions.

Wait here for now, if you please. We aren't done yet, I conveyed silently. They all nodded and started discussing the situation quietly.

Colin, who had waited until things calmed down some to talk to me, said, "Can you believe what Aidan did? I wasn't even aware he'd come into his powers yet."

I looked over at Derek and Aidan, who still had their heads together, murmuring quietly to each other. "He's a remarkable young man, but Aodh always was distinctive among us for his even temper and kindness."

"I don't remember him," Colin said, regretfully. "I feel as if I should, though, as if we had a special rapport once."

I didn't remember that, but they must have known each other in the realm of the gods—they were brothers, after all. Although, I wouldn't think the Irish god of fire and the Norse god of war would necessarily have had a reason to associate so closely.

A moment later, Aidan approached us and held out his hand to Colin. "Týr, it's great to see you again."

Colin and I both froze, though for different reasons.

Bollocks, I thought. I never thought to warn Aodh that Father wanted Colin to discover his true identity for himself, but I hadn't known before this abduction had occurred that Aidan would manifest as an adult in his god form.

"What did you call me?" Colin asked, his heart pounding so hard I could hear it.

Aodh looked puzzled, slowly lowering his hand when Colin didn't return the gesture. "Uh, Týr?"

Colin glowered at me suspiciously. "You knew who I was all along and didn't tell me?"

"I only recently remembered it, and Father didn't want me to tell you; he wanted you to remember on your own," I said. "I never expected Aodh to be here and call you by name."

Aodh looked back and forth between us with a worried expression on his face. "It's sorry, I am. I had no idea it was a secret, although I thought it peculiar when you disappeared from the god realm, Týr. Or I could call you Uncle Colin, even though you're my brother. It's confusing, it is."

Colin and I stared grimly at each other and didn't answer him.

"Right, I'll leave you two to figure it out and go to my room." He walked away and we hardly noticed.

Colin stomped away from me, whirled around and stomped back, getting into my face. "I'm fucking pissed off at you right now, Brother, 'cause I would think you wouldn't want me to remain in ignorance, when you know it's bothering me so damn much!" he growled.

It was tough holding onto my own temper. I didn't answer him until I'd taken a few deep breaths to calm down. "Look, Colin, since you still don't remember being Týr, or remember residing in the god realm, you don't realize what our father can be like. He's *God!* You don't just *ignore* God's direct instructions—and he specifically told me not to tell you."

Colin turned away from me with his shoulders hunched, and I waited impatiently while he worked through his anger. Even though he was unbiased and equitable, rarely giving in to temper (reflecting, unknowingly, his god aspects of upholder of law and order and dispenser of justice), he was primarily the god of war, and unquestionably revealing it now.

It took a few minutes for him to look at me again. "How in the hell did I end up being a *Norse* god, of all things?" He pointed to his swarthy face. "Look at me. I'm not blond and fair-skinned and neither is Beli. We could be from the Mediterranean, or the Middle East."

"Remember, Beli is a Welsh god. There are many Welshmen who are dark due to Spanish ancestry," I said mildly. "But the reality is, we're gods, not humans, and our physical appearances don't having anything to do with 'ancestry.'"

Colin continued as if I hadn't spoken, "...and wasn't Týr known as the one-handed god? I'm not missing a hand, so what's up with that?"

I didn't respond. This situation had gotten so far out of control I had to fix it at once. I stopped time and rewound it back to the moment Aidan/Aodh had approached us.

* * *

Aodh walked up and held out his hand to Colin, preparing to greet him as he had before. As he opened his mouth, I intervened. *Aodh, you mustn't tell Colin that he's Týr. God has forbidden it. He wants Colin to discover his real identity on his own.*

He glanced at me without surprise, having felt my manipulation of the timeline. *Apparently, I already did and it caused an uproar. I'm that sorry for it. Thanks for fixing things.*

He turned to smile at Colin, who had no idea what had occurred, and shook his hand. "Nice to see you, Uncle. Thanks for being here to welcome us home."

"Oh, uh, no problem, Aidan, glad you're back safe and sound. Sorry, I'm feeling dizzy. I think I need to sit down."

Colin started to look for a chair to drop into, but I stopped him. "It will pass, I promise you."

I turned to address everyone left in the room. "We're all forgetting something vital—we still need to find and rescue Arthur, retrieve Beth, and destroy Sam's body so he'll have to return to the Hell realm where he belongs."

* * *

Gwen had felt uncharacteristically bitter toward the family when they seemed to throw themselves wholeheartedly into celebrating the children's return. That is, two children and one newly-turned adult.

It wasn't that she resented their relief or their happiness, but she did resent that they had apparently forgotten about Arthur. She'd glanced at Merlin and he'd looked as perturbed as she felt. Truthfully, more, considering the history he and Arthur shared, not to mention his paternal bond with Arthur.

Normally not a crier, Gwen felt tears overflow and trickle down her cheeks, causing the mascara she had so painstakingly applied yesterday to run.

"Honey, it'll be alright, you'll see. Merlin will find him."

Gwen swung around and was enveloped in a reaffirming hug. Em gave a brief half smile as she held her close. "I understand, because I'm terrified for my son."

They were both reassured when Merlin announced his intention to renew the search for Arthur.

* * *

Emotions—mine and everyone else's in the family, in the room or not —swirled around me, inundating and stifling me, emotions that hindered me from finding my son.

Em and Gwen watched me closely, their own fears and yearning for Arthur so strong that their combined emotions alone threatened to engulf me.

Without another thought, I mentally stepped back from the maelstrom into the peace and serenity of spirit inside me, repelling the emotional storm like water off a duck's back. I was removed from it all and figuratively took a deep breath for the first time in ages. I wasn't denying or rejecting emotion permanently, just putting it aside temporarily.

For years, I had been so focused on my life here in this realm that I had seldom taken advantage of my position as the only fully realized god on the planet, and incorporated my unique abilities as such. I hadn't even utilized to their furthest extent the abilities I'd had before my transition. It seemed ridiculous to me now. How had I lost track of myself that way?

I would have to put aside my soul-searching—I couldn't wait any longer to find Arthur and Beth and contend with Sam.

CHAPTER 55
Moab, Friday, November 10, 2023, Morning

Colin felt his brother trying to get himself back on track emotionally and spiritually. He put his hand on Merlin's shoulder and squeezed gently. "Hey, I'm here and I'll help you with whatever you need. What's our next step?"

Merlin turned his head and Colin was riveted by the intensity of his gaze. "I've been going about this all wrong, once again forgetting that we needn't limit ourselves to human methods of investigation or even basic god powers. I won't need your help, but I do appreciate your offer. I know what to do."

Even though he was a god himself, Colin shivered at the unimaginable power shining through Merlin's eyes and amplified through his voice. It was as if Merlin had merged with their father and had access to the vast knowledge of eternity.

Merlin smiled. "Exactly. I have merged with the energy of the earth, the sky, the water and the air, and with every creature and structure. It will be a simple matter to determine where they are. The universe, and everything in it, is one, and I am one with the universe."

Colin gulped. "Oh, God."

Merlin winked and smiled as he disappeared into blinding white Light.

* * *

I found Arthur and Beth here in Moab, literally under our noses. They had been at Sam's apartment all along. I now understood how we'd missed it. He had utilized a convoluted series of spells and wards which would not only divert and repel any investigations by humans, but also any efforts by the gods to uncover his whereabouts. But he hadn't counted on my infiltrating the very atoms and molecules he and his dwelling place were made of.

I reincorporated myself into my physical form, which felt strange after having no limitations whatsoever. "I know where they are. Let's go."

All of us—Colin, Beli, Llyr, Portunus and I—appeared in Sam's apartment without warning. Beth was unconscious on the floor, close to death. Sam and Arthur stood side by side, ready to go out the door, which I barricaded with a thought.

Beli, get Beth out of here and have Seth heal her. He immediately picked up Beth's limp form, and vanished.

The rest of us arrayed ourselves in an arc with Sam and Arthur in the center, their backs against the door. They remained silent, exhibiting the same ugly, belligerent expression on their faces.

Arthur didn't seem pleased to see me, and it was evident that he had joined forces with my evil brother. I couldn't tell whether it was by choice or coercion.

"I'm not going with you, Merlin," Arthur snarled. "I'm done with you and your stupid plan to save the world. Why bother? I will *rule* the world instead, with humanity enslaved."

How could my son choose to dominate the world with the embodiment of evil at his side, rather than save it, with me? Part of me was devastated, but my father's will and the energy of the universe still ran through me, overruling my personal feelings with a prodigious optimism. I wasn't going to give up without a fight. I quickly surrounded Arthur with a shield of Light, intending to transport him back home. At the same time, I targeted Sam for destruction.

"I don't think so, Merlin," Sam uttered, and before I could act, he disappeared, taking Arthur with him.

"No!" I screamed, my hopes and dreams of the last 1600 years crumbling to dust. My recent optimism disappeared as my mind told me it was too late.

Colin grabbed my arms. "Don't you dare give up! This isn't over yet!"

All my brothers surrounded me and buoyed me up, reminding me that I wasn't alone in this, transforming the single, most devastating tragedy of my life into the biggest challenge I had ever faced: Get Arthur back and go on to save humanity.

EPILOGUE
Arthur

As I slowly regained consciousness, I swallowed convulsively, my throat parched. My thought processes were so sluggish I felt as if I was underwater. I tried to move my arms and legs but they weren't cooperating, even though I could tell I wasn't physically bound to the uneven surface beneath me.

As fuzzy as my mind was, I recognized that I had been abducted, although the details escaped me—except for who had done it: Satan, Merlin's infamous brother, also known as Sam.

I lost focus again and drifted. Eventually my mental fog began to lift and the first thing I became aware of was that my bodily needs hadn't been met in a long while. I was very cold, and I desperately needed to urinate. My muscles ached from prolonged inactivity.

I looked around and frowned. Where the hell was I? I was in a cavern, but I couldn't remember such a place being in Utah. A single torch was burning somewhere behind me, which would explain the distorted shadows on the wall. The ceiling was lost in darkness above me. The large flat boulder beneath me was hard and brutally uncomfortable.

I was utterly alone.

There was no sign of Sam. I had no idea what he wanted from me, or how he had been able to control me. A stray thought burgeoned into a flood of information and I realized what must have happened. Sam—no, I should call the bastard Satan—had to have infiltrated every cell in my body from the moment I'd been conceived to have such absolute power over me. I'd heard the story of Merlin and various magically endowed members of the family performing an epic spell to remove the evil from my nephew Morry's cells back in 2014, but it was Nimue, not Satan, who had been the villain that time. Or the truth was that Nimue had infected Morry at Satan's behest.

With surprising composure considering that I was being held

against my will, I recognized that every significant negative emotion or attitude I'd ever had in my current life was most likely due to Satan's influence. From the very beginning.

I wondered why my father had never noticed the evil growing in me. After all, Merlin wasn't merely a sorcerer, he was an extremely powerful god, and supposedly God's favorite son.

Unless Merlin was as vulnerable to Satan's influence as anyone else —a possibility that would have disturbed me greatly if I could feel anything.

I remembered the cruel things I had said to my father when he and the other gods had arrived at Satan's heavily warded apartment to rescue me. Someone else had spoken through my mouth, and who else could it have been besides Satan uttering those vile words. I, Arthur, would never have done so, no matter how angry I was with my father. Merlin had looked shocked and heartbroken, and yet I still couldn't bring myself to *care*, even taking into account the growing understanding and clarity I was experiencing. Had Satan blocked my emotions or permanently destroyed some vital part of me?

As deserving of further deliberation as those topics were, I put them aside for now and concentrated on my immediate needs. First of all, it was imperative that I destroy the binding spell holding me immobile and empty my bladder, and second, I needed to figure out how to get out of this abominable prison. It was pathetic that something as mundane as needing to urinate superseded an escape plan, but there it was.

Several hours later, I was at my wit's end. I'd tried everything I could think of to get free of the invisible bonds, or spell, or whatever it was Satan had used to immobilize me. And I was starting to imagine increasingly horrific scenarios. What if he came back and killed me? That wasn't probable, since I was an immortal demigod and couldn't die. No, that wasn't true; I could die but would come back to life. A horrifying thought occurred to me. Satan had decapitated my half sister, Adrestia—and there was no coming back from that.

Abject fear swamped me and I broke out in a drenching sweat despite the winter-worthy temperature of the cavern. I forgot all of my past bravery and accomplishments as a warrior and panicked, thrashing about on the unforgiving surface until I was a mass of bruises.

My heart pounding from the exertion, I lay still as it occurred to me that I might never see my wife, my mother and siblings, or my loyal knights again. Nor reconcile with my father. Tears clouded my vision as

I realized that I hadn't told them lately how important they are to me, how much I loved them.

It seemed that I hadn't been stripped of my emotions after all.

Drained, miserable, and feeling increasingly hopeless, I closed my eyes and waited for sleep to come. It didn't take long, but my slumber was plagued by disturbing images of roiling black clouds disgorging one monster after another, which pursued me until I finally turned and made a stand with Excalibur held high, only to find that my mighty sword was nothing but a slender, fragile branch.

And then, somewhere in the midst of my darkest nightmares, a bright Light ignited inside me, and I felt a warm reassurance, as if I was a baby again, cradled lovingly in my father's arms.

"Dad," I murmured in my sleep.

I'm coming for you, Arthur.

LIST OF CHARACTERS
(In Alphabetical Order)

ADRESTIA AMBROSIUS: Merlin's daughter by Nimue. Mordred "Morry" Colburn's biological mother. She is also Beli's granddaughter.

AIDAN COLBURN: Derek and Sarah's red-haired son, who has the soul of Aodh.

AISLING COLBURN: Unborn daughter of Derek and Sarah Colburn.

ANN OGILVIE: Mother of Lainie Ogilvie, descendant of Merlin, and a competent witch.

AODH (Pronounced Ay and rhymes with hay): Merlin's brother, the Irish god of fire and the underworld (Aidan Colburn's true identity).

ARTHUR PENDRAGON AMBROSIUS: The son of Uther Pendragon and King of Camelot in the fifth century, and the reincarnated son of Merlin in the twenty-first century. Remarries Guinevere.

BELI (Pronounced Bell-eye): Merlin's brother, the Welsh god of death, who normally lives in the god realm as an incorporeal spirit. At odds for millennia, he and Merlin reconcile when they are lost in the past without their memories in *The Shape of Time*.

BEN REESE: Tom and Sandy Reese's younger son, who is currently the caretaker (property manager) of Merlin's estate in Wales.

BETHANY "BETH" DOUGLAS: Owen Douglas's half sister, who works at the newspaper with Gwen and Morry. She has the soul of Morgause Pendragon.

BONNIE AND BRADY COLBURN: Morry and Lainie Colburn's shapeshifter twins.

CADENCE CAMPBELL: Unborn daughter of Lumina and Josh Campbell.

CARA PENDRAGON: Bastard daughter of Uther Pendragon in the fifth century and Derek Colburn's biological mother. She died in a fire when Derek was a baby.

CARLOS SUN CHASER: Native American shaman who traveled to Wales to give Merlin a warning. He died during a dragon attack when Merlin first awoke in 2013 (*The Heart of Magic*), and his spirit gave Merlin information about finding a new portal to Avalon.

CATHY GRANT: Twin sister of Chris Colburn. She was chronically ill for years until she participated in a drug trial that temporarily alleviated her condition. Seth MacAdam cures her shortly after she returns to Moab. Marries Colin Campbell.

CHLOE: Friend of Beth Douglas for many years.

CHRIS GRANT COLBURN: Derek's first wife and original owner of The Moab Herbalist, twin sister of Cathy Grant, and eventually the wife of Seth MacAdam.

COLIN CAMPBELL: Detective and then lieutenant with the Moab City Police Department, he thinks he's a distant relative of Merlin's. Later, he discovers that he is actually Merlin's brother and therefore also a god.

DEREK COLBURN: Merlin's son by Uther Pendragon's bastard daughter, Cara. Also known by his birth name, Emrys Ambrosius, he was born in the fifth century and brought to the present time as a baby by Llyr, to be raised by foster parents until he met Merlin as an adult. Since he is the son of Merlin, the god Myrddin Emrys, Derek is a demigod.

EDDA SMITH: Police officer and then a detective with the Moab City Police Department, she is Colin Campbell's partner.

ELAINE "LAINIE" OGILVIE: Morry Colburn's wife and Ann Ogilvie's daughter, she is a witch and a shapeshifter.

EMILY CRANDALL REESE: A law enforcement ranger at Arches National Park until she meets and marries Merlin, who goes by the name Michael Reese. Derek's best friend for years, daughter of Rae and

Jack Crandall, mother of Lumina and Arthur, and stepmother of both Derek and Seth. Runs the family business, The Moab Herbalist.

FRED BAKER: Police chief for the Moab City Police Department, and Colin's, Edda's, and Owen's superior.

GOD: The Creator of the universe and the father of all the gods and goddesses.

GUINEVERE "GWEN" PENDRAGON: Queen of Camelot in the fifth century, known as Gwen Singleton in the twenty-first century, "twin sister" of Jim Singleton who was killed by Morgana and her minions. Marries Arthur Pendragon Ambrosius.

GWEN SINGLETON: Acting as the "twin sister" of Jim Singleton, she was Jim until he died. She took his place at the newspaper office and is the alter ego of Guinevere Pendragon Ambrosius.

HELEN AND ROGER THOMPSON: Morry's and Sarah's foster parents (Morry and Sarah were foster brother and sister growing up).

JACK CRANDALL: Rae's husband and Emily's father, who is later taken over by Satan.

JC: Merlin's other brother.

JEN REESE: Tom and Sandy Reese's daughter in Wales.

JIM SINGLETON: Morry's friend and supervisor at the newspaper who has the soul of the queen of Camelot. He is tortured by Morgana's minions and later dies in Merlin's arms. Merlin resurrects him in his original female form, Guinevere Pendragon.

JOSH CAMPBELL: Colin Campbell's son and Lumina Ambrosius Reese's husband. Since his father is a god, Josh is a demigod.

KEN WILSON: Worked as a law enforcement ranger at Arches National Park with Derek Colburn, and was Derek's friend, and for a short time, his lover. He is killed by a dragon in 2014, brought back to life by Merlin, then later is killed by Morgana. He exists now as a disembodied spirit.

LILITH AMBROSIUS: Merlin's human mother in the fifth century.

LISA COLBURN: Derek's adoptive mother, who is a wizard.

LLYR/ LIR: Merlin's brother, who is both the Welsh and the Irish god of the sea.

LUMINA AMBROSIUS REESE: Merlin and Emily's daughter, who is a minor Roman goddess. Marries Josh Campbell.

MAGGIE CAMPBELL: Colin Campbell's first wife.

MERLIN AMBROSIUS: As the Sorcerer of Camelot, Merlin had been unaware that he was actually Myrddin Emrys, the Welsh god of magic and healing. In the current time, when he discovered he was a god, he thought Llyr was his father. He traveled to Moab looking for a new portal to Avalon to reunite with King Arthur.

MICHAEL REESE: Merlin's persona in Moab as the proprietor of The Moab Herbalist. Tom and Sandy Reese had allowed Merlin to use their deceased son's identity when he first awoke in the Crystal Cave in 2013.

MORDRED "MORRY" COLBURN: Derek Colburn's son by his half sister Adrestia. A sorcerer and shapeshifter, he is considered a demigod. Born in the fifth century, he was brought to the present time as a baby by Llyr. Raised as an orphan, he and Sarah Gordon had been fostered by Helen and Roger Thompson in California.

MORGANA PENDRAGON: Arthur's half sister in the fifth century, a witch proficient in dark magic. She appears in the twenty-first century doing Satan's bidding by leading a group of wizards and other practitioners of magic who had once supported Merlin during the Battle of Matheson Preserve (*The Heart of Magic*).

MORGAUSE PENDRAGON: Arthur's half sister in the fifth century, a witch, although not as proficient or as evil as Morgana. She has been reincarnated as Beth Douglas, who has no magical powers that we know of.

MRS. O'KELLY: Morry and Lainie's sweet but nosy neighbor who is unaware that the Colburns are magical shapeshifters.

MYRDDIN EMRYS (Pronounced Mur-thin Em-ris): The Welsh god of magic and healing, Merlin's alter ego.

NIMUE (Pronounced Nim-way): Daughter of Merlin's brother Beli, the Welsh god of death. Merlin's nemesis beginning in the fifth century after she had an affair with him, and unbeknownst to him at the time, conceived their daughter, Adrestia. As a young sorcerer, Merlin had no memory of being a god and didn't know Nimue was his own niece.

OENGUS (Pronounced Ungus): Rae Crandall's Elven grandfather who is the leader of the Fae High Council of Elders, which is composed of Elves. Emily gave Merlin Oengus's ring to wear as his wedding ring.

OWEN DOUGLAS: Beth Douglas's half brother and Colin Campbell's CSI assistant at the Moab City Police Department. Randy Hartwell's roommate.

PATTY: An annoying young woman who had worked with Morry and Jim Singleton, and now works with Morry, Gwen, and Beth Douglas at the newspaper office. She was into the Goth scene, but has now outgrown that affectation.

PORTUNUS: Merlin's brother, the Roman god of keys, doors, ports, and livestock, also known as his neighbor, Rod. As Rod, Portunus shapeshifts into the black cat that had assisted Merlin in the Battle of Matheson Preserve.

RAE CLARK CRANDALL: Emily's mother, who comes to live with her and Merlin after Emily's father, Jack Crandall, threatens her life.

RANDY HARTWELL: The son of Seth's Fae uncle and therefore his first cousin, and a distant cousin of Chris MacAdam through her Grant ancestors. Randy is a Fae changeling who grew up in Moab and is Owen's roommate.

ROB REESE: Tom and Sandy Reese's older son.

ROSE CAMPBELL: Colin Campbell's daughter.

SAMAEL: Merlin's brother, also known as Lucifer or Satan, he is the god of the underworld and the Hell realm. Goes by the innocuous nickname "Sam," which is misleading since he is the epitome of evil.

SARAH GORDON COLBURN: Derek Colburn's second wife and the mother of his son Aidan. Morry's foster sister who is now his stepmother.

SETH MACADAM: Merlin's half-Fae son and Chris Colburn's husband. He is the grandson of the King of the Seelie (Light Court) Fae, a prince and heir apparent to the throne.

SHARONE REESE: Ben Reese's wife, who had to adjust to the reality of serving the immortal sorcerer, Merlin.

SIR GAWAIN/GARY GARDNER: Original Knight of the Round Table, reincarnated in the present time in a different body but with the same appearance.

SIR LANCELOT/RYAN JONES: Original Knight of the Round Table, reincarnated in the present time in a different body and altered appearance.

SIR LEON: Original Knight of the Round Table, physically brought to the current time from the fifth century by Llyr.

SIR PERCIVAL: Original Knight of the Round Table, physically brought to the current time from the fifth century by Llyr.

SORCHA MACADAM: Unborn daughter of Seth and Chris.

TOM AND SANDY REESE: Merlin's caretakers (property managers) for his Welsh estate when he awoke in the Crystal Cave in 2013.

TÝR: The son of Odin and the brother of Thor, Týr is the Norse god of war, law, and justice and is Beli's twin. Merlin remembers that this is Colin Campbell's true god name, but God has forbidden Merlin to tell Colin, who must discover the truth for himself.

UTHER PENDRAGON: Father of Arthur, Morgana, Morgause, and Cara (illegitimate), and the first King of Camelot.

GLOSSARY OF TERMS AND PHRASES

Aboot: The way Seth pronounces "about."

Abscedere (Latin, pronounced approximately, ab-seh-dare): One of Merlin's old spells that means "to avoid."

All-fired (American slang): From the year 1829, said to be a euphemism for "hell-fired."

Awa' (Scots): Away

Aye (Scots): Yes

Beannachd Leat (Scottish Gaelic, pronounced approximately, bee-on-ocht laht): Farewell

Bean sidhe (Irish Gaelic) or *ban sidhe* (Scottish Gaelic), (pronounced ban-shee in either language): Supernatural being in Celtic folklore whose mournful wailing at night was believed to foretell the death of a member of the family who heard the lamentation.

Bide a wee (Scots): Stay a little while.

Braw wee bairn (Scots): Fine-looking little child/baby.

Couldna (Scots): Couldn't

Croese i Gymru (Welsh, pronounced approximately, croy-zaw ee gumree): Welcome to Wales.

Desino (Latin, pronounced approximately, deh-see-no): This is one of Merlin's early spells that prevents the subject from moving.

Didna (Scots): Didn't

Dinna (Scots): Don't

Dinna fash yersel' (Scots): Don't upset/disturb yourself.

Diolch (Welsh, pronounced approximately, dee-olch, emphasis on the second syllable, the ch similar to the ch in loch, like a breathy, soft k): Thanks

Diolch i Dduw (Welsh, pronounced approximately, dee-olch ee thoo): Thanks to God.

Fer or ***Fur*** (Scots): For

Halò (Scottish Gaelic, pronounced hallo): Hello

Ken, Kent (Scots): Know, Knew

Lloniannau (Welsh, pronounced approximately, thlon-ya-nah): Cheers

Madainn mhath, ciamar a tha thu (Scottish Gaelic, pronounced approximately, mah-ten vah, kim-mer uh ha oo): Good morning, how are you?

Marrit (Scots): Married

Mayna (Scots): May not

Mo bràthair (Scottish Gaelic, pronounced mo bray-her): My brother

Mo chridhe (Scottish Gaelic, pronounced mo chree): My heart

Mo fàthair (Scottish Gaelic, pronounced mo fay-her): My father

Mo leannan (Scottish Gaelic, pronounced mo len-nan): My lover, my sweetheart

Mo màthair (Scottish Gaelic, pronounced mo may-her): My mother

Mo muirninn (Scottish Gaelic, pronounced mo mwere-neen): My darling

Nay or ***nae*** (Scots): No

Ne'er (Middle English or Early Scots, first used in 13th century): Never

No' (Scots): Not

O fy Duw (Welsh, pronounced approximately, oh vih doo): Oh, my God.

Sae (Scots): So

Shouldna (Scots): Shouldn't

Sláinte (Irish Gaelic, pronounced slawn-che): Cheers or to good health.

Slàinte mhath (Scottish Gaelic, pronounced slan-ja vah): Cheers or to good health.

Stramash (Scots): A commotion or upset.

Sut wyt ti (Welsh, pronounced approximately, suit wit tee): How are you doing?

Tá (Irish Gaelic, pronounced taw): Yes

Tae (Scots): To

The noo (Scots): Just now.

'Tis (English, first used in 1555 according to Merriam-Webster): Literary, archaic or colloquial form of "it is."

Tha gaol agam ort (Scottish Gaelic, pronounced ha ge-ill ah-kum orsht): I love you.

Tha gu math, tapadh leat (Scottish Gaelic, pronounced ha guh mah, tah-pah laht): I'm fine, thank you.

'Twas (English, first used in 1555): Literary, archaic, or colloquial form of "it was."

'Twould (English, first used in 1555): Literary, archaic, or colloquial form of "it would."

Veniat ad me (Latin, pronounced approximately, ven-ee-at add me): An old spell of Merlin's that means "come to me."

Verra (Scots): Very

Weel: The way Seth pronounces "well."

Whit's fur ye'll no' go past ye (Scots): Literally, what's for you will not go past you; in other words, what will be, will be.

Willna (Scots): Won't

Wouldna (Scots): Wouldn't

Ye, Yer, Ye're (Scots): You, Your, You're

CARYL SAY is a writer living in Moab, Utah. She is an avid reader of several different genres, including fantasy, science fiction, mystery, and paranormal fiction. She enjoys working on her family tree and has traveled to Ireland, Scotland, England, and Wales. She loves to hike in the magical red rock country of southeast Utah. She is currently working on the fifth book in the Merlin in Moab series. You may contact Caryl by email carylsay.author@gmail.com, on her website www.carylsay.com, or on Facebook www.facebook.com/AuthorCarylSay.

THANK YOU for reading *The Winds of Change*. As a special bonus for Merlin in Moab fans, I had made a short story available when the third book, *The Shape of Time*, was published, and would like to offer it once again. You can get it here: **http://carylsay.com/tsot-bonus/**

Reviews help authors gain more visibility online, and your review helps other readers like you find books they will enjoy. I appreciate all reviews, both positive and negative.

Thanks, and happy reading!

Made in United States
Troutdale, OR
11/18/2023

14706623R00236